THE FAMILY WAY

Tony Parsons is the author of *Man and Boy*, winner of the Book of the Year Prize, and translated into 38 languages. His subsequent novels – *One For My Baby*, *Man and Wife*, *Stories We Could Tell* and *My Favourite Wife* – were all bestsellers. He lives in London.

Visit www.AuthorTracker.co.uk for exclusive information on Tony Parsons.

Praise for Tony Parsons:

'Heartwarming and highly recommended . . . His most sensitive book yet' *Heat*

'Funny, serious, tender and honest . . . Tony Parsons is writing about the genuine dilemmas of modern life' *Sunday Express*

'It has it all – parent/child conflict, professional intrusions on personal space, serious illness, life-threatening accidents – a one sitting read' *Mirror*

'He takes as his specialist subject contemporary emotional issues which almost every other male writer has ignored' *Guardian*

'Memorable and poignant – nobody squeezes more genuine emotion from a scene than Tony Parsons' *Spectator*

'Unashamedly touching . . . funny and well-written'
Telegraph magazine

'As ever, [Tony Parsons] is in impressively depth-charging, straight-talking form. A broadsheet mind with a tabloid tongue, he remains one of the few male writers prepared to look beyond his own navel in search of answers' *GQ*

BY THE SAME AUTHOR

Man and Boy
One For My Baby
Man and Wife
Stories We Could Tell
My Favourite Wife

The Family Way

Tony Parsons

HARPER

Harper
An imprint of HarperCollins*Publishers*
77–85 Fulham Palace Road,
Hammersmith, London W6 8JB

www.harpercollins.co.uk

This paperback edition 2006
1

First published in Great Britain by
HarperCollins*Publishers*

ISBN 978-0-00-785589-6

Set in Sabon by Palimpsest Book Production Limited,
Grangemouth, Stirlingshire

Printed and bound in Great Britain by
Clays Ltd, St Ives plc

For Jasmine

part one:
the world is her biscuit

one

'Your parents ruin the first half of your life,' Cat's mother told her when she was eleven years old, 'and your children ruin the second half.'

It was said with the smallest of smiles, like one of those jokes that are not really a joke at all.

Cat was an exceptionally bright child, and she wanted to examine this proposition. How exactly had she ruined her mother's life? But there was no time. Her mother was in a hurry to get out of there. The black cab was waiting.

One of Cat's sisters was crying – maybe even both of them. But that wasn't the concern of Cat's mother. Because inside the waiting cab there was a man who loved her, and who no doubt made her feel good about herself, and who surely made her feel as though there was an un-ruined life out there for her somewhere, probably beyond the door of his rented flat in St John's Wood.

The childish sobbing increased in volume as Cat's mother picked up her suitcases and bags and headed for the door. Yes, thinking back on it, Cat was certain that both of her sisters were howling, although Cat herself was dry-eyed, and quite frozen with shock.

When the door slammed behind their mother and only the trace of her perfume remained – Chanel No. 5, for their mother was a woman of predictable tastes, in scent as well as men – Cat was suddenly aware that she was the oldest person in the house.

Eleven years old and she was in charge.

She stared at the everyday chaos her mother was escaping. Toys, food and clothes were strewn across the living room. The baby, Megan, a fat-faced little Buddha, three years old and not really a baby at all any more, was sitting in the middle of the room, crying because she had chewed her fingers while chomping on a biscuit. Where was the nanny? Megan wasn't allowed biscuits before meals.

Jessica, a pale, wistful seven-year-old, who Cat strongly suspected of being their father's favourite, was curled up on the sofa, sucking her thumb and bawling because – well, why? Because that's what cry-baby Jessica always did. Because baby Megan had hurled Jessica's Air Stewardess Barbie across the room, and broken her little drinks trolley. And perhaps most of all because their mother found it so easy to go.

Cat picked up Megan and clambered onto the sofa where Jessica was sucking her thumb, for all the world, Cat thought, as if she was the baby of the house. Cat hefted her youngest sister onto her hip and said, 'Come on, dopey,' to the other one. They were just in time.

The three sisters pressed their faces against the bay window of their newly broken home just as the black cab pulled away. Cat remembered the profile of the man in silhouette – a rather ordinary-looking man, hardly worth all this fuss – and her mother turning around for one last look.

She was very beautiful.

And she was gone.

After their mother had left, Cat's childhood quietly expired. For the rest of that day, and for the rest of her life.

Their father did all he could – 'the best dad in the world', Cat, Jessica and Megan wrote annually on his Father's Day cards, their young hearts full of feeling – and many of their childminders were a lot kinder than they needed to be. Years after they had gone home, Christmas cards came from the ex-au pair in Helsinki, and the former nanny in Manila. But in the end even the most cherished childminders went back to their real life, and the best dad in the world seemed to spend a lot of his time working, and the rest of the time trying to work out exactly what had hit him. Beyond his restrained, unfailingly well-mannered exterior, and beyond all the kindness and charm – 'He's just like David Niven,' awe-struck strangers would say to the girls as they were growing up – Cat sensed turmoil and panic and a sadness without end. Nobody ever sets out to be a single parent, and although Cat, Jessica and Megan never doubted that their father loved them – in that quiet, smiley, undemonstrative way he had – he seemed more unprepared than most.

As the oldest, Cat learned to fill in the gaps left by the parade of nannies and au pairs. She cooked and childminded, did some perfunctory cleaning, and a lot of clearing up (many of their kiddie-carers refused to do anything remotely domestic, as if it were against union rules). Cat learned how to program a washing machine, knew how to disable a burglar alarm and, after a few months of frozen meals and fast food, taught herself to cook. But there was one thing she learned above all others: before she was in her teens, Cat Jewell had some idea of how alone you can feel in this world.

So the three sisters grew.

Megan – pretty and round, voluptuous, her sisters called her, but the only one of them who would always have to watch her weight, academically brilliant – who would have thought it? – with all the fierceness of the youngest child.

Jessica – the doe-eyed dreamer, the sensitive one, prone

to laughter and tears, who turned out to be the unexpected boy magnet of the three, looking for that one big love behind the bicycle sheds and in the bus shelters of their suburban neighbourhood, quietly nursing a desire for a happy home.

And Cat – who quickly grew as tall as their father, but who never outgrew the small-breasted, long-limbed dancer's body she had as a girl, and never outgrew the unspeakable rage of being abandoned, although she learned to disguise her scars with the bossy authority of the eldest child.

They clung to each other and to a father who was rarely around, missing their mother, even when things were bad and they hated her, and after a while the fact that Cat had forsaken her childhood seemed like the least of their worries.

Cat loved her father and her sisters, even when they were driving her nuts, but when the time came, she escaped to Manchester and university with a happy sigh – 'As soon as someone left the door slightly ajar,' she liked to tell her new friends. And while Jessica married her first serious boyfriend and Megan moved in with her first real boyfriend, Cat lost herself in her studies and later her work, in no rush to build a home and start a family and return to the tyranny of domesticity.

She knew all about it. Family life meant nothing in the fridge, a mother gone, Jessica crying and baby Megan squawking for 'bis-quits, bis-quits'.

Family life was their father away working, the au pair shagging some new boy out in the potting shed and not a bloody bis-quit in the house.

More than either of her sisters, Cat had seen the reality of a woman's work. The hard slog, the thankless graft, the never-ending struggle to keep bellies fed and faces clean and bottoms wiped and eyes dried and washing done.

Let Jessica and Megan build their nests. Cat wanted to fly away, and to keep flying. But she was wise enough to know that this wasn't a philosophy, it was a wound. As a student, emboldened by one term at university, Cat angrily confronted her mother about all that had been stolen from her.

'What kind of mother were you? What kind of human being?'

'Your parents ruin –'

'Ah, change the record.' Cat was deliberately loud.

Megan stared with wonder at her big sister. Jessica prepared herself for a good cry. They were in a polite patisserie in St John's Wood where people behind the counter actually spoke French and shrugged their shoulders in the Gallic fashion.

'You were our mother,' Cat said. 'We were entitled to some mothering. I'm not talking about love, Mummy dearest. Just a little human decency. Was that too much to ask?'

Cat was shouting now.

'Don't worry, dear,' her mother said, calmly sucking on a low-tar cigarette and eyeing up the young waiter who was placing a still-warm pain au chocolat before her. 'One day you'll have fucked-up children of your own.'

Never, thought Cat.

Never ever.

When she was certain that her husband had settled down in front of the football, Jessica crept into his study and stared at all his pictures of Chloe.

It was turning into a shrine. The few carefully selected favourites were in their silver frames, but there were more propped up on bookshelves, and a fresh batch was spilling out of a Snappy Snaps envelope and fanning out across his desk, burying a VAT return.

Jessica reached for the envelope, and then hesitated, listening. She could hear Bono and U2 singing, 'It's a beautiful day'. He was watching the football. For the next hour or so it would take a small fire to get Paulo off the sofa. So Jessica reached for the latest pictures of Chloe, and thumbed through them, frowning.

There was Chloe in the park, in the baby swings, one vicious-looking tooth glinting at the bottom of her wide, gummy mouth. And here was Chloe looking like a beady-eyed dumpling on bath night, wrapped up in a baby version of one of those hooded towelling outfits that boxers wear on their way to the ring. And here was Chloe in the strong, adoring arms of her father, Paulo's younger brother, Michael, looking ridiculously pleased with herself.

Chloe. Baby Chloe.

Bloody baby *Chloe*.

Somewhere inside her, Jessica knew that she should be grateful. Other men furtively pored over websites with names like *Totally New Hot Sluts* and *Naughty Dutch Girls Must Be Punished* and *Thai Teens Want Fat Middle-Aged Western Men Now.* Jessica was certain that the only rival she had for Paulo's heart was baby Chloe – the child of Michael and Naoko, his Japanese wife. Jessica knew she should have been happy. Yet every picture of Chloe was like a skewer in her heart. And every time that Paulo admired his shrine to his niece, Jessica felt like strangling him, or screaming, or both. How could a man that kind, and that smart, be so insensitive?

'Michael says that Chloe's at the stage where she's putting everything in her mouth. Michael says – listen to this, Jess – that she thinks the world is a biscuit.'

'Hmm,' Jessica said, coolly staring at a picture of Chloe looking completely indifferent to the mushy food smeared all over her face. 'I thought all Eurasian babies were pretty.' Cruel pause for effect. 'Just goes to show, doesn't it?'

Paulo, always anxious to avoid a fight, said nothing, just quietly collected his pictures of Chloe, avoiding his wife's eyes. He knew he should be hiding these pictures in a bottom drawer, while Jessica knew it hurt him too – the younger brother becoming a father before he did. But it didn't hurt him in the same way that it hurt her. It didn't eat him alive.

Jessica loathed herself for talking this way, for denying Chloe's unarguable loveliness, for feeling this way. But she couldn't help herself. There was a large part of her that loved Chloe to bits. But Chloe was a brutal reminder of Jessica's own baby, that baby that hadn't been born yet, despite the years of trying, and it turned her into someone she didn't want to be.

Jessica had left work to have a baby. Unlike both her sisters, her career had never been central to her world. Work was just a way to make ends meet, and, more importantly, to perhaps meet the man she would make a life with. He was driving a black cab back then, in the days before he went into business with his brother, and when he stopped to help Jessica with her car, she thought he would be all chirpy cockiness. *Going my way, darling?* That's what she was expecting. But in fact he was so shy he could hardly look her in the eye.

'Can I help?'

'I've got a broken tyre.'

He nodded, reaching for his toolbox. 'In the business,' he said, and she saw that slow-burning smile for the first time, 'we call it a *flat* tyre.'

And soon they were away.

On her very last day at work, before she set off for her new life as a mother, her colleagues at the Soho advertising agency where she worked had gathered round with balloons, champagne and cake, and a big card with a stork on the front, signed by everyone in the office.

It was the very best day of Jessica's working life. She stood beaming among her colleagues, some of them never having said a word to her before, and she kept smiling even when someone said perhaps she should go a little easy on the booze.

'You know. In your condition.'

'Oh, I'm not pregnant *yet*,' Jessica said, and the leaving party was never quite the same.

Jessica's colleagues exchanged bewildered, embarrassed looks as she beamed happily, the proud young mum-to-be – as soon as she conceived – examining the card with the stork, surrounded by the balloons and champagne, among all the pink and the blue.

That was three years ago, when Jessica was twenty-nine. She had already been married to Paulo for two years, and the only thing that had stopped them trying for a baby the moment the vicar said, 'You may kiss the bride,' was that Paulo and his brother were trying to start their business. It wasn't the time for a baby. Three years ago, when the business was suddenly making money and Jessica was about to leave her twenties behind – that was the time for a baby. Except nobody had told the baby.

Three years of trying. They thought it would be easy. Now nothing was easy. Not sex. Not talking about what was wrong. Not working out what they might do next. Not feeling like complete failures when her period came around, with a pain that all the Nurofen Plus in the world could not smother.

Those paralysing, indescribable periods. That was when she felt alone. How could she ever describe that white-knuckle pain to her husband? Where would she start? What did he have to compare it with? That was one kind of pain. There were others. Traps were everywhere.

Even what should have been a small, simple pleasure like looking at pictures of her niece had Jessica in torment. One day she found herself weeping in the fifth-floor toilets of

John Lewis, the floor where the baby things are sold, and she thought, am I going insane? But no, it wasn't madness. Swabbing her eyes with toilet roll, Jessica realised that she had never had her heart broken before.

She had been hurt in the past – badly hurt, long before Paulo. But no boy or man could ever hurt her like their unborn baby did.

Jessica had believed that conception was a mere technical detail on her way to happy, contented motherhood. Now, after all this time trying, ovulation came around like a demand for rent money that she didn't have.

Now, when the Clear Plan Home Ovulation Test ordained that the time was right, Jessica and Paulo – who had imagined that they would be young, enthusiastic lovers for ever – grimly banged away like minor offenders doing community service.

That very morning Jessica had peed on her little white plastic oracle and it had duly decreed that her 48-hour window of fertility was opening. Tonight was the night. And tomorrow night too – although Paulo would have given it his best shot, as it were, by then. It felt like a cross between a date with destiny, and an appointment with the dental hygienist.

Paulo was settling down to the north London derby, a cold Peroni in his hand. He looked up as she entered the room, and the sight of his face made her heart give an old familiar pang. Although their sex life was now performed with a kind of numbing obligation, as if it were a form of particularly tiresome DIY, closer to putting together self-assembly furniture than creating a new life, Jessica still loved her husband's dark, gentle face. She still loved her Paulo.

'I don't know the score,' Paulo said, sipping on his Italian beer. 'So if you know who won, don't tell me, Jess.'

She knew it was a goalless draw. A typical grim north London derby. But she kept it to herself.

'I'm going up to bed now,' said Jessica.

'Oh, I say!' said the man on the television.

'Okay,' said Paulo.

Jessica nodded at the beer. 'Go easy on that stuff, will you?'

Paulo blushed. 'Sure.'

'Because . . . it makes you tired.'

She said it with the smallest of smiles. Like one of those jokes that are not really a joke at all. The way, thought Jessica, my mother would always let slip some unpalatable truth. The worthless old cow.

'I know,' said Paulo, putting down the beer. 'I'll be up in a minute.'

'You've got to admire the spirit of these youngsters,' said another man on TV. 'They're not giving up just yet.'

Something told Jessica that she had to harden her heart if she was going to get through this thing. Because what happened if the baby never came? What then? She didn't know how she could stand it, or what kind of life she would have with Paulo, who wanted children as much as any man could want children, which was almost certainly not as much as she wanted children, or how this marriage could endure with disappointment haunting their home like a malignant lodger.

'See you in a bit then,' Jessica said.

'See you soon, Jess,' Paulo said, not quite catching her eye.

She used to drive him crazy. Now he acted as though sex was an exam he hadn't prepared for.

'Oh, my word,' said the TV commentator. 'He's never going to get it in from there.'

A cone of golden light fell on Megan at her crowded desk.

She looked up from her computer screen at the skylight in the ceiling of the tiny room. To Megan it looked like a window in the kind of prison where they locked you up and threw away the key. The light and noise that filtered down indicated another world out there but it felt a very long way away. Yet she loved this room – her very first office in her first real job. Every morning she felt a shiver of pleasure when she walked into the little room. Smiling to herself, Megan got up from her desk and climbed on her chair. She was getting good at it now.

Three times a day she stood precariously on her swivel chair, its cushion worn threadbare by the buttocks of all those who had sat there before her, and she clung to the frame of the skylight, craning her neck. If she stood on tiptoe, she could see most of the school playground that backed onto the rear of the building. Megan loved to listen to the sound the children made at playtime. They were little ones, as noisy and smooth-skinned as babies. They sounded like a flock of ecstatic birds. She realised she had never had much experience of small children. She was so used to being the youngest.

'Doctor?'

Megan spun round, almost toppling off her chair.

A crumpled-looking woman was standing in the doorway, nervously fingering a piece of wet kitchen towel. A child in some kind of miniature football shirt was shrieking at her feet. The woman watched red-eyed as Megan descended to her desk.

'They told me to go in, doctor. The lady on the desk.' The woman looked shyly at the ground. 'Nice to see you again.'

Megan's mind was blank. She had seen so many faces recently, and so many bodies. She got a name, a date of birth and took a quick look at her notes. Then it all started to come back.

The woman had been here a few weeks ago with this same small child, who was then in his other outfit of a grubby grey vest, and chomping on a jam sandwich.

The brat had run his sticky paws through Megan's

paperwork while she examined his mother, confirming her pregnancy. The woman – Mrs Summer, although as far as Megan could tell, she wasn't married, and she didn't have a partner called Summer – had received the news like it was a final demand from the taxman. Not much older than Megan, who was twenty-eight, Mrs Summer was already beaten down by motherhood. The apprentice hooligan with the jam sandwich was her fourth from a rich variety of men.

'How can I help you?' Megan asked now, relieved that the brat seemed more subdued today.

'There's been some bleeding, Dr Jewell.'

'Let's take a look at you.'

It was an early miscarriage. The woman had been depressed by the news of the pregnancy, but this was infinitely worse. Suddenly, catching Megan off-guard, Mrs Summer seemed to be choking.

'What did I do wrong? Why did it happen?'

'It's not you,' Megan said. 'A quarter of all pregnancies end in – Here. Please.'

Megan pushed her box of Kleenex across the desk. Mrs Summer's scrap of kitchen towel was coming apart, and so was she. Megan came out from behind her desk and put her arms around the woman.

'Truly, it's not you,' Megan said again, more gently this time. 'The body runs its series of tests. It finds some abnormality in the embryo. Why does it happen? The honest answer is – we don't know. A miscarriage comes out of the blue. It's horrible, I know. The thought of what might have been.' The two women stared at each other. 'I'm sorry for your loss,' Megan said. 'I really am.'

And Megan was sorry. She even sort of understood how Mrs Summer could be terrified at the prospect of another baby, and yet devastated when the baby was abruptly taken away from her. A fifth child would have been a disaster. But losing it was a tragedy, a death in the family that she wasn't even really allowed to mourn properly, except for these shameful tears in a doctor's surgery the size of a broom cupboard.

Megan talked quietly to Mrs Summer about chromosomal and genetic abnormalities, and how, hard as it was for us to accept, they were simply incompatible with life.

'You and your partner have to decide if you want any more children or not,' Megan told her. 'And if you don't, then you need to start practising safe sex.'

'I do, doctor. But it's him. It's me . . . partner. He doesn't believe in safe sex. He says it's like taking a shower in a raincoat.'

'Well, you'll just have to discuss it with him. And condoms are far from the only possibility, if that's what he's referring to.'

Megan knew perfectly well that condoms were what he was referring to. But now and again she felt the need to adopt a magisterial tone, to reassert her authority, to keep her head above the sorry human mess that pressed its way into her surgery.

'What about the pill?'

'I blew up. Fat as a fat thing. Got thrombosis. Blood clots. Had to come off it.'

'Coitus interruptus?'

'Whipping it out?'

'Precisely.'

'Oh, I don't think so. You haven't met him. I've tried, doctor. Tried all the safe sex. What do you call it? The rhythm section.'

'Rhythm method, yes.'

'Tried that one when the doctor said it was the pill that was blowing me up. But it's when I'm asleep. He just helps himself.'

'Helps himself?'

'Jumps on top of me and he's away. Then snoring his head off the moment it's over. You would never get a condom on him, doctor. I wouldn't like to try. Honest I wouldn't.'

It was another world out there. The sprawling estates that surrounded the surgery. Where a baby was still a bun in the oven and the men still helped themselves when some poor cow collapsed at the end of another busy day.

'Well, you tell him he can't help himself. It's outrageous behaviour. I'll talk to him if you want me to.'

'You're nice, you are,' the woman told Megan, and grasped her in a soggy bear hug. Megan gently prised her away, and talked about the glories of an intrauterine device.

Women liked her. She was by far the youngest doctor at the surgery, a GP registrar only a month into her final year of vocational training, yet easily the most popular.

She had spent the last seven years preparing for this job – six of them at medical school, and the last year as a house officer in two London hospitals. Now, in a surgery where the other three doctors were all men, she was finally in a position where she could make a difference.

When women came in complaining of period pains that made them feel like throwing themselves under a train, Megan didn't just tell them to take a painkiller and get a grip. When young mothers came in saying that they felt so depressed they cried themselves to sleep every night, she didn't simply tell them that the baby blues were perfectly natural. When a nuchal scan said that the possibility of Down's syndrome was high, Megan discussed all the options, aware that this was one of the hardest decisions that any woman would ever have to make.

When Mrs Summer was gone, Dr Lawford stuck his head around her door. In the confines of the tiny room, Megan could smell him – cigarettes and a cheese and pickle bap. He bared his teeth in what he imagined to be a winning smile.

'Alone at last,' he said.

Lawford was Megan's GP trainer – the senior doctor meant to act as her guide, teacher and mentor during the year before she became fully registered. Some junior doctors worshipped their GP trainers, but after a month under his tutelage, Megan had concluded that Dr Lawford was a cynical, bullying bastard who hated everything about her.

'Chop chop, Dr Jewell. Your last patient was here for a good thirty minutes.'

'Surely not?'

'Thirty minutes, Dr Jewell.' Tapping his watch. 'Do try to move them in and out in seven, there's a good chap.'

She stared at him sullenly. Growing up with two older sisters had made Megan militant about standing up for herself.

'That patient has just had a miscarriage. And we're not working in McDonald's.'

'Indeed,' laughed Dr Lawford. 'Dear old Ronald McDonald can lavish a lot more time on his customers than we can. Here, let me show you something.'

Megan followed Lawford out into the cramped waiting room.

Patients sat around in various degrees of distress and decay. A large woman with a number of tattoos on her bare white arms was screaming at the receptionist. There were hacking coughs, children crying, furious sighs of exasperation. Megan recognised some of the faces, found that she could even put an ailment to them. She's cystitis, she thought. He's hypertension. The little girl is asthma – like so many of the children breathing the air of this city. My God, she thought, how many of these people are waiting to see me?

'You're going to have a busy morning, aren't you?' Dr Lawford said, answering her question. 'A good half of these patients are waiting for you.' Chastened, Megan followed Lawford back to her office.

'It's Hackney, not Harley Street,' he said. 'Seven minutes per patient, okay? And it doesn't matter if they have got the black plague or a boil on the bum. Seven minutes, in and out. Until God gives us forty-eight hours a day, or we get jobs in the private sector, it's the only way we can do it.'

'Of course.'

Lawford gave her an exasperated look and left her alone.

To get to this little room, Megan had worked so hard, but she wondered if she could make it through this final year with Lawford watching her every move. She had heard the only reason that surgeries welcomed a junior registrar was because it meant they were getting a doctor for nothing. But none of the old quacks, no matter how penny-pinching or cynical, wanted a bolshy GP registrar who was going to make their lives even harder. They would be better off without her. Megan felt that Lawford was waiting for her to do something stupid, so he could cut his losses and get shot of her.

And that was ironic because Megan suspected that she already had done something stupid. Something so stupid that she could hardly believe it.

In the morning, during one of her regular breakfast meetings with Lawford – Megan was obliged to meet him twice a week so that they could discuss her progress, or lack of it – she had quickly excused herself and run off to throw up her almond croissant and cappuccino in a café lavatory smelling of lemon-scented Jif.

But it was on her way home to her tiny flat, her feet and back aching, that Megan really believed that she had done something stupid.

She knew it was impossible, she knew that it was far too soon. But it felt so real.

The kick inside.

two

'Oh, you're far too young to be having a baby, dear,' Megan's mother told her. 'And I'm certainly too young to be a grand-mother.'

Megan estimated that her mother must be sixty-two by now, although officially she had only been in her fifties for the last six years or so.

In Megan's surgery she often saw grandmothers from the Sunny View Estate who were the same age as Cat and even Jessica – all those 'nans' in their middle and early thirties, who started child-bearing in what Mother Nature, if not the metropolitan middle class, would have considered their child-bearing years. But it was true – Olivia Jewell didn't look like anyone's idea of a grandmother. And Megan thought, why should she? She had never really got the hang of being a mother.

Olivia Jewell still turned heads. Not because of the modest fame that she had once enjoyed – that had evaporated more than twenty years ago – but because of the way she looked. The massed black curls, the Snow White pallor, those huge blue eyes. Like Elizabeth Taylor if she had won her fight against the fat, or Joan Collins if she had never made it to

Hollywood. An elderly English rose, wilting now, it was true, but still with a certain lustre.

'They take over your life,' Olivia said, although her voice softened as she contemplated her youngest daughter. 'Darling. You don't want anyone taking over your life, do you?'

When their parents had met at RADA, it was Olivia who was the catch. Jack was a tall, serviceably handsome young actor, ramrod straight after two years' National Service in the RAF and moonlighting as a male model (cigarettes, mostly – the young Jack looked good smirking in a blazer with a snout on the go).

But Olivia was a delicate porcelain beauty, like that other Olivia, Miss de Havilland, already a bit of a throwback in those years of post-war austerity, when large-breasted blondes were suddenly all the rage.

Olivia was swooned over by her teachers, her classmates and, later, the critics, who loved her as a petulant, foot-stamping Cordelia in Stratford. It was widely predicted that Jack would always work, but that Olivia was destined for true stardom. In the mocking passage of time, it had worked out very differently.

After a few years where he scuffled around in the background of British films nostalgic for World War Two – playing the pipe-smoking captain in a chunky sweater who goes down with his shipmates, or the knobbly-kneed POW who gets shot in the back by the Hun while attempting to escape, or the RAF squadron leader with the gammy leg anxiously scanning the blue skies of Kent – Jack Jewell stumbled on the role of a lifetime.

For almost twenty years he played a widowed father in the long-running BBC fishing drama, *All the Fish in the Sea* – played it for so long that Megan, his youngest child, had little memory of her father being around when she was growing up, he was so busy playing a doting father to his screen children. By the time they reached their teenage years, Jack Jewell's kindly, knowing face had become one of the cherished icons of the nation, while Olivia's big starring roles had never materialised.

'Dad would be pleased,' Megan said, deliberately provoking her. 'Dad would be happy to be a grandfather.'

Olivia shot her daughter a look. 'You didn't tell him, did you?'

'Of course not. But he would be happy, I bet.'

Olivia Jewell laughed. 'That's because he's a big soft bastard. And because he doesn't care what it would do to your life. Not to mention your lovely young body, dear.'

Megan and her mother were in the café in Regent's Park, ringed by all the white Nash houses, the most beautiful buildings in London, Megan thought, like architecture made out of ice cream. They were on one of their dates – drinking tea and watching the black swans glide across the lake, smelling freshly cut grass and the animal mustiness of the nearby London Zoo.

Megan was the only one of her daughters that Olivia saw on a regular basis. Contact with Jessica was sporadic – Jessie was too easily hurt for a sustained relationship with someone as selfish as Olivia – and Cat hadn't spoken to their mother in years.

You had to make an effort with her, Megan always thought. That's what her sisters didn't get. Their mother was all right if you made the effort.

'In the early sixties there was a darling little Maltese man off Brewer Street who used to take care of girls who got into trouble.' It still mildly surprised Megan every time she heard her mother's voice. She had a self-consciously cut-glass accent, the kind of accent that made Megan think of men in Broadcasting House reading the news in their tuxedos. 'God – what was his bloody name?'

'It doesn't matter, I'll be all right,' Megan said, pushing a napkin halfway across the table. Olivia covered her daughter's hands with her own, and gently rubbed them, as if to make them warm.

'Well – anything I can do, dear.'

Megan nodded. 'Thank you.'

'A woman's body is never the same after giving birth. I had a body like you when I was young. Not petite like Jessica. Or skinny like Cat. More like you. All curves.' Olivia squinted at her daughter. 'Perhaps not quite so *plump*.'

'Thanks a million.'

'Did you know that Brando once made a pass at me?'

'I think you mentioned it. About ten thousand times.'

'Dear Larry Olivier admired my Cordelia. The dress I wore to the premiere of *Carry On, Ginger* caused a sensation. I was the Liz Hurley of my day.'

'Then that makes Dad Hugh Grant.'

'Hughie Green more like. That man. I dreamed of Beverly Hills. He gave me Muswell Hill.'

It was strange, Megan thought. Their mother was the one who walked out. Their mother was the one who shacked up with a second-rate ham in a rented flat. Their mother was the one who left the raising of her children to their father, and whoever he could hire, and to Cat. And yet their mother was the one who acted bitter. Perhaps she could never forgive their father for becoming a bigger name than she would ever be.

Her career had been a peculiarly English affair. If Olivia Jewell had ever needed a job description, then *plummy crumpet* would have just about nailed it down. In the fifties she had screamed her way through half a dozen Hammer Horror movies – strung up in her nightdress in a Transylvanian dungeon, the mad doctor lurching towards her, wicked experiments on his mind – and then moved into whatever ramshackle provincial theatre would have her when the times and the accents changed, and the public wanted actresses to be more working class and northern (the kitchen sink dramas), or exotic and foreign (James Bond and his bikini-clad harem).

Although only twenty-two when the sixties began, Olivia Jewell seemed to belong to another era. But she would never admit to the long years of rep and resting. In her conversation, and perhaps even in her feverish head, she was all that her teachers at RADA and Kenneth Tynan had predicted she would ever be.

Olivia's star burned brightest the year after she left home for ever. Fleeting fame, when it came for their mother, arrived late. She was pushing forty – and admitting to thirty-two – when she landed the part of the posh, nosy neighbour in the mid-seventies ITV sitcom, *More Tea, Vicar?* The man in the back of the cab was the male lead, playing a diffident young priest who had an electrifying effect on his female parishioners, and in the sweltering summer of 1976, while London seemed to melt in the heat and Cat cooked for her sisters and tried in vain to find this new group the Sex Pistols on the radio, Olivia and her dirty vicar appeared together on the cover of the *TV Times*.

Then her star faded, and within a few short years the humour of *More Tea, Vicar?* swiftly seemed as though it came from some older England that was now embarrassing, racist, and ludicrously out of time.

The characters in it – the eye-rolling Jamaican, the goodness-gracious-me Indian, the bumbling Irishman and, yes, the plummy old crumpet from next door, who must have been a bit of a goer in her time – were all swept away on an angry tidal wave of jokes about Mrs Thatcher and bottoms.

Eventually the man in the back of the cab left Olivia alone

in the rented St John's Wood flat and went home to his wife and children. But somehow Olivia never seemed cowed by time and experience. The haughty grandeur she had mastered in the fifties had never deserted her. Megan believed in her.

'What am I doing, Mum?'

'You're doing the right thing, dear.'

'Am I? I am, aren't I? What else can I do?'

'You can't be tied down, Megan. You've got your whole life in front of you. And what if you meet some young buck? Some handsome young surgeon?' Olivia's huge eyes twinkled with delight at the thought of this Harley Street hunk. Then she scowled, furiously stubbing out her cigarette, angry with her youngest daughter for throwing away this perfect match. 'He's not going to want to take on some other man's child, is he?'

'It's not a baby yet,' Megan said, more to herself than her mother. 'Jessica wouldn't understand that. That's why I can't tell her. Or even Cat. It still has a tail, for God's sake. It's more like a prawn than a baby. Admittedly, it would grow –'

Her mother sighed.

'Darling, you can't have some screaming little shit-machine holding you down. That's what went wrong for me. No offence, dear. But you can't have this brat.'

Megan's eyes stung with unexpected tears.

'I can't, can I?'

'Not now, darling. Not after passing all those exams. And being such a clever girl at medical school. And emptying bedpans in those horrid hospitals in the East End.' Her mother looked pained. 'Oh, Megan. A baby? Not now, chicken.'

Megan knew exactly what her mother would advise. That was why she had wanted to see her. To hear that she had absolutely no choice. To be told that there was no other way out. That there was nothing to even think about. Perhaps the reason that Megan was closest to their mother was because she remembered her the least.

The last meeting of Olivia and all of her daughters had been more than fifteen years ago. Megan was a bright-eyed, still boyish twelve-year-old, Jessica a shy, pretty sixteen, pale and quiet after getting mangled on some school skiing trip – at least, that's what they told Megan – and Cat at twenty was clearly a young woman, emboldened by two years at university, openly bitter and keen to confront their mother over the designer pizzas.

When their mother casually informed them that she would not be attending the prize-giving day at Megan's school – Megan was always the most academically gifted – because she had an audition to play a housewife in a gravy commercial ('Too old,' they said when she had left, 'too posh.'), Cat exploded.

'Why can't you be like everybody else's mother? Why can't you be normal?'

'If I was normal, then you three would be normal too.'

Megan didn't like the sound of that. Her mother made normality sound scary. Maybe if she was normal then school-work wouldn't come so easily to her. Maybe she wouldn't be collecting a prize from the headmaster. Maybe she would be as slow and stupid as all the other children.

'But I want us *to be normal,' Jessica sobbed, and their mother laughed as though that was the funniest thing in the world.*

'How is my little Jessica?' said Olivia.

'This is a tough time for her,' Megan said. 'She's been trying for a baby for so long. She would feel terrible about – you know.'

'Your abortion, yes.'

'My procedure.'

Olivia never asked about Cat, although she sometimes

offered an unsolicited, and unflattering, opinion on her eldest child.

'I tried to speak to Jessica on the phone recently. Pablo said she was sleeping. Bit of tummy trouble, apparently.'

'*Paulo*. His name is Paulo.'

'Of course. Lovely Paulo with those gorgeous eyelashes. Like a girl, almost. I heard they were taking away her womb or something.'

'That's not it. She just needs some tests. She gets these excruciating periods. God, Mother, don't you know that?'

Olivia looked vague. 'I never really had much to do with Jessica's *cycle*, dear. But you're right, of course – you can't talk to her about your, you know, condition.'

Megan stared out over the lake. 'This should be happening to Jessica. This should be happening to her. She'll be a terrific mum.'

'Who's the father?' said Olivia, lighting a cigarette.

'Nobody you know.'

And Megan thought – nobody I know, come to that. How could I have been so stupid?

'My baby,' Olivia said, and she touched her daughter's face. Unlike her sisters, Megan had never doubted that her mother loved her. In her special way. 'Get shot of the bloody thing, okay? You're not like Jessica. The little woman who can't be fulfilled until she has a couple of screaming brats sucking her tits to the floor. You're not like that. And you're not like Cat – determined to be a spinster wasting herself on some inappropriate man.' Her mother smiled triumphantly. 'You're more like me.'

And Megan thought, is that really what I am?

Paulo hadn't been expecting the magazines. They were a surprise. Who would have thought the NHS would provide you with a bit of porn to help you fill your little plastic jug?

Their attempt for a baby had been so overwhelmingly unsexy, so stripped of anything resembling passion or lust – saving up your sperm as though they were points in Sainsbury's, only doing it when the ovulation test decreed, his wife's tears when it turned out that the act had all been in vain – that Paulo was stunned by the sight of what he thought of as dirty magazines.

Blushing like a teenager, he grabbed one called *Fifty Plus* and headed for his cubicle, wondering if that was their chest size, their age or their IQ.

The doctor had assured Paulo that his sperm test wasn't really a test at all.

'I don't want you to feel under any pressure. Nobody expects you to actually *fill* the little plastic jug.'

But just like any other exam, a sperm test came with the promise of either success or failure. Or it wouldn't be a test, would it?

So Paulo prepared. But instead of practising three-point turns or studying the Highway Code, he did everything to increase the number of potential lives swimming about inside him, and everything he could to ensure that they would be heading in vaguely the right direction.

Loose pants. Cold baths. Zinc, vitamin E and selenium, all purchased in health shops where both the staff and the clientele looked uniformly and spectacularly unhealthy.

He read all the literature. And there was an amazing amount of it. The human race was forgetting how to reproduce itself. Tap in 'sperm' on the search engine, and you almost drowned in the stuff.

The vitamin pills, the roomy pants, the nut-shrinking cold baths – apparently all these were good for the number of sperm, and their motility – their ability to wiggle around in the required fashion. But what was the pass mark? How many million did you need to get the nod?

Surely, Paulo thought, when the sperm hits the egg, all you really need is one?

The examination room was the toilet in an NHS hospital. Paulo had heard rumours that if you had your sperm test done in Harley Street, your wife was allowed to go in there with you and give you a hand.

But in this sprawling NHS hospital, which felt more like some untamed frontier town than a place of healing, where cancer patients in their dressing gowns hungrily sucked cigarettes outside the main reception, and tattooed men with head wounds regularly attacked the young nurses who were caring for them for not caring quite quickly enough, you just went in the toilets and made sad love to your little plastic jug.

And yet the event seemed momentous to Paulo. This was something new. This was masturbation for some greater good. After years of doing it behind locked doors – and how he recalled the shame and the fear that his parents would catch him red-handed emerging from the bathroom with a copy of a Sunday paper stuffed down his shirt – he was actually being encouraged to strangle the one-eyed trouser snake, choke the monkey and beat the meat. The world was saying, go ahead, Paulo. Wank yourself stupid.

There was a list of instructions – as if any man needed advice on how to fiddle about with himself – but basically it was just you, your jug, and some pornography, provided by the state.

So much was riding on this ridiculous act. It didn't feel like his sperm they were testing. It felt like his future, and the future he might have with Jessica. He unzipped his trousers, then immediately zipped them up again, taking deep breaths.

He had it easy. He knew that. He had to ejaculate into a little plastic jug, and he was allowed to do it in the privacy of an NHS toilet. Jessica had had so many examinations that she said she felt like her private parts were now in the public domain.

All these tests, all these judgements – as if it wasn't up to them if they loved each other, but to some much higher power, ancient and cruel.

Paulo flicked through the pages of *Fifty Plus*. He hadn't seen any of this stuff for years. At school, there was a boy known as Spud Face, a cackling, habitual masturbator – thick specs, red cheeks, always giggling inanely by the corner flag during games – who had regularly brought to class what he pronounced 'good wank fodder'.

Paulo, a shy, thoughtful boy who preferred magazines featuring motors, had always stayed at his desk, reading the latest edition of *Car*. But one day Spud Face had called Paulo across to the leering, cheering mob that always surrounded his dirty magazines during break.

'Oy, Baresi, come and look at this, you big poof. Here's something you can't get from cars.'

Paulo had caught a glimpse of the magazine and almost fainted – a bearded Asian man with no clothes on was doing something unbelievable to a goat who clearly couldn't believe his luck. While all the other goats in the neighbourhood were no doubt being beaten and mistreated, this goat was getting a blow job. That goat must have felt like he had won the goat lottery.

It was enough pornography to last Paulo a lifetime. He didn't like it then, and he didn't like it now. There was just something a bit too gynaecological about it for his straight-forward tastes.

Paulo closed his copy of *Fifty Plus*. Although he felt like he was semi-retired from his sex life – making love and making babies were clearly two very different things – the women in *Fifty Plus* did not remotely stir him.

Paulo closed his eyes. He got a grip of himself. And he thought about his wife.

Which made him a different man to all the other wankers in there.

The way Megan found out that her boyfriend was sleeping with somebody else was that she caught him with his hand on her arse. And Megan couldn't say that he looked exactly unfamiliar with the territory.

Will and Katie were on the up escalator at Selfridges just as Megan was coming down – perfectly placed for a view of Will's hand casually exploring the valley of the little tart's bottom. Katie had the decency to gasp when she saw Megan. Will went white, his hand frozen on Katie's rear, like someone caught with his fingers in the till.

Megan thought, what am I going to do? I just lost my best friend.

'A woman's biological destiny is to have a baby,' Will said. 'A man's biological destiny is to plant his seed in as many women as he can. But that doesn't mean I don't love you.'

This is what he told her. He told her all the other stuff too – that it didn't mean a thing, that he loved her, that they had been together for too long to chuck it away because of one mistake. And they had been together for a long time. Megan and Will had been med school sweethearts, living together when most of their contemporaries were playing doctors and nurses at every opportunity. But what it came down to in the end was that he had slept with Katie because the survival of the human race depended upon it.

'What can I do? I'm programmed to spread my seed. It's the biological imperative.'

'That's on your hard drive, is it? Sticking your miserable dick in strangers?'

'Katie's hardly a stranger. You've known her since med school.'

'She was a slapper there, too. Plenty of junior doctors did their advanced biology on Katie.'

'We grew very close working in accident and emergency at the Homerton. These things happen. You get thrown together.'

'You mean – *oh, no, I've slipped! And now my penis has got stuck in Katie! How on earth did this happen?* Is that what you mean, you rotten bastard?'

Megan thought that she should have expected something like this. She had noticed a sudden decline in Will's sex drive when he was doing those six months' vocational training at the Homerton, while she was off doing her six months' VTS in paediatrics at the Royal Free.

She had put it down to Will witnessing stab wounds on a regular basis, for the Homerton is in Hackney, and their A & E is busy every night of the year. Now Megan felt she should have guessed that Katie was wagging her tail in the doctors' mess during tea break. One of the first things that every medical student learns is that the average hospital has the sexual mores of a knocking shop when the fleet's in. All those extremely young doctors and nurses working all hours of the day and night in a highly stressed environment, most of them too busy for a proper relationship – it did something to the hormones.

As part of her vocational training, Megan had done six months at the Homerton's A & E herself, and it had done nothing for her libido. She had felt as though she was seeing the world as it really was for the first time in her life. But perhaps she had more imagination than Will and Katie.

He attempted to put his arms around her but she shrugged him off, almost baring her teeth. He really didn't understand that it was over. How could he? He wasn't like Megan. His parents had stayed together.

Nobody left in his home. Nobody decided to cut their losses and bolt. He had never seen the rotten, messy aftermath of fucking around.

Will had grown up as the youngest child in a tight, loving family in Hampstead Garden Suburb. That was one of the things she had loved about him. The intact, secure world that he came from, the long Sunday lunches and the gently mocking humour and the years of unbroken happiness. At weekends, and at Christmas, he took her home to his parents and they made her feel like she belonged, and she wanted to be a part of this other family, this other life, this better world.

These kids from their nuclear families made her laugh. Will thought he would always be forgiven, he thought that trust could never be broken and love could never be pissed away. Like all the saps from happy homes, Will believed in his right to a happy ending.

But she snapped the suitcase shut, hefted it from their bed and placed it at his feet.

'Megan? Come on. Please.'

She saw him now as the rather pathetic figure he had always been. Will was one of those good-looking short guys who are destined to a life of discontent. Sweet enough but totally unreliable, bright but lazy, socially charming but academically listless, he truly wasn't cut out for a career in medicine. He desperately wanted to be, and his parents – a silvery, gym-fit eye surgeon father and a blonde, well-preserved paediatrician mother – desperately wanted him to be, but during the long years of training their good-looking boy had struggled at every stage.

Will had been one of the unhappy minority of medical students who have to resit their finals, finally scraping a pass only to discover that dealing with death, sickness and gore on a daily basis gave him a funny tummy, and minor league depression. Even his depression was half-hearted. Now a part of Megan wanted to strangle him. But she also felt sorry for him. Poor Will. He was wrong for this life. Just as he was wrong for her.

And there was something else he was wrong about. It was true that she was not led around by a part of her anatomy, the way Will's penis apparently dragged him around like an insane tour guide, taking him to places he had never in a million years planned to visit.

But there were times when Megan's craving for that kind of human contact was just as urgent. There were days when her yearning – for love, for sex, for something better than both – was far stronger than anything Will could have felt when he bent Katie over in the darkened doctors' mess at three in the morning. She had a biological imperative of her own.

The big difference was that Will's craving was determined by a little pink courgette that was on call twenty-four hours a day, vulnerable to the whim of anything in a mini-skirt that took a shine to him. And when it came, Megan's craving was determined by something far more powerful than that.

It was on one of those craving nights, about two weeks after she had sent Will home to his bitterly disappointed parents in Hampstead Garden Suburb, that Megan went to a party for the first time in ages, and met a young Australian who, after taking a look at the world, was soon to go home to sun and surf, Sydney and his girlfriend.

What was his name again? It didn't really matter now. She was never going to see him again.

Where Will was small, dark, with cheekbones that really belonged on a woman, the man at the party was tall, athletic, with a nose that had been broken twice playing rugby in college, and once falling off a bar stool in Earls Court.

Not really Megan's type at all.

But then look what her type had done to her.

Cat Jewell loved her life.

Every time she entered her Thames-side flat, Tower Bridge glittering just for her beyond her windows, it felt like she was taking a little holiday from the world.

Almost twenty years after leaving home, she had finally found a place of stillness and silence and fabulous riverside views, a place that felt like the home she had been looking for all these years.

In an underground car park, there was her silver Mercedes-Benz SLK, and although her brother-in-law Paulo, who knew about these things, made gentle fun of her – 'That's not a sports car, Cat, it's a hairdryer' – she loved zipping about town in a car that, rather like her life, was built for two. At the very most.

It was true that her flat was the smallest one in the riverside block, and the car was five years old and etched with a beading of rust. But these things filled her with a quiet pride. They belonged to her. She had worked for them. After escaping from the prison of her childhood, she had made a life for herself.

When she had come back to London after university, the woman who gave Cat her first proper job told her that you could get anything in this town, but sometimes you had to wait a while for a good apartment and true love. At thirty-six, she finally had the apartment. And she believed she also had the man.

Over the years Cat had had her fair share of sloppy drunks, premature ejaculators and the secretly married – on one memorable occasion, all on the same date – but now she had Rory, and she couldn't imagine being with anyone else.

Cat had met him when he was teaching Megan wado ryu

karate. He was standing in the corner at a party celebrating Megan's end of term at medical school, and Cat had taken pity on him. You could tell he didn't have it in him to start a conversation with anyone.

To Cat he had seemed an unlikely martial artist – soft-spoken, socially awkward, no swagger about him. Then as the party rapidly degenerated into what Megan said was a typical med school do, full of legless nurses and young doctors off their faces on half an E, Rory explained to Cat how he came to the martial arts.

'I was bullied at school. The tough guys didn't like me for some reason. They were always pushing me around. Then one day they went too far. I had concussion, broken ribs, a real mess.'

'So you decided to learn – what is it? – kung fu?'

'Karate. Wado ryu karate. And I enjoyed it. And I was good at it. And soon nobody pushed me around any more.'

'And you mashed up the bullies?'

He grimaced, wrinkling his nose, and she realised she liked this man. 'It doesn't really work like that.'

Thirty years on, you could still glimpse the quiet, bullied kid he had once been. Despite his job, all those days spent teaching people to kick and punch and block, there was a real gentleness about him. A strong but gentle man. The kind of man you might want to have children with, if you were the kind of woman who wanted children.

Which Cat Jewell was most certainly not.

Rory's body was fit and hard from the endless hours of wado ryu karate, but there was no disguising the inner wariness of a divorced man in his forties. He had done the whole happy families bit for so long, it hadn't worked out, and he was in no rush to do it all again. He had been there, done that, and was still paying the child support. And that was fine by Cat.

Rory was more than ten years older than Cat, living across town in Notting Hill with a son who came to stay, usually when he had argued with his mother and stepfather.

Since his divorce, Rory had dated plenty of women who all seemed to have the alarms ringing on their biological clocks – women in their early thirties who had yet to meet Mr Right, women in their late thirties who had met Mr Right only for him to turn out to be Mr Right Bastard. It was too much. The last thing a man wanted to hear about on the third date was how much the woman wanted a husband and a baby. It would turn off any man. Especially a divorced man. After all of that, Cat was a sweet relief.

She didn't want him for a husband, or a father. She loved her life, and didn't need some ageing Prince Charming to change it. If their relationship was going nowhere, then that was fine. Because they were both happy with the place that it had arrived at.

And that was just as well, because Rory wasn't in the position to give any woman a baby. Cat had heard all about it the night, a month after Megan's party, that they had slept together for the first time.

'I'll wear a condom if you want me to, Cat. But there's not really the need.'

She stared at him from the other side of the bed, not trusting him and wondering what line she was being spun.

'I mean, I'll wear a condom if you want me to. Of course I will. But you don't have to worry about getting pregnant.'

He wasn't going to promise to pull out before he came, was he? Yeah, right. And the cheque's in the post.

'I've had the cut,' Rory said.

'What?'

'The snip, the cut, the operation. You know. A vasectomy.'

For some reason she knew he was telling the truth. There was just something about the way he hung his head, smiling ruefully, saying the words that she knew he must have rehearsed.

'I had it just before my marriage broke up. My wife and I – well, things were bad. We were both getting older. We knew we didn't want any more children. So I had it done. And then she got pregnant by her tennis coach.' The rueful smile. 'So it was perfect timing, really.'

'Did it hurt?'

'A bit like getting your balls caught in a nutcracker.'

'Okay. We don't need to talk about it any more. Come here.'

It was strange at first – the feeling of a man coming inside her, and knowing she didn't have to worry. Cat had spent so many years trying to avoid getting pregnant, enduring the various indignities of coil, cap, condom, pill and pulling out, that it was a load off her mind, and a load off her menstrual cycle, to be able to stop worrying about all of that. Rory was a considerate, experienced lover, and yet not one of those men who absolutely insist on the woman coming first, as though anything else would be awfully bad manners. They even had their own running gag about their contraception arrangements, or lack of them.

'How do you like your eggs, madam?' Rory would ask, and Cat would cry, 'Unfertilised!'

She began to see his inability to have children as another one of the good things in her perfect life. Like the flat with the view of Tower Bridge, and the beat-up little sports car, and her job as manager of Mamma-san, one of the most fashionable restaurants in London, where tables were in such short supply that, when you called the reservation line, they just laughed at you and then hung up.

Unencumbered – that was a word Cat liked.

She was free to lie around all Sunday in her dressing gown, reading the papers, or jump on a plane and go to Prague for the weekend, or stay over at Rory's place when the mood took her. Unencumbered – and that was just how she wanted it. Because after their mother had walked out, her childhood had been as encumbered as can be. She never wanted to be that tied down, that domesticated, again.

She didn't want children, and could go for, oh, months, without even thinking about the subject – until someone implied that it was somehow abnormal to want to hold on to a life you loved – and she was too successful, and too fulfilled, to feel as though she was missing anything. Cat didn't consider herself childless, she considered herself child-free. Big difference.

She wasn't like those other women. She wasn't like her sister Jessica. Cat didn't need a baby to make her life worthwhile, and her world whole.

Where did it come from, that addiction to the idea of motherhood, that need to be needed? Cat knew where it came from – it came from men who didn't love you enough. Men who left a hole in your life that a woman could only fill with some adorable, eight-pound crying and crapping machine.

So she lay in the dark with Rory sleeping by her side, and she thought to herself, this is perfect, isn't it? This is a good, unencumbered life. *Unencumbered* – the most beautiful word in the English language.

Why would anyone ever want anything more?

three

Paulo and Michael grew up in one of the rougher parts of Essex, their father an engineer at Ford in Dagenham, and their childish dreams were full of cars.

More than half the men in their neighbourhood worked at the plant. Cars were everything here. Cars meant jobs, a wage packet, a glimpse of freedom. Cars were how the boy became a man. A teenager's first Ford Escort was a rite of passage as momentous as any tribal scar. Yet although the brothers both loved cars, they loved them in very different ways.

Paulo was fetishistically obsessed with V8 engines, camshafts and the life of Enzo Ferrari. Michael's interest veered more towards what he called 'pussy magnets'.

Paulo loved cars for themselves. Michael loved them for what they could get you, the sweet illusions they projected, and the dreams they made come true.

Michael liked girls as much as he liked cars. His specialist subject, even when he was a spotty little virgin, sharing a bedroom with his slightly bigger brother, was 'what drives them wild'.

While Paulo learned about Modena and Le Mans, Michael

read top-shelf magazines and absorbed the lessons of 'shallow fucking' ('You don't put it all the way in – drives them wild, it says so here') and locating the G-spot ('Put a moistened finger inside and then move it as if you want someone to come towards you – drives them wild, Paulo, apparently').

They both covered the walls with pictures of Ferraris, but Michael had Sam Fox sandwiched between the Maranellos and the Spiders. Until one day their devout mother saw her.

'I'm not having the Whore of-a Babylon in my house,' she said, pulling down the poster with one hand and deftly cuffing Michael around the ear with the other. She knew it wouldn't be Paulo putting up Whore of Babylon pictures. 'Put up our Holy Mother.'

'No jugglies on the wall, lads,' their father quietly told them later. 'They upset your mother.'

And the brothers thought – jugglies? What would their old man know about jugglies?

Their parents had come across from Napoli as small children, landing within a year of each other, although you would never know it. Their father, another Paulo, sounded every inch a working-class Londoner, all glottal stops and talk of West Ham and Romford dogs, while their mother, Maria, had never lost the accent and the attitudes of the old country.

Maria – who was called 'Ma' by both her husband and her sons – didn't drive, never saw a bill and never had a job. 'My home is my job,' she said. Yet she was the volatile, undisputed emperor of their little terraced home, giving her sons what she called 'a clip round the earhole' as often as she kissed their cheeks with a fierce, moist-eyed passion. The boys couldn't recall their father ever raising his voice.

As a child, Paulo felt most Italian when he visited the homes of his friends. That's when he knew his own family was special, not because they attended Mass or because they ate baked ziti or because his parents spoke to each other in a foreign language, but because they resembled the type of family that was dying out in this country.

Some of his friends lived with just their mother, one of them lived with just his father, many were in strange patchwork families, made up of new fathers, half-brothers and stepmothers. His own family was much more simple, and old-fashioned, and he was grateful for that fact. It was the kind of family that Paulo wanted for himself one day.

There were only ten months between the brothers, and many people mistook them for twins. They grew up unusually close, dreaming of going into business together one day – something with cars. Racing them, mending them, selling them. Anything. This was what they had learned from their father and all those long years at Ford. 'You can't get rich working for somebody else,' said the old man, again and again, just before he fell asleep in front of the ten o'clock news.

After leaving school at sixteen, the brothers drove taxis for ten years, Paulo in a black London cab after passing the Knowledge, and Michael working the minicabs, until finally they had enough of a stake to get a loan from the bank.

Now they sold imported Italian cars from a showroom off the Holloway Road in north London. They brought in small quantities of pre-ordered merchandise from Turin, Milan and Rome, driving the cheaper left-hand-drive cars back to the UK themselves, doing the conversion to right-hand drive in their body shop, or else they bought second-hand in the boroughs of Islington, Camden and Barnet. Above their modest showroom a row of green, white and red Italian flags streamed in the weak sunlight of north London, above the name of the firm – Baresi Brothers.

They made a good living, enough to support both their

families, although like many small businessmen they found there was either not enough work or more than they could handle.

Now when trade was slow, Michael produced the latest pictures of his daughter, Chloe, and spread them across the gleaming red bonnet of an old Ferrari Modena. If marriage to Naoko had calmed Michael down, Paulo thought, then the birth of Chloe seemed to have tamed him.

As they admired the latest portraits of Chloe, the brothers were joined by Ginger, the showroom's receptionist. Ginger was married and somewhere in her late thirties, and Paulo couldn't help noticing that Ginger's breasts seemed to rise and fall in slow motion as she sighed with longing at the sight of baby Chloe in all her gummy-mouthed glory.

'Oh, she's *gorgeous*, Mike,' Ginger said.

And Michael smiled proudly, completely smitten by his daughter. Ginger looked all dreamy-eyed, as she went to put on the kettle.

'They love it if you've got kids,' Michael told his brother when they were alone.

Paulo smiled. 'I guess it's a sign that your wedding tackle's in full working order, and you're a good provider, and all of that. You know – a good mate.'

'Yes, all that old bollocks,' Michael said, as he considered his daughter's pouting beauty. 'It drives them wild, doesn't it?'

Megan didn't remember too much about the party. A crumbling Victorian house big enough to provide a home to half a dozen trainee doctors. The sweet and sickly smell of dope. All these people she knew acting ten years younger than they really were. And all this really bad music – or at least music she didn't know.

Then suddenly there was this guy – Kirk, definitely Kirk – and he was different from the other people there.

For a start he wasn't as unhealthy-looking as all the young doctors. He didn't drink as much, or smoke as much. He didn't have the cynical line in chat that Megan's contemporaries had developed as a way of dealing with the parade of disease and deprivation that was suddenly passing through their lives, expecting to be saved.

He just stood there, a fit, good-looking Australian boy – more reserved than you would expect a guy like that to be – smiling politely as the finest minds of their generation got stoned and drunk while talking shop.

'Everybody's so smart,' he said, and it made her laugh.

'Is that what you think? I thought this lot were just good at passing exams.'

'No, they're really smart. Got to be smart to be a doctor, haven't you? I don't understand what they're talking about half the time. All these medical terms. Someone was talking about a patient who was PFO.'

Megan smiled. 'That just means, *Pissed – Fell Over*,' she said.

He frowned. 'It does?'

She nodded, and let him into the secret language of medical students. Raising her voice above the bad music, while he tilted his handsome head towards her, Megan told him about ash cash (money paid to a doctor for signing cremation forms), house red (blood), FLKs (funny-looking kids), GLMs (good-looking mums) and the great fallback diagnosis, GOK (God only knows) – all the mocking slang that protected them from the sheer naked horror of their jobs.

'But you still got to be smart, though,' he insisted.

What an open and honest thing to say, she thought. And so unlike all the people she knew, who couldn't open their mouths without trying to make some cynical little joke. She looked at him – really looked at him – for the first time. 'What do you do?'

'I teach,' he said. It was the last thing she would have expected. 'I teach people how to dive. You know – scuba dive.'

She gestured with her glass, taking in the party, the flat, the city.

'Not around here.'

His wide white smile. Megan loved his smile. 'In sunnier places. You ever dive?'

'No, but I've got a certificate for swimming a length in my pyjamas. Not really the same thing, is it?'

He laughed. 'It's a start.'

He liked her. She could tell. It happened quite a lot. She knew she wasn't as pretty as Jessica, who had a kind of baby-faced beauty about her, or as tall as Cat, who was as long-limbed and rangy as a dancer, but men liked Megan. They liked all those curves and a face that, because of some genetic accident, somehow looked slightly younger than her age. They liked that contrast. *A girl's face and a woman's body,* Will always said excitedly, heading straight for Megan's breasts.

She smiled at Kirk, and he did her the honour of blushing. It felt good to have this kind of contact after being with Will for so long, and having to make sure she didn't send out the wrong signals. Tonight she could send out any signal she liked.

Then suddenly there was finally a song she knew and loved – the one where Edwyn Collins sings, '*Well, I never met a girl like you before.*'

'That can be our song,' Kirk said, grinning sheepishly, and usually such ham-fisted flirting would have turned her right off. But she let him get away with it because she liked him too. Right at that moment, she liked him a lot. He wasn't part of her world and that was fine. She was ready for a break from her world.

And then there was that moment she had almost forgotten about after all the years as someone's girlfriend – the look of recognition in the eyes of someone you don't know yet – and suddenly his face was an irresistible object, and their heads were slightly tilting to one side, and finally they were kissing.

He was a good kisser and that was nice too. Enthusiastic, but not trying to clean your tonsils with his tongue. A really good kisser, Megan thought – just the right amount of give and take. She liked that too. But what she liked best was that he could have probably fucked any girl at that party, but he clearly wanted to fuck her.

And Megan thought, you're in luck, mate.

So they found themselves in one of the bedrooms, and Megan started to relax a little when she saw there was a lock on the door, and soon she was fulfilling her biological destiny on a stack of coats, while downstairs Edwyn Collins sang, '*I never met a girl like you before,*' and, yes, somehow it felt like it was just for them.

Megan smiled to herself as her sister came through the turnstile.

Jessica looked gorgeous passing through the crowd, Megan thought, like a woman without a care in the world among a mob of tube-weary commuters. Men of all ages turned for a second look – checking out the slim legs and that effortlessly size 10 frame and the round baby face that often made strangers believe she was the youngest of the sisters.

Looking at Jessica made Megan feel shabby and fat. That was the trouble with curves. You had to watch them or they got out of control. Megan was suddenly aware that she had only fingercombed her hair that morning, and that she had to stop keeping Mars bars in her desk.

They hugged each other at the ticket barrier.

'Look at us,' Megan said, linking arms with her sister. 'Grace Kelly and a crack whore.'

Jessica sized up her sister.

'You look exhausted, Dr Jewell. Doesn't that sound great? *Dr Jewell, Dr Jewell.*'

'I've been pretty busy. It feels like every woman in the East End wants me to look up her fanny.'

'Oh, I know the feeling. Are you still okay for lunch? We could have done it some other time.'

'We're fine, Jess.'

'And they *do* give you a four-hour lunch break, don't they?' Jessica said.

She was wide-eyed with concern. There was an innocence about her that both her siblings lacked, as though she had been spared most of life's sharp edges. The middle child, buffered by the presence of the big sister and the baby.

Megan just smiled. It was true that her morning surgery ended at twelve, and her afternoon surgery didn't begin until four. But her morning surgery usually overran by almost an hour – she just couldn't seem to get her consultations down to the required time – and before afternoon surgery began, she was expected to make her round of house visits.

'I've got us a table in J. Sheekey's,' Jessica said. 'Is fish all right for you?'

Fish and a few glasses of something white would have been fine with Megan. But she really didn't have time for an elaborate lunch in the West End. In truth, she just about had time to grab a sandwich at the nearest Prêt à Manger, but she didn't want to cancel lunch with one of her big sisters.

'It's not really *all* lunch break, Jess,' Megan said gently. 'I have to see someone in their home before surgery starts again.'

'You mean sick people?'

'Sick people, yeah. I've got to see a woman this afternoon. Well, her little girl.'

'You visit sick people in their homes? Wow, that's terrific service, Meg. I thought they only did that on Harley Street.'

Megan explained that the sick people with a doctor on Harley Street didn't need someone to come round to see them. Those people had cars, taxis, spouses who drove, even chauffeurs. Her patients in Hackney were often afflicted by what was known as *no means*. No cars, no money for cabs. Many of them were stuck at the top of a tower block with a bunch of screaming kids, and all this stuff in their heads about it getting worse if they sat in a doctor's waiting room. So house calls were actually far more common at the bottom end of the market.

Megan didn't tell Jessica that the older, male doctors at the surgery all hated making house visits, and so farmed the majority of them out to her. Despite being four years younger, Megan had always felt the need to protect Jessica from the horrible truth about the world.

'Somewhere closer then,' said Jessica, trying not to sound disappointed.

'Somewhere closer would be good.'

They bagged the last table in Patisserie Valerie, and after they had ordered, the sisters smiled at each other. Because of Megan's new job, it had been a while since they had seen each other. They both realised that it didn't matter where they had lunch.

'How's Paulo and his business?'

'Good – business is up eighty per cent on last year. Or is it eight per cent?' Jessica bit her bottom lip, staring thoughtfully at the mural on the Pat Val wall. 'I can't remember. But they're importing a lot of new stock from Italy. Maseratis, Ferraris, Lamborghinis, all that. People here order them. Then Paulo and Mike go and get them. How's Will?'

'Will's sort of out of the picture.'

Jessica flinched. 'Oh, I liked Will. He was really good-looking. For a short guy.'

'He wasn't so short!'

'Kind of short. I suppose it's hard to keep a relationship going when you're both working so hard.'

'Will's never done a day's work in his life. It's actually hard to keep a relationship together when one of you is a slut hound.'

'Oh. Oh, I'm sorry.'

'Don't be. Best to find out these things before – you know. Before it's too late. Before you go and do something stupid.'

'But you loved Will, didn't you?'

'I think I was grateful that somebody seemed so interested in me,' Megan said. 'Especially such a good-looking short guy.' They laughed. 'Don't worry about it. Really. It was never one of the great love matches. Not like you and Paulo.'

'Still – it's sad when people break up. I hate it. Why can't things just stay the same?'

Megan smiled at her sister. Jessica – last of the great romantics. She was exactly the same when they were growing up. Jessie always had Andrew Ridgeley on her wall, and some unreachable boy she had a hopeless crush on.

'You look good, Jess.'

'And you look worn out. Nobody would guess that I'm the ill one.'

'You're not ill!'

'Got this bloody test coming up. Where they drill a hole through your belly button, for God's sake.'

'The laparoscopy. Who's doing it?'

Jessica named an obstetrician and an address on Wimpole Street.

'He's good,' Megan said. 'You'll be fine. Everything okay with Paulo's sperm?'

A businessman at the next table turned to look at them. Megan stared back at him until he looked away.

'There's a slight mobility problem.'

'Motility problem. That's not the end of the world. It just means some of them are lazy little buggers. You would be amazed what they can do with lazy sperm these days.'

The businessman stared at them, shook his head, and signalled for his bill.

'I'm not so worried about Paulo.' Jessica idly ran her fingers through some spilled sugar on the table in front of her. 'What I'm worried about is me, and what they are going to find when they cut me open.'

Megan had her own ideas about what they might find when they looked inside her sister. But she smiled, taking her sister's sugar-coated hands in her own, saying nothing.

'I feel like I've got something wrong with me, Meg.'

'You're lovely. There's nothing wrong with you.' Megan shook her head. Nobody who looked like her sister should ever feel this sad. 'Look at you, Jess.'

'I feel defective.' Jessica gently released herself from Megan's grip, and considered the small crystals of sugar stuck to her fingertips. 'That I don't work the way I should work.' She carefully placed her fingers in her mouth, and grimaced, as if the taste wasn't sweet at all.

'You and Paulo are going to have a beautiful baby, and you're going to be the best mother in the world.'

The waitress arrived with Jessica's pasta and Megan's salad, and that's when the wave of nausea struck. Megan pushed back her chair, shoved her way through the crowded café, knocking aside an authentically French waiter, and just about made it to the toilet before she threw up.

Back at the table, Jessica hadn't touched her lunch.

'What's wrong with you, Megan?'

'Nothing.'

Jessica stared at her with a sullen stubbornness that Megan knew from their childhood.

'What *is* it?'

'Just really tired, that's all. Working too hard, I guess. It's nothing. Eat your pasta.'

Megan couldn't tell her sister.

Jessica had to be protected from this secret, more than she had ever needed to be protected from anything.

How could she ever tell Jessica? Megan's baby would only break her heart.

It wasn't as though she was planning to keep it.

'I tell you, doctor – I'm so knackered today I ain't hardly got the energy to light up.'

Megan soon understood why the other doctors were reluctant to make house visits.

It was hardly ever the truly sick and infirm that demanded a doctor come to their door. The pensioner crippled with arthritis, the single mum with a disabled child, the middle-aged woman who had just been told that there were cancer cells throughout her body – these people somehow struggled to the overcrowded waiting room of the surgery.

The ones who called you out were invariably the loud ones who talked a lot about their rights, the ones who managed to be both self-pitying and egocentric. Like Mrs Marley.

She was a large woman in a small council flat in the bleak heart of Sunny View, one of the most notorious estates in London. If you didn't live among these concrete warrens, then you didn't venture into the Sunny View Estate unless you were buying drugs, selling drugs or making a concerned documentary. Apart from summer, when the annual riots came round, even the police gave the Sunny View Estate a wide berth. Megan didn't have that option.

She had been frightened before. During her year as a

hospital house officer she had spent six months attached to a consultant at the Royal Free, and then six months working in casualty at the Homerton.

The Royal Free was a breeze – her consultant, a paediatrician, was a kind and generous man, and the children of Highgate and Hampstead and Belsize Park were mostly beautifully behaved little children who wanted Megan to read them Harry Potter. But casualty at the Homerton was another world.

After the first shift Megan felt that she had seen more of the world than she ever wanted – stabbed teenagers, beaten wives, mangled bodies pulled from car wrecks. Meat porters with hooks in their heads, pub drinkers who had been glassed at closing time, drug entrepreneurs who had been shot in the face by a business rival.

It was Megan's responsibility to assess the level of injury when the patients crawled, hobbled or were carried in. Seeing those wounds and that misery, and having to make an instant judgement about what needed to be done – that was as scared as she had ever been. Somehow walking through the Sunny View Estate to see Mrs Marley and her sick child was worse. How could that be? Hormones, Megan thought. It's just your hormones going barmy.

At the foot of the stairwell to Mrs Marley's flat, a group of teenagers were loitering. With their unearthly white skin and hooded tops, they looked like something out of a Tolkien nightmare. They didn't say anything when Megan passed through them, just smirked and leered with their generic contempt and loathing. They stank of fast food and dope – a sweet, rotting smell coming from under those hoods.

'You look a bit young to me, darling,' Mrs Marley said suspiciously. 'Are you sure you're a proper doctor?'

Megan was impressed. Most people never questioned her authority. 'I'm a GP registrar.'

'What's that then?'

'I have to do a year under supervision before I become fully registered.'

Mrs Marley narrowed her eyes. 'Next time I want a proper quack. I know my rights.'

'What appears to be the problem?' said Megan.

The problem was the woman's daughter. An impossibly cute three-year-old – how do such repulsive adults produce such gorgeous children? – who lay listlessly on the sofa, staring at a Mister Man DVD. Mr Happy was having the smile wiped off his yellow face by all the other inhabitants of Mister Town. Megan knew the feeling.

She examined the child. Her temperature was high, but everything else seemed to be normal. Megan saw she was wearing small diamond studs in her ears. They couldn't wait for their children to grow up on the Sunny View Estate, although with their casual clothes and recreational drugs and loud music, the Sunny View adults seemed to stew in a state of perpetual adolescence.

'What's your name?' Megan said, pushing the child's hair from her moist forehead.

'Daisy, miss.'

'I think you've got a bit of a fever, Daisy.'

'I've got a kitty-cat.'

'That's nice.'

'I've got a puppy.'

'Lovely!'

'I've got a dinosaur.'

'I just want you to take it easy for a couple of days. Will you do that for me, Daisy?'

'Yes, miss.'

'Are her bowel movements normal, Mrs Marley?'

'Shits like a carthorse, that one,' said the mother, running her fat pink tongue along the edge of a cigarette paper.

Megan stood up and faced the woman. When she spoke she was surprised to find her voice shaking with emotion.

'You're not smoking drugs in the presence of this child, are you?'

Mrs Marley shrugged. 'Free country, innit?'

'That's a common misconception. If I discover you are taking drugs in front of this child, you will find out exactly how free it is.'

'You threatening me with the socially serviced?'

'I'm telling you not to do it.'

The woman's natural belligerence was suddenly cowed. She put down the cigarette papers and began fussing over Daisy as though she was up for mother of the year.

'You hungry, gorgeous? Want Mummy to defrost you summink?'

Megan let herself out. That woman, she thought. If Daisy were mine I would feed her good nutritious food and read her Harry Potter and never pierce her little ears and never let her wear cheap jewellery and –

Her eyes suddenly filled with tears. Daisy was not her child. She was just her patient, and she had three more to see on the Sunny View Estate before the start of afternoon surgery.

Megan pushed through the hooded youths at the foot of the stairwell. They didn't laugh at her this time, even though their ranks had been swollen by a number of smaller hooded creatures, who looked like elves on mountain bikes.

These people, thought Megan. The way they breed. Like rabbits.

It was lucky she was here to save them.

Cat's boss was the woman with everything.

Brigitte Wolfe had a business she had built from nothing, a boyfriend she had met in one of the more exclusive resorts in Kenya and, above all, independence.

If Cat's dream on leaving home was pure, unencumbered liberation, then surely Brigitte was closer to achieving that dream than anyone she had ever known. There was no husband to answer to, no children to prevent her jumping on a plane to anywhere she felt like going. Nobody owned Brigitte. Unlike most people on the planet, Brigitte wasn't trapped by her past.

So Cat was surprised to walk into Brigitte's office at Mamma-san on Saturday night and find her boss feeding a shoebox full of photographs to a shredding machine.

Brigitte held up her hand, requesting silence. Cat stood there and watched her deleting a box full of memories.

Brigitte would select a photograph from the shoebox, give it a cold smile, and then feed it to the growling shredder. A wastepaper basket overflowing with coloured streamers indicated Brigitte had been at her work for some time. Cat noticed that the photographs were all of Brigitte and her boyfriend. If a forty-five-year-old property developer called Digby could reasonably be called a boyfriend.

There had been a string of men in the past, all that bit older and bit richer than Brigitte, and she tended to stick with them for two or three years, and then trade them in. 'Like cars,' she told Cat. 'You get a new one before the old one fails its MOT.'

Digby had been around for longer than most. Brigitte always said that he could stay until she found a vibrator that liked going to galleries. Now Digby was clearly out, but it didn't look as though it had ended the way these things had for Brigitte in the past.

Brigitte had taught Cat everything she knew about the restaurant business, and a lot of what she knew about life.

So while Brigitte fed her relationship to the shredding machine, Cat stood there in patient silence, as if she might learn something.

Cat owed her career to this woman.

When she had first met Brigitte Wolfe, Cat was a twenty-five-year-old freelance journalist eking out a minimum wage by knocking out restaurant reviews for a trendy little listings magazine. Write about what you know, they all told her, and after feeding her younger sisters thousands of meals when they were growing up, what Cat knew about was food.

And by now she also knew about restaurants, because the well-brought-up public school boys she met at university had all wined and dined her before attempting to take her to bed. It was a different world from the one she knew – the restaurants she had occasionally glimpsed with her father and his actor friends had seemed more concerned with drinking than eating – but she took to it immediately. Usually the food was better than the sex. What she liked most of all was that you didn't have to cook it yourself.

When she met Cat, Brigitte Wolfe was nearly thirty, and was the owner, accountant and head cook of Mamma-san, a tiny noodle joint on Brewer Street where young people queued out on the narrow pavement for a bowl of Brigitte's soba and udon noodles.

Over the next ten years London would become full of Asian restaurants that were neither owned nor run by Asians – bright, funky places with menus that served Thai curry and Vietnamese noodles and Chinese dim sum and Japanese sashimi, as if that continent was really just one country, with a cuisine that was perfect for beautiful young people who cared about their diet and their looks. Mamma-san was among the first.

Cat joined the noodle queue on Brewer Street, and wrote a rave review for her little listings magazine. When she came in again, not working this time, Brigitte offered Cat a job as manager.

As the listings magazine took a very casual approach to

paying its contributors, Cat took the job. The magazine went out of business soon after. Mamma-san moved up-market and out of Soho, although Cat believed that the clientele were still the same ragged-trousered kids who had queued up on Brewer Street all those years ago before going dancing at the Wag, just ten years older and, a decade into their careers, a lot more affluent. Brigitte seemed to enjoy her restaurant as much as they did.

'A great man once said, *Arrange your life so that you can't tell the difference between work and pleasure.*'

'Shakespeare?' said Cat.

'Warren Beatty,' said Brigitte.

It was love at first sight. Cat had never met anyone who could quote Warren Beatty, although her mother claimed that he had once touched her arse backstage at the London Palladium. Brigitte had more fun than anyone Cat had ever known. After the domestic drudgery of her childhood, here was life as it ought to be lived.

When most of the city was still sleeping, the two women toured the markets – Smithfield for the restaurant's meat, Billingsgate for their fish, New Spitalfields for vegetables. Red-faced men in stained white coats shouted at each other in the pre-dawn gloom. Cat learned how to hire good kitchen staff, and how to fire the bad ones when they turned up drunk or stoned, or couldn't keep their hands off the waitresses.

Cat learned how to talk to the wine merchant, the VAT man, the health inspector, and to be scared of none of them. Although she was only four years older, Brigitte felt like the closest thing to a mother that Cat had ever had.

Brigitte was one of those European women who seem to discover a lifestyle they like in their middle twenties, and then stick with it for ever. She had never married. She worked harder than anyone Cat knew, and played hard too – twice a year she flew off to walk in the foothills of the Himalayas or dive in the Maldives or drive across Australia.

Sometimes she took Digby with her, and sometimes she left him at home – more like a favourite piece of luggage than a man. Brigitte enjoyed her life, and for years she had been Cat's North Star, guiding her way, showing her how it was done. This unencumbered life.

But now Brigitte selected a photograph of Digby and herself on a blinding white beach. The Maldives? Seychelles? One last look, and she fed the photo to the shredding machine.

'What's he done?' Cat said.

'He wants to be with someone who can bring something new to a relationship.'

'Like what?'

'Like, for example, a pair of twenty-four-year-old tits.'

Cat was speechless. And outraged. Men didn't treat Brigitte like this. She was the one who did the dumping.

'Some well-stacked slut from his office.' Brigitte calmly fed the shredding machine a Polaroid of Digby and herself atop a couple of drooling camels, the pyramids shining in the background. Dry-eyed, Cat noticed with admiration. Even now, Brigitte seemed in control. From the floor below they could hear the clatter and din of Saturday night at Mamma-san.

'I just wanted to tell you there are a couple of footballers at the desk. They haven't booked.'

'Alone?'

'Two women with them. They look like lap dancers. Although of course they could be their wives. What should I tell them?'

'Tell them to call ahead next time.'

'Could be good publicity. There are a couple of photographers outside.'

'It's even better publicity if we turn them away.'

'Okay.'

Cat turned to leave. Brigitte's voice caught her at the door.

'Do you know what I am this year?'

Cat shook her head.

'Forty. I am forty years old. How can I compete with a big bouncing pair of twenty-year-old tits?'

'Twenty-four. And you don't have to compete. You're a strong, free woman who has seen life, and lived life, and all that kind of stuff. You don't need to latch on to some man to prove you exist. *She* has to compete with *you*.'

Brigitte began to laugh. 'Oh, my darling Cat.'

'She's not the catch,' Cat said, warming to her theme, 'you are!'

Brigitte stared wistfully at a photograph of Digby and herself at a crowded party – New Year's Eve? – and then gave it to the shredder.

'The trouble is, Cat, as women get older, the pool of potential partners gets smaller. But for men, it gets bigger.' She fed the shredding machine a picture taken on a bridge in Paris. 'So where does that leave women like us?'

And as the roar of Saturday night boomed beneath her feet, Cat thought, women like us?

four

It was his favourite moment of the week.

When the city streets were starting to empty, and the lights were going out all over London, Cat would ease her long body into his car, closing her eyes as soon as her head touched the passenger seat.

'Boy,' she said. 'I'm bushed.'

'We'll be home soon,' he said.

He always picked her up at the restaurant on Saturday night. By the time Mamma-san closed for business, and the last drunken customer had been decanted into a taxi, and the kitchen staff and waitresses had all been fed and watered and packed off in a fleet of minicabs, by the time Cat locked up Mamma-san, it was always the early hours of Sunday morning.

These Saturday nights and Sunday mornings were among their favourite times. They would have a drink back at his place, shower together, and make familiar lazy love before expiring in each other's arms.

Sunday meant brunch just off the Fulham Road, surrounded by the papers and fresh bagels in a little café they felt was their own private secret, where they could watch the world go by and pretend it was Chelsea in the swinging sixties. In these luxurious hours of doing nothing very much, their dreams coincided. Cat found the freedom she had craved since childhood, and Rory found the quiet life he had searched for since the end of his marriage.

But not tonight. Rory let them into the flat, and there were lights and music that shouldn't have been there. Bright lights, loud music.

'Jake must have let himself in,' Rory said.

Jake was Rory's fifteen-year-old son. He usually stayed with Rory's ex-wife, Ali, at the weekend, and lived with Rory during the holidays. The exceptions to this rule were the nights when hysterical screaming rows ended with Jake storming off to his father. Rory frowned. What was it this time? He turned to Cat with an apologetic smile.

'Hope you don't mind,' Rory said.

'It's fine,' Cat said.

She had been looking forward to being alone with Rory and shutting out the world. But what could she say? Her man had a child, and if they were going to be together, she had to live with the fact. Besides, she liked Jake. When she had first met him, three years ago now, he had been a shy, sweet-natured twelve-year-old boy who had reacted to his parents' divorce as though the sky had fallen in. Cat loved him instantly, and saw echoes of her own childhood wounds in the boy. Jake was clingy with Rory, and easily moved to tears, and you would have needed a heart of stone not to warm to him. But Cat had to admit it was hard to equate that sunny-faced twelve-year-old with the hulking teenager that Jake had become.

'What's this music?' Rory smiled brightly, as he came into the room with Cat. 'Nirvana?'

Jake – spotty, lanky and hooded, hormones in turmoil – was draped all over the sofa with a hand-rolled cigarette dangling from his lips.

'Nirvana?' he sneered. *'Nirvana?'*

There was another youth by his side, wearing a woolly hat. Cat thought, why do they wear outdoor clothes inside? What's cool about that?

'Nirvana,' the youth chortled. 'Nirvana!'

'It's White Stripes,' Cat said. 'Something from *Elephant*, isn't it? "Ball and Biscuit", is it? Shame on you, Rory. Hello, Jake.'

'Sounds a bit like Nirvana,' Rory said sheepishly.

Jake rolled his eyes to the ceiling. 'It does *not* sound *anything* like fucking *Nirvana*!'

'Tone down the language a notch,' Rory said. 'And please open the window if you have to smoke that stuff.'

'Mum doesn't mind.'

'Mum doesn't live here. Don't you say hello to Cat?'

Jake grunted.

'Hi, Jake, how's it going?' Cat said, in that affable voice she seemed to reserve just for him.

The friend was called Jude. Jude had been planning to stay the night with Jake until there was some dispute with Jake's mother. The details were unclear. As far as Cat could make out, it was something to do with three-day-old pizza, unwashed socks and treating the place like a hotel. So Jake and his friend had escaped to Dad.

Cat felt sorry for Jake. She knew what it was like to have your mother and your father living different lives in different homes. She knew how trapped a teenager could feel. She struggled to remind herself that Jake was still the same vulnerable child she had known not so long ago.

But her Saturday night was shot, and it was hard to fight the feeling that your parents ruin the first half of your life, and then somebody else's children ruin the second half.

How her mother would have laughed.

* * *

There was no lazy lovemaking for Rory and Cat that night, and the glass of wine they shared in the kitchen felt perfunctory, like a ritual that was getting old.

They bolted down the wine, as in the living room White Stripes gave way to hip-hop blaring from the TV, and she tried her best to hide her disappointment from Rory, because he was by far the kindest, most gentle man she had ever met, and she supposed she loved him.

She was bone tired. When they crawled under Rory's duvet, they made spoons, and she soon fell into a fitful sleep, despite the boom-boom guns-and-bitches racket coming from the TV set.

When she woke in the early hours she was desperate for water, and wearing just her pants and a white karate jacket snatched from the dirty laundry, she padded her way through the now silent flat to the kitchen.

When she turned on the light she gasped. Jake and Jude were in their boxer shorts, munching toast.

'Oh, excuse me,' Cat said, grabbing a bottle of Evian from the fridge, and deciding not to get a glass because going to the cabinet where they were stored would have meant getting closer to all those gawky white limbs of the two teenage boys.

As she closed the bedroom door behind her, she heard the voice of Jake's friend Jude, and their graveyard laughter.

'Not bad for an old girl,' he said.

Michael pushed his smile into his daughter's filthy face.

'She's a mucky pup,' he observed. 'And she's a chubby bubba. She is, she is! Ooza lovely chubby bubba? Ooza lovely chubby bubba? Chloe is, Chloe's a lovely chubby bubba!'

Chloe stared blankly at her father.

Then she burped, and the burp evolved into minor projectile vomiting, a milky stream of mashed organic vegetables erupting from her mouth and then dribbling down that dimpled chin.

And Jessica thought, forced to listen to this mindless gibberish, who wouldn't throw up?

'Oooh, has Daddy's chubby bubba got an upset yummy-yummy tum-tum? Has she? Has she?'

It can't be good for her, thought Jessica. Talking to a baby as though you have just had a full frontal lobotomy, it just can't be good for her development.

But then again, thought Jessica, what do I know about it?

Nothing, that's what.

While Naoko cleaned the bile from her baby daughter's face and clothes, Michael rushed off to get the £1,000 digital camera that he had bought to record Chloe's vomiting for future generations.

Naoko lifted Chloe from her high chair and gently placed her on her feet. Chloe was walking. Well, not exactly walking. More like staggering really, Jessica thought, as she watched her niece shuffle around with the grim purpose of a drunk trying to establish sobriety, her parents on either side of her like kindly, concerned policemen.

'She'll be adorable when she gets some hair and teeth,' Jessica said.

Michael, Naoko and Paulo shot her a look, as if she had uttered some unforgivable blasphemy.

'Even more adorable,' she added quickly.

'She has hair and teeth.' Naoko smiled, stroking the light brown bum fluff on the top of her daughter's head. 'Don't you, Chloe-chan?'

Chloe smiled, revealing four tiny white teeth, two up two down, in the centre of her wet pink mouth. And then she collapsed onto her nappy-covered bottom, her brown eyes wide with shock. Four adults rushed to attend to her.

'Come to your Uncle Paulo.'

But Chloe didn't want to come to her Uncle Paulo. She clung to her mother and howled with outrage, staring at Paulo as though he had just climbed in through the window with a chainsaw.

Chloe was changing. A few months ago, when she was still indisputably a baby, Chloe didn't care who picked her up and gave her a cuddle. But now, one month short of her first birthday, with babyhood already being left behind, she was clinging to her parents and regarding anyone else with suspicion. Not so long ago, she was content to lie back and be admired. But already, she was becoming her own little person, stingy with her affection and wary of the world.

Paulo was crushed. He had fondly imagined that Chloe would grow up loving him, just as he loved her. But she was dumping him already.

Jessica was glad that Chloe's cuddles were off limits. When she had held her as a newborn baby, something strange happened inside her. It was far more than wanting a baby of her own. It was the terrible knowledge that she had been born to give birth in her turn, and that she might never fulfil that destiny.

For Jessica, there were a thousand humiliations in any visit to Michael, Naoko and Chloe. She couldn't stand the pity of her brother- and sister-in-law. They were decent-hearted people, but it was bad enough feeling like a defective woman, without having to put up with all the concerned, sympathetic looks at her lack of fertility. The fact that the sympathy was genuine, and meant well, only made it worse.

She could understand their delight in their daughter – if Chloe were her baby, Jessica was certain she would never leave her side. But where did understandable, unbridled joy end, and unbearable, insufferable smugness begin?

Yet she had to be the good guest – expressing wonder at how much Chloe had grown since she had last seen her (seven days ago). Listening with rapt interest as Michael discussed developments in Chloe's bowel movements, or Naoko went on (and on and on) about her daughter's eating habits, and her apparently whimsical changes of taste.

Give me a break, thought Jessica. It's bad enough that I can't have one of my own. Do I really have to give a standing ovation to everybody else's baby?

Jessica knew that Naoko was a good woman, and that Paulo was as close to Michael as she was to her two sisters. And, objectively, she could see that Chloe was a lovely baby – good-humoured, robust and adorable. In a bald, toothless, incontinent-old-geezer sort of way.

Jessica really didn't want to come here for Sunday lunch any more. It was just too hard.

'Excuse me,' she said, with the fixed grin that she wore as protection around other people's babies.

She fled the room with Naoko holding the red-faced, crying Chloe, and Michael stroking his daughter's (when you thought about it) alarmingly large head, and Paulo keeping a respectful distance, like a minor courtier. Nobody even noticed her leave the room.

Jessica desperately needed to get to the bathroom, but there were these bloody baby gates all over the house. Now that Chloe was on the move, disaster had to be averted on every landing and stairway. Because of an eleven-month-old child who could just about make it from the sofa to the coffee table (the numerous remote controls were a source of endless fascination to Chloe's sticky fingers), the Victorian terrace had been turned into a maximum-security prison.

Chloe certainly wasn't getting through these gates. They

were hard enough for an adult. You had to find the little button on top, press it down and lift up the gate all at the same time. Then you had to step over the bottom of the gate without falling flat on your face. Jessica made it through three gates and locked herself in the bathroom, where she confirmed what she already knew. Her period had started.

One more month of failure. One more month of feeling like she should be recalled by whoever had manufactured her. One more month of seeing that disappointed look in her husband's eyes, neither of them daring to say what was in their hearts – that this marriage might be childless for ever.

And, just to rub it in, her period brought one more bout of teeth-grinding pain that would have had a grown man begging for it to stop.

I'm not crying, Jessica thought. They're not going to see me cry.

But she had to get out of here. She had to find a place where she could remove the fixed grin and take a shower and let her husband hold her. So she almost ran out of the bathroom, stumbled over the metal bar of an open baby gate and, with a shocked intake of breath, fell flat on her face.

By the time Jessica presented herself in the living room, Michael was on his knees playing peek-a-boo with Chloe, who was now dry-eyed and shrieking with delight – talk about violent mood swings – and Naoko was alerting Michael to the latest bulletins from the kitchen.

'I tried her on broccoli blended with sweet potato but the funny thing is that she refuses to eat anything green and – my God, Jessica, are you all right?'

Jessica laughed gaily, a lump the size of a tennis ball throbbing on her forehead, a bruise pulsing on one of her shins, the palms of her hands red and sore from carpet burns.

'Oh, I'm fine, fine, just fine,' she said, turning brightly to her husband. 'Is that really the time?'

They sat in the car and Paulo listened to her pouring it out.

'Have you noticed that everyone's having a baby these days?' Jessica said. 'Gay men. Lesbian couples who wouldn't touch anything with a penis. Sixty-year-old Italian grandmothers with one wonky ovary. I even read that they might start making babies from aborted foetuses – how about that? Someone who has never even been born can have a baby. But I can't.'

They were sitting outside Michael and Naoko's house in Paulo's blue Ferrari. The car was a perk of the Baresi Brothers, but also a necessity. Michael always told Paulo that you couldn't sell imported Italian cars when you come to work in a Ford Mundano. Michael's red Maranello sat in the drive, as well as a BMW with a baby seat in the back.

'They don't do it to hurt you. To hurt us. They don't mean to rub it in our faces. But they're just so happy with their baby, they can't help it. They don't mean to hurt us.'

'I know,' she said, hanging her head.

We would be the same, he thought. If Jessica and I had a baby, we would love it so much that we wouldn't care who we hurt. It seemed to Paulo that having a baby made you care less about the rest of the world.

Because the baby became your world.

'Do you know what my brother told me? He said that he hasn't had sex with Naoko for seven weeks.'

Jessica stared at him. 'Are you listening to me?'

'I'm listening to you. I'm just saying.'

'What? What are you saying?'

'I'm saying that it's not perfect in there. I know Chloe's great. I know how much you want a baby of your own.

Our own. But I'm just saying. Something's happened to them. I don't know how to explain it. It's like since Chloe was born, they have something between them now.'

'She's younger than me,' Jessica said, not listening to him. 'Naoko. Four years younger. Same age as Megan. When Naoko is the age I am now, Chloe will be starting school.'

'It's not perfect in there,' Paulo insisted.

His conversation with Naoko had shocked him. His sister-in-law had a PhD from Reading University. She had been an archaeologist when she met Michael. And now all she talked about was how this week Chloe preferred brown mush to green mush.

Paulo loved his little niece. He had loved her from the moment he saw her. He knew that he always would. But in a secret chamber of his heart, he had his doubts.

He didn't mind the indignities of making love to a plastic cup. He didn't feel less of a man because apparently some of his sperm were dozy bastards who couldn't find one of Jessica's eggs if you gave them an *A–Z*.

The doctor had told him they just needed to keep banging away. Plenty of people conceived babies with far worse odds. And whatever his wife had to go through – the endless scans and tests, the laparoscopy, whatever new humiliation they came up with – Paulo would be right there at her side. He would always be there. She was the one for him. He had known from the first time he had seen her face.

But he wondered if he would really be any good at this fatherhood lark – the endless games of peek-a-boo, and in-depth analysis of 'pooing' (Jesus, his brother – the arch shagger, the great womaniser, the Don Juan of Dagenham – was suddenly talking like a little kid), and watching it – the baby – every waking second, so that it – the baby – didn't collide with the coffee table, or crawl out of the window, or swallow the remote control.

It was like you created this new life, but your life was over. Mother Nature had finished with you.

And here was the funny thing. Paulo's sex life with Jessica had become bleak and desperate because they were trying for a baby. But Michael's sex life with Naoko was non-existent because they had a baby.

Once Michael had been crazy for Naoko. The only reason Michael gave up Sunday morning football in the park was because it gave him an extra ninety minutes under the duvet with Naoko. But that was before they had a baby.

Paulo still wanted a child with Jessica.

But the most pressing reason he wanted it was because he knew it would make her happy. And was that a good reason to bring a baby into the world?

five

The job was too much for her.

Megan could handle the workload, but not at the pace required. Her patients still filled the waiting room long after the other doctors had gone to lunch, and more were there when she came rushing back late from her house visits. So it was no surprise when Lawford came into her office and told her, 'There's been a complaint about you.'

All those years at med school. All those blood-splattered hysterical nights in A & E at the Homerton. All the tired flesh she had pressed, all the dicky hearts she had fretted over, and all the rubber gloves she had donned to probe some ancient and decaying rectum.

And now the ancient rectums she worked with were kicking her out.

She wondered which of the surgery doctors had lodged the complaint. They had some nerve. Bastards, she thought. Rotten bastards the lot of you.

No wonder female patients flocked to her, away from these old men with hair in their ears and stains on their trousers and contempt for their patients and their talk of 'plumbing problems', as if the aftermath of an ectopic pregnancy was no different from having a leaking pipe, as if crippling period pains were somewhat similar, when you thought about it, to having a broken boiler.

Megan could deal with any of it, all these things that she had never experienced herself, only studied in a classroom at medical school. But she just couldn't do it in the few fleeting minutes allowed. She needed time.

She was just about to tell him to take his job and stick it up the terminal part of his large intestine when he spoke.

'I think you're doing a terrific job,' Lawford said.

'What?'

'So do the other doctors.'

'But the complaint . . .'

'It's from a patient.'

'A patient? But my patients love me!'

'Mrs Marley. Remember her? The large woman from the Sunny View Estate? One of your house visits.'

'I remember Mrs Marley. And Daisy.'

'Daisy's the problem. You diagnosed a fever, correct?'

'Her temperature was a bit high. She was listless. I thought –'

'She was rushed to hospital the next day. It turned out to be a thyroid condition. Daisy's hypothyroid. Hence the lethargy.'

Megan could feel her heart pounding. That poor child. She had failed her.

'A thyroid condition?'

'We all get it wrong sometimes. We're doctors, not God.'

'How's Daisy? What will they do?'

'Give her some Thyroxine pills and she should be back to normal.'

'But she will have to take them for life.'

'In all probability.'

'Are there any side effects?'

'Side effects?' Lawford was suddenly impatient. 'Yes – they make her well.'

It was the response of a vastly experienced doctor. *Are there side effects to these pills, doctor? Yes, they make you well.* Megan filed it away for future reference. She knew she would use the line many times in the coming years. If she ever became a fully registered GP.

'Don't worry about Daisy. She'll be fine. Mrs Marley's the problem. You don't want a complaint of negligence on your record. Doesn't look good at all.'

'What do I do?'

'You apologise to Mrs Marley. Grovel a bit. As much as necessary, in fact. Admit you're only human. As you know, this year is a continuous exam for you. I'll be writing a summative assessment. I don't want a misdiagnosis on your record, Megan.'

It was the first time that Lawford had ever called her by her first name. She could see that he was trying to get her out of this thing with her career intact, and she felt a flood of gratitude.

'You're not just apologising because it will get Mrs Marley off your back,' he said sternly. 'You're apologising because it's the right thing to do.'

'Of course.'

Lawford nodded and headed for the door.

'Thank you, Dr Lawford.'

He turned and faced her.

'How far along are you?'

She placed a protective hand on her stomach. 'Is it so obvious?'

'The constant vomiting was a clue.'

'Eight weeks,' she said, finding it difficult to breathe.

'Are you planning to have the baby?'

'I don't see how that's possible. I can barely look after myself.'

I'm not going to cry, Megan thought. I am not going to cry in front of him.

'I do want children,' she said. 'Very much. But not now.'

Lawford nodded again. 'Well,' he said, suddenly shy. 'That's it then.' He smiled with a softness that Megan had never seen before. 'I'll let you crack on.'

I *do* want children, Megan thought when he had gone. And one day I *will* have children, and I will love them far more than our mother ever loved my sisters and me.

But not now, not when I have just started work, and not with some man I fucked at a party.

Yes, she would apologise to Mrs Marley.

But Megan felt like she should really be apologising to Daisy.

And to this little life that would never be born.

Bloody doctors, Paulo thought. They never tell you what you are letting yourself in for. If they did, they would all go out of business.

Paulo carefully steered his Ferrari through the streets of north London as if he had a cargo of painted eggshells on board. Jessica was sleeping in the passenger seat, white-faced and exhausted by the events of the morning.

They had made the laparoscopy sound as routine as having a tooth filled. But Jessica was dead to the world – pumped full of drugs so they could drill a hole in her belly and send in their camera to find out what was wrong.

He slowly drove home with one eye on the road and one eye on his wife, and he knew with a pure and total certainty that he loved this woman, and that he would not stop loving her if they couldn't have children. He would love her even if she found it impossible to love herself. He would love her enough for both of them.

When they got home Paulo undressed Jessica and put her to bed, her sleeping face as white as the pillows.

Then he went into his study and took down all of his pictures of Chloe.

When Megan left the surgery, a young man stepped into her path.

He was big and good-looking, in a bashed-in, careless kind of way, and at first she thought he was one of those charity muggers – chuggers, they called them – who increasingly ambushed you with their clipboards, stepping over the homeless to assault you with their good causes and direct debit forms. She tried to swerve past him, but he moved quickly to intercept her. She shot him her look of cold magisterial fury, usually reserved for patients refusing to take their prescribed medication.

'Megan?'

And then all at once she realised that it was him. The man from the party. The father of her child.

'Oh – hello, Kurt.'

'It's Kirk.'

'Of course.'

'It's great to see you, Megan.' A lovely accent. Full of wide-open spaces and healthy living and Christmas on the beach. 'You look fantastic.'

'Thank you.' She gave him a quick smile. He was a nice guy, and she had liked him a lot, and she had no regrets – apart from the fact that a doctor who spent her days lecturing teenage mums about contraception should probably never leave her own family planning to the fates. But there was no time left for anything more.

'Nice bumping into you, Kirk. But I really must be –'

'I had to see you,' he said, and at last she understood that this man had actually been waiting for her.

Megan's head reeled with the insanity of the situation. Here she was carrying his baby inside her and here he was angling for a second date.

She didn't know him. And he didn't know her. Yet even in the cold light of Hackney, without one too many Asahi Super Drys inside her, Megan could recall very clearly how they had ended up in bed, on a pile of coats dumped by the guests. He was tall, athletic but with a kind of genial innocence about him. His children will be beautiful, Megan reflected, and the unbidden thought made her feel like weeping.

'I thought you were going back to Sydney.'

'I am. I will be. But I wanted to see you before I go.'

She had to be strong. He might be making beautiful babies one day, but they would not be with her.

'Why's that then?'

'Because, well – I like you. It was terrific, wasn't it? It was great, wasn't it?'

'It was okay.'

'It was unbelievable!' He grinned, shook his head. 'I don't usually do that kind of thing.'

'I am sure your girlfriend is delighted about that.'

He had let slip the girlfriend early on in their conversation, but she had been quietly forgotten when he started reading Megan's signals, cottoning on that – maybe – she was interested. Now he had the decency to blush. He did that quite a bit for such a good-looking man.

'I just wanted to say goodbye. That's all. And say that I hope we see each other again.'

'How old are you, Kirk?'

'Twenty-five.'

'I'm twenty-eight. I'm a doctor. Remind me what you do again?'

'I teach.'

'What subject?'

'Scuba diving.'

'Right – so you're a young scuba diving instructor living in Sydney, and I'm an elderly GP practising in London.'

'You're not so old.'

'I just – I really don't see how anything can come of it, do you?'

He hung his head, and Megan had to fight back the urge to take him in her arms, taste some more of those good kisses, and tell him the truth.

'Just wanted to see you. That's all. I don't usually do things like that. Get pissed and fall into bed with a complete stranger.'

'Could you speak up a bit? I think one of the old ladies at the bus stop across the road didn't hear you.'

Kirk hung his cropped blond head, knowing at last that coming here had been a bad idea.

'Take this,' he said, handing her a scrap of paper with a scrawled telephone number. It looked like long distance. Very long distance.

'If you ever need me. Or, you know, come to Australia.'

'Thanks.'

'As I said – I just like you.'

'Yeah, well. I like you too.'

'Well – like the song says – I guess I'll see you next lifetime.'

'Yes,' she said. 'See you next lifetime, Kirk.'

As soon as she had disappeared around the corner, she began ripping the telephone number into tiny pieces, her eyes blurring with tears.

Young, dumb and full of come, she thought. On his way home to his girlfriend and their beautiful babies without me ever telling him, without ever knowing, without ever being asked to carry his share of the load. And he was right – it had been fun while it lasted.

But he should consider himself lucky. She didn't want a family with this man.

She had a family already.

In some other family, they might have drifted apart by now. In their late twenties and thirties, other sisters might have found the demands of work and home life closing in on them, clamouring for attention, taking up all their time. In some other family, men and jobs might have got in the way.

But although Jessica had her husband, her house and her dreams in one of the leafier parts of town, and while Megan and Cat had their demanding jobs at either end of the city, they clung to each other now as they had clung to each other as children, growing up in a home where the mother was absent.

They didn't talk about it. But when Cat had first started with Rory, he had been surprised to discover that, no matter what was happening in their lives, the sisters spoke on the phone every day and tried to meet for breakfast once a week. 'That's unusually close, isn't it?' he said, with that gentle, querulous Rory-smile on his face. But of course to Cat – and to Megan, and to Jessica – it seemed perfectly normal.

This is what Cat thought about it – nobody loves their family more than someone from a broken home.

They always tried to meet in a restaurant that was equidistant from their lives.

When Megan was at the Imperial College med school, and Jessica was living in Little Venice with Paulo, they had met in Soho, in the shabby opulence of Cat's private club, where the members were as frayed as the carpets.

Now that Megan was working in Hackney, and Jessica was up in Highgate, the axis had moved east, to a restaurant next to the meat market in Smithfield. Cat's suggestion. It was a place where young foreign waiters dressed in black served traditional British fare such as bacon butties, porridge and fried breakfasts as if they were exotic delicacies, and every hot drink came in a mug, rather than a cup and saucer. Everything was authentically working class, apart from the sky-high prices.

Cat was the first to arrive, and through the huge windows of the restaurant she saw white-coated porters who had worked all through the night hauling massive slabs of fresh meat onto the waiting vans.

Jessica turned up next, and together they watched the porters of Smithfield at their work.

'In ten years this will probably all be gone,' Cat said. 'All pushed out to the suburbs, and Smithfield turned into another Covent Garden, full of clothes shops and street performers and little cafés.'

'Oh, that'll be nice,' Jessica said, picking up the menu.

Cat stared at her. 'It will be bloody awful, Jess.'

Jessica shrugged. 'I suppose you prefer all these men walking about carrying cows. I suppose that's atmospheric, is it?'

Megan arrived, glancing at her watch, already dreading the dash back to the East End and morning surgery. She snatched up a menu.

'Did you get your results?' she asked Jessica.

Jessica nodded. The black-shirted waiter arrived, and they placed their orders, pointing at the menu as he couldn't understand their English. When he was gone, Megan and Cat watched Jessica, and waited for her to speak.

'It's endometriosis,' she said, pronouncing the word as if it had been new to her until quite recently. 'The results of the laparoscopy say that I've got endometriosis.'

'That explains the pain you get,' Megan said, taking her sister's hands. 'That terrible pain every month.'

'Endometriosis,' Cat said. 'That means – what? That's to do with your period, right?'

Megan nodded. 'It's a menstrual condition. Fragments of membrane similar to the lining of the uterus are where they shouldn't be – in the muscles of the uterus, the Fallopian tubes, the ovaries. Basically, all these horrible, inflamed bits that bleed when you bleed.'

'It stops you getting pregnant,' Jessica said. 'And it hurts like hell.'

'They can't cure it?' Cat said.

'It disappears after the menopause,' Megan said.

'That's something to look forward to then,' Jessica said.

'You can control it by taking the pill. You stop the periods, you stop the pain. And stop the condition from deteriorating. But the best cure for it . . .'

Jessica looked at her, smiling bitterly. 'This is the funny bit, Cat. I love this bit.'

'The best cure for endometriosis,' Megan said quietly, 'is getting pregnant.'

'It stops you having a baby,' Jessica said. 'But it only goes away if you have a baby. Isn't that perfect?'

'Symptoms disappear when you get pregnant,' Megan said. 'But it's true – the symptoms make conception difficult. Not impossible, Jess. Please believe me.'

Megan put her arms around Jessica, and her sister pressed her head against her. Stroking Jessica's head, Megan glanced out of the window, and saw the slabs of bloody meat being carted into the fleet of white vans. All the headless, yellow-white carcasses and the panels of bloodied flesh. The men with their bloody, Jackson Pollock-splattered white coats.

Their breakfasts arrived at that moment and Megan gasped, the vomit rising in her throat. She pushed her sister away and quickly fled from the table. When she returned from the bathroom, Cat was tucking into her sausage sandwich, but Jessica hadn't touched her pancakes.

'What's wrong with you, Megan?'

'It's nothing.' She looked at her porridge and felt like being sick again.

'Megan,' Cat said, the stern elder sister demanding the truth. 'What's happening?'

Megan looked at her sisters and knew that it was madness to think she could keep this thing from them. They were her best friends. They would understand.

'I'm pregnant,' Megan said.

Cat put down her bagel. 'How long?'

'Eight weeks.'

'How does Will feel about it?'

'It's not Will's.'

'Okay,' Cat said. 'Okay.'

Jessica struggled to speak. 'Well – congratulations,' she said eventually. She stroked her sister's shoulder, smiling through a thin film of tears. 'I mean it, Megan. Congratulations.'

Cat shot Megan a look.

Megan shook her head. 'No.'

'You'll be a terrific mother,' Jessica said.

'But you're not . . .' Cat's voice trailed off.

'No,' Megan said. 'I'm not keeping it.'

Jessica looked at her.

'I'm not keeping it, Jess. How can I? I hardly know the father. And even if I did, I still wouldn't keep it. I'm not in love with him, Jess. And this is the wrong time. It's just completely the wrong time for me to have a baby.'

'The wrong time?'

'I've just started work. I just did six years at medical school – six years! – and another year as a house officer in hospitals. I'm not even fully registered for another year.'

'You just started work?' Jessica said. 'Wait a minute – you're going to have an abortion because you just started *work*?'

'That's right,' Megan said, angry that she had to justify herself.

'Do you know what it means to go through an abortion?' Jessica said.

'Jess,' said Cat, trying to stop her. 'Come on.'

'I almost certainly understand the procedure better than you do,' Megan said.

'I wouldn't be so sure,' Jessica said. 'Some things you can't get from books. They hoover the baby out of you. That's what it amounts to. They get a fucking hoover, and they hoover this baby out of you, then stick it in a bin, or they burn it, they throw it away like a piece of *rubbish*. That's how they will get rid of the baby, Megan, just so you can carry on with your precious career.'

'And do *you* know what it means to go through a pregnancy without a father?' Megan said. 'Or to go through life as a single parent? I see them every day in my surgery – women with the life sucked out of them. You sit out in Highgate waiting for Paulo to come home, and you have no idea what women are going through in the real world. I'm sorry, Jessica – that's not going to happen to me.'

'So selfish. So bloody selfish. You think I'm not in the real world? What makes you think that Hackney is any more real than where I am?'

'This is not about you, Jess,' Cat said. 'It's not about you and Paulo and your baby. This is Megan's decision.'

'It just makes me sick,' Jessica said. 'These women treating abortion like it's just another form of contraception.'

'These women?' Megan said.

'As though it's no different to a condom or a pill or something. Why did you let it get this far? Why did you have to make a baby? Why did you have to *do* that?'

'It's not a baby,' Megan said. 'Not yet. And I can't cope with my work as it is – it just wouldn't be fair on the baby.'

'You think that *killing it* is fair on the baby? You don't care about the baby, Megan. You care about your career.'

Jessica stood up. Cat tried to stop her, but Jessica shook her off.

'That poor little thing, Megan. That poor little thing.'

Jessica threw some money on the table and walked out. Megan and Cat let her go. A couple of porters whistled at her.

'It's natural, isn't it?' Megan said. 'Not to want this baby?'

Cat stared out of the window at the meat market. All this would be gone soon. She suddenly felt exhausted.

'It's the most natural thing in the world,' she said.

six

Far above the South China Sea, Kirk suddenly felt the plane jolt, drop and his stomach fall away.

The fasten seat belt sign pinged on and flight attendants began passing through the cabin, waking the sleepers and making them strap themselves in. The Aussie captain's calm, reassuring voice began murmuring over the intercom, as soothing as a lullaby.

Kirk closed his eyes and touched the fastened buckle of his seat belt. The plane shuddered, more violently this time, and again seemed to sink through the sky. Now there were cries of mild alarm, and the unspoken paranoia of the modern traveller – *what if?* Kirk took a deep breath, his eyes shut tight.

It's just a bit of turbulence, he thought. I am a seasoned world traveller.

But he again touched the buckle of his seat belt, and did what he always did when he felt there was a faint possibility that he could die on a plane within the next few minutes. He tried to remember all the women he had ever slept with.

He had started early, at fourteen, with the family's babysitter. One. Then there had been a fallow period of a few years until he was seventeen, and started with his first proper girlfriend. Two.

By the time that ended three years later, he was a dive instructor, and every day at the office there were women in swimwear. Three to ten.

Then he spent a summer in the Philippines, and discovered bar girls – eleven to nineteen, or was it twenty? When he got back to Sydney that September, there was an older married woman whose family owned a flower shop. He met her there every Sunday morning between eight and nine o'clock, while her husband and sons slept on upstairs, and he was dressed and gone by the time they got up and started getting ready for church. Twenty or twenty-one.

Then there was a surfer girl he really liked and the sister of a friend . . . but hadn't he forgotten someone? He knew there had been the odd brief encounter that sometimes slipped his mind, but faces and bodies and beds seemed to blur and merge, and some names were already lost for ever.

At twenty-five, he was already unsure of the number. He guessed it was somewhere in the high twenties. Not that many really, when you considered that sometimes a period of monogamy had lasted for years, sandwiched between bouts of wild promiscuity.

And now he came to think of it he recalled the days of madness when, as one relationship ended, and another began, and a limited offer suddenly presented itself, he had somehow squeezed in three women in one day. He still didn't understand how he had done it. It wasn't the physical demands that took the toll. It was all that travelling.

But for the last two years he had been faithful to his girlfriend back home. Remarkable really, when he remembered that his travels had taken him to bars in Bangkok and clubs in Tokyo and parties in half a dozen European cities, including Warsaw and Stockholm, where there was a beauty on every corner. He had been faithful to the girl back home through all those temptations.

Up until the night he met Megan.

What was it about this one? Why was she special?

Because he was keener than she was. That was a first. She ticked all the boxes – she was hot, funny and smart (although 'smart' was a box that Kirk didn't necessarily need ticked). But the clincher was that she just didn't care as much as he did, and that had him hooked.

As his plane trembled and shook somewhere over Indonesia, Kirk asked himself all the questions that are the stirrings of love in the male heart.

How can I win her? How many have known her?

And when will I see her again?

Digby walked into Mamma-san with Tamsin on his arm. Cat glanced across at Brigitte drinking with a couple of regulars at the bar and saw her visibly flinch, as if she had been slapped.

Cat glared at Digby, and thought, how could you? But the terrible thing was, she sort of understood. Not how Digby could come here and rub Brigitte's nose in his new relationship – such casual cruelty was beyond her comprehension – but she could understand how Digby had ended up with Tamsin. Cat had seen Tamsin in Mamma-san back in the days when she was just another party tart hoping to bump into a footballer at the bar, and she could see the appeal.

If Tamsin's body language could be summarised in two words, it was *fuck me*. Whereas Brigitte's natural demeanour – proud, strong, glamorous Brigitte – suggested *fuck you*.

Cat watched Digby and Tamsin at the lobster tank, choosing their main course. When she looked back at the bar, Brigitte had fled into the kitchen. She decided she wasn't going to allow anyone to humiliate her friend. Not in this place.

Digby, who Cat thought was good-looking but with charm so oily you could fry noodles in it, had the self-consciously puffed-up look of the older man with the younger woman. Steeling himself for applause, or laughter.

Tamsin also did her bit to fit her sexual stereotype, clinging to his arm as if he were the hot one, not her, as if a black American Express card was superior to gilded youth. She was really that stupid.

Abbreviated skirt. Strangely immobile breasts. Unfeasibly blonde. Digby had dumped Brigitte for this little fuck puppet? It was like choosing an inflatable doll over a real woman.

Cat crossed the restaurant with a friendly smile, knowing that the promise of staying friends was impossible for a man like Digby. It wasn't enough to break up with a man like that. They had to make sure their ex was unhappy.

'Digby, how good to see you.'

'I know the one I want, Cat,' Digby said.

Tamsin bent over, pressing her snub nose against the fish tank, her skirt rising up her golden thighs. Men at the adjacent tables held their breath, their chopsticks quivering with longing. A gang of lobsters waved their pincers at Tamsin in slow motion.

'But I thought they was pink,' she said.

'Only when boiled,' Cat said.

'I like them when they're fresh,' Digby said, pressing his fleshy face against the tank, considering the lobsters. 'I'll take that one, Cat,' he added, pointing at the biggest crustacean.

'I'll make sure it's as you like it, Digby.'

After indicating to the chef the lobster they had selected, Cat found them a good table. She took their orders for drinks – white wine for Tamsin and Asahi Super Dry for Digby. Cat watched them whispering their giggly secrets, and Digby slipped his tongue in Tamsin's ear, giving it a good clean. Then she went into the kitchen to check on Brigitte.

'Are you all right?'

Brigitte attempted a laugh, but didn't quite make it. It sounded more like she was clearing her throat. Cat was shocked to see her this undone. The unencumbered life was meant to be pain-free.

'I bet she fucks his brains out,' Brigitte said.

'Didn't know he had any. Excuse me.'

Cat went off to talk to the chef.

And she made sure that she was standing close by when the lobster, sunburn pink now and peacefully reclining on a bed of shredded horseradish, was served up to Digby and Tamsin on a wooden Japanese platter.

There was an instant when nothing happened – when the diners and their beady-eyed meal seemed almost hypnotised by the sight of each other. Then Cat saw the smiles vanish from their faces as, with considerable effort, the lobster lifted itself from the wooden platter and began crawling from the plate, its claws trailing thin white slivers of horseradish.

Tamsin screamed. Digby snatched up his butter knife, as if to defend himself and his fuck puppet. The lobster slowly toppled from the wooden platter and began its slow march across the table towards Tamsin, who was shrieking with terror now, and her inflatable breasts.

'Do you want some wasabi on that?' Cat said.

It was scary to be too unencumbered, she thought later. The whole unencumbered thing could go too far. Cat saw that now. You had to get the balance right.

A person needed to be unencumbered but not cast adrift, free but not lost, and loved but not smothered. But how do you manage all that?

'We're going clubbing,' Brigitte told Cat. 'It's DJ Cake versus the Glitter Twins at Zoo Nation. Want to come?'

It was almost one in the morning. The restaurant had closed, and the staff were grimly shovelling food into their tired faces. Their minicabs were already lined up outside, waiting to take them home. A brace of pierced, dyed blond young waiters hovered deferentially behind Brigitte, watching Cat expectantly.

'Oh, come on,' Brigitte said excitedly. 'It'll be fun.'

Maybe a few years ago, Cat thought. Maybe before I had someone to curl up with and cuddle.

'You have fun with the boys and DJ Cake,' she said. Through the plate-glass window of Mamma-san Cat could see Rory pulling up outside. 'I'm going home.'

'Bring Rory.'

'He's more of a Sting man,' she said.

Cat didn't feel sorry for Brigitte. She was good at having a good time. But personally Cat couldn't think of anything that she would like less than being in a black hole listening to crap music with drugged-up people fifteen years her junior.

Cat thought, is this what happens? If you don't settle down when the world tells you to? Do you end up taking drugs in a club when you are forty?

So unencumbered it hurts.

Jake had moved into Rory's place.

A purely temporary measure until things were smoothed out with his mother and stepfather, who had apparently – as always, the hard facts about the domestic tiff were somewhat hazy – caught him sacrificing virgins in the conservatory or something.

In many ways, Rory was the most easy-going man Cat had ever known. She came and went from his flat as she pleased, she worked late without explanation or apology, she felt no inclination to report her whereabouts when they were not together.

Loved without being suffocated – wasn't that exactly what she wanted? He wasn't as possessive as some other men had been, or as clingy as many of them, and not as fixated on her sexual history as all of them.

He wanted to make this relationship work, and to last, and to make them both happy. She could see it twinkling in those shy, amused eyes. But she couldn't utter even the mildest criticism of his son. That was the one thing that wasn't allowed.

Since Jake's latest row with his mother, Cat wasn't even allowed to suggest that Rory slept over at her place. Because Jake – Mr Sensitive – might think she wanted to avoid him (like the plague, actually, for she had come to the conclusion that the sunny-faced twelve-year-old was gone for good). Rory fretted constantly about something called Jake's self-esteem. Cat wondered if her mother had given her self-esteem a second thought as she turned her back on her three daughters and caught a taxi to her new life.

'Hi, Jake, we're home!' Rory called, as they came into the flat to find Jake fondling the breasts of a thin, droopy girl on the sofa. The place stank of stale pizza, teenage sex and what Cat identified as Moroccan Red. Cannabis had never been to her taste, but a large proportion of her kitchen staff had a spliff during their tea break.

And my kitchen staff are grown-ups, she thought. Not just past puberty.

'Can't you fucking knock?' Jake snapped, and Cat almost laughed at that – the idea of someone knocking before they came into their own home. She tried to find something else to look at while the girl fastened her training bra and pulled down her T-shirt and Jake adjusted the rise in his Levi's. Cat saw that the girl was wearing one of those modern, ironic T-shirts where the same slogan is repeated endlessly.

I blame the parents
I blame the parents
I blame the parents . . .

'Hello, Misty,' Rory said, 'does your mother know you're here?'

'She don't care, the old cow.'

The young folk had a snigger at that.

'Well, please let her know if you stay over. Will you do that?'

Misty's stoned gaze seemed directed at a point over Rory's shoulder.

'Would you kids like something to eat?'

'I'm so not hungry,' Jake said, choosing to take it as an insult, as he did everything his father said.

'Well – good night then.'

But they were already lost in the banal materialism of their TV show. Big cars, white mansions, bikini-clad babes by the pool. At least we dreamed of freedom, Cat thought. When did the dreams of children become the same as the dreams of middle-aged men?

'Drugs?' Cat said. 'I'm no prude, Rory – God knows, you get all sorts in a kitchen – but aren't they a little on the young side for drugs?'

'I wish that was true,' Rory said sadly. 'But the drugs have found them by the time they're fifteen. And Ali and I agreed that we would rather he did the soft stuff under our roofs, than the hard stuff somewhere else.'

Ali and I, Cat thought, and it made her blood boil. They had been divorced for years, and Rory still talked as though they were some kind of partnership. Because of their overgrown, overindulged child.

'I hate the way he talks to you,' Cat said to Rory as they undressed. It was a listless kind of undressing. They were not going to have sex tonight, she could tell. 'And I hate the way you talk to him.'

'How do I talk to him?'

Keeping his voice neutral, not wanting to fight.

'As if you're apologising for existing.'

'Is that what I do? I don't mean to. I love him, that's all. He's my son. Maybe if you had children . . .'

'Maybe. But I'm not going to have them with you, am I?'

He turned his head away, stung, and she was immediately sorry she had said it. She didn't want to hurt him. And she didn't want children with him, or anyone else. Did she? At the same time she didn't want to end up going to clubs when she was forty. Oh fuck, sometimes she didn't know what she wanted.

'That's true, Cat. You're not going to have children with me.'

'Oh, Rory, you know I don't want kids.'

'I worry about him, that's all. I have always worried about him. Before he was born I worried that his mother might miscarry. Then when he was a baby I worried that he would suffocate in his cot. I couldn't bear to leave him alone, it was physically painful to leave him sleeping there alone. Then when he was growing up I worried about drunk drivers and sexual perverts and killer diseases. These things happen to real children.'

'I know they do,' she said. But she felt like screaming, *but what's this got to do with us?*

'And now I worry about the divorce and what it has done to him – how much it has hurt him, what it will do to his relationships and happiness. I worry about what the world might do to him, and I worry about what I have done to him. When a baby is born – no, nine months before that – you get the fear of God in you, and it never goes away. Not when you're a parent.'

In the living room, Cat could hear the callous laughter of the children. She didn't want to argue with this good man.

'Don't listen to me,' she said. 'I've had a bad night.'

She told him about Digby turning up at the restaurant with Tamsin. He smiled that rueful smile when she told him about the lobster and her revenge.

'Digby's threatened by Brigitte,' Cat said. 'That's why he left her for this little tart. He can't handle a successful woman.'

'Well . . . it's not necessarily that Digby's *threatened* by Brigitte,' Rory said cautiously, not quite sure if he wanted to get into all this. 'Sometimes men don't want a replica of themselves. Someone who is – you know – successful, driven, work-obsessed, all of that.'

Cat began pulling off her clothes.

'But Brigitte's formidable. What about education, earnings, professional achievements?'

'It's not a job application, Cat. Sometimes a man wants a woman who can bring something new to the table.'

She threw her T-shirt at him.

'Oh, you mean like a big pair of twenty-four-year-old tits?'

She kicked off her trousers and walked into the room's en suite bathroom.

'I'm just saying.' He began folding her T-shirt. 'It's wrong to think that men only want a copy of themselves. Where's the law that says men can only want women their own age?'

She came out of the bathroom in just her pants, her toothbrush in her hand. She felt his eyes run over her long limbs and saw him catch his breath.

'And what do you want?' she said.

'You know what I want, Cat. I want you.'

Maybe they were going to have sex after all.

Megan was changing.

Her hair was becoming less oily, her skin was becoming smoother and her breasts, always abundant, were becoming fuller and rounder, almost an embarrassment of riches. The chronic, all-consuming sickness was easing now, yet becoming more selective. She couldn't walk past a Starbucks or McDonald's without wanting to throw up. Wow, she thought. It's an anti-globalisation foetus.

The doctor in her knew that the baby was hardly there at all – so small that it almost didn't exist, despite the tightness around her waistband. Just three centimetres long from head to bottom. Not a child. Not a baby. A problem that would be dealt with tomorrow morning. Certainly not murder.

And yet, and yet.

She knew that a scan would show minute fingers and toes. The eyes were already forming, and so were the nose, the arms, and the mouth. The internal organs were already there. It was difficult to kid herself that she was ridding herself of something other than another human life.

She stood at the window of her tiny flat looking down at the streets of Hackney, still swarming with people going about their pleasures way after midnight.

Her eyes were suddenly brimming with emotion. And Megan thought, oh, God, please let me get it over with. What else can I do?

She put on her pyjamas and opened a bottle of white wine. Then Jessica rang her doorbell.

Megan buzzed her up, amazed that her sister hadn't been relieved of the Prada handbag she was clasping, and somehow not surprised to see her. It was almost as if Megan had been expecting her.

Jessica sat on the sofa that had been used by countless other tenants, trying not to look disapproving. Megan found another glass and poured them both a drink.

'Should you be . . .' Jessica stopped herself, and held out her hand for a glass. 'Thank you.'

Megan wearily took a slug. 'I think my drinking while pregnant is rather academic, don't you? Please don't lecture me, Jess. I'm not in the mood tonight.'

Jessica's face was pale and beautiful, her features a chorus of perfect symmetry. Our mother, Megan thought. That's why Jessie is so good-looking. She's the one who looks like our mother.

'I didn't come here to lecture you,' Jessica said. 'I just wanted you to know that you're wrong about me. You think I'm jealous of you. Paulo and I try so hard for a baby – and then you get knocked up just by looking at some guy.'

'There was a bit more to it than that,' Megan said gently.

'You know what I mean. You think I'm taking my disappointment out on you.'

'I wouldn't blame you. I know it must seem unfair. And it is unfair – but that's the random nature of the whole thing. People who want babies can't have them, people who don't want them get knocked up on a one-night stand. Mother Nature is a heartless old bitch.'

'I'll drink to that.'

The sisters clinked glasses.

'But there's another reason why I was so upset,' Jessica said. 'You think I'm some kind of innocent, don't you? Married, having my nails done when you're curing sick people, dreaming of nothing more than my own baby.' Jessica raised a manicured hand, overruling her sister's objections. 'I know it's different from your life. And from Cat's life too. But I'm not as innocent as I look.' Jessica took a drink, took a breath. 'I had one.'

'What?'

'I had an abortion. Long time ago. When I was sixteen. God, I was so stupid.'

'I never –'

'Of course you didn't. You were twelve years old. You

were a little girl. Cat knew. She helped me. Came down from Manchester to help me. I was meant to be on a skiing trip with the school.'

'I remember that trip. You got hurt. Your knee.'

'There was no trip. I was somewhere else. Getting rid of my baby.'

'Jesus, Jess.'

Jessica shook her head, and Megan could see that it was all still raw. This wasn't a long time ago for her sister. It wasn't some other life. It was still happening.

'Dad – you could tell him anything. He was a good dad, he did his best, but you know what he was like.'

'Maybe if he'd had sons,' Megan said. 'Maybe it would have been different. Maybe he would have been closer to sons.'

She was still in shock. Jessica – pregnant? Jessica – having an abortion, and Cat helping her, while Megan did her homework and played with her dolls and rode her bike? I never knew, Megan thought, I never knew.

She wished she could have helped her sister then, and she wished she could help her now. But back then she had been a child, the baby of the family, and now she was about to go through exactly the same thing as Jessica. She would even have Cat by her side, taking care of her.

'I'm not sure I could have got away with it with a full set of parents,' Jessica said. 'Or maybe they are all that trusting, maybe nobody wants to believe these things about their little girl.'

'Who was it?'

'Some guy who already had a girlfriend. Some guy I thought I loved. Some guy on the football team who thought he was God's gift. Fuck him, Megan – I hope he's having a miserable life with a fat wife. He's not important. The important thing is – I got pregnant, didn't I? I proved I can do it. But now that I want to – I can't.'

'There's no link between what you went through at sixteen and what you're going through now.'

'See, I think you're wrong. They sell abortion like it's – I don't know – this pain-free, clinical procedure. And it's not like that at all. It's like having the best part of you torn out. We mess around with our bodies, Megan. We cut them up. We throw away babies. We do, we do. And then we're all surprised when we can't have another one on demand.'

Megan sat down on the sofa and put her arms around Jessica. She hugged her so hard that a bone clicked.

'What else could you do, Jess? You couldn't have a baby with that boy. You couldn't become a mother while you were at school. You must know that.'

'I know, I know. But we do it too much. We chop our bodies about because we're not ready, because it's the wrong time, because it's the wrong guy. And then we act all amazed when we can't have a baby when we really want.'

Megan wiped her eyes on the sleeve of her pyjamas. Then she wiped her sister's eyes.

'This is a tough time for you. And for Paulo too.'

'I just wanted to tell you that it's not just envy and hurt. I worry about you. I worry about this thing you're going to do. And I love you.'

'I love you too, Jess. Don't worry. You'll have your baby, and when you do you'll be a terrific mum.'

'You know what I really want? I just want to be myself again.'

Megan heard those words from sick people every day in the surgery. *This is not really me. I want to be myself again. Where did the real me go? I want my life back.*

'Yes,' said Megan. 'Me too.'

Jessica stayed the night.

It was too late to go home, and anyway she said she

wanted to be with Megan at her appointment. When Megan was twelve, she had been far too young to be a part of what Jessica had to go through. But now the sisters were grown. Now they could stick together. Now they could help each other.

Without even needing to discuss it, they slept together in the same bed, just as they had when they were children.

Megan tucked herself into the curves of her sister's body, holding on to her until sleep came, almost as if the younger sister felt the need to protect the older one from all the things that were out there, moving in the darkness.

Cat was waiting at the clinic.

When Megan walked in with Jessica, it all came back. Jessica at sixteen, her world unravelling. 'In trouble', as they still called it back then. The boy and his friends on the corner, smirking as the sisters passed by in Cat's rusty Beetle, on their way to Jessica's fictitious skiing trip. The waiting room just like this one, as antiseptic and clinical as a dentist's. And Jessica later, after the abortion, hiding in Cat's halls of residence for a week like a wounded animal, years younger than Cat and her friends, shattered and shivering, as though it was not the tiny life inside her that had been drawn out, but her own. Too young for this experience. Much too young.

Cat thought, why should it all come back? This was different. Megan was a grown woman. A doctor – or about to become one. Megan was clear-eyed and calm when she arrived. Nobody's victim. A woman, not a girl. A woman who knew what she had to do.

'Can I help you?' said the old lady at the reception desk, and the three sisters ignored her. Megan and Jessica sat down either side of Cat, their bodies so close that she could feel their warmth.

'There was this woman at my surgery,' Megan said. 'Mrs

Summer. From one of those estates. The Sunny View Estate – the worst one of the lot. A bunch of kids and another one on the way. It would have been hard having this baby. This new baby. But then she lost it. And the strange thing is – that was even worse.'

Yes, it was very different this time, thought Cat, suddenly understanding.

Because this time her sister was keeping the baby.

seven

We are all miracles, thought Paulo.

What were the odds against a life? Any life? All of our lives? When you thought of all the untold billions of sperm that fell on stony ground, and the eggs beyond number that were destined to make their lonely journey unfertilised, and the virtual impossibility of any sperm and any egg ever meeting, it was a wonder that anyone ever got born at all.

Every last one of us, thought Paulo. A walking miracle.

He flipped the switches and the lights went off in the showroom. The four cars in the window gleamed in the glow of the street. Two Maserati Spyders, the Lamborghini Murcielago and the fairest of them all, the Ferrari Maranello.

Paulo paused for a moment, his heart aching at the sight of all that low-slung, metallic Italian-built beauty. Then he punched in the numbers for the alarm system.

It had always been Michael's responsibility to lock up for the night. That changed after Chloe was born. Now Michael had taken to disappearing early, and Paulo happily shouldered the extra workload. When you had a kid, thought Paulo, work was different. Not so central to your life. Let Michael go home and enjoy some quality time with his beautiful baby girl. For the first time in his life, Paulo envied his brother.

With the alarm's warning signal buzzing, Paulo headed for the door, the keys in his hand. Then he paused. There was a sound that shouldn't be there. It was coming from Michael's office.

Paulo quickly punched in the code again and the alarm fell silent. He could hear the low murmur of voices. He glanced at the showroom. How much was this lot worth? In this neighbourhood convenience store clerks were frequently knifed for a fistful of till money, and pensioners were battered for a purse containing nothing but coins for cat food. The rent was cheap around here, and so was life.

There was a toolbox behind the reception desk. Paulo opened it as quietly as he could and pulled out a wrench. Then, conscious of his shallow breathing and hands that shook with fear, he edged towards the darkened office, holding the wrench like a club.

Shouting more from fear than rage, Paulo threw open the door to Michael's office and turned on the lights.

And there was Ginger on top of the desk on all fours, her skirt pushed up above her breasts and her thong pulled down around her knees, and hammering away behind her when he was supposed to be home with his wife and child, there was his brother Michael.

When they were alone – and Ginger had set an Olympic record for getting on her bra and pants – Paulo slapped Michael's face, slapped him as hard as he could, this brother who had always been able to beat him up. Paulo didn't care tonight. He felt wild and out of control, as if something priceless had been insulted here.

'You idiot. I don't believe you. You've got a perfect life, and you're pissing it all away.'

Michael's face twisted into a bitter grin. There was a red mark throbbing on his stubbled cheek.

'What do you know about my life?'

Paulo tried to slap him again but Michael easily swatted away the blow.

'What don't I understand, Mike? That things are not what they were at home? Get over it. You're a father now.'

'You don't understand how they change. *Women.* When they have had a baby. You don't understand how they change.'

Paulo felt the argument slipping away from him. Michael was making it sound complicated. And it wasn't complicated at all.

'Of course they change. You're not the centre of their world any more. That's the way it should be.'

'Easy for you to say.' Suddenly Michael seemed like the angry one. He towered over his brother, his fists clenched by his side. 'I can deal with the broken sleep – night after night, month after month. This permanent state of being totally knackered – I can live with that.'

'That's big of you.'

'I can even handle Naoko going off sex,' Michael said. 'Or being too tired to even think about it. Or not fancying me any more. Or whatever it is. I can handle that.'

'Michael – you've got this beautiful little baby. For once in your life, stop thinking about getting your end away.'

When they had both been a lot younger, Paulo had admired Michael's easy way with women. The way they flocked to his brother, the way they fell for him, and the way that he was always moving on. Now it seemed like a burden. Paulo had thought Naoko – so physically different from the blondes that Michael had knocked around with in Essex – would put an end to all that. Now Paulo wondered if it would ever end.

'When a woman has a baby, everything is different,' Michael said, quietly now. He wanted his brother to understand. 'You can never mean as much to her again. You can never take up so much space in her heart.'

'You've got this perfect family,' Paulo said. 'You really want to break it up? Is that what you want? You want Chloe to grow up without her dad around? Like so many of the poor little bastards around here?'

Michael shook his head. 'You think it's so simple, don't you, Paulo? You think you get the job, get the girl, get the house – and get the baby. And then live happily ever after.'

'What more would you want? You should be grateful. You should consider yourself lucky.'

'Don't lecture me. I love my daughter, you self-righteous fuck. And I love my wife. I love her as much as I can love anyone.'

'Funny way of showing it.'

'But a baby doesn't complete your world. Not if you're a man. A baby is a *rival*. And you can't compete, you just can't compete.' Michael took the wrench from Paulo's hand and placed it gently on the table. 'She's found someone much more loveable than me. Our daughter. So where does that leave me?'

'Go home, Michael. And count your blessings.'

'When a woman has a baby, she changes. I don't know how to explain it.' Michael smiled sadly at his big brother. 'It's almost like she has fallen in love with someone else.'

'My poor baby,' said Megan's mother. 'It's a rotten thing to go through, I know.'

Olivia let her youngest daughter into her flat. Heels and make-up, thought Megan, as her mother clicked across the floor. She even wears heels and make-up when she's home alone.

'We all have these little accidents. I had to have myself seen to before we shot the second series of *Vicar*. And long before that – before your father, even – there was a photographer who was helping me put a portfolio together.' Olivia, who rarely touched her children, rubbed Megan's back, gauging her daughter's condition. Still beautiful, thought Megan. She could understand why men her own age turned for a second look at her mother.

'I have to say, dear, you really don't look too bad.'

'I'm keeping it.'

'What?'

'I didn't go through with it, Mum. I'm keeping the baby.'

'But – why would you do a thing like that?'

Megan shrugged. She couldn't tell her mother about Mrs Summer. She couldn't explain that having this baby was hard, but not having it would be infinitely harder. How can you explain that feeling of being torn? She sat down on the sofa. The bouts of nausea were passing, but she was starting to feel tired all the time.

'I want to have it,' Megan said simply. 'I want this baby.'

'But – you're too young to have a child!'

'I'm twenty-eight, Mother. A bit older than you were when you had Cat.'

'I was married, dear. With a ring on my bloody finger. And it was still a fucking disaster.'

'This isn't going to be a disaster.'

'Where's the father? Is he in the picture?'

'No, he's out of the picture.'

'Megan, do you have any idea what you're taking on? The sleepless nights, the exhaustion, the screaming and the shitting and hysterical fits?'

'And that's just the mother, right?' Megan let out a breath. 'I know it will be hard. I know it will be the hardest thing I've ever done.'

'You have no idea. It's hard enough if you've got a husband and a nanny and a few bob in the bank. Try doing it alone on whatever pin money the NHS is chucking your way.'

'Jessica says she is going to help me.'

'Jessica has got her own life.'

'She means it. I know she does. She says she gets sick of going shopping and having facials and waiting for Paulo to come home. Jessie will be glad to look after the baby while I'm at work.'

'And what if Jessica finally gets knocked up?'

Megan hadn't thought about that. After all the sights she had seen in hospitals and doctors' surgeries, was it really possible her mother knew more than she did? Megan felt a shiver of fear. What if there was no one to help? What was she getting into? She saw the years stretching ahead – an eighteen-year sentence. Then she saw her mother's painted face twisted with anguish and she thought, perhaps you are never free of your children.

'What about your career? What about all those years at college and all those exams?'

'I'm going to keep working.' She didn't sound quite so sure of herself now. 'Of course I am. I can't afford not to. As you say, I don't have a ring on my finger.'

'You little fool, Megan.'

Her mother's voice was thick with disapproval.

'Why are you so *angry* with me?'

'Because you're throwing your life away!'

'Is that it? Or is it that you hate the thought of being a grandmother? Because it will be the final confirmation that you're no longer in the first flush of youth.'

'Oh, don't be ridiculous.'

'Please. I don't want you to be angry with me, Mum. I want you to be happy.'

'Happy? My daughter acts like some stupid little shop girl and she wants me to be happy?'

'I want you to love this baby. I want you to be happy.'

'Then go,' said Olivia. 'If you want me to be happy – just go.'

So Megan went, and for the first time the hard practicalities of her new life crowded in. Where would this nameless, unimaginable baby sleep in her tiny flat? Would the music played by the neighbours downstairs keep it awake? What would actually happen when Megan was at work? Would Jessica really be able to care for it during the day, every day, as if it was her job? What would the nights be like with the baby sleeping – or screaming – by her side?

Then Megan had her first scan, and although the doubts and the dark stuff did not disappear, someone or something seemed to whisper, *the right thing, the right thing, you are doing the right thing.*

Cat changed after Megan decided to keep the baby.

Rory couldn't understand it, but suddenly she seemed to act like his operation was a big deal.

The cut. The snip. The bollock-tampering. That had never been the case in the past. She didn't want children! God knows, he didn't want children. So the vasectomy was, if anything, a bit of a bonus. Then Megan cancelled her appointment at the clinic and things were somehow different.

Perhaps it had as much to do with his ex-wife as with Megan. One day Ali turned up to claim Jake with her five-year-old, Sadie, in tow.

There was undeniably something impressive about Ali. Rory had to admit that, even though their love was dead and buried years ago.

Ali was small and blonde, but she had made a little go a

long way – she was tanned and toned, with a prettiness that had made it into middle age without seeming absurd. She had an air of quiet authority about her. Jake was almost meek in her brisk, bossy presence, as she stood there watching him gather his belongings, and lug them out to her big BMW X5 off-roader – perfect for taking Sadie to her ballet class.

'Why has Jake-Jake been staying here, Mummy?' asked Sadie.

'He's just been spending a little time with his daddy, darling,' said Ali. 'Now it's time to come home.'

'He's welcome any time, the old boy,' said Rory, clapping his son on the back.

Stooped with teenage self-consciousness, Jake carried on gathering up the CDs that were strewn all over the coffee table, not meeting his father's eyes.

'But maybe next time he could leave his Rizlas at home,' Cat said quietly.

Rory and Ali stared at her.

'Mummy?' said Sadie.

Cat knew it was a mistake to say anything. But she couldn't help herself. Just because Rory and Ali were forced to negotiate an emotional minefield, that was no reason for her to pretend that Jake wasn't a walking nightmare.

'What are you suggesting?' Ali said.

'That Jake's too young to take drugs,' Cat said.

'*Cat*,' Rory said.

'How dare you?' Ali said. 'How dare you push your face into my family's business?'

'I can't help it. Sorry. I'm just saying – you let him get away with too much.'

'I'm ready, Mum,' Jake said.

Sadie took his hand, beaming up at her big half-brother. 'Jake-Jake,' she said.

'My son has been under enormous pressure,' Ali said, trembling with emotion. 'But I wouldn't expect someone like you to understand.'

'Someone like me?'

Ali smiled thinly. 'Someone who has never had a family of her own.'

'I've got a family,' Cat said, trying to keep her voice calm. 'I don't have children, it's true. But don't you ever tell me I haven't got a family.'

Then they were gone, and Rory was trying to make up. Too late. Cat was furious – with Rory, for letting his ex-wife walk all over him. With Jake for coming into their life. With Ali, for being such a cold, self-righteous bitch. And with something else that she couldn't name. It was something to do with the limitations of her life. She didn't want limits put on her life. She wanted her options to be permanently open.

'Cat?'

'I'm going.'

'Stay! Come on. We've finally got the place to ourselves.'

'She really kept *her* options open, didn't she?'

'Who?'

'Who? Your ex-wife. Ali got a second chance to get it right, didn't she? Another marriage, another kid, another life. You and her – that was just her starter marriage. Her dry run. She got another go.'

'Why are you so mad at me?'

She turned on him, white with fury and tears in her eyes. It frightened him. He was losing her, and he didn't want to lose her.

'Why did you have that stupid operation? Why? Cutting yourself up like that. Doing it for that cold bitch who went straight out and had a kid with the next man who came along. Why?'

Rory held up his hands. 'Because – because we didn't want any more children. Because it seemed like the right thing to do at the time.'

'So she got another go. But you don't. You're stuck with the past, and all its fucking mess. And me too. I'm stuck with your past too. You didn't just limit your options, Rory. You limited mine.'

'What's this all about? Megan's pregnant, so you suddenly want a kid of your own? You're talking like you want a baby.'

'It's not that. Where would I put a baby, for God's sake? But why couldn't you keep your options open? Ali did.'

'I can't give you a baby, Cat. You knew that when we started.'

'I know. And why should you? You've done it, right? Done it and got the T-shirt. And I don't even want a baby, do I?'

'So what's the problem?'

Cat shook her head. She couldn't explain it to him. She didn't suddenly want a child. She really didn't. But she wanted to be part of a family. When Ali had told her she didn't have a family, it had cut her to the core.

Cat was starting to understand that children gave you a stake in the future, and they gave you a family. They gave you a new family just when your old family was starting to drift apart, when your old family was starting to go its own way, making new families with their husbands and their babies. Without children all you had was now, and reminders of the past.

Rory stared at Cat, watched her anger fading away. He knew he didn't want any other woman, only her. But when she walked out the door, he didn't try to stop her.

Women got it wrong, Rory thought. They believed that they were victims of some ticking biological clock, and yet men could go on having children for as long as they liked. And it just wasn't true.

Because you got tired. You made that journey – from the nights when your child stayed awake teething, to the nights when your child stayed awake taking drugs – and it exhausted you. It just wore you out.

Even without his operation, and the divorce, and all the poison between him and his ex-wife, Rory would have found it hard to go through all that again. Time performed its own kind of surgery on you. And even if it was a possibility, which it wasn't, it would be absurd to choose to go through all of that again at his age, wouldn't it? By the time the kid was sixteen, he would be well into his sixties. It was tough enough dealing with a teenager in your forties. How could you do it as an old man?

It would take a lot to decide to go through all that again.

You would really have to love someone.

Megan gripped Jessica's hands as the sonographer put cold jelly on her belly and pressed down hard with the scanner.

The pressure felt too hard, far too hard, but the twinge of anxiety was forgotten because suddenly there it was on the screen, Megan's baby, this unplanned little human, looking like an alien in a snowstorm.

Its head too big, fingers like threads in a spider's web, and lidless eyes, unseeing and all-seeing. Megan and Jessica laughed out loud, laughed with delight and disbelief. Megan looked at her sister and was filled with gratitude for her love, and for her generosity, and for the fact that she was there to hold her hand and share this moment. Jessica was as thrilled, and as moved, as Megan. It was almost, Megan thought, as if the baby belonged to both of them.

Megan looked at the hazy profile on the scan and felt a connection that she had never felt with another human being.

The baby was part of her flesh and blood and yet entirely separate, at once as familiar as her own face and yet as mysterious as an angel. It was just a fuzzy black-and-white image on a screen. That's all. The sonographer probably did a dozen a day. And yet it provoked feelings inside Megan that she had never known existed.

Maybe the neighbours downstairs would play their music too loud. Maybe there would be days when Jessica couldn't baby-sit. Maybe it would be harder than Megan could possibly imagine. But these worries all seemed to diminish in the presence of that blurred image. How could you worry too much about the neighbours or sleepless nights when you were in the presence of magic?

When Megan left she was given a slip of shiny black paper with the baby caught in heartbreaking, big-headed profile. That little alien in a snowstorm. The first picture of the baby.

Megan was told a date for the birth, a day that seemed ridiculously distant, almost meaningless, as though it had been plucked from the calendar at random. But she knew it would come.

And she knew it was a date with another kind of life.

Jessica and Paulo talked to their doctor about going for IVF.

Paulo had been shocked by the discussion – shocked by both the cost (thousands) and even more the odds (about a one in three chance of success, and that was the most optimistic prognosis). Most of all, he had been shocked to hear that there was no time to waste.

'But she's thirty-two!' he said to the doctor.

'Exactly,' said the doctor. 'A woman is born with the only eggs she is ever going to have. And there's a marked deterioration in fertility after thirty-five. Best to get started before you get too old. Who knows how many cycles you'll need?'

'I want to do it,' Jessica said on their way home. 'I don't

care what we have to do to get the money. I don't care how many times we try. But I want to do it now.'

'What does your sister say?'

'Megan?'

'Does she think IVF is a good idea?'

'I didn't talk to her about it. She's got enough on her plate. I don't want to worry her that I won't be free to look after her baby. You know. When I get pregnant from the IVF.'

So that's what they were going to do. Their GP referred them to a private clinic out in rural Essex with one of the best rates of success in the world. And Paulo went along with it because he would do anything for Jessica. Almost anything.

'I'm not going to let this baby thing break us up, Jess,' he said when she came into the bedroom that night.

'What?'

'I've never complained. And I never will. All the tests and the consultations. All the wanking into little jugs and the rest of it. All the text messages telling me to come home and shag you because you're ovulating. I'll go along with all of it. You want IVF treatment? Fine. But I'm not going to let this break us up.'

'Why would it break us up?'

He sat on the bed and took her face in his hands. He loved that face.

'Because it has become more important than anything. More important than you and me. This baby thing – it's taken over our world.'

'You know how much this means to me.'

'Of course I do! But if it doesn't happen, if it never happens – well, I'll still be in love with you. I know you want a kid. Me too. But it's not the most important thing in my life. Because you are, Jess.'

She shook her head.

'It can't be like it was before. When we could make love when we felt like it. You don't understand, Paulo. If I don't have a kid, then what's the point of me?'

'The point of you? If you never have a kid, you're still beautiful. You're still smart, and kind, and sexy.'

'I'm not sexy.'

'Yes, you are, you sexy little bitch.' They were both smiling now. 'I know you want a kid, Jess. So let's go for the IVF. And if it doesn't work, let's try again. And again. And if we have to sell everything to keep trying, then we'll do it.'

She placed a hand on his upper arm and squeezed it, massaging the curve of the muscle, feeling the bone beneath. This was the man she wanted to be with for the rest of her life.

'Thanks,' she said.

'But if it doesn't happen, if it never happens, then let's not stop loving each other. Because I couldn't stand that.'

'Me neither.'

'I promise you we'll spend every penny we have on the IVF thing, but I want you to promise me something.'

'What's that?'

'That once in a while, just every once in a while, we will stop thinking about all this baby stuff and make love not because we want a baby, but because we still fancy each other.'

Her smile was broader.

'I promise.'

So they kissed for a while and then took off their clothes and she put on her high-heeled Jimmy Choo shoes – her husband was a very conventional man, and she knew how much he liked high heels in the bedroom – and then they stood up, positioning the wardrobe door just right so that they could see themselves in its full-length mirror.

And that was the night that Jessica and Paulo made their baby.

eight

Jack Jewell was still recognised.

All the Fish in the Sea had ended ten years ago, but he had never stopped working and there had been enough roles on television – the retiring cop forced to work with the reckless rookie, the gentleman jewel thief swindling the gullible widow, the private dick with exquisite table manners and Sherlock Holmes tendencies – for it to cause a minor stir when he walked into a restaurant in Chinatown.

Today he didn't notice the double takes, the affectionate smiles, the startled murmurs of 'Isn't that . . . ?'

Today all he saw was his daughters.

He was so proud of them. They were so beautiful, they had always been so beautiful, and he was the one person in the world who could see on the women they'd become the imprint of the children they had once been.

Megan, pretty and round, as if she was made up of circles (he knew she worried about her weight, but she was always gorgeous to him). Jessica, the conventional beauty, with her lush black hair, compact frame and baby face (he could understand why people thought she was the youngest, and smiled when he remembered how that used to drive her crazy). And Cat, his darling Cat, tall and slim, all arms and legs, with those wide-set brown eyes that seemed to see right through you.

What was the old song? Something about when you are the father of boys you worry, and when you are the father of girls you pray. He was never worried about them, the girls, but only what men – his lying, cunning, cheating tribe – would do to them. But now he felt that it was all going to work out fine.

He liked to joke about what a trial they had been, but it was the defence mechanism of a man who felt he hadn't been there often enough for the children in his sole charge. He loved them more than he loved anything in his life. But he knew that the hard work, the day-to-day drudgery and graft, had been mostly done by Cat and a series of hired hands from the poorer parts of the globe.

'So you're their mother *and* their father,' women would say to him when the girls were growing up.

But he had never been a mother to them. A man doesn't become a mother just because the mother is not around. He hadn't even been a good enough father.

It would be different today. Men were different. More capable of taking on different roles. But back then, in the mid-seventies when Olivia walked away, Jack had been type-cast as an old-fashioned kind of father. Designed to go out into the world and make a living while his children were brought up by someone else. A parade of long-forgotten nannies, au pairs, housekeepers and, above all, his oldest daughter.

Jack Jewell had been too busy earning a living to always be there for Megan, Jessica and Cat. But it was more than the demands of work. Unlike his ex-wife, and unlike most actors, Jack had never had years of resting. There had always been a market for his well-mannered decency, his old-world charm. 'David Niven lite', one critic called it, trying to be unkind, but Jack had taken it as a compliment. Sometimes he took jobs not because they needed the money but because he needed the self-esteem and sense of worth that came from making his mark in the working world.

When Olivia left him, his sense of self had taken a terrible blow. He thought less of himself as a man when she walked out. The only way he could recover his sense of self was through work, and by taking to bed the women that work brought his way.

Helping Cat with her homework, taking Jessica to ballet class, teaching Megan to dress herself – these things would not have helped Jack Jewell put himself back together. He needed his work. It was so much easier to make a success of your career than your marriage.

And now two of his children were to have children of their own. The news filled him with nothing but happiness. It seemed to Jack that grandchildren would put stabilisers on their little family, and ensure its survival.

What stability had he given his daughters? He was there in theory, the sole carer. In practice he was constantly on set, or attending to his needs with some love-struck make-up girl or recent graduate from RADA. To his buried but abiding shame, Jack Jewell knew that he didn't have it in him to be a full-time parent. It would have driven him insane. But perhaps – no, definitely – even back then he could have struck a healthier balance between home and work. There were jobs he could have resisted, women he could have walked away from. And gone home early to his three daughters. It was too late now. Thank heavens it had worked out all right in the end. He knew that Megan and Jessica would make good mothers. Megan was smart and tough. Jessica was loving and kind. They would be everything that their own mother had not been.

If he had been sometimes preoccupied by work, and distracted by starlets, then Olivia had been something worse. From the moment she left, it was as if she wanted no reminders of her old life. Contact was sporadic, and then almost non-existent. The children, it seemed to Jack, were expected to make all the effort. Olivia made none. She had more important things to consider – the struggle with her weight, her botched second face-lift, and again and again the man of her dreams turning out to be a lazy, freeloading loser.

Jack had known plenty of fathers who had behaved that way to their first family. Olivia proved that a mother could be just as cruel and pitiless. A barnyard animal would not have been so callous to its offspring.

Jack could never explain such wanton malice to his children, and neither could he articulate his own feelings about how he had failed them as a father. He could hardly explain these things to himself.

Bloody actors, Jack thought. No good to anyone without a script.

Megan always told her patients that pregnancy was a bit like flying. Take-off and landing. They were the tough parts. If things were going to go wrong, that's when it usually happened.

When the three of them sat down with their father in their favourite restaurant in Chinatown, Jessica was in – what? Week four? Most women wouldn't even know they were pregnant by then. Most women would be looking at the calendar and starting to think, *funny that. A bit late.* Or perhaps most of them wouldn't even notice that their cycle was a bit out.

Unless of course they were waiting. Unless they were trying, and had been trying for a long time.

'You're going to be a *grandfather*,' Jessica said again, laughing with delight. 'Twice over, Dad. Can you handle it?'

'They can't be any harder than you three.' He smiled, embracing Jessica. 'And at least at the end of the day I'll be able to give them back. Congratulations, darling. I know how much you wanted this. You and Paulo.'

Then he attempted to do the same to Megan, but it was much more awkward because she was holding a spring roll with her chopsticks, and she didn't have a partner, and she nearly stabbed him in the eye.

'Well done, darling,' he said, and Megan felt as if she had just got another A+ in another exam.

Megan smiled. Dear old Dad. Week four and week twelve was all the same to him. But it wasn't the same to her. During take-off and landing a few short weeks could be the difference between life and no life at all.

For like all doctors, Megan counted pregnancy in weeks. It was only the rest of the world that counted in months.

Megan thought, oh Jessie, week four; it's far too soon to be telling people. But nothing in this world could stop Jessica blurting out her news. She had waited so long. And it was hard to urge caution in the face of such unbridled joy.

Megan hugged her sister and congratulated her, but in her heart she thought, the plane is still on the runway. And anything could happen.

'It was a Sunday morning,' Jessica told their father. 'Paulo had been for a run. And when he came back, I was sitting on the stairs. He looked at my face. And he just knew.'

And there was something else. On some level of sibling rivalry, Megan knew she was jealous.

She was happy for Jessica. She couldn't have been happier. But Jessie had her husband and her house and her life. And, yes, the ring on her finger. Their father had walked Jess down the aisle – given her away, as they say. There was

Paulo to go running on a Sunday morning and to come back home and hear the good news and to cuddle Jessica at night.

Megan thought – I have no Paulo, no ring, and no room in my flat for a little pink or blue nursery. All I've got is the bun in the oven and a rented room in Hackney.

Megan was in week twelve while Jessica was in week four or five. Megan had just sailed through her nuchal scan – there were no chromosomal abnormalities, there was no risk of Down's syndrome. The heartbeat was strong and steady, the baby looked normal and happy. The date Megan had been given seemed more real with every passing day. *This is your captain speaking. We have lift-off. You may unfasten your seat belts and wander about the cabin. You are definitely going to have a baby.*

Jessica was still a couple of months away from a nuchal scan. Megan didn't think her sister had any comprehension of how momentous that test would be, or how awful that paralysing wait when you hold your breath until they give you the odds of Down's syndrome. Less than 300 to one and you needed further examination – an invasive test, they called it, to find out if the baby was really likely to be disabled or not.

But this was the heartbreaker – an invasive test, an injection into the baby's neck, could kill a healthy baby. If the bookies of the medical profession gave you odds of less than 300 to one, did you go for an invasive test, and risk killing a healthy baby? Or did you take the risk of disability? And how could anyone ever make those choices about something as innocent and defenceless as their unborn baby, and know for certain that they were doing the right thing?

Megan was over that particular hurdle. If there were others, they were likely to occur nearer to the date they had given her. During landing.

At week twelve Megan's foetus was undeniably human.

On the scan it – Megan still thought of this thing growing inside her as *it,* although the *he* or *she* had already been genetically programmed – could be seen crossing its legs and wiggling its fingers. The head was enormous – almost half of Little It was taken up by that great bulging bonce, nodding forward as if it was far too heavy to hold up – and, incredibly, unbelievably, Little It seemed to be sucking a thumb. Little It was around eight centimetres long and weighed in at eighteen grams.

At week four, Jessica's foetus was still too small to see without a magnifying glass – about a fifth of a millimetre long. Was it even a real baby yet? It was to Jessica.

'Paulo's going to tear out his study,' Jessica said. 'Just throw it all out and turn it into a nursery. He has started already. All the shelves have gone. It's going to be the most beautiful nursery in the world.'

Although her condition still seemed slightly unreal, the doctor in Megan knew that nothing much could stop her baby being born now, while Jessica's baby was still fighting for its life.

And yet here was the funny thing.

Somehow Jessica's baby felt like the one whose future was secure.

Cat sipped her champagne. Only she and her father were drinking the bottle of Mumm that had been produced from the bottom of the Shenyang Tiger's fridge. And as she watched her two pregnant sisters – Jessica spilling over with joy, Megan far more reserved, yet apparently happy that she taken the decision to have this baby – Cat knew that she had let her personal life drift.

Megan had a career and a baby on the way. Juggling the needs of both would be tough, but next year she would be a fully registered doctor and a mother. No matter how hard it got in Hackney, there was something enviable about a life so full.

And Jessica – Cat had never seen anyone so happy. She had the final piece of her jigsaw. The man, the marriage, the home – and now the baby. Cat was glad for her. Because she knew that for her sister, the rest of it would have grown sour and meaningless without a child.

Cat thought, what about me? What do I have? What will make next year any different from this year?

It was almost funny. She had always been completely ruthless in her professional life. Working hard, knowing when it was time to move on, finding a mentor in Brigitte, and then doing all she could to please her.

But in her private life Cat now felt she had been hopelessly passive, allowing herself to drift where the wind blew her. Cat liked to think of herself as an intelligent woman. But existing on automatic pilot – how stupid was that?

'The next generation of Jewells is on the way,' said their father, holding the hands of Jessica and Megan, but staring at Cat and lifting a wry eyebrow. 'You're next, Cat.'

'Not me,' she said. 'I'm a bit more careful than they are.'

Rory – what was all that about? He was kind, attentive, and clearly mad about her. But Rory's past wouldn't lie down and die. It couldn't. Not ever. Because there was a child involved. Because the ex-wife would always be there. Because of that stupid operation.

And as Cat watched her sisters with their father, she thought, what do I need to be happy? A job I love, a good flat, my own space. Children had never been on the list. And they were not on the list today. But perhaps she needed the possibility of children.

Even if Cat never had any of the little bastards, it would be nice to think she could if she really wanted to. If she ever changed her mind. That was the problem with Rory. She was not used to having her options limited.

Yet, as she sat listening to her sisters' tales of fatigue, sickness and swollen breasts – and as she guessed at Megan's fears of bringing a baby into a one-bedroom flat in Hackney – Cat felt a clearly identifiable emotion wash over her, and almost swooned with the force of it.

Relief.

Then suddenly Megan had to go. There were house visits to make on the Sunny View Estate before afternoon surgery. And Cat had to get back to Mamma-san. So they said their goodbyes on Gerrard Place, next to the long line of fire engines in Soho's fire station.

Jack and Jessica lingered, both reluctant to go home. They drifted across to John Lewis and went up to the fifth floor, losing themselves among the prams, cots, push chairs, Grobags, babygros and many things they didn't even recognise – tap protectors, bottle warmers, nappy wrappers, the products of an industry that had sprung up since Jack Jewell's daughters were children.

They didn't talk about it, but they both knew what they wished for Jessica's baby, and for the baby that Megan was at this very moment carrying around the Sunny View Estate, and it was a wish that grew within the walls of every broken home.

A family that was built on far stronger ground than the one they had known.

Rory went to see Megan. She saw him in her surgery after hours, a small favour to her old martial arts teacher. Neither of them told Cat.

'I had an operation. Towards the end of my marriage. You know. A vasectomy.'

Now she understood why he didn't want to talk on the

phone. This was a big thing in his life. You didn't resolve it with a phone call.

'I think my sister may have mentioned it.'

'And now – well, I'm not sure it was the right thing to do. I mean, I knew I didn't want any more children with my wife. Ex-wife. And she certainly didn't want any more children with me. But perhaps it was too drastic.'

'It's a common problem.'

He was stunned.

'It is?'

'We're good at controlling our reproduction. But not so good at controlling our personal lives.'

'You mean you have seen this before?'

'What? Regrets from a man who has had a vasectomy? More times than I can count. I've also seen women who are sterilised, and live to regret it.'

'I thought perhaps – I don't know – I was the only one. It sounds stupid when I say it like that.'

'It's not stupid. Nobody talks about these things. Because what does it say about you?'

'That I am a complete idiot who has made a total mess of his life.'

'That's a bit harsh. I was going to say, it shows you have made one or two bad choices. Although I am sure it seemed like a good idea at the time. But how can I help you, Rory?'

'I want to know if it's possible to reverse what's been done to me.'

Megan had seen it all before. Even with her limited experience in a surgery, this conversation was not new. Perhaps this is how you become a proper doctor, she thought – seeing the same scenarios of human pain and sadness and illness again and again, until your response became automatic. What was different this time was that this man was in love with her sister.

'First off, they should have told you that the procedure is designed to be irreversible.'

'They did.'

'Secondly, you should never have had it done if you thought there was the remotest possibility that you would live to regret it.'

'I know. I do.'

'All that said – of course life changes. You wake up one day and the world looks different. You don't want children with the woman you are married to. Years later, you meet someone you think you would like to have children with. Like, possibly, I don't know – my sister.'

'So they can reverse this operation? They can do it?'

'Happens all the time. Reversing it is not a problem. But it's far from certain that you would be able to produce a child. Your sperm are unlikely to have the degree of motility they had before. Maybe, maybe not. But there's one thing I've learned since I left medical school.'

'What's that?'

'You never know your luck. I have to tell you, in all honesty, it's a long shot. That's the reality. I'm sorry I can't be more positive.'

'That's okay.'

'And anyway – oh, this has got nothing to do with me.'

'Go ahead.'

'I don't think my sister wants children.'

'That's fine. That's great. Because you know what? Neither do I.'

nine

Endings sneak up on you, Cat thought.

You think you are in control. You think you can decide when it's all over. And then suddenly it all slips away, and you are reminded that you are not in control at all.

It was just the two of them now. Just how she liked it. Jake was back with his mother, his stepfather and his half-sister – complicated or what? – and Cat could sleep over at Rory's place without bumping into anyone with acne.

But late one night, as he poured two glasses of something red and full-bodied, she noticed that he had cleared out his spare room. This was where he kept the stock for his business – the white karate tops and trousers, the coloured belts in their cellophane wrappers, the black and red leather pads for kicking and punching. Now it was all gone, replaced by a flatpack from IKEA. A single bed.

'I thought I'd prepare a room for Jake,' he said, joining her in the doorway. 'It's not fair on the boy, expecting him to always sleep on the sofa.'

'But – but what about all the stuff you need for your business?'

What she meant was, *but what about us?*

Rory handed her a glass, and shrugged. 'I can keep it at the dojo. The important thing is that Jake feels welcome here.' He stared at her, his face hardening. 'What is it?'

'Nothing.'

'Come on, Cat. You're pissed off because I'm making a room for Jake. I can tell. I've got a son – can't you understand that?'

'And I haven't got a son. Can't you understand that?'

'I'm not going to argue with you. I can't apologise for having a child.'

'I'm not asking you to apologise.' Suddenly she felt an overwhelming sadness. This wasn't what she wanted. 'Just – I don't know. I just wish the present mattered to you as much as the past.'

'Look – it'll be fine. The pair of you used to love each other. It's just a difficult age.'

'For him or me?' Cat shook her head. 'This is no good, is it? Of course you want to make your boy feel at home. There's nothing wrong with that. What kind of heartless cow could object to that? I just think – we should maybe not see quite so much of each other.'

His face fell. 'Because I want to make some space for my son?'

'Because I need some more space for myself. It's not your fault. It's mine. Wanting your son to feel at home – it's only natural.'

And leaving him then felt natural too. If she was going to find something else in her life, then she had to allow herself – what did they call it in all the magazines?

Search time. They called it search time.

As part of her vocational training scheme, once a week Megan caught the bus to the local hospital and sat around with a dozen other GP registrars, discussing their problems.

Trainee quack coffee mornings, Megan thought, though she could see their value. She always came away from these gab sessions thinking, oh, it's not just me then. It's a screaming nightmare for all of us.

The other GP registrars were from every class and race – almost half of them were from Asian backgrounds – and yet Megan had no doubt that they were all people like her. Late twenties, bright-faced high achievers, academic virtuosi who were starting to look a little worn around the edges. Megan thought it was wise of their masters to set up this ritual. Because they couldn't talk to their friends and family about what they were going through. Nobody else would understand.

'I've got this patient who is being bashed about by her husband,' said one young woman, a blonde with pony clubs and privilege in her every vowel. 'Comes in once a week, cuts and bruises, the occasional cracked rib. I don't know whether to alert the authorities or not.'

A fat Chinese boy peered at her through black-rimmed spectacles. 'What's stopping you?'

'Arranged marriage,' sighed the blonde. 'If the police turn up at the door, I'm afraid that hubby or his family will kill her.'

'Cultural diversity,' smirked a smooth young Indian man. 'Don't you just love it?'

'Don't tell anyone,' snapped the Chinese. His accent was that strange mixture of Cockney and Cantonese. Everything sounded like a command. 'She'll never press charges, and it will just make it worse for her. That's what they're like round here.'

'I hate it when my patients tell me to fuck off and die,' said a Pakistani girl in a mini-skirt who looked as though she should still be doing her A levels. 'Have you noticed? They tend to do it when you refuse to give them their pill of choice.'

'Temazepam,' drawled the Indian. 'They always tell me to fuck off and die when I decline to dish out the Temazepam on demand.'

Megan took a deep breath and blurted it out.

'I'm pregnant,' she laughed.

They stared at her. And kept staring. Megan found herself grinning into the embarrassed silence.

After a few months in general practice, these young doctors thought they had seen and heard it all. The man with a hamster bite in his rectum. Wives who slept with a hammer under the pillow, not to protect themselves from burglars, but to protect themselves from their husbands. The brother and sister who were left to fend for themselves when their parents went dancing.

In Ibiza.

A grotesque parade of feral children, thieving junkies, neglected pensioners, men with their cocks stuck inside vacuum cleaners, more men with assorted fruit and vegetables stuck up their back passage, women who had been beaten and bashed by men who were drunks, or religious fanatics, or jealous to the very edge of murder, all the abusers and the abused.

In rotting neighbourhoods full of baseball bats where not one single person played baseball, the finest minds of their generation tended to the sick, the diseased and the dying. They had seen it all, and written the prescription.

But one of their band of high-flying, straight-A brothers and sisters *pregnant*? They had never heard anything like it.

'I think it will be fine,' Megan said, smiling with a confidence that she didn't feel. 'The baby will be born towards the end of vocational training, so I will probably be breastfeeding during the final MRCGP exam, and the father's out of the picture, but I really think I can handle it. You know?'

They didn't know what to say.

They had all come so far, and all worked so hard, and seen so much, and were now struggling through their final year before full registration. A baby on top of all that? A baby *now?* It seemed perverse – like an exhausted marathon runner staggering into the stadium, and deciding to do the final lap on his hands.

The other young doctors stared at Megan in silence, offering neither congratulations nor commiserations. They had seen some strange sights on the front line of the NHS – but this? It was as if they didn't quite believe her. Megan looked at all those different-coloured faces wearing exactly the same expression. *She's kidding, right?*

Megan knew how they felt.

Sometimes she couldn't quite believe it herself.

'Once they've got their baby, it all changes,' said Michael. 'Not just their body – although there's certainly that – but their entire outlook.' He drained his beer and signalled the bartender for another one. The bartender ignored him. 'The baby becomes the centre of their world. And the man barely shows up on the radar.'

They were in a pub just off the Holloway Road. It was close to their business, but they had never visited it before. Neither of them were drinkers – 'There is no word in Italian for *alcoholic*,' their father had always told them, when their English friends were all growing beer bellies in their late teens – and both of them had somewhere they would rather be. But Michael was increasingly reluctant to go home. Not that staying out made him happy.

'Do you think that's what happened to our mum?' Paulo said. 'She lost interest in our dad?'

Michael shot him a look. 'Don't talk about Mum that way.'

'I'm just thinking. She always seemed like such a real mum

to me.' Paulo smiled at the memory. 'Cooking, and bossing us around, and all that stuff.'

Michael smiled too. 'Yeah, she was good at it. Good at being a mum.'

'Maybe she changed. Maybe when we came along we became the most important thing in her world. And maybe Dad was glad. They always seemed happy together, didn't they? Happier than couples now.'

'It's different these days. Men like the old man, they courted the first girl that came along, they got married, and that was it. Work and home and no rumpy-pumpy in between. Now we've got all these temptations. Now there are all these women out there who like sex as much as men do. Until you marry them.'

Paulo watched his brother staring moodily into the gloom of the Rat and Trumpet, and he realised how close he still felt to him, how much he still cared about this man. How much he still loved him.

'Let me get this straight,' said Paulo. 'It's not actually your fault you were taking Ginger from behind. It's your wife who's to blame.'

'Keep your voice down, will you?' Michael glanced around nervously, a hunted man. 'I'm just saying – they go all mumsy on you. The big difference is not living together or living apart. It's not being married or being single. The big difference is being childless and then having a kid.' Michael stared at his brother defensively. 'I love my daughter, I couldn't love her more.'

Paulo placed a hand on his brother's arm. 'I know that. So stop shagging around. You don't want a divorce, do you? You don't want Chloe to grow up with you not around. You want her to have the same sort of family we come from, don't you? A family as solid as that.'

'It can never be like that any more.'

'But it's madness to chuck your family away for the sake of a quick poke. It doesn't make any kind of sense. You love your family, Mike. You don't want to lose it.'

'Ginger's very special.'

'Well, they're all special when you've got a boner, Michael. But it wears off, doesn't it? That boner. That passion. That – I don't know – that hunger. It melts away. You know it all better than me, the number of girls you've had. But what you've got with Naoko is something to build a life on.'

Michael hung his head. 'I love Naoko. And I love Chloe. But since she's been born, I just wonder – how can you have so much love in your life, and so little joy?'

'Is that your idea of joy? Meaningless sex with a virtual stranger?'

'Well, it's a start.'

'You stupid bastard. She's the one who is supposed to get postnatal depression. Not you.'

Paulo thought, it will be different for us, for me and Jessica and our baby.

I don't care about the sleepless nights, or the teething problems, or changing nappies, and whatever else it is you have to do. And I don't even mind if the baby becomes the most important thing in my wife's life and we only have sex by appointment. I *want* her to love our baby that much. A baby deserves to be loved more than me.

Whatever is happening with Michael and Naoko and Chloe will never happen to us. We are going to be fine. The only thing we have to do, thought Paulo, is get through the next nine months. That's all.

Then he left his brother in that miserable pub and went home to his pregnant wife, and gently pressed his ear against her still-flat abdomen, and it was the best thing in the world, both of them smiling and full of unalloyed joy, listening for that tiny heartbeat, waiting for some small signal from the centre of the universe.

Week fourteen, thought Megan, heaving her weary legs down the steps of the surgery. She could hear a shaven-headed man in a grubby vest shouting at the receptionist that he knew his rights.

Week fourteen, she thought, lightly running the palm of her hand across her abdomen, a gesture of reassurance, although Megan had no idea if she wanted to reassure the baby or herself. The bump was starting to show. Her clothes were tighter. The baby was learning to suck its tiny thumb. It was really happening.

In the surgery there was a leaflet called 'The First Trimester' for next year's mothers, full of sensible sound bites for women with a bun in the oven and perfect lives.

Involve Your Partner. Try to Fit in a Daily Nap. Give in to Your Exhaustion. Get Fitted For a Proper Maternity Bra. Get Your Partner to Give You a Soothing Massage. Swim Regularly. Talk to Your Partner. Don't Suffer in Silence.

Megan often looked at the leaflet when she wanted a good laugh.

'Megan?'

It was Will, all shy and anxious, and for a few moments she was absurdly pleased to see him. Involve Your Partner, she thought. Get Your Partner to Give You a Soothing Massage. But Will wasn't her partner any more, and he wasn't the father of this child. He had sent her a barrage of text messages that she had deleted without reading. What was there to say? And still she felt the sweet and sour pang of regret for a road not taken.

If he had loved only her, they would still have been together. They would probably have drifted into marriage and, eventually, had some sweet-looking children who would have spent Sundays with their doting grandparents in Hampstead Garden Suburb. Now she wouldn't even look at his text messages. Megan thought, how we rush to forget those we once loved.

'You look good, Megan.'

They had been so close. That was why she was happy to see him. She wasn't sure she would ever be that close to a man again. They had all that precious time to waste during their student years. Nights when they talked for hours and told the secrets of their soul and the stories of their life. Nights when they didn't sleep because they couldn't stand to be apart. Nights when they smoked and drank and watched the sun come up.

It wasn't that Megan couldn't find a better man than Will. It was that she would never again have all that time to waste. She realised how lonely she had been.

'I want you back, Megan.'

Not possible. Because of what he had done. Because of what she had done. Best to get it out of the way.

'I'm pregnant, Will.'

His jaw fell open.

'It's not yours,' she added quickly.

Megan had always thought that scene in *Four Weddings and a Funeral* was a bit unrealistic, the one where Andie MacDowell tells Hugh Grant about her sexual history, and all he does is look a bit sheepish and say, 'Oh golly gosh, matron, oh bugger me.'

Megan always felt that was a little too enlightened.

'You slut, Megan,' Will managed, his face red with rage, not very Hugh Grant-like at all, and trying to stop himself from crying. 'You bloody slut!'

Men didn't expect virginity these days, Megan thought, but they certainly expected the illusion of purity. *The truth? They can't handle the truth!*

'Who is he, you filthy slut? I'll kill him!'

Virtual purity, Megan thought. That's what they all wanted.

Impossible when you were in the family way.

Jessica entered From Here to Maternity with shyness and pride.

Women at various stages of pregnancy moved slowly around the store, lifting maternity clothes from the racks – combat trousers with huge expanding, elasticated waistbands, flowery smocks, austere black business trousers, again with one of those expanding waistbands. All kinds of maternity clothes for all kinds of lives, and all kinds of future mothers.

The women occasionally made that protective double or triple stroke of their pregnant bellies, that gesture that Jessica had caught herself doing – the Masonic handshake of pregnant women.

From Here to Maternity was different from other clothes stores. There were no bored husbands and boyfriends sitting around sighing. Nobody seemed to be in any mad rush. The women seemed to have all the time in the world. Occasionally they would talk to the sales assistants, and their conversations seemed like a mixture of the trivial and the momentous. *Can you get these combat trousers in khaki as well as green? Oh, I'm due next month.* Jessica couldn't stop smiling to herself. Because she belonged here.

Jessica picked a pink, flower-print dress from the rack. She could see that some of these clothes were no different from what young, non-pregnant women would wear to a bar or club. Okay for Megan perhaps, but not her. But the pink, flower-print number was exactly Jessica's idea of what a maternity dress should look like.

'It's pretty, isn't it?' an assistant asked.

Jessica smiled. 'I love it.'

'There's no reason why you can't look stylish and sexy when you're pregnant. From Here to Maternity wants you to show off that bump with pride.'

Jessica glanced down at herself.

'Don't worry.' The assistant smiled. 'The bump will get bigger, I promise you. So you're around three months, I guess?'

'Not quite, actually.'

'Would you like to try it on?'

Why not? Jessica was part of the club now. And even if her normal clothes still fit her, there was no reason on earth why she should not start preparing her wardrobe for the coming months. She always did things a bit early.

She left work to have a baby before she was pregnant. She told the world about her pregnancy before she reached three months. And now she was shopping for maternity clothes when she was still only a size ten. And this was because Jessica couldn't wait, she just couldn't wait to hold her baby, to start a proper family, for everything to be okay again.

She was in the changing room, still fully dressed, when she felt the wetness in her shoes. That's what she didn't understand. The wetness was in her shoes. That's why she didn't realise she had started bleeding. Because the only sensation was the wetness in her shoes.

The fear rising, Jessica started to remove her clothes and that's when she saw the blood. All that blood. On her hands, on the unbought dress. She felt the panic flood her heart.

There was all that blood and the wetness in her shoes and the dress with flowers still in her hands, somehow flecked with red.

My lovely baby.

ten

At first he thought she was his wife.

There was something about the curve of her face, the set of her eyes that for just a moment made Paulo think, *there she is.*

From the other end of the hospital corridor, it was an easy mistake to make, what with his nerves still jangling from the mad drive, and with this terrible need to see her. But it was one of the sisters. It was Megan. Sipping a cup of coffee she didn't want. Waiting for him. She looked up as he ran towards her.

'Is she all right? Is she all right?'

'Paulo, Jessica's going to be fine, okay? But there's been a lot of bleeding. They have to do what's called an ERPC.'

He struggled to understand her. How could this be happening?

'It's standard procedure. Very straightforward. An ERPC is a short operation. Nothing to worry about. It means evacuation of retained products of conception.'

'But she's going to be okay?'

'Yes, Paulo. I promise you Jessica's going to be okay.'

'And the baby's going to be okay?'

Megan stared at him, took a breath. 'Paulo – Jessica lost her baby.'

'What?'

'Jessica had a miscarriage.'

'A miscarriage?' He shook his head, looked away, struggling to grasp it. 'Our baby's gone?'

'I'm so sorry.'

'But – she's having this operation, isn't she?'

'The ERPC is just – it's to clear out the uterus. We – they – can't leave anything inside Jessica. Because that can lead to infection. We have to wait for a few hours before she can be given anaesthetic.'

Paulo seemed to unravel before her eyes. 'We lost the baby?'

'You and Jessica will have a beautiful baby one day.'

He shook his head again. How could this be happening? 'But what did we do wrong?'

'You didn't do anything wrong. I know this is a terrible thing. But it happens every day. One in four pregnancies –'

'Where is she? Where's my wife?'

Megan indicated the door behind her. Paulo nodded, wiped his eyes with the palm of his hand, and went inside.

Megan took out her mobile phone and, ignoring the withering looks from a couple of passing nurses, called Cat yet again, and again got nothing but the metallic voice of the woman on the answer machine.

My lovely wife, he thought.

The room was lit by nothing but the buzzing bar of fluorescent light behind Jessica's bed. But even in this sterile twilight, Paulo could see it all written on her face. The loss of blood. The grief. The exhaustion. And on top of it all, the terrible weight of the lost life.

She was propped up on pillows, but seemed to be sleeping.

Paulo pulled a chair close to the bed and took her hand. Then he buried his face in the covers of the hospital bed, sobbing into the starched sheets, choked with grief.

'Sorry,' Jessica said.

'You have to use a condom,' Cat said.

The boy smiled, and tugged at the edge of his woolly Justin Timberlake hat. 'But I want to feel myself inside you.'

He reached for her and she lightly held his wrists. 'Well, you can feel me through a condom, or tonight you'll be feeling nothing but your fist.' She smiled, friendly but firm. 'Your choice.'

'I'll see what I can find,' he grumbled, and went off to wake up his roommate.

He had taken his shirt off as soon as they walked into the flat. Perhaps he thought his tanned, pumped-up torso would take her mind off his peeling, shagged-out accommodation. Now she was alone, she suddenly felt out of place. There were takeaway pizza boxes and stacks of dirty laundry and the remains of a spliff in an ashtray. She had gone home with him to wake up her body. But did she really want it to wake up here?

They had met in a club frequented by the kitchen staff of Mamma-san. She had admired his hat. They had danced. She had asked his name and soon forgotten it – Jim? John? – then been too shy to ask again, and not caring anyway.

They had necked – ridiculous, Cat thought, kissing like a couple of teenagers, but nobody looked twice at them. Conversation had been minimal, their shouted introductions and small talk drowned by the music, but that was okay too. She was tired of talking.

He came back with a packet of three, scratching the eagle tattooed on his biceps, and she realised she wanted to go home. Her body definitely needed waking up, but she thought she would let it nap for a little longer. And there was something else, although she knew it was crazy.

If she was going to wake up her body, she sort of wished it could be with Rory.

'I'm sorry,' she said. 'But I have to go.'

'Why?'

She shrugged helplessly, and remembered a line she had once learned under grey Manchester skies.

'*Desire makes everything blossom; possession makes everything wither and fade.*'

'What?'

'I just got my period.'

She was afraid he might turn nasty, but he just took off his woolly Justin hat and shook his shaved head. He even called her a minicab.

'You modern girls make me laugh,' he said as she was leaving. 'You don't know what you want, do you?'

She couldn't argue with that.

The next morning, when she had breakfast alone in the Starbucks at the end of her street, Cat thought – it's easy to meet someone. But how do you meet someone who doesn't wear a woolly hat unless it's a bit chilly outside?

How do you meet someone good?

Then Cat switched on her phone, and listened to Megan's messages, and turned her face away from the boys and girls who had not yet gone to bed, so they would never guess that she was nothing like them.

Paulo drew the curtains, and double-locked the front door, and shut out the world.

He went into the living room and checked on Jessica. She was still on the sofa with her feet up, idly leafing through one of the glossy magazines he had bought her.

'I'll make us something to eat,' he said, and when she

looked up at him and smiled, her face drained of all colour, he felt his eyes and his heart filling up again. He was going to have to stop doing that.

'What do you fancy, Jess?'

'Anything,' she said, shaking her head, still smiling.

He went into the kitchen and began searching through the freezer for something that would make her strong. Meat sauce and pasta, and maybe a little green salad if there was anything in the fridge. Some red wine. He wanted to make a good meal for his wife.

People thought he loved her because of the way she looked. And of course that's how it begins, he thought. But there was a quiet kind of bravery about Jessica, she wasn't as fragile as she seemed, you could see it in the way she lifted her face when every instinct must have been telling her to look down and hang her head.

She raised her chin when she looked at you, and he thought of that simple gesture as he cooked their dinner, occasionally going to the door of the other room to make sure she was okay. And every time he appeared in the doorway, Jessica would look up from her magazine and smile, lifting her chin, the way she always did, and he would smile back at her.

They didn't need to say anything.

When the meal was ready, he came into the living room with a tray containing two steaming plates of spaghetti, two side salads made of limp lettuce and squashy tomatoes, and a bottle of the best wine they had in their rack.

'Speciality of the house,' Paulo said. 'The famous Baresi Bolognese.'

He was afraid that she would tell him she wasn't hungry, but she dropped the glossy magazine and rubbed her hands.

'Do you want to eat at the table or on our laps?' she said, swinging her legs round so she was sitting on the sofa. He looked at her bare feet and felt a pang of longing.

'What do you want?' he said, placing the plates on the coffee table. He began uncorking a bottle of Barolo. You're meant to let it breathe, he thought.

'I'm happy here,' Jessica said.

'Then let's have it here.'

So they sat in front of the television eating their dinner, sipping red wine and talking about what he had to do at work the next day.

The doors were locked, all the curtains were drawn, they were safe and warm and well fed, and it was almost as if there were just the three of them left in the world.

Jessica and Paulo and their unimaginable child.

'What's that song you keep singing?' Jessica said.

She was sitting at the top of the stairs. At the bottom, Chloe was on her hands and knees, huffing and puffing towards her as if climbing her own private Everest while Naoko followed close behind, ready to catch her daughter if she fell. As Chloe slowly scrambled up the stairs, grunting through the Hello Kitty dummy she had stuck in the side of her mouth, throwing her little arms high above her head in a swimming motion as she dragged her pink knees onto the next stair, Naoko sang to her in Japanese.

Maigo no
Maigo no
Koneko-chan.
Anata no ouchi wa dokodesuka?

'It's a really silly nursery rhyme.' Naoko smiled. 'It's about a policeman, who happens to be a dog, right, and he finds this lost kitten.'

'She loves it.'

It was true. Chloe had been in a cranky mood all week,

with a large tooth pushing its way through her sore gums, and only a few of her favourite things soothed her.

She liked chomping hard – definitely not sucking – on her Hello Kitty dummy. She liked the climbing-the-stairs game. And she liked this lilting Japanese song.

Chloe never tired of the things she loved. She wanted them endlessly repeated, and was ready to kick up a fuss if her orders were not obeyed. Naoko and Chloe had come to the house every day that week. In their different ways, Jessica and Naoko were lonely. Alone all day with Chloe, Naoko craved adult company, while being around Naoko and Chloe seemed to salve some raw wound deep inside Jessica. The arrangement suited all of them. Naoko could have a conversation that didn't consist of baby noises. Jessica was happy to have company in a house that would be silent until her husband came home.

Jessica would keep Chloe amused while Naoko mashed up her food – the milk was being phased out and she was on solids now, but squashed to the kind of chewy pulp that four teeth could accommodate. Jessica could change her, bath her, persuade her to have a little afternoon nap. The only thing that Jessica couldn't do was sing the special song. But she felt that she almost knew the words by now.

Maigo no
Maigo no
Koneko-chan
Anata no ouchi wa dokodesuka?

'The kitten can't tell the cop where she lives or what her name is,' Naoko said, as Chloe ran out of puff near the top of the stairs, and began roaring with frustration. 'All she can do is cry.'

Maigo no
Maigo no
Koneko-chan
Anata no ouchi wa dokodesuka?

Ouchi o kitemo wakaranai
Namae o kitemo wakaranai.
Meow meow meow meow
Meow meow meow meow!
Naite bakari iru koneko-chan.
Inu-no omawari-san
Konatte Shimatte.
Woof woof woof woof
Woof woof woof woof!

Chloe got her second wind and scrambled up the last couple of stairs. Jessica snatched her up and kissed her fiercely on her cheek. As always, the newness of the child shocked her. That heartbreaking mint-fresh milkiness. Jessica held Chloe on her lap and Naoko sat beside them. There was an easiness between them now. They were real friends at last.

'Tell me what it means,' Jessica said.

'I'll try,' Naoko said, and translated the song with a smile on her face.

Being lost, being lost – you dear little kitten.
Where is your home?
She doesn't know where her home is.
She doesn't know what her name is.
Meow meow meow meow
Meow meow meow meow
She only keeps crying.
But the dog cop is lost too.

Woof woof woof woof
Woof woof woof woof!

'I guess it loses something in translation,' Naoko said.

'Not at all,' Jessica said. 'I didn't expect the dog to be lost too. So they're both lost – the man and the woman.'

'Well – the dog and the cat.'

'It's lovely, Naoko.'

They sat there for a while not feeling the need to talk, waiting for Chloe to catch her breath and indicate that she was ready to return to base camp and attempt another ascent.

Then Jessica said, 'I saw my baby. She was in a little creamy-coloured sac. A tiny, tiny thing. But a real baby. They tell you it's not a real baby yet, and that's just not true. She was a real baby – I saw her. Among all that blood. She didn't have a name. And I don't even know if she was a she. Might have been a little boy. I don't know. But there was a real baby inside me, and now it's gone and this is what they don't understand when they talk about having another baby and how you ought to snap out of it and not take it so hard – I'll never have *that* baby again. *That* baby's gone. They don't understand that. The doctors, the nurses. They think you're crying for yourself. They don't understand that you're crying for the baby who will never be born. For *that* baby.'

She looked at Chloe wriggling in her mother's embrace, growling to herself, anxious to be free. Ready to play the climbing-the-stairs game again.

'Michael's having an affair,' Naoko said.

It was all she had to give her.

Jessica stared at Naoko.

'How could he do that to you?'

'It's not me he's done it to. It's our family.'

'How do you know?'

'The woman wrote to me. I would show you the letter

but I've thrown it away. She's pregnant.' She laughed bitterly. 'If you saw her, you would think she was too old for all that. It's the woman where they work. The woman on the front desk of the showroom.'

Jessica had seen Ginger, and she had always thought, she must have been quite a looker once upon a time.

'He swears it's over. Says she's left the firm. Promises on his mother's life he's never going to see her again. But how can I believe a word he says?'

Naoko lifted her baby up and buried her face in her neck. Jessica knew that she was smelling it too – that impossible newness. It took your breath away. How could anything be that pure and unspoilt?

'It's not easy to walk away when you've got a kid,' Naoko says. 'It's her life too. It's her family I'd be breaking up.'

Jessica watched Naoko carry Chloe to the bottom of the staircase and carefully place her on the carpet. Then she came back up the stairs and sat next to Jessica. Chloe grinned up at them, amused at the prospect of climbing the stairs without a chaperone.

'It's okay,' Naoko said. 'She's not going to fall. She's good at it now.'

'Da,' Chloe said, pointing a finger the size of a matchstick at her mother and Jessica. 'Da.'

It was her first word, her only word. Michael insisted it meant *daddy*, but he was wrong. It meant *look at you*. It meant *what's all this?* It meant *this is a funny old life*. It meant everything, and would do so until Chloe learned her second word.

'What's going to happen?' Jessica said.

'I don't know,' Naoko said. 'Michael says it's over and I want to believe him but I think he's lying. I could ask him to leave but then Chloe grows up without a father. Or I can let him stay and then I know I am living with a husband who prefers going to bed with someone else. Either I lose or my baby loses. So I don't know what happens now.'

Jessica and Naoko sat on the stairs together, and as the baby began her ascent of the staircase, they started singing the song she loved so much, Jessica hesitantly following Naoko's lead, as they watched Chloe's determined little face and the evening gathered around them.

Maigo no
Maigo no
Koneko-chan
Anata no ouchi wa dokodesuka?

The two women laughed as Chloe crawled up the stairs towards them, her angel eyes shining, her new teeth gleaming, and never tiring of the game.

part two:
a family of two

eleven

The Here Pussy Pussy bar is on P. Borgos Street in the heart of Manila's red-light district.

The bar has stood on the same spot since the Vietnam War. Originally its clientele were American soldiers looking for rest and recreation. Today the men are usually expatriate businessmen in search of intercourse and intoxication. After more than thirty years, only the music has changed at the Here Pussy Pussy.

Young women in bikinis still sway and smile on the stage, while men in short-sleeve shirts still nurse a San Miguel beer and watch the lazy dancing, never quite knowing if they are the hunter or the game.

Kirk became a regular at the Here Pussy Pussy after he was laid off by the dive school in Cebu. The British owner was very apologetic – only months earlier he had persuaded Kirk to move from Sydney to the Philippines. But the spate of terrorist bombs had frightened away the tourists, and on most days Kirk was alone on the dive boat.

Maybe he should have felt angrier with his boss. The truth was he had been glad to get out of Australia. His girlfriend kept talking about *where they were going* and Kirk knew in his bones that it would never be where she wanted to go. He had never doubted that he would marry this girl, but he had been wrong. Kirk just couldn't pretend it was the same as when he had left. Two years away had changed him. Meeting Megan had changed him too.

He had lost his girlfriend in Australia and his job in the Philippines. So now he propped up the bar in the Here Pussy Pussy, watching all those acres of golden female flesh, and trying to stave off that point of drunkenness where he would pay some girl's bar fine – the fee paid to the Here Pussy Pussy for losing an employee for the night – and take her back to his hotel.

'Where you from? What hotel you stay?'

A slender woman in a green lycra string bikini had appeared by his side. She lightly touched his arm.

'You very *gwapo*,' she said, framing his face with a thumb and index finger.

'Thank you,' Kirk said, though he knew she would have told the Elephant Man he was *gwapo*, meaning handsome.

Like most of the girls in the Here Pussy Pussy, she was a strange mix of shy and shameless. After the introductions were over, she was stroking her side and wiggling her hips, her frail body swaying on her towering high heels.

'I never enough,' she said. 'Oh! Ah! I never enough.'

He smiled politely and looked back at the stage. Usually the girls at the Here Pussy Pussy moved as though they were sleepwalking. This was part boredom, and part exhaustion. Although they all had youth on their side, none of them older than their middle twenties, if nobody paid their bar fine they were expected to dance until four in the morning. Yet occasionally the Here Pussy Pussy DJ put on a record that made them burst into life, and when that happened they laughed and swung their long black hair and moved with real joy and abandon, no longer dancing for the men in the bar, now dancing for nobody but themselves.

There was no rationale behind the songs they loved. Although the Here Pussy Pussy dancers were all dedicated students of popular music, the songs that moved them were as likely to be years old as they were to be last week's number one. They were way beyond fashion.

The girls at the Here Pussy Pussy came to life for 'Jump Around' by House of Pain. 'Without You' by Eminem. 'Sex Bomb' by Tom Jones and Mousse T. 'See You When You Get There' by Coolio. 'Macarena' by Los del Mar. But most of all they went wild when the DJ played, 'A Girl Like You' by Edwyn Collins.

That girl, Kirk thought. That girl Megan.

It was stupid. He knew it was stupid. It was only one night, but she had got under his skin. He wasn't over her. Maybe because it was only one night. Maybe because he never had the chance to get her out of his system. But probably because he cared, and she really didn't.

Megan, he thought, looking at fifty other girls, all of them half-naked, any of them his for a night for pin money. He could have two of them if he wanted, or even three, if he could afford it, and if he had been eating his greens. But that wasn't going to happen.

Megan, Megan, Megan.

After another few San Miguels, the bar girl was still by his side, a small, proprietorial hand laid on his arm. Even in the pulsating gloom of the Here Pussy Pussy, he could make out the Caesarean scar on her stomach.

Most of them have babies, these girls, he thought. Why else would they be here? Because they enjoy it? Because the guys that come here have such terrific personalities?

Seeing him watching her, she closed her eyes and opened her mouth, winding and unwinding her slender hips.

'Oh, I never enough!'

He knew he would not be seeing Megan tonight, or possibly ever again. So he paid the girl's bar fine to one of the Here Pussy Pussy's mamma-sans, and waited while she went to the dressing room. When she finally returned he felt an enormous wave of tenderness. She had changed from her professional bikini and heels and was now dressed in the heartbreakingly ordinary T-shirt and jeans of her civilian life. From whore to girl next door, in just one costume change.

Once they were out of the Here Pussy Pussy, away from the bar's bouncers and the smiling owner who kept a shotgun in his desk, the girls were at the mercy of their customers. They walked into strange hotel rooms with middle-aged Germans and Scandinavians and Brits, or even young Australians, and were expected to negotiate a price, an act, and still get out with their life.

Kirk didn't negotiate. He just gave her everything he had in his wallet and told her to buy something for her child. She was grateful.

'I never enough, Dirk,' she whispered in the steaming darkness of the Manila night. 'Oh, Dirk, I never enough.'

And he knew it was true. This would never be enough.

Megan wearily climbed the concrete steps of the Sunny View Estate.

Inside her, the baby was sleeping. She – and Megan knew it was definitely a she – always slept when Megan was moving, the rocking motion of the working day soothing the unborn baby girl to sleep. It was only when Megan was attempting to sleep herself that a tiny fist or foot would be slammed with alarming force against the wall of her uterus.

That's my girl, Megan thought, giving her enormous stomach the protective, possessive double stroke that was second nature to her now.

Poppy. My daughter, Poppy. She was running out of space in there.

At twenty-nine weeks, Megan no longer recognised her body. There were thick blue veins visible in her new breasts. Stretch marks on her stomach and thighs that brought with them an unbearable itchiness. She slept in one-hour shifts, woken by the need to scratch, or pee, or Poppy giving her a firm right hook.

Near the top of the stone stairway, with all the grimy sprawl of Hackney stretching out below her, Megan felt the contraction.

The sensation was uncomfortable rather than painful, and although her heart fluttered with panic, she knew this wasn't the real thing. This was a Braxton-Hicks contraction. False labour – a bit like a dress rehearsal for opening night.

She sat down on the cold stone stairs and waited for the discomfort to pass. A pale thin child in a baseball cap wheeled an enormous bike past her as she sat rotating her ankles and gently stroking her bump.

'Not yet, Poppy,' she whispered. 'Not yet.'

Wearily pulling herself up, Megan made her way to Mrs Marley's door. Thrash metal was playing loud enough to rattle the windows. Sighing, Megan knocked. No response. She knocked louder and longer. Mrs Marley opened the door. The music hit Megan's face like a blast of hot air from a suddenly opened oven and she felt herself recoil. Mrs Marley regarded Megan with a cold stare, a cigarette dangling from her lower lip.

'Daisy's inside,' she grunted. Then her sneer turned to a smirk as she regarded Megan's bump. 'Left you in the lurch, did he, dear?'

Megan ignored her and went into the flat. It was even more squalid than usual. Dirty clothes and the stinking debris of takeaways beyond number were strewn around. There were broken toys underfoot and, inexplicably, perhaps a dozen TV sets and DVD players pushed into the corner of the room. Daisy was reclining on the sofa, a Hello Kitty duvet pulled up to her chin, a half-eaten Egg McMuffin in her little paw.

Megan knelt by her side, smiling.

'Do you think you could turn that music down?' Megan said, not looking round.

'It's me brother,' Mrs Marley said. 'It's Warren. He says you can't appreciate it if it's too low. It's why he got slung out of his council flat.'

A shiftless, scrawny young man in Adidas tracksuit bottoms came into the room, lighting a cigarette. He leered at Megan, scratching his crutch.

'Could you turn it down, please? The music?'

'I don't give a fuck,' the young man said. 'I've got the fucking right, haven't I?'

He went into the bedroom, trailing cigarette smoke and outraged resentment. Megan turned back to Daisy, giving up.

The child had been complaining of stomach pains. Megan examined her, took her temperature and then watched her quickly inhale the rest of her Egg McMuffin. There was nothing wrong with her appetite.

'Daisy?' Megan said.

'Yes, miss?'

'Is anyone being nasty to you at school?'

A pause. 'Elvis takes me sweet money.'

'That's horrible. Can you try talking to your teacher? Or Elvis's mummy?'

Silence.

'I reckon it's her appendicitis,' Mrs Marley diagnosed. 'I reckon she wants it out.'

'There's nothing wrong with Daisy,' Megan said, standing up. 'She's being bullied.'

‘You got it wrong before, didn’t you?’ Mrs Marley flared. ‘Think you’re so smart. Coming round here. And you got it *wrong*, didn’t you? Nobody bullies my Daisy.’

‘Mrs Marley,’ Megan said. And then she saw it. Poking out from under the ragged sofa. As casually discarded as a pizza box. The syringe. Megan crossed the room quickly and picked up the phone.

‘Who you calling, Lady Muck?’

‘Social services,’ Megan said.

Mrs Marley didn’t stick around to argue. She went into the bedroom to get her brother. Megan was vaguely aware of pandemonium being played out behind her. Raised voices, thrash metal, the sound of a child sobbing.

A pre-recorded voice was telling her to press the star button twice when he grabbed her from behind. An arm lock around her neck, dragging her down and away from the phone.

I should be able to deal with this, she thought. Four years of wado ryu karate. I should know what to do. Smash his knee with my heel. Grab a hunk of flesh from the top of his thigh. Seek out the nerves in his wrist. But her mind was blank. She could not remember the lessons that Rory had taught her every Wednesday night for all those years.

And then Warren Marley was screaming obscenities as he slammed her head hard against the wall, then pulling back and doing it again. Like a battering ram.

‘I’ve got the right, you cow,’ he was raving. ‘I’ve got the fucking right to do whatever I fucking well like.’

Four years studying in a dojo with Rory and she didn’t remember a thing. Endless martial arts classes and she was as helpless as a punch bag. Four years of striking, kicking and blocking, of white pyjamas and war cries, and she couldn’t find it in her to put up a fight. It felt like she had just been pretending to be tough, and now she was in the real world.

All Megan could do was cover herself and think, but what about my daughter?

It was way after midnight but the infamous Greek resort of Ratarsi was still swarming with people.

Almost all of them were tanned, drunk and British. Pierced, pissed and tattooed. Modern boys and girls having fun in the sun. Which largely consisted of turning a five-hundred-year-old fishing village into an al fresco vomitorium.

Cat was at least ten years older than most of them, although she was in better shape than all of them. Junk food, junk sex, buckets of alcohol – it took its toll.

But what really made her different to the young folk in the streets of Ratarsi wasn't the fact that she was older, but that she was sober.

And alone.

It wasn't meant to be this way. Cat wasn't meant to be going on holiday by herself. Brigitte was meant to be coming with her. But then Digby begged Brigitte to take him back, and suddenly Brigitte's plans changed, and Cat was off to Ratarsi all alone.

'What happened to Digby and the bimbo?' Cat had said.

'It didn't work out.' Brigitte smiled. 'I think his recovery time was a problem.'

'Recovery time?'

'You know. The time it takes a man to be ready to go again.'

'Go again? Oh – *go* again.'

'These young girls are not like us, Cat. They might be easy for a guy like Digby to pick up, but they expect to get fucked two or three times a night. Digby is forty-five and a prime candidate for a dicky heart. Even with his half an aspirin a day. You seem surprised.'

Cat tried to keep her tone neutral. But she thought of

Brigitte's holiday photos with Digby, and how they had looked being passed through the shredder.

'I'm not surprised it didn't work out between them,' Cat said. 'I'm surprised you're taking him back. After what he did to you.'

But Brigitte was upbeat, as if this was a practical decision, and not the stuff of humiliation.

'Well. He doesn't crowd me. He makes me laugh. We get on. To be honest, I'm not sure you can hope for much more than that. It's what growing up is all about, isn't it?'

Cat hoped she would never be that grown up.

So she went to Ratarsi alone and walked through its sticky streets, appalled at the sight of her countrymen on holiday, and wondering why she hadn't chosen to go hiking in the Lake District with all the well-behaved German and Japanese tourists. And then she saw him. Propped up against a wall, his Hawaiian shirt ripped, an Alcopop in each hand.

Rory's son. Jake.

Some mocking, mini-skirted girls were standing in front of him, impersonating his legless state.

Cat got him to his feet and led him away from the jeering girls. She waited at the end of an alley while he emptied his guts into an overflowing dustbin.

Then she took him to the last good hotel in Ratarsi and guided him on his rubber legs into the dining room. It was almost empty. Ratarsi was no longer the place to come for fine dining and delicate wines.

'Can we just get some coffee?' Cat asked a waiter.

The waiter visibly shivered. Must think I'm some game old bird with her toy boy, thought Cat.

'Coffee only with meal,' said the waiter.

'Then we will have a meal,' Cat said, the hint of steel in her voice that she used on bolshy kitchen staff. 'Think you could hold down some food, Jake?'

The boy nodded uncertainly. When the waiter had reluctantly escorted them to a table, Jake seemed to recognise her for the first time.

'I think I got a bad kebab,' he said.

Cat laughed. 'Yes, we all get a lot of bad kebabs at fifteen.'

'Sixteen,' he said. 'Last week. This is my birthday present from my dad. Ten days in Ratarsi with my friend Jude.' He looked around the restaurant at the thin scattering of sunburned middle-aged tourists. 'Don't know what happened to old Jude.'

'Wow, a holiday in Ratarsi as a birthday present. Whatever happened to a nice bicycle and an Action Man?'

Jake shrugged. 'I dunno.'

'How's your family?'

'My mum's not so good. She lost a baby. You know. What do you call it? A miscarriage.'

Cat wondered how old Ali must be by now. Forty-five? Forty-six? And she already had a boy and a girl. But some women couldn't get enough of it. They couldn't see that it was time to stop giving birth to children, and start bringing them up.

The waiter returned.

'Ready to order?'

Jake examined the menu with wary respect, as if he had never seen one before.

'I'll have, er, some vinaigrette.'

The waiter stared at the ceiling. He sighed audibly. Then he was silent.

'Me too,' Cat said into the silence.

'*Vinaigrette*,' spat the waiter, 'is a *salad* dressing.'

'We know,' said Cat. 'We're on the Atkins diet.'

The waiter left. Cat and Jake smiled at each other. It had been a long time since that had happened.

The waiter returned with coffee and two silver bowls of vinaigrette.

'Spoons?' he said.

'Please,' Cat said.

Together they sipped their salad dressing and pulled a face.

'Horrible,' Jake said.

'Yes, but you'll know next time,' Cat said.

He stared into his coffee. 'Thanks for – you know. Getting me.'

'That's okay, Jake.'

'You've been so nice to me.'

'Yes,' Cat said. 'You're lucky I'm not your stepmother.'

He guffawed, uncertain how to respond. She saw that he was still just a child.

'And what about your dad?'

'My dad's fine,' Jake said.

'That's good. Give him my – you know. Tell him I said hello.'

'I'll do that.'

Cat tried to imagine Rory's life, but it was beyond her imagination. Was he settled down in some cosy, long-term relationship? Was he screwing around? Either possibility made her heart go pang. It must be strange being a man who could no longer have children. Did every turning feel like a dead end? Cat was suddenly furious with herself.

She refused to accept that a relationship could only be serious if it included children. Because if that was true, then what did that make what she had had with Rory? That made it just a joke. And it wasn't a joke.

She stared across the table at Jake, and for the first time saw the shadow of his father's craggy face in those abashed teenage features. She missed him. She had never realised she would miss him this much. It was more than breaking up with the latest man.

Cat felt like she had lost one of her family.

* * *

Paulo and Jessica followed the estate agent into the enormous garden.

The suburban night was still and peaceful. In the darkness the lights of the swimming pool made the water sparkle and shine, the perfect blue flecked with shimmering gold.

'It's large for a private pool,' the estate agent said.

'It's beautiful,' Jessica said. 'The lights under the water. I love it.'

'Not everybody wants one,' the estate agent said, with one of those flashes of honesty that she used to temper her sales pitch. 'There's a certain amount of maintenance – although, that said, I think there are some excellent pool guys around here. And then there's the safety issue, of course. You don't have children yet, do you?'

'Not yet,' said Paulo, turning in time to see his wife flinch. He felt a wave of despair. Why can't the world just leave her alone?

'Can we see the rest of the house?' Jessica said.

After the doctor told them that Jessica was over her miscarriage, they had gone ahead with the cycle of IVF. But Jessica would never be over her miscarriage, and the IVF hadn't worked.

Jessica had dutifully injected herself with fertility drugs every night, her tummy slowly becoming covered with a patchwork of bruises, as her egg production went into overdrive. There were countless scans, becoming more and more frequent as the great egg harvest day approached.

Paulo thought his contribution seemed pathetically trivial – a quick wank into a plastic tube on the day that they took the eggs from Jessica. His wife did all the work.

They removed twelve good eggs and they were all successfully fertilised. Two of them were placed inside Jessica but when she took a pregnancy test two weeks later, it was negative. A scan showed that the two fertilised eggs had simply melted away, like teardrops in the rain. And that was it.

It wasn't like the miscarriage. There was a crushing disappointment, and the depressing knowledge that all those injections and trips to the doctor and hours with her legs in the air had been in vain.

But it wasn't like losing a baby. There wasn't the blood and the unused milk to deal with. The IVF cycle was more like an endurance test followed by a beautiful dream, a dream that she eventually had to wake from.

For an unknown number of days, or maybe only hours, or even minutes, or seconds – who would ever know? – there had been two fertilised eggs inside her. Potential babies? No – babies. Her babies.

Then they were gone, as if they had never existed, and after a low-key commiseration with the obstetrician, suddenly Jessica and Paulo were back on Harley Street, just the pair of them, a childless married couple, watching a woman and a man load a newborn baby into a car seat.

'Never again,' Jessica had said.

'You'll change your mind.'

'Watch me. IVF? It doesn't work, and when it does, they don't know what it does to the baby.'

'Come on, Jess. That's not you talking. That's some tabloid scare story.'

'They *don't* know what it does to the baby. How can they? They've only been doing it for a blink of an eye. I've read all this stuff that says IVF is a genetic time bomb.'

'There are plenty of kids who were conceived naturally that get sick. Nobody can ever guarantee that a baby wouldn't have problems. Is that honestly what you're afraid of? Or are you afraid of failing again?'

Jessica turned her head away.

'Leave me alone. You're horrible to me.'

'You did brilliantly. You did everything you could. But we can't give up after one try. There are other places, better places.'

'And what are the odds at these better places, Paulo? A twenty-five per cent success rate? A thirty per cent success rate? And that's at the very best places. What kind of odds are they?'

'But that's counting everybody. Older women. Women that have had serious illness. That's not you, Jess. Your odds are a lot better than that if we have another go.'

'We?' She almost laughed. 'What's this *we* business?'

'I'd go through it with you, if I could. Have some of those injections. Fill myself with some of those drugs. I wish I could.'

She stared at the pavement. 'I know you do.'

'One more try?'

She shook her head. 'No more tries.'

'Oh, come on, Jess.'

Already he could tell it wasn't going to happen. He could see it in that face he loved so much. This thing had beaten her, and it broke his heart.

'Because whatever odds they give you, the chances are that it's not going to work. Failure is what happens, and what you should expect. And I just can't take any more failure, Paulo. I'm sorry. But I already feel like the best part of me is missing.'

So now they spent all their spare time looking at houses on the edge of the countryside, the part of the countryside that was full of people who wanted to escape London but couldn't afford to escape too far. The city in the country, the estate agent called it. Apparently it was the hot new thing.

Jessica said it was because their greenish little bit of London was going downhill. Even there, you now got gangs and drugs, as the city got meaner, and harder to keep at bay. But Paulo knew it had nothing to do with the crime outside their front door.

It was because of the room at the back of the house, the room with the new carpet and the yellow walls and the cot from the fifth floor of John Lewis. They had to escape because before Jessica's miscarriage they had prepared a room for the baby, and now they could never change that room. They didn't have a reason to use it, and they didn't have the heart to redecorate it. They could only run away from it.

Paulo turned away from the heavenly light of the swimming pool and went inside the house. It was a beautiful place – one of those substantial homes built just before the war for affluent city dwellers in search of somewhere cleaner and greener. But what would they do in all this space? Just the two of them?

He followed the voices of Jessica and the estate agent to a room on the first floor. He froze when he entered the room. It was a nursery.

There were baby toys all over the floor. A child-sized frog. Some sort of musical teddy bear. And lots of these half-destroyed my-first-books where you pulled a tab and a grinning cardboard animal appeared. A white cot sat at the end of the room like an altar.

'Nice high ceilings,' said the estate agent, crushing a clockwork pig under her heel.

Paulo was at his wife's side. 'Jess?'

He realised he didn't give a damn where they lived. He just wanted to be with his wife. To shut their front door and make everybody go away.

She was staring at the cot.

'It's perfect for when you hear the patter of tiny feet,' said the estate agent. 'And there are some terrific schools around here.'

Jessica nodded thoughtfully, as if agreeing with some internal voice rather than the estate agent.

'I am tearing all this out,' she said. 'Gutting it.'

Her voice was calm and businesslike. But her husband saw her eyes, and knew her heart, and was in no doubt that his wife was choked with a grief that he could never imagine.

Paulo thought that maybe his brother was right. Maybe women changed after they had a baby. Maybe they changed in ways that you would never believe possible.

Paulo didn't know about that. All he knew was that his brother should come round to his place sometime.

And see what happens to a woman if she never has a baby.

twelve

Dr Lawford had never been to her flat before. Megan was embarrassed by the shabby pokiness of the place, and her pants drying on the radiator, and the medical books she had casually left on the floor.

But as his strong, bony fingers lightly examined her face, most of all Megan was embarrassed to need his attention.

Embarrassment, Megan thought. What bloody good is embarrassment to a doctor?

She was scratched down one side of her face, but apart from a throbbing lump on her forehead, the pain was mainly in her arms, where she had taken most of the blows. She knew that much, at least. So perhaps the lessons with Rory were not completely wasted.

Lawford started to take her blood pressure when someone buzzed up from the street. She saw Jessica and Cat in the grimy little monitor and let them inside. 'My sisters,' she told Lawford. They clumped up the stairs. Jessica took one look at Megan and burst into tears.

'It's okay, Jess.'

'Those bastards,' Cat said. 'Don't they respect anything?'

'Not a lot,' said Megan. 'Not on the Sunny View Estate.'

'What about the baby?' Jessica said.

'The baby's fine,' Megan said. 'I'm fine.'

'The baby's okay? Poppy's okay?'

'She's good. I had a scan. At the hospital. Everything's normal.'

'You can't work in that place, Megan,' Cat said. 'It's too dangerous.'

'That's exactly what I keep telling her,' said Lawford. The three sisters looked at him. 'These animals don't deserve our Megan,' he went on. 'She should get out and find herself a nice little private practice on Harley Street.'

Megan didn't know if he was joking or not.

'Come on,' he said. 'Let me take your blood pressure.'

Megan made the introductions and settled herself on her single bed, rolling up her sleeve. Cat put her arm around Jessica and they all watched in silence as Lawford took the reading.

'We're going to have to watch this,' he said.

'What is it?'

'A hundred and eighty over ninety-five.'

'That's the same as at the hospital. It should be down by now.'

'Yes.'

'Well,' Megan said, taking it in. 'Someone tried to beat me up. That's not going to relax you, is it?'

'In which case we would expect the reading to be temporary,' Lawford said. 'But if it doesn't come down – well. Let's wait and see, shall we?'

Megan nodded. 'Let's wait and see.'

Jessica wiped her eyes. 'What's happening? What's wrong with your blood pressure?'

'We'll keep an eye on it,' Lawford said. 'Excuse me, I have to talk to the police. After that young man had finished with you, they delivered him to the nearest casualty ward so he could get his prescription filled. When they were a bit too slow with the methadone, he assaulted a nurse. Nice meeting you, ladies. I'll see you back at the surgery, Megan.'

He left them alone. Cat went to put the kettle on.

'Megan?' Jessica said. 'What's wrong? What's all this with your blood pressure?'

'Do you know what pre-eclampsia is, Jess?'

Jessica shook her head, and Megan thought, of course not. Jessica had read thousands of words about endometriosis. She was an expert on what it was like to go through a miscarriage and an IVF cycle. She could tell you all about sperm motility and fertility drugs. She knew everything there was to know about trying to have a baby. But Jessica knew nothing about all the things that could go wrong when you were about to have a baby.

And why should she?

'Pre-eclampsia is prenatal hypertension,' Megan said. 'High blood pressure, when you're pregnant. In many ways it's indistinguishable from what your average, stressed-out, overweight executive gets – except pre-eclampsia has nothing to do with being fat or the pressures of modern life. It's the kind of high blood pressure that you only get in pregnancy.'

'This milk is a week old,' Cat said, coming back into the room with a battered carton. 'Do you want me to run down the shops for you?'

'I don't really want any more tea,' Megan said. 'Are you really interested in any of this, Jess?'

'Of course I am! You're my sister! Poppy's my niece!'

'Okay. It's to do with the blood supply to the placenta – essentially how the mother sustains the baby in the uterus.'

'But – this moron attacked you,' Jessica said. 'Your blood pressure – it's bound to be up, isn't it?'

'Sure. But it shouldn't stay up like this. Nobody really knows what causes pre-eclampsia. If there's a trigger. If something like this could be a trigger. So now we're hoping it doesn't stay up.'

'And what if it does?' Cat said.

Megan thought of the premature babies she had seen during her training at the Homerton. Tiny, wrinkled little creatures huddled up in woolly hats because they were too small to keep their own body warmth. And their parents, watching them through the plastic of their incubators. She thought about the ones that lived – that went on to be perfectly normal healthy babies. And she remembered the ones that didn't.

Megan took a breath. She was suddenly very tired. And tired of explaining it all.

'If my blood pressure remains high, then it's pre-eclampsia. And the baby will have to be born early. I'll have an emergency Caesarean because the baby will be too small for anything else.'

'But she'll be all right?' Jessica said anxiously.

Twenty-nine weeks, Megan thought. Her daughter wasn't ready for the world. Nowhere near it. The baby's lungs weren't strong enough to breathe yet – they wouldn't be for weeks. If she was born any time over the next two months, she would still be considered premature. If she was born over the next seven days, she would be fighting for her life. Megan and Poppy would have to hold on for as long as they could.

'I hope so. She could be a little undercooked. We have to prepare ourselves for that.'

'A bit small, you mean?'

Twenty-nine weeks. And the scan showed that the baby was light for twenty-nine weeks. Megan's obstetrician had told her at the hospital that the baby was currently just under a kilo. A little human life that weighed less than a bag of sugar. Megan's daughter.

'Yes. Poppy might be a bit small.'

Megan tried to sound reassuring. She didn't tell her sisters about eclampsia. She didn't tell them that when women and their babies died during childbirth in the good old days, eclampsia was usually what killed them.

Toxaemia of pregnancy, they called it back then – literally, poisoned blood, poisoned pregnancy. Convulsions during childbirth, the placenta tearing, and mother and baby bleeding to death within fifteen minutes. It was rare these days, because doctors did everything in their power to stop the pre-eclampsia ever advancing that far. But it could happen. For all their modern technology, the same cruel rules of life and death still applied.

But Megan didn't tell her sisters any of that. It was one of the unspoken tenets of her profession. You didn't have to tell them everything.

'I called Dad,' Cat said. 'He's really worried.'

'Oh *Cat*,' Megan said, suddenly the kid sister again. 'I really don't want him to come back for this. I'm fine. The baby's fine.'

'I'll call him again. Tell him you're okay. You and the baby.'

Their father was in Los Angeles for a couple of auditions. Jack Jewell hadn't been on a movie set since 1971, when he had a bit part in *Not Without My Trousers* ('Dreadful spin-off from the shockingly unfunny TV series' – the *Daily Sketch*). One was a very long shot – the part of an evil British terrorist, the British being the one nation who would never complain to Hollywood about racial stereotyping.

Megan began impressing on Cat that she didn't want her father to know what had happened, but that was when someone buzzed from the street.

'It's probably Mum,' Jessica said.

Cat groaned with disbelief.

'Well,' Jessica said. 'You called Dad. I called . . . her.'

She went to the door and let their mother into the flat, bringing with her the smell of Chanel and Marlboro. She was carrying a bottle of red wine, as if she were going to a dinner party.

'Do you know there's a horrible man with dreadlocks sleeping in the lobby?' Olivia said. 'I do believe he's some kind of tramp. Can't we get security to toss him out?' Olivia approached the bed. Cat and Jessica quickly stood up, and edged back to give her space. Handing Jessica the bottle of wine, Olivia kissed Megan on the cheek that wasn't scratched.

'What have they done to you, my baby?'

'I'll go and buy that milk,' said Cat.

She was on her way down the rickety staircase when her mother's voice called her name. Cat kept going. Moving surprisingly fast for someone of her age on heels, Olivia caught her at the bottom of the stairs, repeating her name but not touching her. Cat turned and stared at her mother.

Olivia looked a lot older than she remembered. The war paint was being laid on with a trowel these days. How long had it been? Five years. Since Jessica's wedding. And it was easy to avoid someone at a wedding.

'You've got some nerve, my girl,' Olivia said.

'And why's that?'

'Do you honestly believe I don't have the right to see my own child?'

'Do what you want. That's Megan's choice. But I don't have to sit there and watch you play the concerned parent.'

'You don't stop caring.'

'Then go and show Megan how much you care.'

'One day you'll thank me. You and your sisters.'

Cat had to smile. 'And why's that?'

'Do you have any idea what other women are like with

their daughters?' Her voice became a mocking, working-class singsong. *'Why aren't you pregnant yet? When are you going to become a mum? Where's the lickle bay-be?* I spared you all of that. Gave you room to grow.'

'Is that what you gave us?'

'I was never that kind of stultifying, brat-obsessed mother.'

'Perhaps you shouldn't talk about brats when Megan is in there fighting for her baby's life.'

Suddenly her mother changed gear. The painted lips parted to reveal a dazzling smile, the voice was soft as a sigh.

'Look at it this way. I allowed you – and your sisters – to be yourself. You must be able to see that. Not some dull, dreary mother whose self-esteem is tied up in the kids she dropped.'

Cat could smell her mother's perfume and cigarettes. It felt like it was suffocating her.

'Excuse me. I've got to get some milk.'

Cat turned away, stepping over a man in dreadlocks who was asleep in the doorway.

'What did your father expect?' Olivia said. 'These men. They get a beautiful girl who is full of life and then expect her to change into some little housewife as soon as she has children. You'll see one day, Cat.'

Cat bought a pint of semi-skimmed milk from a 24-hour shop with wire-mesh guards on all the windows. Then she waited on the corner until a minicab collected Olivia, and she knew there was no one in the flat except her family.

'Isn't she gorgeous?' Michael said, leaning against a Maserati and watching Ginger through the glass of the front office. 'All that pale flesh. All those freckles. Do you know what I did once? I tried to count them. Is that crazy or what?'

'You shouldn't have asked her to come back to work here,' Paulo said. 'It's all wrong.'

'Which one of her replacements would you like back? The fat one who forgot to post the VAT form? Or the one with glasses who couldn't take messages from Italy because they "talk all funny"?'

Paulo shook his head. It was true that the receptionists who had attempted to take Ginger's place were disastrous for business. But having her back felt like it would end up in a far bigger disaster.

'What if Naoko finds out she's back? What if Jessica finds out?'

'They won't. My wife's too busy with Chloe to come to the showroom. And your wife is out on your country estate.'

'It's not a country estate. It's just a big house in the suburbs.'

'And even if they found out, it's perfectly innocent. I told you not to worry, Paulo. I'm not having sex with her any more. She is back with her husband and his Saturday night specials. So what's the problem?'

Michael suddenly smiled, lowering his head, leaning his broad, well-muscled body in close and Paulo felt the raw physical presence of his brother, that old-school rugged charm, the way he had of making you feel that the two of you were separate from the rest of the human race. Paulo could understand why women liked his brother, why they let him get away with murder.

'It works with Ginger back, doesn't it?' Michael said. 'We get our messages, we get our post delivered.'

'Let's just hope she's back for business not pleasure.'

Michael frowned with irritation. Despite his usual cockiness, Paulo knew that his brother had been badly shaken by Naoko's discovery of Ginger. Michael had come very close to losing his family, and it had terrified him.

Paulo looked at his brother's tired face, saw clearly all the exhaustion from the running around and the lying and the never-ending fear of getting caught, followed by the discovery, and the endless tears and the late-night talks and the slamming of the bedroom door when Naoko made him sleep on the couch. Paulo had no trouble believing that his brother's affair with Ginger was truly behind him. Who had the heart or the stomach to go through all of that again?

Paulo believed that if only his brother could get on the right track, then he could be a good husband, and a great father, and what he had always been as a child. Michael could be loveable again.

'You can't have both, Mike,' Paulo said gently. 'You've got to see that. The family life and the playing around. They don't go together.'

'I told you – don't worry,' Michael said. 'I'm not fucking her any more.'

'If you do,' Paulo said, 'then we are all fucked. Have you got those customs forms for that Alfa Romeo? I need them now.'

'I think they're in the back office. I'll have a look.'

Paulo watched his brother's former girlfriend, if that wasn't the wrong word, answering the phones in the front office.

He thought that Ginger was still a good-looking woman, but there had probably never been anything momentous about her, nothing about her that made you understand how Michael would be prepared to play Russian roulette with his family. There was nothing about her to make you think that she had the power to turn a man's world inside out.

Paulo wondered how it could ever be worth it. To build a family – a wife, a child, a home – and then put it all at risk for the excitement of someone new. It was true that Paulo was a different man from his brother, that he had never been the cock artist that Michael had once been, and probably still was in his heart, despite his recent vow of celibacy, and perhaps always would be until his knob withered with the years.

But still – how could any new woman be worth that degree of heartache? How could any new woman make you put your family on the line? Nobody was that good in bed.

Paulo couldn't explain it, but he felt that more than his brother's family had been put at risk. Michael's reckless behaviour somehow seemed to endanger everything they had worked for. And he loved what they had built here. He loved their business. The smell of the cars when he arrived at work in the morning, that glorious scent of leather and oil. The trips to Turin and Milan, then the long drive back through the Alps, across France and then England and home. The clients who loved these beautiful objects as much as he did – and as much as his brother did.

They had no boss, they were making good money, they were living out their boyhood dreams – working for themselves, working with cars. Paulo knew that they were lucky men. But his brother couldn't see beyond his next erection.

Michael returned with the customs forms.

'Don't lose Naoko and Chloe,' Paulo said to his brother. 'Ginger's not worth it. No new woman is worth it.'

'I *told* you. I haven't laid a finger on her since she came back.'

'And I'm telling you. Love your family the way they deserve. Stop trying to be the little stud you were back in Essex.'

'You don't understand, do you?'

'Explain it to me.'

'You don't want to hear it.'

'Go ahead.'

'Okay – mothers are mothers first and women second,' Michael said.

Ginger caught his eye and laughed, before returning to her work with a little smile.

'What does it take to get you?' Michael said. 'What does it take to get any man?'

'I don't know,' Paulo said. It wasn't the kind of thing he thought about.

'It takes the legs, the breasts, the flesh.'

'Are you talking about choosing a woman here?' Paulo said. 'Or choosing a chicken? Because you sound like you're in the poultry department.'

'Come on. Why were you attracted to Jessica? Because she's a babe! Jessica's a babe!'

Paulo felt his heart swell with pride. It was true. Jessica was the babe of babes.

'Her car broke down,' Michael said. 'You were in your cab. You looked at her and you fancied her. Come on – admit it.' Michael lightly punched his brother's arm, and they both laughed. 'That's how it *works*. That's how it *always* works. If she had weighed a ton, you wouldn't have even slowed down.'

Paulo couldn't help himself. He was happy to hear that his brother thought Jessica was a babe. After all, Michael was so much more experienced with women.

'We agree what it takes to get you,' Michael said. 'But what does it take to keep you? *The baby.* And the love for the baby – this big love, the biggest, the love of your life. You can't imagine how big that love is, Paulo, you can't guess at the love inside you that pours out when you have a child. That's why you stay.' Michael shook his head. 'It's so easy to walk away when there's no baby. You just go. There's no anchor, no ball and chain. But then there's a baby, and it's impossible.'

'People do it. Plenty of men do it.' He thought of Jessica's mother, could see her smoking a cigarette in an expensive

St John's Wood apartment where there were no children to spoil the carpet, or fill the silence, or remind you of the passing years. Jessica had only taken him there once, when they were just back from their honeymoon. It was enough. 'And women too.'

'I know they do,' Michael said quietly. 'But I don't know how. I'm never going to leave Naoko and the baby. They're going to have to leave me.'

Perhaps it would have been different if Ginger had had her baby. Then Naoko and Chloe would have had to compete for Michael's heart with Ginger and her baby. But Ginger didn't have her baby after all.

A false alarm, Michael had said.

No, thought Paulo. Not a false alarm. Wishful thinking.

'She's not as pretty as Naoko,' Paulo said.

'This is true,' Michael said.

'And she's not as smart. And she's a lot older.'

'Can't argue with that.'

'Then – why did it ever happen? How could it happen? I don't get it.'

But his brother didn't have to think about it.

'She's dirtier. And isn't that what men really like? When you get right down to it. Isn't that what gets the pleasure trigger going?'

'The pleasure trigger?'

'We want women to be dirty – but we don't want the mother of our children to be dirty. Look – I don't make the rules, okay? Ginger – I take one look at her, and I want to make like Father Christmas.'

Paulo looked confused.

'To empty my sacks,' said Michael.

'But it's not fair, is it? It's not fair on your wife. She deserves better. Look how much you hurt her, look at the pain you caused.'

'Yes,' Michael said, avoiding his brother's eyes. 'She deserves a lot better. And that's why I go home when we finish work. That's why I don't go to the Hilton for a couple of hours. I walk the line, because I have a wife and child. But home's not quite the same these days. Naoko still doesn't want to sleep with me. Not after – you know. We have separate bedrooms. I'm in the guest room. She's with the baby in our old room.'

'That's sad.'

'She'll come around eventually,' said Michael. 'When I've suffered enough. Look, I love Naoko – in my way. Oh, it's different from when I first met her. It's different from when she was a young student and I had never been out with an Asian girl and she was so different from all the rest of them and we couldn't get enough of each other. It's another kind of love now. And I am not sure it's any worse than millions of other marriages. I love her the way a lot of men love their wife, the way a lot of men love the mother of their children. I love her like a sister.' Michael looked at his brother. 'And maybe that *is* a bit sad. Because who wants to fuck their sister?'

'Jessica's not like my sister.'

'Give it time. This is what we are all afraid to admit, even to ourselves. *If you want to fuck them, then you don't want a baby with them. And if you want a baby with them, then you don't want to fuck them.*'

Then maybe Jessica and I are better off alone, Paulo thought.

He never wanted to be like his brother and all those other unhappily married men – grimly serving out their life sentences like cynical old lags.

Paulo believed in romance. He believed that love could last a lifetime. He still believed that he could have it all with Jessica. He believed in Jessica and himself as a couple, despite all that aching longing for something they had never had, despite the sadness, and the secret tears behind closed doors, and the hurt that chewed them up alive when his mother yet again smiled and yet again asked them when they were going to start a family – as though the pair of them were currently just a cheap impersonation of a family.

But if we never have a child, he told himself, then maybe nothing will ever come between us. Maybe nothing will ever kill our love, or ever force us into separate bedrooms.

Yet he couldn't believe it. Because he knew that Jessica would never be happy without a child. Paulo suddenly realised he had to find Jessica her baby. Their baby.

If he had to search the whole wide world.

thirteen

London. Bloody London. Christ, he had forgotten how cold this place could be. And wasn't this what the Poms called summer?

As Kirk walked through the West End in search of a job and a girl – any job would do, but only one particular girl – the wind whipped down Oxford Street and chilled him to the bone.

But the worst of it wasn't the cold or the clogged traffic or the psychotic cyclists or the kebab vomit or the urban foxes that howled outside the window of his tiny studio flat as they scavenged for discarded fast food.

It was those flat white London skies that sapped his spirit, it was that deathly light – like early closing day at the mortuary. It was the light that made Kirk feel like running back to Manila, or all the way back to Sydney.

Yet like many men who had treated commitment as their own private Kryptonite, he dreamed of an end to the running. That's why he had come back. To find the girl and to put an end to the running. It had to end sometime, didn't it? That life of fun and travel and fucking around? Because how could it go on for ever?

Kirk had always had a cold dread of family life. Not because he was one of those sad bastards whose parents had split up. But because he was one of those sad bastards whose parents had stayed together.

He loved his mother and father, but only individually. Together, as a married couple, they were a disaster. He loved them – but separately. Under the same roof, he couldn't stand the sight of them, the sound of them, the smell of what his father called 'Scottish knockout drops'.

There had been times in his childhood when he felt he would never escape. From his father's drinking. From his mother's anger. The one endlessly feeding off the other, on and on, year after year, the drinking and the anger getting worse as the decades slipped by.

Why did his father drink? Because his mother was angry. Why was his mother angry? Because his father drank.

This is what he remembered, this is what he had always run from, this is why he had left the girl in Australia, why he had fled to the beaches and the bars of the Philippines. It was only during that brief period in London that he felt he had glimpsed the possibility of another life. A life so different from the married hell of his parents.

His father was this borderline alcoholic, a man who was actually a sweet enough guy when he wasn't in his cups, a sober taxi driver by trade, a kind and attentive father who only drank to sink some nagging, unnameable disappointment in his life. And his mother was this housewife on a hair-trigger, all fixed smiles and brittle charm at the supermarket or the school gates, but flying off the handle at the dinner table, screaming in the kitchen, throwing anything to hand. But Kirk couldn't help loving her – she could be affectionate and gentle when her husband was at work or comatose from the Scottish knockout drops. His mother could be a very loving person. Especially if you were a dog.

His parents should have split up when Kirk was grown and gone, teaching both locals and tourists how to scuba dive by the time he was sixteen. But his parents stayed together, and it made you believe in the sanctity of divorce.

Kirk looked at the restaurant matchbox in his hand, the place where he was told there might be work. *Mamma-san.*

That was a funny name for a restaurant. Maybe they thought they were being authentically Asian – putting together the Anglo colloquialism with the Japanese honorific *san,* maybe they thought it meant respected mother. And perhaps it did in this neighbourhood.

But in the bars of Asia, it meant something very different. Over there, the mamma-san was the old woman who helped you to find your girl for the night. Or an hour or two. Or a quick fifteen minutes in some blacked-out VIP room. The mamma-sans, who were mostly like a cross between your dear old granny and a hardened pimp, had taught Kirk that he wasn't paying the bar girls for sex. He was paying them to go away when it was all over.

Now he believed that he had had his fill of recreational sex, and commercial sex, and sex with scuba-diving tourists that you didn't want to talk to the moment you surfaced. Now he truly believed he might finally be ready to settle down with this incredible girl at the party – this Dr Megan Jewell.

It was true that he sometimes found it hard to remember her face. They had both been pretty drunk. But he remembered enough. Something about her – and how can you ever explain it? – had got deep in his bones, and even when he was on the other side of the world, even when he was in bed with other women, even when he was paying for sex, Megan just wouldn't go away. You could never explain that feeling, but you couldn't mistake it for anything else. He thought of it as love.

He liked it that she was a doctor. Loved it, in fact. He found it impressive, and sexy. He knew that was dopey, but he couldn't help himself. This hot young woman who dealt in matters of life and death – it gave her an authority that the other women he had known just didn't have. And unlike everyone else at that party, she had not treated him like some dumb beach bum with sand for brains.

He really thought she might be the one. But in some secret chamber of his heart he suspected that he only felt that way because he had never had the chance to fuck her out of his system, and because he knew it would be almost impossible to find her again in a city of ten million souls.

Kirk asked himself the question that all men must ask when they have had lovers beyond the counting.

When he got what he wanted, would he ever want it again?

The women Rory saw were younger than him.

A lot younger. He hadn't planned it that way, but that's what was on the market, that's what was available. All these women who were young enough to be his – well, girlfriend.

He couldn't imagine what the women his own age – forty-nine and three quarters – were doing with their evenings while he was out on a date. Following around their teenage children, maybe, telling them they couldn't go out dressed like that. Thinking about the rotten men who had fucked up their lives, possibly. Perhaps they were relieved to finally be beyond all the horrors and humiliations of the mating game. And maybe they were happy at last – happier than he could ever be. Whatever they were doing, it was a different world, a parallel universe that he could never be a part of.

Younger women were easier to meet. They were relaxed about their lives. It was only the older women – that is, women around ten years younger than Rory himself – who were deafened by the sound of their biological clock. And not just the ones who had never had a child. The single mothers were just as bad. The happily divorced women with children were just the same.

Their bodies were in extra time, their eggs were still hopeful of a penalty shoot-out. But even if they had a kid or two already, they wanted one more baby, and one more chance at a perfect family.

Rory couldn't blame them. He understood. His lonesome heart ached for exactly the same thing.

A proper family at last.

Rory looked at the shattered fragments of his former family, and he yearned for the impossible – to somehow make it whole again. He had no trouble at all understanding the urge to build a family home. And yet so many of the women wanted too much, too soon. After one dinner, one movie, and one trip to bed, he could sometimes feel them sizing him up as partner material, and it always made him feel like bailing out. There was something peculiarly old-fashioned about many of these modern women – the equation of sex with marriage and children. And of course because of the minor surgery on his testicles, Rory wasn't having children with anyone.

One of the older women – cresting thirty-nine, that fatal shore – actually cried when he told her about his vasectomy.

'That means I'll never have your baby!'

This after some Japanese fish, one German film, and a rather uninspiring fuck.

So he stuck to the younger women. Not for the reasons that were usually advanced – the firmness of their flesh, the springy youthfulness of their bodies – but because they didn't feel as though time was slipping away.

He couldn't have kids? Fine. Because they didn't want

kids with him. They didn't want kids with anyone. Not *now*. Not *yet*.

'A baby is something with a big mouth at one end and no sense of responsibility at the other,' asserted one Cambridge graduate who was currently organising minicabs at the BBC. She was twenty-nine. Rory knew that she would lose the smirk and change the tune somewhere over the next ten years. They all did. But he would be long gone by then.

Men of his own vintage – sixties and seventies kids, veterans of the divorce courts, sometimes more than once – assured Rory that it was perfectly natural to be seeing younger women.

One of them – a fifty-year-old lawyer who was seeing a thirty-two-year-old literary agent – declared that to find your perfect partner (always assuming you were a middle-aged male with a large disposable income) you had to halve your age, and then add seven years.

So a trim thirty-year-old man should be seeing a twenty-two-year-old woman. And a well-preserved guy of forty should be involved with a twenty-seven-year-old. And a fifty-year-old groover should be seeing a woman of thirty-two.

It was perfectly natural for a man of his age to see younger women, Rory was told – however clichéd it felt, and however reluctant he was to be typecast as a dirty old man. It was one of the cruel rules.

'As men get older, there are more and more women to choose from,' said the lawyer. 'For women, it is the other way round. And that's true no matter what toy boy Joan Collins or Demi Moore is going out with this week.'

The last woman Rory had been seeing was thirty-two – half his own age, plus seven – perfect. At first it was good. She treated his snip like a party trick, as if a vasectomy was rather like being double-jointed. She wasn't desperate to fulfil her biological destiny. Not right *now*. Not with *him*. She thought she had all the time in the world. And she was happy to put away the condoms.

Rory let her down gently after a couple of months. There was nothing wrong with her. She was smart, funny, and great fun under the duvet. But in truth, the sex didn't feel so very different from getting a takeaway pizza. More and more, that's what modern sex reminded him of – like an American Hot with extra pepperoni. A moment of pleasure that dissolved in the memory, and soon enough you were famished again. Beyond satisfying that moment of animal hunger, what was the point? Perhaps there wasn't any.

It wasn't always this way.

Back in the dark days of his marriage, before his operation, sex always carried with it the promise of something more. After his cut, as the marriage collapsed, sex and procreation were for ever separated – just as society separated them, he always thought. Sex for him would never again mean family, just as the sex you saw in glossy ads never meant family.

The sexual images we are bombarded with every day – what did they have to do with the possibility of a new human being, another life, building a family of your own?

Nothing at all.

All sex was fast sex now, junk sex, quick and easy sustenance – for Rory, for the world – quickly consumed, and just as quickly forgotten. A feverish rut up against the refrigerator while you were slurping down your Häagen-Dazs ice cream.

Instant gratification, disposable pleasure.

And once it had meant far more than that. Once upon a time it had been everything it was today – the hunger, the fever, losing yourself in the body of another human being – and yet infinitely more.

Since his marriage had ended, Cat was the only woman

who had made sex feel like something better than a take-away pizza.

Oh, he wished he had met her first, he wished she was the mother of his son. He ached with all of that empty, pointless wishing. And he missed her. In the end, it was that simple. He missed her so much. Her fierce spirit, her goofy smile, her strength and her kindness. The length of her limbs, her soft breathing when she slept, and the way she looked on a Sunday morning when they were reading the papers and they didn't need to say a word. He missed it all.

Since it had ended, he had been out with women who were younger, prettier, and wilder in bed, and yet none of them were in the same league as her. That was the mystery that we would never understand, he thought. You couldn't rationalise it. You could never explain why the heart chose to love who it loved.

He had been truly in love with her – he saw that now – but as much as he missed her, he knew that he could live without her. That was the worst thing about growing older. That was the worst thing of all. Realising that you could keep living without anyone, when it came to the crunch, when it came to goodbye and good luck, take care of yourself and let's be friends, realising that we are all ultimately alone, taking our pleasures where we can.

When you finally know that you can't die of a broken heart, he thought, then you know you are truly middle-aged.

So Rory stuck with his younger women. And the irony was that he had never had this much success with women when he was a virile young man.

They liked his body, the way it looked after all the years of constant exercise. They liked his gentle manner. And most of all they liked the sad fact that he could live without any of them.

Once you have used up your store of love, he knew now, you can live without anyone.

That was one of the cruel rules, too.

Paulo swung the Ferrari into the drive and immediately slammed on his brakes.

He slowly reversed back out, the gravel crunching under his wheels, noting the presence of the gardener, the swimming pool guy, a telephone engineer, two unidentified white vans – plumbing? – a couple of cars he didn't recognise, the builder's big black BMW X5 and an overflowing skip that hadn't been there this morning. It was like trying to park on Piccadilly Circus.

There was an empty double garage on the far side of the drive but negotiating a path to it would have been like organising the evacuation of Dunkirk. So Paulo parked out on the road again. As he opened his door a car whistled past him, angrily sounding its horn. After a lifetime in the crawl of city traffic, the speed of these suburban roads appalled him.

The door to their new home was open.

Paulo stepped inside and was assaulted by noises and smells. Banging, welding, something heavy being dropped. Raised voices and laughter. Fresh paint and wet plaster. Chewing gum and cigarettes. Feeling like a stranger in his own home, Paulo leaned against the banister, his hand instantly recoiling from its stickiness, his palm covered in a coat of magnolia emulsion.

'They say moving is as stressful as bereavement and divorce,' mused their builder, lighting up a hand-rolled snout. 'Give me bereavement and divorce any day of the week. Looking for the little lady, Paul, mate?'

Jessica was in the back garden, under the parasol of the Indian Ocean garden furniture, considering what looked like architectural drawings with a man Paulo didn't recognise.

The man was naming a price for a kitchen. At first Paulo thought he had misheard – the price seemed far too high, more like the price of a car. But then the man said that it actually wasn't that expensive for a kitchen of this quality. And Paulo wondered when the world had changed, and what his mother would say about a kitchen that cost as much as a car.

The man was having to raise his voice because there was a bevy of shirtless young gardeners wielding what looked like hand-held vacuum cleaners, skirting the fringes of the huge garden, blasting stray leaves and twigs into submission. Beyond them the swimming pool guy was dragging the water with a giant fishing net, removing scraps of debris that were being blown into the water by the gardeners. The messy striving for perfection was everywhere.

Paulo looked at his wife. Her perfect features were arranged in a mask of concentration as she studied the drawings. He loved watching her when she didn't know he was there – he could never believe his luck, really, that this was the woman he got to share his home, his bed, his life with. He always declared that he could watch her for ever, although Jessica always insisted with a smile that fifteen minutes would be closer to the mark.

No, Paulo thought, watching her now with the kitchen man. For ever is much more like it.

Then she suddenly looked up at him and smiled. Always happy to see him again, even after all this time.

'Jess? Can I have a word?'

But Jessica wanted to introduce Paulo to the kitchen man and, for quite a while, the three of them sat there pondering the virtues of different kinds of wood, granite, tile and kitchen appliance, until the man finally had to rush off to his next appointment.

There was a little shed at the end of the garden, part

summerhouse, part storage space. Overriding her protests – she wanted to talk to the chief plumber about taps – Paulo steered his wife to the shed.

'It will be a beautiful kitchen,' Jessica said, her eyes shining with excitement.

'I know, Jess.'

She frowned with concern.

'Are we all right for money?'

'If this is what you want, we can always find the money.'

She threw her arms around his neck. A builder whistled.

'You're so sweet.'

He lightly kissed her mouth. 'I just want you to be happy.'

He meant it. If this new place would make her happy, then he would find the money somewhere. If this new kitchen, which would cost more than the home his mother and father lived in, the house they had raised two boys in, was what it took, then show him where to sign. He would give his wife all the things she wanted. But deep in his heart, he wondered if that wasn't part of the problem.

We are so used to getting the things we want, he thought. All of us. So how do we cope when there's something we can't have? Something we want more than anything?

'Watch out for the staircase,' she said. 'The paint's still wet.'

'I'll be careful.'

He realised they were still having to raise their voices because of the gardeners and their leaf machines. But he could not wait until they were really alone. This had to be done now. There was no time to waste. So down in the little summerhouse he showed her the brochure that he had brought home.

There was a colour picture of an Asian baby on the cover, wrapped up in someone's arms. A woman's arms. In the background, in black and white, was a generic Asian image, the curved roof of a Buddhist temple, misty green mountains.

Adopting in China, it said on the cover. Yellow words on a red background. Chinese colours, Paulo thought. Jessica looked baffled, and then concerned. As if a perfect day was being taken away from her.

'What's this?' Jessica said, shaking her head. 'What is this?'

He had seen his wife looking at so many glossy brochures. For kitchens, bathrooms, bedrooms and every item in them. Beds, sinks, carpets, curtains, tables and chairs. But Paulo knew that these were not the things they needed to turn this house into a home.

There was only one thing that could do that.

'You don't want to try IVF again,' Paulo said.

'IVF is a medical time bomb,' Jessica said, flicking through the *Adopting in China* brochure.

The text was full of black-and-white photographs of frightened-looking Chinese babies, sleeping Chinese babies, smiling Chinese babies. Beautiful babies. Jessica stared at them as if babies were a species she had never encountered before.

'As you know,' Paulo said, 'I think that's all bollocks.'

She turned on him. 'Oh, you're the big expert, are you? You think I'm just afraid to try again, and you're wrong. This stuff is *dangerous*, Paulo. There's research that says IVF causes a greater risk of tumours. That IVF babies are more likely to have low birth weight. Never mind the effects it has on the poor bloody women. Do you know anything at all about the links of IVF to breast cancer?'

Her voice was angry, but there was something else in her, and it felt like fear. He didn't want her to be afraid. He wanted them to get through this thing together.

'I read all those articles too,' Paulo said, as gently as he could. 'And I'm sorry, Jess, but I still think that's not the reason you don't want to try it again. You think babies born normally don't have problems? Jesus, everybody wants cast-iron guarantees these days. Everybody wants a lifetime warranty. And the world's not like that.'

She hung her head, and the sadness in her felt like it would overwhelm them both.

'How pathetic you must think I am.'

'Come on, Jess, you know that's not true. You're the best thing that's ever happened to me.'

'You think – oh, the poor cow has got a Mrs degree. What good is she without her baby? Give her a baby and shut her up. And any baby will do.'

'That's not fair. I'm just saying – I think there are millions of healthy babies born by IVF.'

She lifted her chin defiantly, that patented Jessica gesture whenever she found herself in a fight, and he felt a surge of feeling for her.

'It's my body.'

'Yes, it is – and that's why I want you to at least think about adopting.'

She laughed bitterly. 'Is that what you think I want? A baby that I picked out on the Internet? A little exotic baby from cute-orphan-dot-com that nobody wants in its own country?'

He placed his hands on the brochure she held, as if it might save them.

'Just read about it, Jess. That's all I ask. You know what they say in China? About an adopted baby? *Born wrong stomach – find right door.*'

'Everybody would *know* it's not my baby.'

Her voice pleading with him, trying to get him to stop, almost frantic with the need to stop talking about trying to love somebody else's child, and the terrible implication of that love – that they would never have their own child.

'Who cares what people know, Jessie? Who cares what people think? Who cares?'

Her eyes shone with fury.

'I bloody care!'

'Jess – there's a baby out there somewhere for us. A baby who needs loving parents just as badly as we want a baby. What's wrong with adopting? I'm just saying – think about it. That's all. It's an option.'

Her words were flat and hard, with no hope left, and nothing more to discuss.

'Not for me. It's not an option for me. I want *my* baby. Not a baby that comes from somebody else. Not a baby that doesn't look like me. *My* baby. I don't want some substitute. I don't want second best. I don't want to adopt.'

She handed him back his *Adopting in China* brochure. The cover and the back page had been crumpled and torn in her hands.

'I would rather get a fucking cat,' she said.

fourteen

'Table four,' the chef said, slamming down a plate of tiger prawns. 'Cat's table.'

Kirk looked blank.

'The old guy and the three women. Let's move it, surfer boy!'

Kirk came out of the steaming kitchen and into the crowded, Saturday-night restaurant. There was something oddly familiar about table four. He thought he recognised the old boy – this erect, silvery David Niven type, a real old-school Brit – and – oh, of course – he had definitely met the tall, good-looking woman next to him. Cat, the manager of the place, who he had been briefly introduced to after the chef gave him a job. There were two more women at the table, but he didn't see their faces.

'Your tiger prawns,' he said, making to place the plate on their overcrowded table. 'Careful, they're very –'

Then he was staring into Megan's eyes.

'Hot,' he croaked, the tiger prawns hovering in mid-air.

'Do you mean spicy-hot or cooking-hot?' said Jessica.

He had rehearsed their reunion so many times that he was undone by the reality of the moment. For some reason he had imagined that she would have nursed the same feelings, and that she would be glad to see him.

But there was nothing in her eyes that indicated she even recognised him.

'Sorry, what kind of hot is it?' said Jessica.

He stared at her. 'What?'

'It's okay, we'll be careful,' Megan said, more calmly than she felt, easing the prawns from his grip. What was *he* doing here?

'It's you,' he said, with a weak smile. He had looked for her everywhere. And now she had come to him. But it wasn't meant to be quite like this.

'How are you?' She smiled, as if he were an old acquaintance she couldn't quite place.

Then she did something incredible – she turned away, dismissing him, tucking into the prawns, and he felt his spirits sink. But still he stood there, paralysed by the sight of Megan Jewell. The one-night stand that he would be thinking of on the day he died.

Cat cleared her throat. 'We'll have another bottle of the Bollinger. When you're ready.'

'Right away,' Kirk said.

'Who's that?' he heard the old boy say as he walked away.

'Oh, that's nobody,' said Megan.

They were celebrating.

At sixty-two, Jack Jewell had landed his first Hollywood role. At an age when his contemporaries were scrambling for bit parts as pub fodder in the soaps, Jack was looking forward to three weeks in LA, playing the father in a Vietnam War-era remake of *Little Women*.

'The devoted dad of a difficult, demanding brood of daughters,' he smiled.

'That's going to be a real stretch,' Jessica said.

'Talk about typecasting,' Cat said.

They all laughed, but Megan wondered how close to life it would really be. As much as she loved him, she knew their father had always been quietly bewildered by what he called 'girls' stuff'. As much as he loved them, Jack's daughters had always been a mystery to him.

It had been Cat who had guided first Jessica and then Megan through their debut periods. She guessed that their father had no idea that Jessica had had an abortion at sixteen, or that Megan was on the pill when she reached the same age. Even now there was a look of quiet panic in his eyes when Jessica's endometriosis or Megan's pre-eclampsia came up. Megan had always felt sorry for their dad. A father couldn't become a mother simply because the mother had done a runner.

'*Little Women*,' Jessica said, and they raised their champagne flutes, although Megan's contained only peach juice. 'It's going to be good.'

'It's going to be great,' Cat said.

'Go get 'em, Dad,' Megan said.

It was just the four of them. No boyfriends, no husbands – which really just meant no Paulo, as Jessica was the only one of them with anything resembling a partner. But Paulo was happy to sit it out. When the sisters and their father got together, he always felt like he was gate-crashing some club where he wasn't a member.

'How's the new place, Jessie?' their father asked.

'Five bathrooms,' she said, and they all made impressed noises. It was always the absurd number of bathrooms that she felt compelled to draw attention to. 'It's just so good to get out of the city. It's cleaner, greener, safer.'

'And the people are friendlier, I bet,' their father said. 'More time for you.'

Jessica quickly agreed, even though it wasn't true at all.

She had found that the suburbs were bursting at the seams with smug mums – all these women with Mrs degrees (Hons), fulfilled biological destinies, who saw the world in their little charges. The truth was that she missed her sisters, Naoko, Chloe and the city.

If you smiled at the children in the suburban parks and streets, the self-satisfied mums acted as though you were going to steal their child away. Jessica secretly wished that she had never left their old house, their old life, Naoko and little Chloe. Naoko understood that she would never do anything to hurt a child. Naoko knew she loved children. Naoko knew that she was only smiling.

'I have to pee immediately,' Megan said. 'I mean – now.'

She eased herself out of her chair, and almost immediately heard the explosion of a bottle of champagne hitting the ground.

She stared across the restaurant at Kirk.

And Kirk stared back at her belly.

When they left the restaurant, he was waiting on the street.

'Do you want me to deal with this guy?' Cat said to Megan. 'Jesus Christ, he works for me. I'll kick his butt all the way back to the bush.'

'I'll deal with him,' Megan said. 'It wasn't true. What I said about him being nobody.'

They stared at her, and then at the young Australian.

'He's not – the one, is he?' Jessica said. 'He *is,* isn't he? He's the one.'

Cat took her arm, suddenly seeing it all.

'Come on, Jess.'

Their father stood on the kerb, hailing a black cab with a yellow light, blissfully unaware of all this girls' stuff. A cab pulled up and Megan kissed her sisters and their father goodbye. They reluctantly left her, Cat promising to call tomorrow, Jessica still staring at Kirk, and reminding Megan that she was coming with her for the next round of tests. When the cab had gone, Megan felt him by her side.

'Where do I know that old boy from?' Kirk said.

'My father's an actor,' Megan said coldly, bridling at his mildly insulting small talk. What did he think this was – a date? 'Where do I know you from?'

He grinned, as if she was attempting to charm him.

'That's funny. You want to get a drink or something? There's a bar on the next block.'

'No bars,' Megan said, giving her abdomen that protective stroke. 'No crowds, no cigarette smoke and no alcohol.'

He nodded.

'Stupid of me. Sorry. What then?'

She shrugged.

'You can walk me to my car.'

He looked crushed. 'Sure.'

They made their way to Megan's car, and he awkwardly kept his distance, as if afraid of what might happen if he touched her.

'Is it –?'

She laughed, genuinely amused. Then sighed. 'Yours?'

He looked embarrassed. 'Sorry.'

'Hey – you've got every right to ask.' Megan smiled. 'It's okay. Yes, it is your baby – Kirk, right?'

Was she kidding? She hadn't really come close to forgetting his name, had she? He could never quite tell when she was joking and when she was deadly serious.

'Kirk. Right. But why didn't you *tell* me?'

She avoided his eyes.

'No forwarding address. No phone number.'

'I gave you my phone number!'

She looked up at him, a hint of defiance there now.

'Yeah, but I chucked it away.'

He thought about this for a while. 'God almighty – you're having a baby. What are you – six months gone?'

It wasn't a bad guess. She was impressed. He must have spent some time around women. Married, possibly, or once married. Or maybe he had sisters. Or maybe this had happened to him before.

'Thirty-one weeks. So – a bit more than six months.'

He stared at her bump, his brow furrowed with concern. No, on reflection she didn't think that this had happened to him before. He was too awed by it all. And she could understand that. If you didn't feel awe in the face of this everyday miracle, then you never would.

'Everything okay?' he said.

Megan shot him a sideways look. 'Why should you care?'

He bristled at that.

'Because that's my son you're carrying,' he said quietly.

She smiled. He was a good-looking bastard. And he had a kind enough heart. She could understand why she would want to have sex with him once in a lifetime.

'It's a girl.'

'A girl? A girl.' Somehow he had never imagined that his first child would be a baby girl. But he smiled and nodded, realising that he loved the idea. A girl!

'Then that's my daughter.'

Megan stopped and stared at him. She wasn't quite sure how she should feel about this man. But right now a kind of intolerable impatience seemed just about right.

'But so what?' she said.

He flinched.

'So what?'

'I mean – really, so what? You going to marry me? Make an honest woman of me?'

He looked at her, as if seriously considering it. For a

second Megan was afraid he was going to get down on one knee.

'Is that what you want?'

'No! Jesus!' She took two steps away from him. 'Not exactly perfect husband material, are you?'

'You don't know anything about me.'

'That's true. I don't know anything about you. Apart from the fact that you're this guy who has one-night stands at parties.'

Kirk raised a wry eyebrow.

'Maybe now's the time to get to know me. Now that you're having our baby.'

'No offence, Kirk. But there's no need. You're this – what? This Aussie skateboarder type.'

'I never owned a skateboard in my life.'

'Athletic. Good with the ladies. Getting on a bit now, but still getting plenty of sex. Feeling that there should be a bit more to life than teaching overweight tourists how to dive.'

He seemed pleased. 'So you do remember me.'

'What's to remember? It was one night. Not even that. A quick tumble on top of the coats in a spare bedroom, as I recall.'

'Don't be like that. I thought about you all the time. In Sydney. In the Philippines. I kept thinking about you. I don't know why. You just got under my skin. There's something different about you.'

'That's very flattering.' Megan's voice was brisk. 'But you really don't know me. And I don't know you. I appreciate that you want to do the decent thing. I honestly do. It's kind of nice that you're not heading for the hills and demanding DNA tests and all that. But I can handle this thing alone. With my sisters. I don't need some man who is looking to fill a hole in his life. This is my car.'

She pressed the key and the lights flashed twice.

'I just want to be a part of this.'

How could she explain it to him? He wanted to play happy families. And she didn't even know if there was going to be any sort of family. She might be all alone soon.

'Listen, Kirk – to be honest, I don't know if this baby is going to make it.'

She had one hand on the car door handle. But she wasn't leaving. She watched all those emotions she lived with every day – fear, uncertainty, a horrified disbelief – pass across his handsome face.

'Not going to make it? What does that mean?'

'I don't know if this baby is going to live. I could give birth any day. I could give birth tonight. And if the baby comes this early, she would be fighting for her life. Literally fighting for her little life.' The tears came then, she couldn't stop them, but with the back of her hand she angrily wiped them away. 'Do you know what pre-eclampsia is?'

Then he surprised her.

'My sister had it. It's to do with blood pressure, isn't it? My nephew had to be born early. Emergency Caesarean. He was in an incubator. With a woolly hat on. All wrapped up to keep warm.' He shook his head at the memory. 'Poor little bloke.'

'How far gone was she? Your sister?'

'I don't know.'

'See – that's what counts. The number of weeks. That's *everything*. If it's born at twenty-eight weeks, a baby only has a fifty-fifty chance of survival. Did you know that? Of course you didn't. Where I am, thirty-one weeks, the odds are better. There's a ninety per cent survival rate. But there's still the other ten per cent who don't make it. The babies who die.'

He nodded. For a moment she thought that there were tears in his eyes too. But it was probably just a trick of the streetlights.

‘I’m two months away from full term. That’s a long time. I’m never going to hold out for two more months.’

‘You might do.’

This she didn’t need. Mindless, unfounded reassurance. Megan already had her profession’s exasperation with the layman’s opinion.

‘Are you a doctor? No – you’re a waiter. I’m the doctor. So listen to me. This pregnancy is never going to term. If my baby was born tonight, it couldn’t survive outside of an incubator. That’s a given. The longer I can hold on, the better for both of us. And I am not talking about you and me, Kirk.’

‘I understand.’

Now she wanted him to understand. Now she wanted him to know. This was the most important thing in her world, and she needed him to truly get it.

‘Even if I hang on for a few more weeks, pre-term babies have all sorts of problems. Breathing. Feeding.’ She ran her fingers through her hair, and quietly cursed. ‘Look – the thing about premature babies is that their lungs aren’t developed. *They can’t fucking breathe.* You appreciate that’s a problem. Not breathing. Frankly, Kirk, I’ve got enough on my plate without you hanging around trying to play daddy.’

He spread his hands helplessly.

‘I just want to help you. Any way I can. That’s all, Megan. Is that such a bad thing?’

She felt so tired now, from putting on a brave face at dinner, from the walk to the car, her back aching from the muscles at the base of her spine loosening in preparation for birth. Who was this strange boy? Why didn’t he just leave her alone? Leave them alone?

‘Listen, Kirk, why don’t you just go and –’

Suddenly the baby seemed to irritably lash out with her tiny foot.

All right, all right, Megan thought. Keep your shirt on.

So Megan gave Kirk her number. And she told him when and where the next round of tests would be. No, she didn't want him to come – her sisters would be with her. But she would let him know how they went. And she even let him place a chaste little kiss on her cheek.

There are none so chaste, she thought, as those we once fucked.

'Megan,' he said, patting her arm. 'The baby is going to make it. The baby is going to be fine.'

Her eyes filled with hot, grateful tears, and this time she didn't try to wipe them away. She so desperately needed to hear that her baby would live. But in her heart she thought – no good. Oh, no good at all. You can't have the pregnancy and then decide to have the relationship. It doesn't work like that.

It's all the wrong way round.

Megan was leaving the hospital with Cat and Jessica when they saw her obstetrician in the lobby. As always when Mr Stewart appeared in public places, there was a buzz of scarcely contained excitement around him. It was more like the personal appearance of a pop star than an obstetrician picking up his mail.

The girl on the reception desk was gazing at him with naked adoration. A couple of midwives were loitering beside him, blushing and giggling, hoping he would notice them. Mr Stewart smiled at Megan, revealing even white teeth, little crinkly lines forming by his blue eyes. His wheat-coloured hair was adorably tousled, as if he had been too busy taking care of women to comb it.

Jessica and Cat stared at him, and then at Megan. She knew what her sisters were thinking. This guy is your obstetrician? This younger Robert Redford? He's a *fanny* doctor?

'There's something I would like you to see,' Mr Stewart said to Megan. 'If you've got five minutes.'

He made the suggestion sound almost casual, but as he led them to the Intensive Care Unit, Megan realised that he had planned it this way. That he must do this with all of them.

The women like her.

The Intensive Care Unit seemed deserted. There were no nurses, and apparently no babies. Just a collection of empty incubators. But they all dutifully washed their hands in a big, industrial-looking sink, and as the three sisters followed Mr Stewart across the room, they slowly realised that it was not empty. The baby, so small that he hardly looked like a baby at all, was all alone on the far side of the ICU.

'This is Henry,' said the obstetrician.

Megan thought it seemed a strange name for a baby that weighed less than two bags of sugar. A big, fat, swinging cock name – the name of kings, a name for a man.

Not a heartbreaking little sliver of life, panting inside an incubator.

It was warm in the hospital's Intensive Care Unit, and yet Henry was dressed for deep midwinter. Wrapped in a blanket, tiny mittens on his hands and feet, and a sort of bobble hat, ridiculously huge on his head the size of a small apple, slipping down over his poor little wrinkled face.

'My God,' Jessica said, hands to her mouth. 'He looks like the loneliest little thing in the world.' She looked around desperately. 'Where is everyone?'

'They're taking good care of him,' Mr Stewart said. 'Don't worry.'

Cat was speechless. I had no idea, she thought. This happens every day, and I had no idea. Jessica clung to her, and couldn't take her eyes from the incubator, and Cat didn't need to look to know that her sister was crying.

Megan looked at Henry and felt the panic rise in her. This is where my baby will come. This is where my baby will live or die. This thing will happen. But she fought to remain the calm, cool professional with ice in her veins. As if all her questions were purely academic.

'When was he born?' she said.

'Two days ago, at thirty-five weeks,' Mr Stewart said. 'He's doing really well. He's a bit of a tiddler, obviously, but the mother had steroids in plenty of time and his lungs are strong.' He smiled sympathetically at Jessica's tears. 'No need to be upset. Look at him – he's breathing unaided.' He turned to Megan. 'The mother had pre-eclampsia too.'

Megan looked at Mr Stewart with new eyes. What a clever thing to do, gently insisting that she came to the Intensive Care Unit to see Henry. What a good obstetrician. What a wise man.

Gently preparing her for life as a mother whose baby was born too soon.

fifteen

And then everything was the baby.

Megan, who had planned to work up until the moment her waters broke, who had imagined that she would still be seeing patients and prescribing antibiotics until the baby poked out her head, found there was no time for anything but preparing for the birth, and delaying it for as long as possible.

Dr Lawford couldn't have been more understanding. He let Megan take her holiday allowance all at once, and told her they would worry about it later if she needed more time. He smiled shyly and said he could always write her a sick note, and Megan thought that it was his first recorded joke.

They didn't discuss maternity leave, or how the baby would affect Megan's summative assessment, or how her new life could possibly work. Could she really become a doctor and a mother in the same year? Nobody knew. But with the baby on the way, Megan didn't see how she could afford to not become a doctor.

She was sick of being a glorified student, and she would never ask her father or her sisters for money. Megan had been the brilliant youngest child for so long, a role that she loved, and she refused to admit that life had beaten her down now.

So this was Megan's holiday, these daily visits to the hospital for blood tests, urine samples, and constant monitoring of the baby's heartbeat and Megan's boiling, pre-eclamptic blood.

She tried but she couldn't imagine what her working life would look like after the baby had come. How long after the birth could she go back to the surgery? Would she really be writing submissions of practical work while the baby slept peacefully in her cot? Would she be breast-feeding during her multiple choice question paper? Would it all be too much, and would she fall at the final hurdle? Megan couldn't imagine any of these things.

She couldn't even imagine her baby.

There were the same questions from midwives and Mr Stewart to be answered again and again. How was her vision? Was it blurred? Did she see flashing lights? Any blinding headaches? Which were all really the same question – is this thing, your pre-eclampsia, turning into something far worse?

She had not cared much for Mr Stewart at first. She had found him too much the showman, too happy to have smitten nurses and midwives gazing longingly at his grinning, golden head. But now she saw that she was lucky to have Stewart as her obstetrician, and behind that Robert Redford demeanour was a brilliant doctor with a profound conscience. As the birth came closer, Megan saw that the humour and charm were merely the bedside manner, and not the man.

As Stewart examined every ultrasound, blood test and urine sample, as he assessed the readings for Megan's blood pressure and the monitoring of Poppy's tiny heartbeat, he was buying as much time as he could for mother and child, fighting for every extra day, giving the baby's lungs time to grow, and all the while dealing with the knowledge that Megan's blood could boil over at any moment and then mother and baby would both be fighting for their lives. He would not let it get that far. Megan was worried about her baby's life. It was left to Stewart to worry about both of them.

Her blood pressure was still high, 150 over 95, chubby-arsed middle-aged executive level, but remaining steady. Every scan showed that the baby appeared happy, although she only weighed a shade under four pounds. She – Poppy – had this habit of crossing her little legs, as if patiently waiting for the big day, like a commuter waiting for the 8.15 to town, and that simple gesture unlocked a love inside Megan that she had never known existed.

There was nothing wrong with Poppy. Megan was acutely aware that she, Megan, the mother, was the problem. She lay on the hospital bed, Jessica by her side, listening to Poppy's amplified heartbeat on the Sonicaid. The little life growing inside her.

'Sure and steady,' smiled the midwife. 'I'll leave you together for a while.' She squeezed Megan's arm. 'Don't worry. She's a beautiful baby.'

When the midwife was gone, Megan turned to her sister.

'Sometimes I feel like I've let her down before she's even been born,' she said.

'That's just silly,' Jessica said. 'You're both doing fine.'

There was a polite knock on the door.

'It's him again,' Megan said. 'Nobody else bothers knocking.'

'Come in,' Jessica called.

'Anything happen yet?' Kirk said, shyly sticking his head around the door.

'It's not going to be cinematic,' Megan said. 'I'm not going to clutch my stomach and scream, "*It's time!*"'

Kirk grinned with embarrassment. Jessica smiled at him with sympathy. This was a good guy, wasn't it? Wasn't this how we wanted a man to be? Attentive, concerned, there by your side? Why was her sister so hard on him?

'Mr Stewart will look at my tests and decide that my blood pressure is too high,' Megan continued. 'Then he will ask the anaesthetist to look for a window in his diary between his golf game and the next poor cow on the assembly line. So don't expect hospital drama, okay? Don't expect George Clooney and white coats.'

He hovered in the doorway, still smiling uncertainly. 'Okay,' he said.

'She's fine,' said Jessica. 'And the baby's fine.'

'I'll get some coffee then for us, shall I?'

'That would be lovely,' beamed Jessica.

'Or if you give me the keys,' Kirk said, 'I could go to your flat and start painting that wardrobe?'

She thought about her little home, and how the baby had already changed it. Megan and her sisters had cleared most of the solitary bedroom for the baby. They had brought in a beautiful Mamas and Papas cot (a gift from Jessica and Paulo) with a Jenny Giraffe mobile (Kirk's contribution), a herd of stuffed toys (from sentimental old women on the reception desk at the surgery), all these stupendously useless bears, dogs and frogs, although they did make the room seem more welcoming, more like a nursery and less like a miserable little rented flat, and a new chest of drawers (from her father) full of clothes (from Cat).

It was the clothes that tugged at Megan's heart. They would be perfect for a newborn baby, but far too big for premature Poppy.

'Megan?' Kirk said. 'Coffee and keys?'

'Just the coffee,' Megan said. 'To be honest, I don't really want you in my flat when I'm not there.'

'That's cool. That's absolutely cool. I'll just get the coffee then.'

She had allowed him in there once – when he had turned up on the doorstep with the Jenny Giraffe mobile – and didn't like the way his eyes wandered all over her home. As though he was disappointed that his daughter was starting her life in this poky flat. As though she was an unfit mother. What was he expecting? Kensington Palace? She was going to be a single mother.

'Why are you so nasty to him?' Jessica said. 'When this baby comes along, you're going to be joined for life.'

Megan stared at her sister. 'Perhaps that's why I'm nasty to him.'

The door opened and Mr Stewart came in with a sheaf of papers. He gave Jessica the full blast of his smile and then sat on the bed, taking Megan's hand.

'Where are we now?' he said.

'Thirty-four weeks,' Megan said. 'That's still too early. She's still too small. Just four pounds. I want to try to make it to thirty-six weeks. Please. Can't we try for thirty-six weeks?'

He nodded thoughtfully. 'Look at this,' he said.

It was just a line on a chart. The line ascended swiftly, then slowly evened off and finally seemed ready to fall. It looked like the flight of an arrow that was just about to drift back to earth.

'The baby's growth rate,' Megan said. 'It's slowing down.'

'Had to happen. Pre-eclampsia affects the blood supply to the placenta. Sooner or later, the baby stops growing. But of course you know that already.'

Jessica anxiously peered at the chart over the obstetrician's shoulder. 'But what does it mean?'

For a few seconds the only sound in the room was the baby's amplified heartbeat. And then Megan spoke.

'It means it's time,' she said.

* * *

Then there was the waiting. And it went on and on, as the anaesthetist's busy schedule and London traffic combined to delay the birth of Megan's daughter. Midwives and nurses came and went, taking blood pressure and murmuring small talk, as if Megan was waiting for a bus, not a baby.

All this waiting. How could anyone be bored on the edge of something so momentous? Megan felt that her life had stopped. That all time was dead time until the anaesthetist had struggled past the Angel in Islington. Cat arrived with premature flowers. Jessica stroked Megan's feet. Jack called and didn't know what to say. Kirk hovered by the window, trying not to get in the way.

Then they were ready for her, and to Jessica it seemed that things moved alarmingly fast. Like those movies you see about death row – the sudden mad rush to get the act done and behind them.

With Cat and Jessica on either side of Megan, holding her hand, two hefty young porters lifted her onto a trolley and wheeled her out of the room and into harshly lit corridors smelling of hospital food and flowers. Into a huge lift and down into the basement of the building, where Mr Stewart was waiting, as beautiful in his blue hospital smock as Robert Redford in his Navy whites in *The Way We Were*.

And then into the holding room, where the anaesthetist was waiting, his voice as soothing as a lover's as he slipped in the needle.

There was a room beyond the holding room, full of happy, chatting people, all wearing the blue uniforms and shower caps. They surrounded a flat table. Under the lights of the operating theatre, it shone like an altar. All the while, her sisters never stopped holding Megan's hand.

The expectant father followed in their wake. They gave him a blue coat, a plastic shower cap for his hair, and a surgical mask. His heart raced. A girl, a girl, it was going to be a girl. This unimaginable child. Soon she would be here. There was nothing he could do. Except prepare to be a good father. And he wondered, what would he tell his daughter about men?

How could he prepare her for their lies, their tricks, and their black hearts? Our black hearts? Her childhood years would fly by, and soon the boys would look at her, his precious baby, in that same calculating way that he had looked at a million girls in thirty countries.

He loved her so much, and yet already this was his greatest fear – that she would one day meet someone just like him. This was the womaniser's bitterly ironic fate – to be the father of an adored, beautiful baby girl.

They wheeled Megan into the brightly lit operating room where there were more people than he had expected. They were young, smiling, all wearing the same blue coats as him.

'Any requests?' one of them said, as if this was a radio show rather than an emergency Caesarean. Kirk remembered the CD in his pocket. He handed it over and someone stuffed it in the operating theatre's ghetto blaster. They busied themselves around Megan – pulling some strangely sexy stockings onto her thin, pale legs, putting an IV drip into her arm, murmuring sweet nothings.

As the anaesthetist leant over Megan, a tiny screen was put across her belly. Kirk stared at it in amazement. He had heard that it was a *tent*. They put a *tent* on the woman's belly for a Caesarean. That's what he had heard, that's what he was expecting. Some huge expanse of canvas that could house a family of Bedouin tribesmen. This was more of a handkerchief. If he lifted his head, he would be able to see everything.

Megan's bulging belly was swabbed with antiseptic and then Mr Stewart bent over her, a thin blade in his hands. Kirk pressed his face close to Megan's face, fighting for breath. It was meant to be a *tent*. What happened to the fucking *tent?*

What would happen if he caught a glimpse of Megan's sliced open belly and he couldn't take it? What if the first thing his daughter ever saw was her daddy, flat out on the floor, fainted clean away? How would that look?

Megan took his hand.

'Don't worry,' she said, mumbling a little through the mist of drugs. 'You'll be fine.'

She heard a song begin to play. That seemed strange, that there was music in here. And the faces swam around her – the faces she knew, and the faces she had never seen in her life – all of them strangely interchangeable, not because they all wore that blue nylon uniform with the mask and the little hat, but because they all looked at her with the same expression. A kind of concerned love, as though she was a virgin bride on her wedding night. It was as if she had suddenly become the most important person on the planet. Or maybe it was the baby. Maybe the baby was the most important person on the planet. Yes, that seemed right.

'Well, I never met a girl like you before.'

Like someone doing the washing up in her stomach. That's what it felt like. Intimate – more intimate than anything she had ever felt – and yet strangely, mercifully distant. The guy – Kirk, his name was definitely Kirk – had his face pressed close to her. Bracing himself for something. He was holding her hand. She suddenly wanted to tell him, better start painting that wardrobe.

But they were inside her now, the song not even half over – *'This old town's changed so much'* – and even through the sweet fog of anaesthetic she was aware of something being pulled from her, something that was her and yet independent of her, and all attention was suddenly elsewhere, on this thing that was her and yet not her.

'Is everything all right?' she said, or maybe she only thought it – but the focus was on this little thing now, and for a few seconds she felt ignored, forgotten, like a bride abandoned at the altar.

Then there was laughter – shocked, delighted laughter – and movement, and her sisters and Kirk were smiling down at her, their heads batting back and forth between her and the little living thing that was being fished from her body – their heads torn between the two of them, back and forth, back and forth, like a cartoon tennis crowd following the action and – how can it be so fast? – then it – *she* – was finally free, the song still not over, as it – *she* – was immediately whisked away from Megan by the midwives to be cleaned and tested and wrapped in swaddling clothes. But the weak little cries reached Megan.

And then there she was, not being held by Jessica or Cat, which Megan would really have preferred but, in accordance with some tribal ritual, by the father.

The baby was tiny – heartbreakingly tiny. More like a sleepy foetus than a bouncing baby. Megan stared at her, too stoned and exhausted to do what she wanted to do, which was take her baby and hold her and love her.

It – she – had a little bashed-in face, like an apple that had fallen too soon, and even after being washed her face was still covered in a sticky film of yellow goo. She looked like the oldest thing in the world, and also the youngest.

'She's beautiful,' Kirk said, laughing and crying all at once. 'She's the most beautiful thing in the world.'

And he was right.

Poppy Jewell's life had begun.

sixteen

It wasn't meant to be this way, thought Jessica.

In all her images of new motherhood, the mother and baby were inseparable – the sleeping tot at rest on her mother's breast, the mother exhausted but quietly ecstatic. An almost Biblical union of mother and child – that's what Jessica was expecting, a bond so close that you could hardly tell where the mother ended and the baby began, as indivisible as they had been when the child was in the womb.

But little Poppy was in the Intensive Care Unit, lying on her belly in an incubator, wrapped up for a winter that only she could feel, and Megan was three floors below – sliced up and spent, inexplicably silent.

One of the nurses had placed a stuffed monkey in the incubator, and it smiled down on Poppy, twice her size. Jessica thought her niece looked like the most vulnerable thing she had ever seen – not yet ready for the world.

'She's about the size of a roast chicken,' said Jessica. 'Poor little mite.'

'Don't worry about our Poppy,' said a cheerful Jamaican nurse. 'She might be a little uncooked, but she's doing fine. Babies with pre-eclamptic mums tend to be tough little buggers.'

'She doesn't look like a tough little bugger,' said Jessica. But she was grateful for the reassurance.

It was true that little Poppy had done well in her first three days of life. She was breathing unaided, drinking tiny quantities of milk – expressed by Megan, but administered by one of the ICU's nurses – and she was putting on some weight.

And there was something else. Even after just a few days, it was clear that there were far harder luck stories than a baby born at thirty-four weeks and weighing just under four pounds.

Jessica hadn't seen any babies smaller than Poppy in the Intensive Care Unit – although she was assured they arrived all the time. But on her first day in the ICU there was also, briefly, a baby boy born with a hole in his heart. And on the second day there had been another baby boy – a fat, healthy eight-pounder – who was born with Down's syndrome.

As the nurses and doctors did what they could for these babies – and Jessica wondered what *could* they do? – the parents stood stunned or quietly sobbing by their newborn. The mother and father of the baby boy with Down's syndrome had a girl of about five years old with them. When you have done it once, Jessica thought, you must relax. You must believe the bad things all happen to other families. And then your world falls apart. And then it happens to you.

Jessica thought she could say a few supportive words to other families with premature babies. She could tell them that their tiny baby boy was a handsome fellow – even as he lay there with his woolly hat falling over his eyes – or that their undersized baby girl was a beauty – even as she lay there like a little pale fillet in the frozen meat department.

But Jessica didn't have any words for the families who had harder things to deal with.

She could not tell the mothers and fathers of the Down's syndrome baby, or the boy with a hole in his heart, that everything was going to be all right. She had no right to say those words, she had no right to offer them cheap, unearned comfort.

Because that's what you learned in the Intensive Care Unit – not everybody who has a baby gets a happy ending.

Jessica watched her niece sleeping. She was getting used to it now – that fretful panting, desperate for life. Like a puppy, or a kitten, the face all mashed up yet somehow heartbreakingly beautiful.

Poppy was going to be fine.

It was Megan that Jessica worried about.

Like a little bird, Cat thought.

Jessica cradled the baby in one arm, and with the other fed her with a small bottle containing a mere drizzle of milk. With her eyes closed, and her surprisingly large mouth wide open – Poppy's mouth was the only big thing about her – Cat thought she looked like a newborn bird in the nest, waiting for its worm.

'There's nothing of her, is there?' Cat said. 'She's hardly here at all.'

'Don't worry about Poppy,' Jessica said. 'She's a tough little bugger.'

'Shouldn't Megan be breast-feeding her? Isn't that better for them?'

'Poppy's too small to breast-feed. She can't do that sucking thing. Can you, darling?'

The baby had fallen asleep, her mouth still attached to the teat of the bottle, her miniature tummy already full. Jessica gently pulled the bottle, and it came away from the baby's fleshy mouth with a quiet *plop*.

Cat stroked the soft down on Poppy's face, as if afraid

to wake her, or perhaps break her. And again she felt it – a sense of complete wonder at this everyday miracle.

'How's Megan doing?' Jessica said.

Cat shook her head. 'She looks like she's been through the mill. I thought that a Caesarean was meant to be the easy option – too posh to push, and all of that. They really sliced her open, didn't they?'

'A Caesarean is major abdominal surgery,' Jessica said, repeating one of Mr Stewart's favourite lines.

'It was a lot more like a scene from *Alien* than I had been expecting.'

The two sisters watched the sleeping baby in silence. Then Jessica quietly said, 'I thought I would feel terrible when I held her. I thought I would come undone. Because Megan had a baby, and I didn't. But look at her – how could you feel anything bad when you hold her in your arms? How could this baby make you feel anything negative? And she's not an idea of a baby any more, is she? There's nothing, you know, theoretical about her. She's undeniably Poppy. She's not some abstract notion. She's Poppy Jewell and she's here to stay. Here, take her for a while.'

Cat awkwardly took the baby.

She wasn't as comfortable holding her niece as Jessica. Not because she was afraid of dropping Poppy on her head – although that was a part of it – but because, unlike Jessica, the feelings the baby stirred threatened to overwhelm her. Who would have believed that was possible? That Jessica would take the birth in her stride, and Cat would be the one who felt the world change?

When Cat held the baby she felt a physical yearning more powerful than any craving she had ever known. It was stronger than any desire she had ever felt for any lover, or job, or possession.

She held a baby so small that it was hardly there at all,

and she wanted one of her own. It was mad – what would she do with it? Where would she stick it? Where would it sleep?

But she couldn't help herself. It felt like she had wasted so many years on things that didn't matter. The pursuit of pleasure and money, the endless, ridiculous yearnings for a better car and a bigger flat, all that time devoted to her latest wants and needs.

I am thirty-six years old, she thought, with her niece in her arms, feeling like she weighed not four pounds, but nothing. I am nearer to forty than thirty, and I am not going to die without one day holding a baby of my own.

All she needed now was – what was it again?

Oh, yes. A man.

Outside the Intensive Care Unit, Olivia Jewell stood in the twilight of the corridor, watching them through the glass. Her two oldest daughters, passing her youngest daughter's baby – Olivia's first grandchild – between them as if they might break her.

The baby was wrapped up like an Eskimo. But as far as Olivia could tell, it was an ugly little bastard. In her experience, all babies were repulsive. But the squashed little puss on this one could curdle milk.

It was different when they were bigger. She had no doubt that she had produced the three most beautiful little girls of all time. But even then they were still a 24-hour job. That was the trouble with children – you couldn't just dress them up and look at them. They kept wanting things from you.

But, oh, she thought of how her daughters looked just before she left – the long-limbed eleven-year-old, the impossibly cute seven-year-old, the pot-bellied three-year-old – and something inside Olivia, something she had long believed dead, began to ache. Then somebody spoke and it was gone.

‘Can I help you, dear?’ said the nurse on the desk.

‘Just looking,’ said Olivia Jewell.

‘He’s got a baby girl,’ Paulo said to the barmaid, at that point in the evening where a man starts freely addressing barmaids. ‘Poppy. She’s called Poppy. She’s a little cracker.’

Kirk grinned with pride, reaching for his glass. But it was already empty.

‘She is, isn’t she?’ he said. ‘She’s a little cracker!’

‘Congratulations,’ smiled the barmaid. Tall, blonde, early thirties. She wiped a wet cloth across the bar. ‘Wait until she starts screaming at three in the morning. And again at four. And again at five. See if she’s a little cracker then.’

They watched her walk away.

‘You wouldn’t think she had children,’ Kirk said.

‘You can’t always tell if they’ve got children,’ Paulo said. ‘That’s what I noticed.’

‘I want her to have a good life. I want her to be the healthy, outdoor type. Not like most of these kids today. Fat. Drugs. I want her to learn to dive! Do you know what we’re going to do when she’s old enough? We’re going to swim with dolphins. She’ll love that. Poppy will love that.’

‘Here’s to you, mate. The three of you.’

‘The three of us,’ Kirk said, contemplating his empty glass. ‘Yes. I’m a father. I can’t believe it. What do I know about being a dad?’

‘You’ll pick it up. How’s Megan? How’s the mum?’

‘She’s great. She’s good. She’s – well – quiet. Not saying very much.’

‘Adjusting. Adjusting to the idea of being a mother.’

Kirk paused, and Paulo was aware that – beyond the euphoria, beyond the beer – this man considered him a stranger. But tonight he had nobody else to talk to.

‘She’s been through a lot. The pre-eclampsia. All those

tests. Not knowing when the baby was going to come. The Caesarean. Jesus – they opened her up like a can of corned beef. Although he's supposed to be very good. Mr Stewart. Leaves a good scar, they say. You hardly know it's there, apparently. And now Poppy is in that incubator. Megan – I don't know. She looks like she's been knocked sideways. Knocked flat and can't get up. Between you and me, I sort of thought she might be a bit happier than this.'

'Still adjusting,' Paulo said. He could not comprehend that a woman could give birth and then not be the happiest woman alive. He waved to the barmaid. 'Can we get a couple of beers over here, please?'

'But what did I expect?' Kirk said. 'We're not like you and your wife. We're not close. Megan hardly knows me.'

The barmaid placed the beers in front of them. 'Wait until the baby gets colic,' she said.

'Give it time. Megan's young. The youngest sister.'

'Yeah, she's young. But she's not *so* young. I mean, our grandparents and our parents wouldn't have thought that twenty-eight was too young to have a baby, would they? They would have thought that was leaving it a bit late.'

Paulo thought about it. 'I guess my mum and dad were middle-aged when they were twenty-eight.'

'It's funny. These days people don't really have children in – what do you call it? – their child-bearing years.'

'True enough. Look at Kylie Minogue. Your countrywoman.'

'God bless her, mate.'

'Widely considered to be one of the most desirable women on the planet. But Kylie is – what? Middle thirties?'

'If she's a day.'

'Kylie looks fantastic. I'll grant you that. I bow to no man in my – you know. Anyway. A woman in the prime of her life. No one's disputing it. But you have to wonder about her eggs.'

'Kylie Minogue's eggs?'

Paulo nodded. 'Kylie Minogue's eggs are no spring chickens. In egg terms, they are well into middle age. Do you know what happens to a woman's eggs after the age of thirty-five? It's not good news. That's what all the bum wiggling is about. Kylie doesn't want a number one record. She wants a baby. But she can't find the right man.'

'That's the big dilemma for these modern girls, isn't it?' Kirk said, reaching for his beer. 'They spend their child-bearing years with guys they don't like very much.'

The barmaid collected their glasses, wiped a desultory cloth in front of them.

'Wait until she starts teething,' she said.

After they had taken the baby away, they gave Megan a photograph. The picture was slotted into a white card with the words, *My name is —* and *I weigh —*, printed on it. Someone had written *Poppy* in the space for a name, but the weight was left blank. Nothing to boast about there, thought Megan.

In the photograph Poppy looked ancient – a wrinkled little old man wrapped up in winter clothes. And Megan thought, you poor little thing. *Who are you?*

There was a light rap on the door and her mother's heavily made-up face appeared.

'Anybody home?' said Olivia.

'Did you see the baby?'

'I looked in. Briefly. She's absolutely gorgeous.' She touched her daughter's arm, carefully avoiding the IV drip that was pumping her full of morphine. 'And how are you, Megan?'

'My scar itches.'

Olivia stared at Megan's midriff. 'I do hope it's well below your bikini line.'

'I think it will be a while before I wear a bikini, Mother. Shuffling to the toilet feels like the long march.'

'What's the matter, darling? Feeling a bit down? Touch of the baby blues?'

Megan shook her head. That was the problem. She didn't really know what the matter was, although she knew it was something to do with failing. She wasn't used to failure.

'I always imagined I would have a natural birth. A Caesarean – it's so hard. They take away your baby. They pump you full of drugs. They cut you open. And it hurts like fucking hell.'

'Don't get too sentimental about the other kind of birth. I had all three of you out of the standard route. There's nothing particularly magical about having stitches in your puss.'

'Do you really have to say "puss"?'

'Oh, all right then – fanny. Are you breast-feeding?'

'She's too small. And I'm not really producing enough milk.' Megan indicated a machine by the side of the bed, fitted with what looked like some kind of vacuum cleaner nozzle. 'I express milk.'

'You what?'

'Express milk.'

'What – you mean, pump it out of your tits and then they give it to her in a bottle?'

'Exactly.'

'Isn't science wonderful? I breast-fed Cat and the little cow almost chewed off my nipples. I swear all our problems start from the time she mistook my nipple for a Farley's Rusk.'

Megan laughed. Only her mother's brand of humour could make her smile in this place.

'It's not the pain I mind. Or the scar. Or even that they took Poppy away and put her in an incubator. It's that everybody expects me to suddenly be a different person. And I can't feel it.'

'I know what you mean, dear. We're meant to turn into a breast-feeding, nappy-changing earth mother as soon as we drop our first brat. No offence to little Poppet, darling.'

'Poppy.'

'Poppy. Of course. Men are allowed to turn their paternal feelings on and off at will. But it's meant to come naturally to us. They expect you to become as selfless as Mother Teresa just because you got knocked up the duff.' Olivia leant close to her daughter, lowering her voice, as if they were sharing some blasphemy. 'Let me tell you, there's nothing remotely natural about giving your life up for another human being. But cheer up – the first eighteen years are the worst.'

'But that's you.'

'Yes, that's me.'

'And I don't want to see my child as some kind of inconvenience, or chore, or bore. I want to love her the way she deserves to be loved. But – I have a baby, and yet I don't feel like a mother.'

'Then you're like me,' said Olivia, with a note of triumph. 'And there's nothing you can do about it.'

Suddenly Olivia's entire body seemed to squirm with pain.

'What's wrong?' Megan said.

Olivia rubbed her arm. 'Nothing, dear. I've been getting these flashes up and down my left arm. It's just old age. Well, middle age.'

'You should get a doctor to look at that.'

There was another knock on the door and Megan choked up when her father's familiar smiling face came into the room, partially obscured by flowers and a large, heart-shaped box of chocolates.

'My baby,' Jack said, hugging his daughter, and she moaned with pain. 'My God! Sorry!'

'It's just my stitches, Dad. They're still a bit raw.'

Jack gave his ex-wife a smile that showed no hint of animosity, or history. Actors, thought Megan.

'Olivia, isn't this a wonderful day?'

'Hello, Jack. Can you believe it? We're grandparents. Doesn't that make you feel like going out and slashing your wrists?'

'No, it makes me feel bloody marvellous, actually.' He turned to Megan. 'And we saw her – Poppy. She's so beautiful! A bit small, of course, but she'll catch up.'

Megan hid in her father's arms, pressing her face against his chest. This was what she needed. Somebody to tell her that it would be all right in the end. Suddenly she realised that her father was not alone. He was accompanied by a tall, smiling redhead around her own age. Megan peeked out at the woman, not understanding, half expecting her to say she was going to take Megan's blood pressure and give her some painkillers.

'I'm Hannah,' said the redhead. 'Congratulations, Megan. She's a little princess. Don't worry – I was born two months early, and I'm just under six feet.'

Megan stared at this Hannah with gratitude. It was the best news she had heard all day.

Olivia was contemplating the tall redhead.

'Hannah did hair on the movie,' Jack said.

'That's how you met?' Olivia said. 'You were touching up Jack's thinning rug? How romantic.'

'Mother,' Megan said.

'You look so good together,' Olivia said. 'Even though you're young enough to be his – what's the word I'm looking for?'

'And you're old enough to keep a civil tongue in your surgically enhanced head,' Jack said.

'Stop it!' said Megan. 'My stomach's just been cut open,

I'm up to my eyes with drugs, I only just stopped pissing through a tube – and all you can think about is this tired old shit that's been dragging on for years. Leave it alone, can't you? For one day at least.'

'You'll have to excuse my daughter,' Olivia said to Hannah, as she got up to go. 'She's not herself today. She's just had a baby.'

Eventually they all went home, even Jessica and Cat, and there was only Megan, wide awake in her room, and Poppy, somewhere in the building high above her, sleeping in her incubator in the Intensive Care Unit, guarded by a stuffed monkey twice her size.

The ICU never closed. The nurses on the night shift were happy for Megan to shuffle up there, rolling her IV drip by her side, and to sit watching her baby sleep. In many ways, the ICU at night was a far more relaxed place than during the day, when it was full of consultants and doctors and friends and family. Megan certainly preferred it at night, because she didn't have to wear her brave and cheerful mask.

'Do you want to do her three o'clock feed?' a Chinese nurse asked Megan.

Megan shook her head, pulling her dressing gown tighter. 'You do it, you're better than me.'

The nurse contemplated Megan with her cat eyes. 'It's good for you to do it. Both of you.'

So Megan let the nurse fish Poppy from her plastic box, but then she cradled the baby in her arms and eased the bottle's teat between her lips. There seemed to be a pitiful amount of milk in the bottle. Her milk supply seemed to be running dry.

Megan, who had always been so capable, who had sailed through everything life had confronted her with – her parents' divorce, medical school, all those exams beyond counting – felt the tears spring to her eyes and thought to herself, *can't I do anything right?*

She held the baby, gently tilting the bottle, until Poppy moaned with exhaustion and her head lolled away, her woolly cap falling over her face.

'That's enough for now,' said the nurse.

Megan pulled the bottle away. And then it happened.

Poppy smiled.

The corners of her wide, little mouth turned up, and for a few shocking moments she bared her newly minted gums. A smile! A smile from her daughter!

'Did you see that?' Megan asked.

'See what?' said the nurse.

'She smiled at me!'

The nurse frowned. 'Probably just the wind.'

The wind, thought Megan. A combination of gas and milk trapped in that stomach the size of a thimble. Or a physical coincidence – a grimace of discomfort or exhaustion that merely resembled a smile. No, Megan couldn't believe any of that.

She would call it a smile.

seventeen

Rory saw Cat enter the karate dojo as quietly as she could and the thing he noticed immediately was that she had tried to make herself look more beautiful.

High heels, lipstick, a special dress. This wasn't the Cat he knew. This was someone who thought she had to make an extra effort tonight.

He was surprised to see her, in here of all places. He realised he was not particularly happy that she thought she could suddenly turn up at his place of work unannounced. But these efforts to make herself look more beautiful pulled at his heart, and filled him with an enormous tenderness.

Over the heads of the twenty children who were facing him, Rory watched her looking for somewhere to sit down. The students ranged in age from five to fifteen, all of them barefoot and in their pristine white uniforms and coloured belts, all of them standing to attention, even the little ones, hanging on his every word, waiting for him to talk a bit more about leg blocking techniques with the feet.

'The inside snapping block – *nami-ashi* in Japanese – is useful if your assailant is attempting to kick you in the groin.'

Cat smiled shyly at him from the back of the room.

Ah, but she doesn't need heels with those legs, Rory thought. And she doesn't need lipstick with that mouth. And a woman like that doesn't need a special dress.

She's beautiful already.

When the class was over, and he was showered and changed, Rory told Cat he knew a little sushi restaurant nearby. The place turned out to be crowded, with reserved signs placed on the two remaining tables, and they were asked if they minded eating at the bar. They conferred, decided they didn't mind at all, and settled themselves opposite the white-capped chef deftly working over slivers of raw fish.

'What I like about Japanese restaurants is that you can eat dinner alone,' he said. 'Because you can just sit at the bar. You can't do that in French or Italian restaurants. Or even Thai and Chinese places. Everybody thinks you're Johnny-no-mates. In a Japanese restaurant, you can eat by yourself and nobody looks twice.'

'But it's nicer if you have someone with you,' Cat said. 'Even here – sitting at the bar. It's nicer if you're with someone.'

He smiled. 'I guess so.'

'I've missed that,' she said, and he could tell that it was not an easy thing for her to say. 'I've missed having someone.'

They sat in silence while the waitress placed miso soup, green tea and a lacquered bowl of sushi in front of them.

'Thanks for looking after my boy.'

'It was no problem.'

'I should have called you.'

The bulk of him seemed to be very close. Cat had forgotten how big he was, how solid. Nothing like all those skinny boys she had found in clubs.

'I've been pretty busy. With work. My sister and the new baby.'

'Megan? She's had her baby?'

'A little girl. Poppy. Poppy Jewell.'

His face lit up with real pleasure. 'That's fantastic. Give her my best.'

Of course, she thought. Megan was once one of his students.

'She must be very happy,' Rory said.

'Well – it's kind of more complicated than that. I wouldn't call it happy. Not exactly.'

'What's wrong?' He thought of his ex-wife, and all the inexplicable tears after their son was born. 'Postnatal depression or something? I'm sorry, it's none of my bloody business.'

'No, it's fine. I know you like Megan, and she's always been mad about you. I'm not sure I know where plain old exhaustion ends and postnatal depression starts. I am not sure anyone does.'

She was unguarded and open with him – all the things he loved about her. Flushed with feeling, full of life. Nothing like the stranger, all disappointed and cold, she had been at the end, at the end of them. This was the Cat he recognised, despite the lipstick and the heels and the special dress. He couldn't resist her.

'Me too,' he said, as he snapped open his wooden chopsticks. 'I've missed having someone too.'

It takes time to learn to sleep with someone, he thought later.

Not just the sex – although there was that too – but the physical act of sharing a bed with someone, of actually spending the night together. The tugs on the duvet. The legs and the arms that could wrap you up or jab you in the ribs. It took months, years, to get it right. But sleeping with Cat was effortless, and he loved that.

He felt physically closer to her than he ever had to any woman – he knew that long body so well, from the funny toes (the middle one all squished up where her shoes hadn't been changed quickly enough when she was a growing child), the long limbs, the small breasts, the goofy smile – all teeth and gums, a smile like the sun coming out of a cloudy sky – all the way up to the ears with their ancient, pinpoint scars of piercing (Jessica with a needle heated up over the stove, when Cat was fourteen and Jessie was ten – the blood was everywhere, apparently). He knew her body as well as he knew his own, and he still hadn't had enough of it. And he was happy and proud that the pair of them knew how to share a bed.

'I want my child to learn karate,' she said into his neck, easing herself into the curves of his body. 'If I ever have one.'

He smiled in the darkness. 'Your child, eh? Have you considered kung fu?'

'I like karate.'

'Why's that?'

'Because I want you to teach her. You only teach karate, don't you? You can't switch about, can you?'

'No, you can't really keep switching about. You choose a discipline and you stay with it for ever.' The voices were soft in the night. This was the terrible thing about breaking up with her, he realised. He had lost his best friend. 'It's a bit like – I was going to say it's a bit like choosing a partner. But how long does that usually last?'

'Ten years,' she said. 'Ten years is how long the average marriage lasts today. I read it in a paper. But that's when people get it wrong. If you get it right, I guess it must be longer.'

He rolled over and faced her.

'What are we doing here, Cat?'

She took a breath.

'I think maybe we should get back together again. And I think that maybe we should have a baby. At least, I think we should try.'

'Cat.'

'I know, I know.'

'Cat, I can't have children. You know that.'

'It's okay. I talked to Megan. She's a doctor, right?'

'Yes.'

'She said you could get it reversed. Get your vasectomy reversed.'

'Do it all again?'

'Not do it all again. Do it the other way round. Have the operation in reverse. A reverse vasectomy. That's what they call it. Instead of cutting your – what do you call them, the tubes?'

'Vases. I think that's it.'

'Instead of cutting them, they stitch them together.'

It was a mistake. A beautiful mistake. He was only going to get hurt again. Better to have made the break and not look back. Too late now.

'And do you know what the odds are of that working?'

'I know it's a long shot. Megan said. I know that when you have it done in the first place, they tell you to consider it irreversible.'

'Exactly. You think I never thought about this? You think I never contemplated getting it reversed? And trying for a kid?'

Just to keep you happy, he thought. Just to keep you.

'But it happens, Rory. Men get this thing reversed and they have a baby. Just like someone always wins the lottery.'

'Do you know the odds against winning the lottery?'

'As I say, I know it's a long shot. But I also know that someone always wins. I think you would be a great dad. Strong, gentle, funny. I think you *are* a great dad.'

'But I'm tired. Do you understand that? I've done it all. Even if it was possible – and I have my doubts – I have done it all before, years ago. I have been through the lot. From sleepless nights and dirty nappies to finding a piece of hash in the sock drawer.'

'But the baby will give you energy. The baby will make you young again. The baby will give you a reason to live.'

She meant it. She wanted it so badly. And really, truly, she wanted to go through it with him. No other man.

They were at the moment when he either had to get dressed and go home, or take her in his arms. So he took her in his arms, and she placed a kiss on his mouth.

'I have missed this,' he said, the heat rising in him again. 'I have missed this so much.'

'I always thought that you learned how to be a mother from your own mother,' she said. 'But that's not true. I see it with Megan and Poppy. It's your child. It's your child that teaches you how to be a mother.'

His mouth was on her, all over her, wanting to know those long limbs, to commit them to memory so he would have them for ever.

'You want it too, don't you?' she said. 'We want the same thing, don't we?'

But by then he was kissing her back, and he couldn't talk, and so Cat's question went unanswered.

Poppy remained in her incubator for three weeks and then she was released into the world.

She had stayed in the Intensive Care Unit for so long that some of the nurses cried to see her go.

They almost feel like she's their baby, thought Megan. And maybe they are right.

The nurses had fed her, clothed her, fretted over her. They had monitored her breathing, and placed a stuffed monkey in her incubator, and come running when she cried in the night.

It was true that Megan had lain there while the baby was plucked from inside her, and it was Megan who squeezed a modest amount of milk from her breasts, but it was the nurses in ICU who had usually been the ones to place the bottle to Poppy's lips. It was the nurses in the ICU who had not been overwhelmed by Poppy's birth.

Megan had left hospital after a week, still feeling like she had been sliced in half and sewn together again, and she had visited Poppy on a daily basis. She felt more like a failure than ever. She wasn't back at work, and she wasn't taking care of her daughter. I'm not a doctor and a mother, she thought bitterly. I'm neither. Lawford and the others see my patients, and the nurses in the ICU take care of Poppy.

Now that time was ending. Now the cot in the bedroom of her little flat would be filled with a real live baby. Now she was on her own. They wrapped Poppy up in her oversized winter clothing, and went out into the world.

One of the nurses held the baby while Megan struggled to fit the car seat in the back of Jessica's Alfa Romeo. In the end the nurses did it for her. Poppy was placed in the car seat, and it dwarfed her. Megan shuddered. Was her baby really going to be driven through London traffic?

Jessica drove home as though she had a cargo of high explosives in the back. Megan sweated and fretted, silently cursing belligerent cyclists who jumped lights and all those Jeremy Clarkson groupies in their white vans and BMWs. Poppy slept through the entire journey.

Kirk was waiting for them outside the flat.

'What's he doing here?' Megan said. 'Is it going to be like this every day? This guy just turning up unannounced and uninvited?'

'Megan,' Jessica said. 'He *is* her father.'

Kirk looked through the car window and got this big foolish grin on his face as he looked at Poppy. 'Don't be too hard on him,' Jessica said. 'He's crazy about Poppy. Give him that.'

When Jessica and Megan were struggling with the straps to the car seat, Kirk stepped in and quickly released the baby.

Megan carried the sleeping baby in her giant throne up to the top floor, and all the noises of her building – Eminem cursing his mother on the ground floor, Sky Sports blasting from the second floor, a man and a woman screaming at each other on the third floor – suddenly appeared in a ghastly new light.

Megan thought, how can I bring a baby into this place?

She felt a creeping sense of shame as she carried her daughter up to her new home, Kirk and Jessica following close behind. And, yet again, that crushing feeling of getting everything wrong. She had always felt that she was on top of her life. And now it seemed as if life was finally and permanently on top of her.

Megan laid the still sleeping Poppy in her cot. Jessica kissed her fingers, and placed them on the baby's tiny brow.

'Congratulations, you two,' she whispered, her voice thick with emotion. 'She's perfect. She's your precious little darling.'

Then she left them.

They watched Poppy sleeping for a while, and Megan had to smile. The baby had made herself completely at home. Three weeks old and the weight of a small fish, yet she looked as though she owned the place. Megan and Kirk crept from the room.

'I hope you don't mind me coming round unannounced,' he said. 'I called the ICU. The nurses told me Poppy was coming home today.'

'It's fine. But maybe in future, you could give me a call?'

'Of course.'

She attempted a fragile smile.

'I mean, it's not as though we're married or anything.'

'No.' He hesitated. 'But you have to understand.'

'What do I have to understand?'

'I want to be a part of this baby's life. I want to support you any way I can. And – I love her. That's all. I love our daughter. She's great, isn't she? She's brilliant! A real little fighter. She's done so well. You've both done so well.'

'It's funny, isn't it? You can love a baby without knowing her. But not an adult. You can't love an adult without knowing them, can you? You can't even like them very much.'

'You're talking about us, aren't you?' He smiled. 'You mean you don't know me.'

He watched her impassive face. How distant they all are, he thought. The women we had sex with in some other time and place. There are none so strange as our old lovers. But there's something Megan doesn't understand, he thought. It's not over between us yet.

'Well, maybe now's the time to start knowing me,' he said.

'Why's that?'

'Because we have a baby, and you're all alone.'

She shot him a look.

'I'm not alone, pal. Don't you ever say that again. I don't need the pity of a part-time waiter. I have two sisters, and Poppy and I are not alone. And I know you well enough already – this ageing surfer boy who wants to play at happy families for a while, because he got bored and jaded with everything else.'

'I'm not a surfer. I'm a diver. And – what? You think you're not easy to read?'

Megan snorted with disbelief. The bloody cheek of the man.

'Let's see you try.'

Kirk folded his arms, sizing her up.

'The youngest child, indulged by everyone in the family. Clever at school, breezes through all her exams. Then the little princess gets her heart broken by her first serious boyfriend.'

'Meets some guy at a party,' she said. 'Has a few too many – as these trainee doctors always do. Gets knocked up.'

'Meets some guy at a party. Goes to bed with him. Because he's a good-looking bloke.'

'Don't kid yourself. He's just in the right place at the right time.'

'Whatever. But maybe he's got a bit more life in him than all the nerds she knows from medical school.'

'You don't know them at all.'

'Nine months later – no, it's only eight months, isn't it? – she's a single parent in Hackney. And – guess what? The little princess discovers she's bitten off more than she can chew.'

'Oh, fuck you.'

'Well, fuck you too.'

From the next room there came a strange, high-pitched mewing sound – small, but unbroken and insistent and feline, like a distant buzz saw.

Megan and Kirk stared at each other.

And then they realised that their baby was crying.

'It softens you, having a baby,' Michael said to Jessica, as they watched Chloe stagger across the floor like a little drunk. 'You realise – *you can't die.* You have to be here for this little thing you created. But at the same time, nothing puts you in touch with your mortality like having a kid. The future belongs to her, not you. And you know – really know for the first time – that your life only has a limited time to run. So life has you hostage. You can't die, but you know you will.'

Chloe was wearing a nappy and a T-shirt. She had a jam-stained DVD in her fist, which she inserted in a portable player that was sitting on the sofa. A big red bus called Beep came over shining green hills, batting its headlamps – its eyelids – and grinning its huge daffy grin. An old nursery rhyme – 'The Wheels on the Bus' – began to play. Chloe began to rock from side to side.

And Jessica thought, this is the world's great divide – not between rich and poor, or old and young, but between those who had children, and those who did not.

'They dance before they can walk,' Michael said, shaking his head with wonder, watching his daughter dance. 'Before they can crawl even. Isn't that strange? Dancing is a basic human impulse. As fundamental as eating, or sleeping. This will to dance.'

There was a time when Jessica couldn't stand to be around Michael. The knowledge that he had hurt Naoko, and put Chloe's happiness at risk, infuriated her. But in her secret heart Jessica forgave her brother-in-law, even though she knew it wasn't her place to forgive him.

She didn't forgive him because she knew he had always liked her, or because he seemed to be trying so hard to make it up with Naoko, or even because there was a rough charm about him, which he always seemed to turn up to ten when Jessica was around. No, Jessica forgave Michael's sins because he was so clearly in love with his daughter. A man who loved his child as much as Michael clearly loved Chloe couldn't be all bad, could he?

Paolo and Naoko came into the room, carrying silver trays

of tiny espresso cups and those hard little Italian biscuits that both the brothers were addicted to.

'What's that incredible smell?' Paulo grimaced, waving a hand in front of his face.

They all looked at Chloe.

She was leaning against the sofa, oblivious to the foul stench emanating from her region, rocking back and forth to *The Wheels on the Bus*. She lifted her left leg off the ground as her nappy slowly began to fill, and continued her rocking dance.

Michael and Naoko and Jessica and Paulo laughed until their sides hurt.

'This is a highly amusing baby,' Michael said, snatching her up and placing a kiss on Chloe's impassive face. Her eyes never left *The Wheels on the Bus*. 'A highly amusing baby.'

When they were back in the car, about to go back to their big empty house, Jessica and Paulo sat in silence for a while. He waited for her to find the words. Finally she spoke.

'All you get is me,' Jessica said.

'That's all I ever wanted,' Paulo said.

eighteen

He came into the surgery with a shy smile, a big man, with a slow, easy grace to his movements.

He looked different from the other men who came into Megan's surgery, and not merely because, in a neighbourhood where beer bellies and junk food pallor was the norm, he was physically fitter than the rest of them. What made him different was his old-fashioned courtesy, the gentleness of his manner, almost unknown in these streets.

The boxer.

'Who are you fighting this time?' Megan said.

'Mexican kid. On his way up. I've seen his films.' Megan knew by now this meant he had watched his opponent on video. 'Good technical boxer more than a scrapper. Unusual in the Mexicans. They usually like to mix it up.'

'Sounds dangerous.'

That shy smile. 'We'll see.'

'Is your daughter coming to watch – Charlotte?'

'Charlotte. No, she'll be with me mum.'

The boxer was a single father. His wife, also a patient at the surgery, had walked out on her husband and child. There was another man, and another baby on the way. Charlotte was cared for by the boxer and, while he was training, by his mother. Without the grandmothers – the nans – it would have been a neighbourhood of orphans.

The boxer had to see Megan for a full medical before every fight. The last time he had a bout, Megan had found traces of blood in his urine sample, signalling internal damage to the kidneys. She had no choice but to note it on his medical records, and prevent him from fighting. He had been bitterly disappointed, but accepted it silently, as one more hard blow from fate. Most of her patients were quick to rant and rave when they didn't get what they wanted. But not the boxer.

Now she took his blood pressure, tested him for HIV, examined his eyes for signs of damage. Listened for signs of slurring in his voice, or an erratic drum beat in his heart. Then she gave him a little plastic tube.

'No problem,' he said.

Megan felt for him. The only way he knew how to support his daughter was by fighting. But the years were taking their toll, the brutal training without end probably more so than the actual fights, and he was finding it increasingly difficult to pass his medical. What could she do? She had to test him. It was the law.

The boxer returned from the toilet with his urine sample in the little plastic tube. Megan picked it up to write his name and the date on, to prepare it for testing in the lab.

And it was stone cold.

She looked at him, and under his coffee-coloured skin, he blushed.

This wasn't his urine sample. If it was, it would have been still warm. And this one felt as though it had been prepared a lot earlier. Megan knew that when the urine was examined, it would contain no traces of blood.

But Megan said nothing, and a few days later she confirmed to the boxer that he had passed his medical.

Because Megan was starting to understand what you would do for your child.

Anything.

'There's something I never told you,' Jessica said.

There was no reason why she should tell him now. No reason why she should tell him tonight. And no reason why she should tell him at all – except she felt that this thing that had gnawed at her for so long should not be a secret between them. There was no reason to tell him, apart from the fact that he had the right to know.

Paulo rolled over on his side, propped himself up on one elbow.

'What is it?'

'I had an abortion.'

Silence between them in the softly lit bedroom. That hard word, hanging between them. And, slowly and painfully, he started to understand.

'You mean – what? You had an abortion before we met? Before me?'

She nodded. 'It was long before us. When I was still at school. Sixteen.'

He tried to take it in. The fact of the thing, and the savage irony. This woman, the woman he loved, who wanted nothing more than she wanted to be a mother, terminating a pregnancy in another lifetime. No – in the same lifetime she had shared with her husband.

'Why are you telling me now, Jess?'

'Because I want you to understand – this is my punishment for the abortion.'

'Your punishment?'

'The reason I can't have our baby is because I killed that baby.'

'Jess, that's not true. This is not your punishment.'

'I messed up my insides. I know I did.' Her voice was totally calm. She had thought about this thing for so long. There was no doubt in her mind, only a bleak acceptance. 'Nothing anybody can ever say will convince me otherwise. It's my punishment. And I deserve to be punished. But I am just sorry you have to be punished too.'

'Jessica – you are not being punished. It's just one of those things. What were you? Sixteen? You couldn't have a baby then – you were still a child yourself.'

'Cat took me. My dad never knew. I was meant to be on a school trip. And I just think – we screw around with our bodies. We kill babies. And there's a price to pay.'

'You didn't kill a baby, Jess.'

'And then we act all surprised when our bodies don't work. I don't know what it is with me, Paulo – whether my insides are messed up, or if God is teaching me a lesson.'

'God's not so cruel.'

'But I know all my problems – all our problems – date back to that day. It's a punishment. What else do you call it?'

'So – what? You loved this guy?'

He wanted to comfort her, he really did. But there was also this rage, this jealousy – someone else with the woman he loved. He wasn't a violent man, but he could have cheerfully hurt this man. No, not a man – a bloody boy.

'He was the school stud. Big football star. Every girl was mad about him – I don't know if you could call it love, although that's what it felt like at the time. God, yes. Sorry, sorry.'

'It's okay.'

He was touched. It didn't stop him loving her. Because nothing could stop him loving her. It wasn't that weak, conditional kind of love.

'We only went together the once. My first time. And then

when I went back to school, he had told all his friends, and they were all laughing at me. Laughing about what a slag I was, although I'd been a virgin. Even when I was still bleeding, they were looking at me and laughing.'

He took her in his arms. 'I love you, and he was never good enough for you, and this is not your punishment.'

As the weeks and months went by after her confession, Paulo felt something change between them. He had feared that the lack of a child would drive them apart. Instead, they felt closer than ever. They stayed close to their home and the people who knew them best. Because once they strayed beyond that orbit, even when they went to visit his parents out where the East End meets Essex, there were too many questions that infuriated them.

'So when are you two love birds going to start a family?' his mother would ask them with a grin, usually after she had told an anecdote about the wonder of her granddaughter Chloe.

'We're a family already, Ma,' Paulo told his mother, told her again and again until she finally got it. 'A family of two.'

In the cot at the end of the bed, Poppy slept.

She looked tiny in there, as though she would never grow enough to fill it – her bald head sticking out of her Grobag and resting on one side, showing off her bulging baby forehead, her arms lifted level with her ears, like a little weightlifter flexing her muscles, her hands the size of matchboxes curled into miniature fists. No sheets on this modern baby's bed – the Grobag was like a sleeping bag with gaps for Poppy's head and arms, completely safe, and yet Megan couldn't escape the sheer terror of believing that her daughter could die at any moment.

So she sat in the kitchen drinking camomile tea, sleepless

for the third night in a row, as out in the early-hour streets of Hackney the residents laughed and bellowed and fought. And as the hopeless tears rolled down her face, Megan thought, *postnatal depression.* What man came up with that one?

She was exhausted, scared witless and feeling like a total failure. How was she meant to feel? Who wouldn't be depressed?

Another blow to her self-esteem was the breast-feeding fiasco. Poppy had been too small to breast-feed at first, her tiny, bud-like mouth not strong enough to make that sucking motion, but the jolly fat health visitor had told Megan – *she* had told *Megan,* this health visitor lording it over a future doctor – that 'baby' (the horrible familiarity of the bloody woman, thought Megan, the infuriating unearned intimacy) was ready to feed directly from 'mother' (oh fuck off, you old cow!).

But Megan – who shamefully remembered all the pious speeches she had made about the glories of breast-feeding to the mothers from the Sunny View Estate who flocked to her surgery ('Full of nourishment and antibodies and completely free, ha ha ha!') – just couldn't get the hang of it. It was supposed to be the most natural thing in the world to a nursing mother, but Megan felt like she had been commanded to sprout wings and fly.

She knew the theory, of course. Knew it inside out, from tit to tonsils. You were meant to get the whole shebang – areola as well as nipple – into the back of the baby's mouth. But whenever Megan attempted it, Poppy acted as though her mother was trying to choke her. Then she screamed blue bloody murder. Megan begged, pleaded and swung her rock-hard breast back into place, catching Poppy in the side of the face and knocking off her little woolly hat. Mother and baby sobbed in perfect harmony.

The baby acted as though she would have called the NSPCC, if only she had been big enough to crawl to the phone, and Megan reached for the bottle, fearing that her daughter would starve to death if she didn't.

It was a different kind of life from the one she had known before. There was no sleep now. When she was a child, Megan remembered how her father had gently admonished his daughters when they were weepy and fretful. *Overtired*, he had called it. That's what I am, Megan thought. Overtired. Too knackered to sleep, and never knowing when the next noisy demand for bottle, cuddle or clean nappy would come.

She had gone back to work two months after the birth. As a doctor, she would have insisted on at least a three-month break before a new mother went back into the working world. But as a new mother herself, she found that all the rules were changed. Beyond the demands of what remained of her year as a GP registrar, Megan discovered she needed work, she needed to remind herself who she had been before her daughter was born.

Her sisters had been great. Cat took Poppy when she was in morning surgery, because Mamma-san didn't open until lunch time, and Jessica was there in the afternoons. Kirk came round with nappies and various pieces of baby equipment – covers for electrical sockets, dummies galore – but sooner or later they all went back to their lives, leaving her alone with her baby and the night, and the overwhelming feelings of disappointment in herself. This mother business – she just wasn't any good at it. It couldn't go on like this for ever, could it? Her sisters standing in for her, the tears when the baby wouldn't stop crying, the crappy little flat and the records played too loud downstairs. Megan was going to have to find a more permanent way of living.

She loved her daughter – there was no question about that. But she couldn't do this thing, it was not in her nature, she was more like her own mother Olivia than she had realised, and the baby deserved someone better. Megan felt like she was giving her all, and her all was pathetically inadequate.

She knew that plenty of women went through pregnancy and motherhood without help. She saw them every day in her surgery. Maternity for one was becoming the industry standard. So why was it so hard for her? Or maybe they all felt this way, all the poor cows going solo. So now she knew what life felt like on the Sunny View Estate.

The end of her GP registrar year was approaching. She had to sit a three-hour exam, which was widely considered to be the easiest part of the summative assessment.

'But what if I fail?' Megan asked Lawford.

'Nobody fails,' he said. 'Only the people who have really screwed up their lives.'

'How do you feel?' Cat said.

Rory arched his back and closed his eyes, his face the same colour as yesterday's bandages. He groaned softly. The painkillers were not working, or there were not enough of them for a man who had just had invasive surgery on his testicles.

He felt like throwing up, but his stomach was empty. Something was ominously wet down there. He could feel the blood seeping through the dressing on his poor, swollen balls. My God, he thought. Those poor bastards have had a few adventures.

'How do I feel?' he reflected. 'Like somebody just sliced open my bollocks and then stapled them back together. As you're asking.'

'But it's worth it, isn't it?' Cat said, taking his hand. 'It's all worth it?'

He nodded. 'Yes, all worth it.'

She placed a soft kiss on his parched lips.

Despite feeling like a freshly neutered tom – ironic really, as the aim of the operation was to make him once more a tom with fully working reproductive tom apparatus – he ran his hand up her leg. On and on it went. The length of those glorious pins never ceased to amaze him, and he loved to wander from knee to thigh. *Measuring me,* she always called it, laughing.

'What happens now?' she said.

He groaned, shifted his weight. 'When I'm healed up, I come in and, you know, ejaculate into a pot of some kind.'

'Talk to my brother-in-law Paulo. I know he's done that lots of times.'

'Cat, if there's one thing a man doesn't need lessons in, it's – oooh!' He gasped and flinched with the eye-watering pain. 'Masturbation.'

'Then they count your sperm?'

'Count 'em. Tickle 'em. See if they can jump through hoops. See if they are there.'

'They'll be there. I know it.'

He smiled at her beautiful, expectant face. And, yes, it was all worth it to have her back in his life. But she acted as though this part, the sperm-meets-egg part, was the difficult bit.

The really difficult bit, in Rory's experience, was keeping a relationship together over the long years that it took to raise a child. Staying together when you were a father and mother was the truly difficult bit, and, in some secret chamber of his heart, he really wasn't sure if he could do it all again.

The thought of becoming a parent once more both excited and appalled him. Because he knew what it took, and it took so much. But he couldn't deny her. If she was going to have a baby with any man, then, please God, he wanted it to be with him.

Later his son sat on the edge of his bed, eating his grapes and wearing a frown.

'So, like, Cat wants children, does she?' Jake said.

Rory moaned, tugged at his bandages to relieve the fire down below.

'In the end,' he said, 'they all want children.'

It seemed to Kirk that the female attitude to the blow job had changed over the years.

When he was a boy, a blow job had been the ultimate prize – bestowed only when a girl (and back then, they were girls not women) decided that you were the one she was going to spend her life with – or at least the next few months of it. When you got a blow job back then, you felt like it was your lucky day. It wasn't like that any more.

Now a blow job felt like you were being fobbed off with some kind of consolation prize. Blow jobs were handed out willy nilly, while real sex, penetrative sex, vaginal sex, old-fashioned sex, was withheld, the dangled carrot, the Holy Grail.

It wasn't as though women enjoyed giving a man a blow job. Unlike the other kind of sex, the penetrative kind, you never heard any of them complaining that a blow job was over a bit too quickly.

'Oh, that blow job was over a bit fast.'

You never heard them say that, did you?

When he was a boy, a blow job felt like a gift. Now that he was a man, it felt more like an act of charity. What had changed? The rise of the blow job couldn't be attributed to a fear of pregnancy, because the teenage girls he had known in suburban Sydney had a sheer terror of becoming pregnant that was not shared by the capable, independent women he knew now, with their coils, caps and morning after pills.

Perhaps the blow job had become a bargaining chip, a

way of ensuring that you found it hard to walk away, and a way of giving the woman the power. If a woman would do that for you, then why would a man ever leave her? What could be better than that?

He touched the hair of the woman kneeling before him. She was from Perth, in London for two years after a period of wandering, getting ready to go back to Australia and her real life.

She had been in Mamma-san on a large drunken table, some kind of birthday bash, and their accents had been like a green light to conversation, a trip to an after-hours bar he knew, and then finally back to his place.

Now the telephone rang and she lifted her gaze to him, making them wide, holding eye contact. A lot of them did that during a blow job. Eye contact was often the trigger that – oh, sweet Jesus. Kirk struggled to breathe. It seemed to work. But the telephone kept ringing, and he realised that nobody should be calling him at this hour.

The answer machine clicked on and he heard Megan's voice. She was upset, he realised with alarm. Something bad had happened.

'I'm sorry to disturb you . . . I need your help . . . if you could come over . . . it's Poppy . . . if you get this message –'

He snatched up the phone.

'Megan? What? Okay. Okay. I'll be there, okay? Soon as I can.'

He slammed down the phone, tearing himself free from the girl kneeling before him. She was still staring up at him, but now there was cold fury in her narrowing eyes.

'You're making a *date* with some *bitch* when you've got your *cock* in my mouth?'

'Sorry,' he said. 'I've got to go. It's my daughter.'

* * *

Megan answered the door in her dressing gown. She looked dead on her feet. From the flat's only bedroom, Kirk could hear the sound of Poppy howling with rage.

'I didn't know who else to ask. I couldn't ask my sisters. They do so much already. And it's so late. What time is it?'

'I don't know.'

There was something about Poppy's crying that chilled his bones. 'What's wrong with her?'

'She doesn't stop,' Megan said. 'She's been fed, winded, changed, cuddled.'

'Is she sick?'

'No fever. No temperature. She's strong as a baby bull.' Megan wearily shook her head. 'And she doesn't stop crying. I'm a doctor, right? I should know why.'

'Well, you're a woman too. That's what I always sort of liked about you.'

Kirk went into the bedroom. It was impossible to believe that something as tiny as Poppy could make so much noise, or express that much anger. Her little face was screwed up with fury, almost purple with apoplexy, and sopping wet with tears. He picked her up and felt the warmth of her through the Grobag, smelled the mint-fresh newness of her skin.

He laughed and his eyes filled with tears. He loved her so much. He had never known he was capable of such pure, unconditional love. His daughter. His baby daughter.

She screamed in his ear.

Megan was in the doorway. 'Do you want a cup of tea or something?'

'A cup of tea would be great. Do you know what I think is wrong?'

'What?'

'I think she's a baby. That's all. That's the only problem.' He patted Poppy's back. Her scent was of milk and her bath time. 'And I think you're trying to do too much by yourself.'

Megan pulled her dressing gown tighter. 'I'll get that tea.'

Kirk held his baby daughter out in front of him, looking at her through a film of tears, a wide, grateful grin on his face. Poppy was becoming undeniably beautiful, losing that scrawny, foetus-faced look she had had at birth, and beginning to look more like a regular baby, all curves and circles and chubby flesh.

But even when she wasn't beautiful, he thought, she was still beautiful. He pulled her close. His beautiful baby girl.

She was as warm as a hot-water bottle, as new as tomorrow. He had to be careful not to squeeze her too tight, she was still so very small. But it was difficult not to wrap his arms around her, and believe he would keep them there for ever, because she made him feel such a fierce, protective love.

Perhaps he did hug her too hard. Because just as Megan came into the room with two cups of tea, Poppy farted like a flatulent navvy on Friday night – a great, big burst of wind that was muffled by her nappy. Then she immediately fell asleep.

Kirk and Megan looked at each other and laughed. Then Megan put a finger to his lips.

'For God's sake, don't wake her up!'

Kirk gently kissed the baby on her cheek. How could anything be that new, that perfect? He placed her back in the centre of her cot.

'Thanks,' Megan whispered.

'She's getting bigger.'

'I reckon another month and she will be out of these preterm clothes. She can start wearing clothes for a newborn baby. All the stuff that Cat bought her.'

'That will be great.'

'It will be the best thing in the world.'

They went into the kitchen and drank their tea, leaving the bedroom door slightly ajar. But the baby was sleeping soundly. Then the tea was gone, and they just sat there, listening to the night. But it was so late now that even the streets of Hackney were finally silent.

'Well,' Kirk said, getting up to go.

Megan stood up with him, gathering her dressing gown around her neck. She placed her finger on his lips again.

'She's got your mouth.'

'Really?'

'Yes. It's really wide. That's why she's capable of making such a racket.'

Kirk placed the tips of his fingers on Megan's chin.

'But she's got your chin. That strong chin. And your eyes.'

He touched her face by the side of her eyes, felt the hard curve of her cheekbone.

'I'm a mess,' Megan said.

She pulled away from him. Not that. She didn't want that from him. She wanted to show him that she appreciated him coming over in the middle of the night, and she wanted to show that there was a bond between them – that there would always be a bond between them. But not that. She didn't want that.

'You're not a mess. You're beautiful.'

'Don't say that. Please. Don't say things that are not true.'

She was self-conscious about her body. It was like being a teenager all over again. Except now, instead of braces on her teeth and a few spots, she had a scar that would never fade dividing her in half, and sore, useless nipples throbbing on painfully hard breasts, those breasts strange and unfamiliar and heavy, and a stomach that still bulged as if there was a baby in there.

'You're beautiful, Megan. You'll always be beautiful to me.'

'No, really. I'm a mess. Look.'

She pulled open her dressing gown, eased her pyjama bottoms down a few inches and cautiously lifted her T-shirt. The scar from the birth was still livid. He took a step towards her and she watched him trace the wound with his finger, not quite touching her.

'That's where our daughter came from,' he said. 'It's not ugly.'

Megan hung her head. She wanted him to stay. But she didn't want that from him.

'I'm so tired,' she said.

'Then let's sleep now.' He carefully pulled down her T-shirt. 'All three of us.'

So she let her dressing gown slip to the floor, and he undressed in the darkness of the bedroom, listening to the steady breathing of their baby daughter. He climbed into the bed. She had her back turned to him but didn't object when he snuggled against her, making spoons.

'I'm so tired.'

'Then sleep now.'

'Maybe in the morning.'

'I'm not going anywhere.'

He put his arms around her, and as they huddled together she felt the warmth of human contact and the glorious blanket of sleep finally closing over her tired bones, and Megan surrendered.

part three:
the most natural thing in the world

nineteen

When Cat was twelve, and Jessie was eight, and baby Megan was a big girl of four, it was decided that the girls would live with their mother.

The decision was not taken by Olivia, or Jack, but by Cat herself, independently and without consultation.

In the year since their mother had left, things had become bad at home. There seemed to be less money than there was before, because their father was away working all the time – although years later Cat saw how people sometimes hid from their home lives in their work lives, so perhaps the problem wasn't money after all.

The new au pair, a great blonde lump from Hamburg, couldn't handle them, didn't know where to start. And suddenly they needed a lot of handling.

There was a fury inside Cat that she couldn't explain, Megan had started wetting the bed again, and Jessie kept bursting into tears, wailing that she wanted things to be how they were before. So did Cat.

Food from tins, that's what Cat remembered about that time. Food from tins and the fury inside.

In her twelve-year-old heart, Cat knew that things could

never be the way they were before. Not after the man in the taxi came for their mother. This was the best she could do.

Take them to live with their mother.

It was surprisingly easy. Cat had already mastered a good impersonation of the haughty indifference their mother had employed whenever speaking to the help, and she informed the dumbfounded au pair that it was all arranged, they were off to St John's Wood for the foreseeable future.

'Aber your farter, Cat-kin . . .'

'My father is quite aware of our plans, I assure you.'

The girls excitedly packed their bags while the big blonde lump tried, unsuccessfully, to reach Jack Jewell. They took only the essentials – pyjamas, toothbrush, a talking frog for Megan, a flock of Barbies and Kens for Jessie, and a Blondie picture disc for Cat. Then they walked to the tube station, holding hands, Cat and Jessie taking turns to carry Megan when she refused to walk any further.

When they were on the tube, Jessica presented her big sister with her secret gift – a fistful of Monopoly money. Cat accepted it with thanks, and didn't tell Jessie that she was a silly little kid. She was going to take good care of her sisters from now on.

St John's Wood was another world, completely unlike their leafy suburb. There were black people here, lots of them – it wasn't until years later that Cat realised they must have been there for the cricket at Lord's – and everyone seemed to be a millionaire. Megan stumbled over some litter on St John's Wood High Street, and it turned out to be a half-smoked cigar, the size of a Wall's sausage.

A fabulously wealthy black neighbourhood. That's what St John's Wood looked like to Cat. She knew that they could be happy here.

That illusion was shattered as soon as their mother opened her front door.

'That's not who I am,' Olivia kept telling Cat – as if she hadn't heard the first time – as she tried to reach her ex-husband on the phone, while Jessie and Megan bumped around the pristine apartment, getting in the way of the Filipina housekeeper – who smiled at them with some sympathy, it seemed to Cat – and touching all the things that were not meant to be touched by the sticky fingers of little girls – 'Megan, *not* my photograph with Roger Moore' – and Cat, increasingly desperate, tried to explain why it was a good idea if they came to live here, following her mother around the flat as Monopoly money fell from the pockets of her jeans.

'But I thought you would be pleased to see us. I thought it would be nice if we were together again. I thought –'

'You thought, you thought, you thought. You think too much, young lady.'

'Don't you *want* to live with your children? Most mothers –'

But Olivia had turned her back on her eldest daughter. She had reached Jack, and now she spoke softly but angrily, urgently, as if convinced that he had planned this invasion just to wreak havoc in her love nest.

When she hung up the phone, Olivia turned to face Cat, and the child looked at the woman and saw that there was no softness in her, no shame, no love.

Years later, Cat had no trouble in turning back the clock to when she was that twelve-year-old girl standing in her mother's rented apartment, her younger sisters now silent on the sofa, the photographs of their mother with various celebrities unmolested, the housekeeper's vacuum cleaner buzzing distantly in some other room, and being told – as her mother furiously snatched up the Monopoly money from the carpet – that all her childish hopes were ridiculous.

'Do you get it yet, Cat?' her mother told her. 'The woman

you want me to be – the mother you want me to be. *That's not who I am.*'

And as she waited for the day in her diary when she would find out if there was a baby growing inside her or not, and all the momentous what-if doubts began to stir – was it ten years too late? was the risk of miscarriage and disability too great? would Rory be happy if she was pregnant, or would he feel trapped? – there was one thing she knew with total certainty.

If she was pregnant, she would never be the kind of mother that her own mother had been. She had to be better than that.

She might not be the best mother in the world – the other date, the potential birthday on next year's calendar both excited and terrified her, she had been childfree for so long – and she might not even be a particularly good mother. She had seen with her youngest sister that the sleepless, milk-stained reality had no resemblance to the expectation.

But she knew she could never walk away from the life she was creating. She could never be so cruel, or selfish, or cold.

That's not who I am, Cat thought.

Here was the problem, as Rory saw it.

Once upon a time a woman had a baby with the first man she met. But these days she was far more likely to have a baby with the *last* man she met.

You could see how having a baby with the first man she met could cause all sorts of problems, and they were mostly the problems of what she would be missing.

An education. A career. Recreational sex. Lots of that, with a wide and varied selection of men. And all those priceless moments when you know that you are young and free and at loose in the world. Watching the sun come up over a beach in Thailand, driving through Paris in an open-top sports car, waking up to the sound of the Caribbean outside your open window . . . and even if Rory's hypothetical woman never did any of these things, then at least the possibility was always there.

But you can't fit a baby seat into an open-top sports car. It just doesn't go.

He knew how it changed your world. His mother had constantly reminded him when Jake was born – *your life is not your own now.*

She was trying to be encouraging. But she made it sound like a life sentence.

So he had no difficulty understanding why the women of the modern world needed a baby with the first man they met like they needed a hole in the head. But had it all gone too far in the other direction? What about the problems of having a baby with the last man she met?

The later maters – that's what they called them, *later maters,* the women who had body-swerved around their childhood sweethearts, and unplanned pregnancy, and their college squeeze, and a ragbag of romances formed on holidays or in offices, clubs and bars. The women who experienced fifteen years or so of being unfettered by maternity, and left a tiny window for babies, a fleeting ten years of fertility.

They had had the education, the career and the recreational sex. And now they were ready to squeeze out a baby while the biological option was still there.

But here was the problem – a lot of the good ones, and maybe even the best ones, were already gone. Surely there was a random element to the last man, just as there was to the first. Rory worried about the later maters. He worried that they were not nearly as smart as they thought. The later maters were like last-minute shoppers on Christmas Eve. There simply wasn't a lot left to choose from.

And what about Rory himself? Was he the love of Cat's life, or just some guy who happened to be there? The thought depressed him. This was no way to bring a new life into the world. And yet he didn't know how to refuse her, or even to say that he had his doubts.

You couldn't tell the woman you loved that you weren't sure you wanted a child with her.

It wasn't natural.

'Nobody will fuck your brains out like a bored housewife,' Michael told Paulo. 'Think about it. The kids are grown or growing. The old man's falling asleep in front of *Match of the Day*. And she suddenly thinks, *what exactly am I saving it for? I go to the gym* – this is her thinking, right? – *I do my Atkins diet. I'm still a relatively young woman. I have my needs.*'

'And then there's you,' Paulo said.

'And then there's me,' Michael said, his voice heavy with resignation. In the end, he had not been able to keep his hands off Ginger. In the end, he had brought her back for more than answering phones and posting VAT forms. Michael could resist everything except the hired help.

My brother the junkie, Paulo thought sadly. Michael thought he was in control, but Paulo knew that was no longer the case. The addiction was taking over. And Paulo saw at last that it wasn't the pursuit of fun that made Michael do the things he did. It was the pursuit of something new, the pursuit of someone who wasn't his wife.

Fun had nothing to do with it.

Paulo knew that Michael and Ginger were slipping off for early evenings in the local Hilton – a time when their absence from their homes was easily explained by bad traffic, work running late – or perhaps not even explained at all.

Paulo felt depressed when he thought of them coupling in that sterile businessman's room, with its little sachets of tea and coffee, the ignored trouser press parked ludicrously in the corner, the Do Not Disturb sign warding off the maid. Paulo could feel the guilt and regret in his brother but it was buried under layers of all of the old cockiness.

Michael thought he was going to get away with it.

'The good thing about married women is that eventually they have to be somewhere,' Michael said. 'It's not like single birds, who want you to hang around and talk about your feelings and go out for dinner. The married woman has to be off pretty sharpish.'

Paulo was tired of hearing about his brother's sex life. There had been a time when he thrilled to hear of Michael's adventures, which he had always dressed up as a kind of personal philosophy, a way of looking at the universe.

Yet that was when they were boys, that was before the promises they had made at their weddings, and now he was sick of it. Let Michael screw up his life if he wanted to. Paulo just wanted to sell cars. He wanted hot shots from the City to come in with their big fat six-figure bonus and talk to him about the Ferrari Pininfarina of their dreams. But business was slow, and most days the showroom echoed with the voices of the two brothers, and nobody looked at the cars for sale.

'There's this motor show in Hong Kong,' Paulo said. 'Baresi Brothers has been invited by their board of trade. Two club class tickets. Hotel.'

Paulo handed his brother a glossy brochure. The cover showed the soaring Hong Kong skyline rising behind next year's F1 Ferrari. A pretty Asian girl in a short skirt was beaming on the bonnet.

'I saw that,' Michael said. 'Yeah. It's going to be pretty big.'

'I thought I would take Jessica. If you can manage without me. It would do her good to get away for a week or so. I'd call it my holiday for this year.'

'Go ahead. There's not much happening here. We'll be fine.'

Paulo nodded. It was settled. He went to turn away, then suddenly stopped. He would have one last try to stop this madness. Before it was too late.

'I watch you with your daughter, Mike. I know you love her. I know you want to be a real family man.'

'I don't want to be a family man. I am a family man.'

'But if you lose Naoko, you'll lose everything. You know that, don't you? Your marriage. Your daughter. Your family. You don't want that, do you?'

Michael was watching Ginger in her little glass box. You would never guess she could fuck someone's brains out in a Hilton. And all before tea time. Paulo saw his brother wince, as if these proceedings gave him physical pain.

'I can't help it, Paulo.'

'Of course you can!'

Michael shook his head.

'You think it's going to end when you fall in love. Or when you get married. Or when you become a father. But it never ends – that *hunger*.' Michael looked at his brother with a sad kind of love. 'You think it's babies that make the world go round. You think that's what it is all about. It's not, Paulo. It's desire. It's fucking. *It's always fucking somebody new.* That's what is at the heart of it all – the whole great game. Wanting it. Desire. Call it what you like. The babies are just a by-product.'

'Not for me. Not for my wife.'

Michael shook his head.

'You think women are any different? They are the same as us. That's the big secret. Women are the same as us. They take their pleasures where they can. And nobody will fuck your brains out like a bored housewife and mother.' Michael paused in thought, and stared out across the empty showroom. 'Unless you're married to her, of course.'

Poppy smiled up at Jessica.

It was a winning smile, gummy and wide, a little shaky at the edges, but definitely aimed at her aunt. For an encore she kicked her legs, as if attempting a backstroke in her cot.

'She recognises me, doesn't she?' Jessica said. 'She's starting to recognise me!'

'Look at the little cow,' Megan said, rubbing the sleep from her eyes. 'All sweetness and light now you're here.'

'Oh, she's not a little cow!' Jessica reached into the cot and lifted Poppy into her arms. The baby gurgled with delight. 'She's a little angel!'

'The little angel's been up screaming half the night. It was so bad the guy downstairs turned up his 50 Cent CD. But there's not a gangster rapper alive who can compete with Poppy.'

The baby regarded her mother with an impassive stare. Kirk came into the room towelling his wet hair.

'We've got to get out of this place,' Megan told him.

'Tell me about it.'

'Is there anything wrong with her?' Jessica said, holding Poppy up for inspection, stroking her wispy hair.

'Colic,' Megan said.

'Colic? That's what horses get.'

Megan nodded. 'Horses and babies. She screams like it's the end of the world. Then she sleeps – but by now you're wide awake. And just as you're finally going off to sleep, she starts screaming blue murder again.'

Jessica said nothing, holding her tongue. She rocked Poppy in her arms, the baby making appreciative noises. And then she said, 'You're so lucky to have her, Megan.'

'I know that, Jess,' Megan said with a tight smile. She wanted to acknowledge the love she felt for her baby girl. But that wasn't the whole story, and she needed her sister to know that it wasn't all happy endings when you had a baby. 'I do know I'm lucky. But I never thought I could be this tired.'

Megan went into the kitchen and came back with two dummies designed to look like the mouths of animals. One featured a smiling bear, the other a tiger licking his lips.

'If she goes absolutely crazy, stick one of these in her gob.'

'Dummies?' Jessica said, as if Megan had produced a couple of spliffs. 'I thought you were *against* dummies? I thought babies became addicted to dummies, and that they weren't good for their teeth, and all of that.'

Megan laughed. 'I was anti-bottle feeding. I was anti-dummy. I was anti-running to the baby every time she cries. Then I had Poppy and you know what changed? Everything. The good intentions, the baby books, the firmly held beliefs about breast-feeding all went straight out of the window. It's all bullshit, Jess. The lot of it. You just have to get through it. You just have to survive.'

Megan placed a hand on her daughter's bulging baby forehead. Poppy snuggled in Jessica's arms, coolly averting her face from her mother.

'Real baby,' Megan said, withdrawing her hand. 'Real world.'

The best thing about teaching people to dive was that moment when a beginner surfaced for the very first time.

A small percentage of first-timers were panicked – tearing off their mask, sucking in air as though they had just been exhumed from some claustrophobic watery grave – but most of them were ecstatic. Raving with joy about the teeming marine life, the psychedelic coral, the sensation of flying that scuba diving so closely resembled.

It was another world down there – a better world, a freer world – and most people loved it at first sight. But you didn't see that feeling in his new job. Seven mornings a week Kirk taught beginners to dive at a swimming pool in the back of a private house in Battersea. And in Battersea everything was different.

No fish, no coral, no sense of all that limitless space containing the shipwrecks of the centuries and mountains taller than Everest and waterfalls bigger than Niagara.

Just a little blue box full of heavily chlorinated water where young women and men – and they were almost entirely in their twenties and thirties, doing the prep for two weeks of summer fun in the Indian Ocean or the Caribbean or the Red Sea – struggled with neutral buoyancy, mask clearing and all the other basics.

In the back room of a dive shop on the Edgware Road, he steered his students through the theory necessary to get their PADI dive card, and it was like trying to explain magic.

There wasn't much money involved. There never was with diving. You did it out of love. But love wouldn't pay the rent so in the afternoons Kirk got on a racing bike that didn't belong to him and delivered sandwiches and coffee to addresses in the City until it was time to go home and take over from Jessica.

Megan knew all about his job teaching in the pool of a house in Battersea. But he didn't tell her about his second job delivering snacks to stockbrokers and bankers and insurance salesmen. He didn't tell her, because he wanted her to be proud of him. The way he was proud of her.

Megan was what he wanted. Poppy was what he wanted – she was a beautiful child and he knew that the endless crying would eventually stop, and things would get better.

But this life in London – the grey streets, the unsmiling faces, the longing to escape even among the people who wouldn't dream of living anywhere else – this was not how he imagined his life would be.

Sex, sleep, sunshine, real diving – all these things, his very favourite things, had somehow been consigned to his past. And he wondered. He really wondered.

How much can you give up for the person you love, and still keep loving them?

Jessica pushed Poppy through the filthy, crowded streets, thinking that most of the mothers around here looked completely worn out.

Old before their time. Stains on clothes that Oxfam would reject. Greasy, untended hair. Knackered beyond belief. They reminded her of someone. With a jolt, she realised that they reminded her of Megan.

But her sister didn't have their anger. These women were angry with the world, with their children – the language they used when the little ones tarried by the sweet counter! More like sailors on shore leave than young mothers out shopping with their children! – and with Jessica herself when she clumsily steered Poppy's trendy three-wheel baby carriage through the mobs of young Hackney mothers and their bawling, whining, underdressed, filthy-faced brood.

'Oy, darling, watch them bleeding wheels,' one of them said, not bothering to take the cigarette from between her lips. 'You nearly run over me fucking foot, innit?'

'Sorry,' Jessica said, smiling politely.

With her trim figure, immaculate clothes, careful make-up and quiet decency, Jessica looked nothing like the effing and blinding brood mares of the Sunny View Estate. And yet she knew they took her to be one of their number, and it made Jessica's heart thrill with joy.

A young mother, on her way to the park, a bit of fresh air for the baby, out in the world with her own flesh and blood.

twenty

In the late morning the playground was taken over by the young mothers of the Sunny View Estate. With their toddlers waddling with solemn purpose between them, and their babies dozing in the prams, the women lounged on the roundabout and swings, and leaned against the climbing frame, talking and smoking.

They had a proprietorial attitude to the playground, because only a few years ago they had been among the teenagers who gathered here in the late afternoon, idly lounging on the swings, or gently twirling on the roundabout, talking and smoking.

Jessica and Poppy remained a little apart from them, concentrating on feeding the fierce East End ducks who lived in the park. Jessica tossed them stale bread, and Poppy's bright blue eyes were wide with awe as the ducks squawked and fought around them.

'She's a little cracker, your one.'

It was one of the young mothers. Barely out of her teens, with a pretty face, and two crop-haired boys milling at her feet. Jessica realised with a start that the woman – a girl was more like it – was talking to her about Poppy.

'A real little cracker,' the woman repeated. She took a long suck on a Marlboro. 'She's – what? – 'bout free months?'

'Five.' Jessica shooed away the ducks, and clutched Poppy closer. 'She was a bit early.'

'Premature? They catch up.' She indicated one of the shaven-headed bruisers in her care. 'Thirty-five weeks, that one. He looked more like a bleeding Kentucky Fried Chicken than a baby. You'd never guess it now.'

The young mothers began making delighted, cooing noises at Poppy, and Jessica found herself drawn deeper into the group.

Looking at the women, you would not expect they were capable of such gentleness. These were, after all, the same women Jessica had seen screaming abuse in the local supermarket. Perhaps, Jessica thought, the children allowed them to show a tenderness that was absent from the rest of their lives.

She perched on a vacant swing while the women fussed over Poppy, as if every new baby was a miracle they couldn't begin to explain. And it was funny – they wanted to know the baby's name, but nobody asked for Jessica's name.

Jessica found she didn't mind at all.

'Don't look like she's just had a baby, does she?' one of the Sunny View mums commented.

There was a murmur of assent. Jessica laughed modestly, bouncing Poppy on her knee. The baby smiled, fighting to keep its head steady.

'You're a little sweetheart, ain't you?' said another young mum, stroking Poppy's rosy cheek with a nicotine-stained finger. 'Do you look like your mum or your dad?'

'Her dad's Italian,' Jessica said, her head thrilling with the lie, and more than half believing it herself. 'He's crazy about her. He calls us *his two girls.*'

'It's nice when they stick around,' said one of the Sunny View mums.

'Jessie?'

Then suddenly Cat was there, in the middle of all the smoking women and their crop-haired toddlers and fat-faced babies, and you could almost see their faces hardening in the presence of this well-dressed, well-spoken, conspicuously childfree stranger.

'What are you doing here?' Jessica said, bewildered.

Cat wagged a bag of pastries.

'Same as you. Feeding the ducks.'

Jessica gathered up Poppy's things – mittens the size of matchboxes, a woolly hat with animal ears, her bottle – and carried the baby while Cat pushed the empty pram.

''Bye, Poppy,' said the woman who had first spoken to Jessica. 'Be a good girl for your mum.'

Cat looked at Jessica.

And Jessica pulled Poppy closer.

On the far side of the lake they sat on a scarred park bench, the bread and the ducks all gone, Poppy sleeping in Jessica's arms. The distant laughter of the Sunny View mothers drifted to them across the water.

'You know that I've been on this IVF cycle,' Cat said. 'The doctor recommended it because of my age. *My* age! Rory's almost fifteen years older than me.'

Jessica studied Poppy's sleeping face. She said nothing.

'Anyway,' Cat said. 'It's been like – I don't know – a marathon with hurdles. All these hurdles, Jess. The injections, the scans.' She shook her head. 'Your mood changing with the weather. All that time, all these hurdles, never knowing if it's going to work.'

'I know what it's like, Cat. I did it myself.'

'Of course you did. I know you did.'

Jessica stared out across the lake, as if lost in her own dreams, not really listening. Cat was talking more quickly now. Getting it out. Wanting her to know. Wanting to get it over with.

'They put two fertilised embryos inside me.'

'Rory's working again, then?'

'Yes, Rory's working again.'

'Good, I've always liked Rory.'

'Then I had to wait, I had to wait two weeks, the longest two weeks of my life.'

'And now you're pregnant.'

Jessica's voice calm and flat, with just a hint of irony. It wasn't a question.

Cat looked at her sister, and she wanted to hold her, to ask her – do you know how much you are loved?

It seemed to Cat that Megan had breezed through life, taking everything in her stride – parental divorce, school, boys and men. Even her youngest sister's postnatal depression, or exhaustion, or whatever it was, had seemed to disappear when Kirk moved in.

But Jessica, thought Cat – right from the start it had all been so hard for Jessica. Cat felt a flush of shame, because she was here to hurt her sister some more.

'And now I'm pregnant, Jess.'

Jessica laughed, and it frightened Cat.

'Do you know how I know? Because you wouldn't come all the way to the East End if it hadn't worked.'

Cat exhaled as if she had been holding her breath for minutes. Perhaps it wasn't going to be so bad after all.

'I wanted you to be the first to know, Jess,' grabbing her sister's arm, suddenly feeling free to touch her. 'Even Rory doesn't know yet.'

Jessica frowned at Poppy, nodding. Then she looked up at her sister, waiting for her to continue. But Cat thought, what else is there to say?

'I never thought it would work,' she said, aware she was

babbling. 'All those hurdles. Rory having to go through an operation just so he could have one off the wrist. It all seemed so fragile, right from the start. What are the odds of success? Less than thirty per cent.' She shrugged helplessly. 'It's a miracle. I never thought it would work for me.'

'That's funny,' Jessica said, not laughing now. 'Because when I had IVF, it never occurred to me that it wouldn't work.'

'Oh, Jessie. I don't want you to feel bad about this baby.'

Jessica took her sister's hands.

'Congratulations, Cat. And thanks for thinking of me.' She smiled, rolling her eyes. 'Don't worry, I'm not going to freak out. I'm not going to run amok. I'm not jealous. I'm not sad. Well, maybe a bit. That's only natural. But I'm happy for you. You'll be a good mother.'

'I'm not sure if this is what Rory wants,' Cat said. She wanted her sister to know – *it's not perfect. Don't think it's perfect.* She was worried about money, about where they would live. But most of all she was worried about the baby's father. *It's not perfect.*

'Rory will be a good dad,' Jessica said thoughtfully, her index finger tracing the contours of Poppy's mouth. 'He's like Paulo. Loves kids.'

Cat was grateful to be the one who needed reassurance, encouraged to spill her heart.

'But I think he's doing it for me. I don't know, Jess. It could all be a terrible mess.'

'When the baby comes, he'll fall in love with it. They all do.' Jessica stared across the water at the playground. The Sunny View mums had gone. Jessica shook her head. 'I wish you well, Cat. And the baby. Of course I do. But don't talk to me about miracles. IVF isn't a miracle – it's big business.' Now her voice was bitter, and her eyes were brimming with the injustice of it all. 'What are they charging these days?

Three grand a go? And you, Cat – you're just a consumer. You suddenly want a baby just like you've wanted a car or holiday in the past. And you get what you want, don't you, Cat? So spare me the talk about miracles, will you?'

Cat slowly stood up, wanting to be away from this place. She had been wrong to come, wrong to try to be the caring big sister. They were grown women with tangled lives. You couldn't just kiss it better any more.

'Jessie, what can I say? IVF gives hope to people with none. That's good enough for me. What? Babies that are conceived naturally don't have problems? Women who conceive naturally don't have problems? Look at Megan. She was ready to top herself. And this isn't really about IVF, is it, Jess?'

Poppy groaned angrily. She began to scream, her face turning first pink, then red, then purple.

'Now look what you've done,' Jessica snapped.

She can't be brave any more, Cat thought. It's too much, it's too hard. My sister has had to be brave for so long. And now all the dark stuff is overwhelming Jessica's brave, kind heart.

'Why do you think I came to you before anyone, Jess? Because I know it must hurt. But I need you. I need you to keep being my sister. I need you to be a wonderful aunt to this baby. Just as you are with Poppy.'

'That's me,' Jessica said, almost drowned out by the baby's screams. 'Auntie Jessica.'

'I have to go,' Cat said wearily. She thought, what am I meant to do? Apologise? I can't do that.

'You should have taken better care of me, Cat.'

'What are you talking about?'

'I was just a kid. Sixteen years old. And a young sixteen. You were twenty. At university. A grown-up woman.' She shook her head. 'You should have taken better care of me.'

Cat was genuinely shocked.

'Are you still thinking about all that old stuff? You've got to get over this thing, Jess. What else could we have done? What were you going to be – a mum at sixteen? It's got nothing to do with anything else.'

'You think an abortion is *good* for you?'

'I didn't say that, did I?'

'Ask your sister. Ask Megan. You career women really make me laugh. You think it's another form of contraception. They tear the baby out of you. With a vacuum cleaner. A fucking vacuum cleaner. What does that do to you? I'll tell you. It ruins you for life.'

'It's not your fault. None of it was your fault. There was nothing else you could do.'

'It ruins you for life.'

'It's not your fault, Jess.'

By now Poppy was apoplectic with rage. Jessica rocked her furiously. Cat had never seen a baby turn that colour. She was howling as though she would never stop.

'Is she all right?' Cat said.

Jessica turned her full attention to the baby, making soothing noises, *sssh-sssh, sssh-sssh*, that sounded like waves or the wind. The baby stifled a snotty sob, and was silent.

'Megan can't do that,' Jessica grinned. 'She just cries and cries all night.' She smoothed the baby's newly minted skin. 'You're driving your mummy mad, aren't you, darling?'

At least we've got each other.

That's what Rory was planning to say to her when IVF failed them, as it surely would.

What were the odds against it? He didn't need a doctor or a bookie to tell him that it was a long shot.

People thought that IVF was something that only the woman went through. And of course it was true that it was

Cat who was pumped full of hormones, who had her body turned into an egg factory. But he was there too – watching her stick those needles into her beautiful flat stomach, he was there seeing her mood change from cautious optimism to bleak despair, holding his breath for all that time, waiting for something to go wrong.

At least we've got each other.

He felt they had to try. And he tried because he loved her. But in his heart he had steeled himself for failure.

They had tried, he told himself, during the longest fortnight of his life, the big countdown, when all they could do was wait to see if both of the fertilised eggs placed inside her had melted away. At least we gave it a go, we did our best, and it would have been great, of course it would, but at least we have got each other. It's not the end of the world and it's not the end of us.

But that's the thing about long shots.

Sometimes they come in.

They stood in the middle of the deserted dojo, smelling the sweat and effort of all those departed bodies.

'You're happy, aren't you?' Cat asked him. 'It's what you want too, isn't it?'

'Are you kidding?' he laughed. 'It's the best thing in the world.'

And as she smothered him in kisses, he forgot all the doubts. The best thing in the world! A little boy – or maybe a girl! – who was half of him and half of her. Another human life created from the love between them. It was the most natural thing on the planet, and yet it felt like something magical. The birth of a child, this everyday wonder.

The bitterness of his divorce from Ali hadn't obliterated his memory of what it was like when Jake was born – the pride they had both felt, the surge of overwhelming happiness, and the love that gets unlocked inside you, all the love that you never knew existed.

He kissed Cat's face, her head in his hands, his feelings for her and their unborn child all one, inseparable.

'You did it,' he said. 'You really did it.'

'I did, didn't I?' she chuckled. 'And you want it as much as me – you're sure about that?'

'It's the best thing in the world.'

And he meant it. He only remembered the nagging uncertainties when Cat had gone off to Mamma-san and he called his son to tell him the good news. 'That's great, Dad,' Jake said, sounding as though someone had changed his world without asking him if it was okay. 'But what does this mean for me? Am I this baby's sort of grown-up half-brother, or a kind of uncle, or nothing at all? Is this my family or some other family you're starting?'

Rory had no answers for his teenage son.

And there was something else. This baby – this magical, unborn child – measured out the boundaries of Rory's life. When Jake had been born, Rory had not thought about how long he would live. It hadn't occurred to him. He had taken it for granted that he would at the very least last as long as it took Jake to grow up – and so it had proved.

But Rory was no longer a young man. Before Cat came to the dojo tonight, he had felt it in his lesson. The aches and protests of joints and muscles that had spent half a century on the planet. He could still do a *mawashi-geri,* a roundhouse kick, that would knock your hat off, but afterwards the burning soreness in his knee told him that time was running out.

By the time the baby came, he would be over fifty. He remembered his father at the same age. An old man, his race almost run, only ten years or so from dying of a massive heart attack.

Rory could tell himself that it was different now, another age. Unlike his father, he had never smoked. Unlike many others of his generation, he had never taken drugs. His job kept him fit – fitter than any man in his middle years had any right to be.

But only an idiot would deny the march of time. And when this baby was in its teens, Rory would be indisputably old. If he made it. If he didn't die at the same age as his father. If he avoided cancer, heart attacks and strokes. If he didn't get hit by a bus.

And what if the things that had happened in the past happened all over again? What if his private history repeated itself? What if he didn't stay with Cat, just as he hadn't stayed with Jake's mother? What if they couldn't hold their relationship together for far longer than any relationship he had ever had?

His generation had grown accustomed to their relationships, their marriages, revolving around the three Fs – fucking around, fucking up and fucking off. The three Fs were considered the norm.

And as a moral philosophy, or amoral philosophy, the three Fs certainly had their advantages.

He would never have known Cat if his ex-wife hadn't fallen in love with someone else. Escaping from the wreckage of his first marriage had left him free to find the love of his life. This new baby would never have existed without his visit to the divorce court.

But what had hurt most about the break-up of his marriage – what had bust his heart wide open, and clawed at it even now – was watching their son change from a bright, sunny-natured child to a withdrawn, frightened boy who trusted no one.

Ali blithely attributed the change in Jake to the miserable transformations of adolescence. But in his bones, and with a guilt that he would feel until his dying day, Rory knew it was because of the divorce.

Ali liked to pretend that the three of them were happier than they had been when they were together. Perhaps lying to herself about their son was her way of coping. Because how could any parent live with the knowledge that they had inflicted wounds on their child that would last a lifetime?

It all came back to him, the fathomless anger and sadness of their divorce, the feeling of having his child torn away from him. He remembered when Ali and Jake had first moved in with the man who was going to restore Ali's happiness. Rory wasn't allowed to call to tell Jake good night – 'An invasion of our space,' Ali said – so Rory would drive to their house, and park outside until he saw the light go off in his son's bedroom.

Good night, good night.

Would he one day park outside some other stranger's home and watch the light go off in this new baby's bedroom?

'This is the best thing in the world,' he had told Cat, gently placing one of his scarred hands on her belly, and he truly felt it.

But he didn't have the words to tell her that the baby also measured out the distance of his life, that little he or little she was a reminder of his own mortality, and nature's way of telling him that everything in this world comes to an end.

twenty-one

'Hilarious,' Brigitte told Cat. 'You're squeezing one out before you hit forty! You're really doing it! Dropping one at the very last minute! I think it's . . . *hilarious.*'

Cat smiled uncertainly. 'Well, I'm not quite ready for the change, you know.'

'No, no, no,' Brigitte said. 'Don't get me wrong. Congratulations to you – and Rory, of course. Who would have thought he had it in him? I just think it's, well, hilarious. Wait a minute.'

Brigitte disappeared into the kitchen. It was early evening in Mamma-san and the restaurant was empty, the only sounds the murmur of the kitchen staff preparing for the night ahead, and the rain lashing against the windows. Cat touched her stomach again. It was good to be inside on a night like this. Brigitte came back holding two glasses and a bottle of champagne.

'Let's drink to you. My clever Cat.'

Cat hesitated.

'I'd love to, but I guess I shouldn't.' She patted her belly. 'You know.'

Brigitte groaned. 'Oh, come *on*. It's a special night. Just one. That's not going to hurt you.'

Brigitte expertly tore off the foil, peeled back the wire and began unscrewing the cork. It came away with a discreet pop. She poured two glasses and held one out to Cat.

'I really don't want to. But thanks.'

Cat reached out to stroke Brigitte's arm. She owed so much to this woman, she didn't want to hurt her. But at the same time – she had to give her baby every chance.

'You're not going to get all prissy on me, are you, Cat?'

Brigitte held a glass in each hand. She took a sip from one of them.

'It's nothing like that. I just – well, it doesn't seem right. But thank you for the thought. Really. Later, okay? After the birth.'

Brigitte swiftly drained her glass, and lifted the other in a salute that was almost mocking.

'After the birth,' she said. 'Of course. Just promise me you're not going to turn into one of those smug, born-again mums who renounces her wild past.'

'I'm not sure I ever really had a wild past,' Cat said. 'But I think I know what you mean. I certainly lived the single life for long enough. The free life. But it gets old, doesn't it?'

Brigitte's face was impassive. She sipped her drink and said nothing. Cat took the empty glass from her hand and filled it with water. There were not many people in this world she would share a glass with – only her sisters and Brigitte.

'I can't say I'll miss it,' Cat said. 'All those men who have either just broken up with the greatest girl in the world or the biggest bitch in the universe.'

'Hmmm,' Brigitte said, non-committal.

'It's funny. When I was growing up, looking after my two sisters, all I wanted was to be free. Nobody holding me down. But being free didn't really work out that way for me. I always felt it should have made me happier than it did. To tell the truth, I was starting to feel desperate. And I hated feeling desperate.'

Brigitte was smiling at her.

'Oh, come on, Cat. You don't think what you're doing is a little bit desperate?'

'What am I doing?'

'Having a baby at the last moment with the man who happens to be handy.'

'It's not the last moment!'

'Well – it's getting there. Come on. It's far more desperate than anything you did as a single woman. And it's hilarious.'

Cat could feel the ice inside. She didn't want it to be this way. She wanted Brigitte to be happy for her.

'Could you please stop saying that?' Hearing her voice trembling with emotion, and hating it. 'Whatever my baby is, I promise you she is not hilarious. There's nothing funny about her.'

'Ah, but it is amusing. Women like you make me laugh, Cat. You really do. All your talk about independence and freedom, and then you grab the first chance you get to play *hausfrau*.'

'I intend to keep working. I can't afford to do anything else. Rory loves his work, but it doesn't pay much.'

'So how's it going to work? Have you thought about it at all?'

Of course she had thought about it. Not as much as she had thought about the doubt she saw in Rory's eyes, and not as much as she had thought about whether the baby would be all right or not. But she had thought about her life as a working mother, even though it all seemed impossibly distant.

'I'll come back to work after twelve weeks. If that's okay with you. My sisters will help. Rory doesn't have classes beyond eight. It will be fine.'

Brigitte finished her champagne. She wasn't smiling now.

'But you'll have to slip off earlier, won't you? Because your baby will be teething, or have the running squirts, or miss its mummy. Or when it gets a bit bigger it will be dressed up as a donkey's arse in the school play at Christmas. And Mummy will have to be there, won't she?'

Cat shook her head, her eyes brimming with hurt. She would never have believed this conversation was possible. Beyond her sisters, and Rory, and her father, there was no one she cared about more than Brigitte. She had taught Cat how to be a grown woman, independent and strong. And now she was withdrawing her love, just as everyone took away their love in the end.

'You act as though my pregnancy is some kind of betrayal.'

Brigitte laughed.

'You don't betray me, Cat. You betray yourself. In two years you'll be pushing a pram down some suburban high street, and you'll wonder whatever happened to your life.'

Cat drained her glass and set it down carefully.

'You know what the real problem is, Brigitte? It's not the smug mums. It's the sour old bags like you.'

'Sour old bags like me?'

'It's all you old firebrands who were afraid that a baby would cramp your style. You should have had a baby, Brigitte. It would have made you a nicer person.'

'Come on, Cat. Let's not fight. I'm not sacking you or anything. You know how much I need you.'

Cat put down her empty champagne glass and picked up her coat.

'I know you're not sacking me, Brigitte. Because I quit.'

Cat didn't turn around when Brigitte called her name, and she walked out of Mamma-san thinking, *oh, very smart.*

She had heard of women who had lost their jobs during maternity leave, plenty of them. But she couldn't recall anyone else who had become unemployed simply by getting a bun in the oven. She stroked her stomach, down-up-down, and wondered what they were going to do. The three of them. Her little family.

Outside the restaurant, Jessica was standing in the rain, waiting for her.

'I don't want to be this way, Cat,' she told her sister.

Cat wasn't sure what Jessica meant. She didn't want to be soaked to the bone? She didn't want to be so full of hurt and anger? She didn't want to be without a child in a family that was suddenly full of mothers?

Cat didn't know exactly what Jessica meant, but she knew exactly how she felt.

So Cat took her sister in her arms, smelling Calvin Klein and coffee, and she held her tight, loving her very much, her own flesh and blood, part of her little family too, and for those moments in the rain outside the deserted restaurant, they were both temporarily unaware of the baby who was already growing between them.

When Poppy wasn't crying she lay there between her parents, and they watched her as if she were an unexploded bomb, capable of going off in their faces at any moment.

The baby slept, but the grown-ups couldn't sleep. They could barely risk breathing, in case it woke up the baby.

There was still something truly stunning about her crying. Who would ever have believed that such a tiny body could produce that ear-splitting white noise, so full of grief and outrage and fury? The baby's parents – exhausted and frightened, incapable of exchanging a word that didn't relate to the baby and her bewildering sleeping pattern – were very impressed.

This was surely the loudest baby in the history of the world.

The first bone-white buds of Poppy's milk teeth were poking through her glistening pink gums, making her tiny, tiny, almost non-existent nose run with transparent baby snot, and it was enough to throw their little home into total chaos.

Megan had eventually slid into an uneasy sleep just after dawn, and soon enough been rattled awake by the alarm.

Now she wearily climbed the stairs of the Sunny View Estate, thinking about the baby, this mysterious squatter who had somehow planted herself at the centre of their world, their lives, so unimaginably changed.

When Jessica had arrived to take care of Poppy, the baby's perfect, freshly made face – the face that made Megan ache with love in a way that no man's face ever had – lit up with delight.

Poppy was happy to see Jessica. The baby recognised her auntie. And as Megan walked down the rubbish-strewn concrete corridors of the Sunny View Estate, she wondered if the baby liked Jessica more than she liked her own mother? Did Poppy even *love* Jessica? But then who could really blame her?

Jessica was relaxed and loving with the baby. Megan was permanently edgy and tense, not the mother she had planned to be at all, and she could not attribute everything to a lack of sleep.

Megan was forever waiting for something terrible to happen. Sometimes, when the baby had exhausted herself with crying and finally fallen asleep, Megan would lie beside her cot, straining to hear her daughter breathe, desperate for the assurance that she was still alive. For hours Megan wanted the baby to sleep more than anything in the world, but then the baby slept as if she was dead, and it terrified Megan.

She had been enslaved by her love for her daughter, and

she knew that she would never be free. It was the first love of her life that she couldn't walk away from, the one love she would never get over, the one love that was endless. The thought both exhilarated and depressed her.

She knocked on a scarred door.

There was no reply, although she could hear music inside – Justin Timberlake promising to funk you all night long. She knocked again, louder and longer. Finally the door was opened and Megan stepped into a scene of unremitting squalor.

Stacks of unwashed clothes adorned the furniture. The air was rank with the smoke of cigarettes and hashish. A scrawny dog was ravaging through the remains of a dozen takeaways.

'I want a real doctor! Fully qualified! I know me rights!'

'I'm fully qualified now, Mrs Marley.'

Mrs Marley's face twisted with suspicion. 'When did that happen?'

'Last week.'

Somehow she had got through her summative assessment. There had been late nights spent writing her submissions of practical work while Kirk cradled their howling daughter, and exhausted mornings in the surgery video-taping her consulting skills – not easy getting the camera to focus when you were examining some pensioner's dodgy prostate gland – while Lawford sat close by, making notes for his trainer's report.

There had also been the exam, the multiple choice question paper, and Lawford was right – Megan, the exam princess, could have passed it in her sleep. Which she almost did, her eyes closing and head drooping over the paper, the yellowed milk stains on her jumper.

'Congratulations, doctor,' sneered Mrs Marley.

'Thank you.'

'Let's hope you don't make any more mistakes now you're a proper doctor.'

Megan didn't tell Mrs Marley that ultimately all she had really done was struggle through her year as a GP registrar, demonstrating what they called 'minimum competence'. All those years of med school and the horrors of Accident and Emergency, then those twelve months as a GP registrar, getting the sick and dying in and out, the Ronald McDonald of the medical profession, and in the end they said you were the proud possessor of *minimum competence*.

That's me all right, thought Megan. Little Miss Minimum Competence.

'What's the problem, Mrs Marley?'

'It's me nerves.' She reared up defensively, arms folded across her expansive bosom. 'It's not mental. I'm not a loony. Just can't get up in the morning. Can't get out of the house.'

'You feel agoraphobic?'

Mrs Marley looked blank. 'Afraid of spiders?'

'You dislike leaving the house?'

She nodded. 'I've been taking the pills. But they're all gone.'

Megan consulted her notes. 'That prescription should have lasted another two weeks.'

'Yeah, well, it didn't, did it?'

'Were you taking them as directed?'

'They weren't fucking working, were they? So I doubled me dose.'

'Mrs Marley,' Megan sighed, 'Dr Lawford prescribed a powerful tricyclic antidepressant for you. It controls the serotonin in your central nervous system. You can't just –'

'I know me rights,' insisted Mrs Marley.

Daisy wandered into the room and began listlessly patting the scavenging dog. Megan went across to her, and knelt down. The child was wearing only a soiled T-shirt. She didn't appear to have been washed for days.

'Daisy, darling, shouldn't you be in school?'

'Mum said I didn't have to, miss.'

Mrs Marley exploded.

'How can she go to school if I can't leave the house? Daft cow.'

Megan straightened up. 'I am really sorry. I don't want to do it. But I'm afraid I'm going to have to ask social services to call round.'

Mrs Marley's face darkened. 'Social workers? I don't want no crappy little do-gooders around here.'

'This child is being neglected. Now I know you're not well –'

Daisy began to cry quietly to herself.

Megan placed a hand on the child's shoulder, and turned to her mother.

'Nobody wants to take Daisy away from you. Not if we can avoid it.'

'If we can avoid it? My brother did you before and he'll do you again!'

Mrs Marley took a step towards Megan, and Megan backed away from the woman and her child. There was a sick, sinking feeling in the pit of her stomach, and it was a different kind of fear to anything she had known before.

Because if something happened to her, then what would become of her baby?

Jessica and Naoko wheeled their pushchairs through the late afternoon crowds.

Poppy was sleeping in a three-wheel pram, while Chloe sat upright in her pushchair, her eyes bright as buttons, a grinning penguin in her arms. Chloe never went anywhere without her penguin.

When the women stopped for coffee, Chloe placed the penguin on the floor and pressed a button on one of its stubby wings. It immediately sprang into life, and began singing in its mechanical voice.

'Bounce, bounce – everybody bounce!
Bounce to the ocean and dive right in.
Bounce, bounce – everybody bounce!
Don't you want to be a bouncy penguin?'

As the penguin leapt up and down, Chloe shook her head, smiling to herself.

'That's new,' Jessica said. 'The head thing.'

'She's just realised that her head moves from side to side,' Naoko said.

When they came out of the coffee shop, they started to say goodbye. Naoko stroked Poppy's sleeping face, Jessica stooped to kiss Chloe and – upon the child's insistence – her penguin.

That is when they saw them.

Michael and the woman were saying their own goodbyes outside the local Hilton, their serious kissing out of place surrounded by all the businessmen and women in their drab corporate grey. Michael and Ginger, the receptionist who wasn't saving it for anything.

Jessica looked at Naoko. Ginger was ten years older than her friend, and nowhere near as pretty. So – why? Why would a man risk losing his wife and child for an old boot like that?

Chloe took advantage of the pause in proceedings to turn on her penguin.

'Bounce, bounce – everybody bounce!'

Naoko bent down and turned off the penguin, saying just one word to her daughter.

'Enough.'

* * *

When the baby finally slept, they made love – nothing like the fierce coupling of their first night, on the coats at the party, but sex that seemed to Megan like it belonged in a library – muffled and hushed, watched by signs saying Silence Please.

But she liked this man who had given her a child, and crossed the world to find them, she liked him more and more.

She knew all about the second job delivering sandwiches, although she never let on, and this menial job didn't make him seem pathetic to her. It touched her heart. It didn't make him look like a loser in her eyes, it made him seem like a real man. He would do anything for them. So she trusted him now.

'I thought I could make a difference around here,' she whispered. 'I really believed that. And look at me. Just like everybody else. Dishing out the antidepressants and calling the social services.'

'You can't help these people,' he whispered back. 'They're too poor, too sick, too far gone on junk food and drugs, fags and booze. Too stupid.'

'No, there are good people around here.' She thought of Mrs Summer and the boxer and Daisy. She thought of all the good and decency that managed to exist in these mean estates. 'They're not all the same.'

'You've got to think about Poppy now. About us. I mean it, Megan. We should get out.'

She smiled at that. It seemed to her that he had spent his life dreaming of going to some new place. Somewhere the sea was bluer, the beaches whiter, and the water cleaner. How the hell did he end up in Hackney?

'Where do you have in mind?'

'I'm serious, Megan.'

'I'm not laughing at you. Honest. I love it. I love the idea of getting away from all this.'

He grabbed her excitedly.

'Somewhere with decent diving. Somewhere I can teach. These are the best places on the planet. Any major diving centre will have me. The Indian Ocean. The Caribbean. Even back home – Australia.'

Suddenly she wasn't smiling.

'You think I want to lie on a beach all my life? You think I'd give up my job?'

'They need doctors everywhere. Why do you have to practise in a place where they don't respect you – or anything else? Where it's filthy, and full of drunks, and ignorant bastards?'

'You hate it here.'

'That's right. But I'm not here for the place. I am here for you. And our baby.'

'This is where I can do the most good. It's not true what you say – and even if it was, what do you think a doctor does? You think I should only treat rich people? Nice people? It doesn't work like that. That's not what I trained for.'

'What did you train for? Not this life. Surely not this life.'

Megan searched her memory. During all those years of study, she had certainly had a vision of herself as a doctor.

In the vision she was calm, kind and endlessly capable. Bringing hope to those in despair. That sort of thing. She had never imagined that she would ever be physically threatened by her patients. She thought that they would be grateful, that they would love her even, or at least respect her. She had never imagined that some of them would see her as a middle-class cow depriving them of the pills they craved, and blighting their lives by calling in the dreaded social workers. And Megan had never guessed that she would ever feel so tired.

'I guess I wanted to make a difference. Yes, that's it. I wanted to make things a little bit better. What's wrong with that?'

'Nothing. But you can't save the world, Megan. Look at us. I mean, just look at the pair of us struggling with the baby every night. This tiny little thing doesn't stop crying and we feel like the sky is falling down.'

The baby stirred in the cot beside their bed.

'Keep your voice down,' Megan whispered.

'How are you going to save the world?' Kirk whispered back. 'We can't even take care of ourselves.'

twenty-two

From their window at the Ritz-Carlton, Jessica could look out on the timeless bustle of Hong Kong harbour.

There was something magical about this place, but what it was felt just beyond her reach. It was a city that was constantly being reinvented, where new dreams pushed aside the old dreams, and everywhere you looked there was land being reclaimed from the harbour, and shining skyscrapers being raised upon it while the soil was still wet.

Out in the harbour there were vessels of every kind and every century. Hydrofoils taking the gamblers to Macao, puffing tugs accompanying giant cruise ships, ancient wooden junks with their orange sails and, always, the green-and-white Star Ferries, shuttling between Central and Wanchai and Tsim Sha Tsui. There was an old film that Jessica had glimpsed late at night, where a man had fallen in love with a girl he first saw on the Star Ferry. Jessica thought it looked like a good place to fall in love.

Framing the chaotic pageant of the harbour were the two shining skylines, the corporate towers of Hong Kong island staring across at the forest of apartment blocks Kowloon side, and beyond them the green hills of the New Territories.

Jessica knew what was on the other side of those hills, and suddenly she realised she wanted to go there, she wanted to see it while she had the chance. Who knew if she would ever be back in this part of the world?

'I would like to see China,' she said.

Paulo didn't reply.

He was lying on their bed, still jet-lagged after five days, listlessly thumbing through a sheaf of glossy brochures from the Hong Kong Motor Show. On the cover of the one he was holding, two smiling Chinese girls in cheongsams were sitting on the roof of some expensive car.

'Paulo? I want to see China.'

'China? Darling, you're looking at it.'

'That's not what I mean.'

'Who do you think Hong Kong belongs to now? Not us, Jess. The British went home. End of empire and all that.'

'I mean the mainland. Across the border. You know. The People's Republic of China.'

He grimaced.

'We can do that, if you want. But I don't think it's as nice as here. I bet those Communists can't make a decent cappuccino. Why can't we just stay in Hong Kong?'

'I'd like to see it anyway. While we're here. Who knows if we'll ever come back?'

He stretched out and smiled, feeling that strangely soporific sensation of being in a five-star hotel room on the far side of the world. He loved the way she looked standing by the window, half turned towards him, the late afternoon light on her beautiful face. He could never refuse her anything.

'Come over here, you little minx, and we'll talk about it.'

'What for?' she laughed. 'You're too tired.'

'Okay, okay, we'll take a look at China.' He yawned and tossed the brochure to one side. 'A day should be enough, shouldn't it? I mean, how long does it take to see China?'

Paulo closed his eyes and Jessica turned back to the view just in time to see a Star Ferry mooring below her. Crowds of sleek, black-haired businessmen and women disembarked, pouring into Statue Square and their working lives in Central.

Most of them probably lived in those endless skyscrapers she could see Kowloon side, sprouting like a forest on the tip of the Chinese peninsula. That's where their families would be waiting when they caught the Star Ferry back home. The husbands and wives. A couple of those beautiful, bell-haired children you saw on the MTR, smart in their old-fashioned school uniforms, looking forward to their future, and the future of this wonderful place.

And suddenly, all at once, Jessica understood the source of Hong Kong's magic.

'You know what it is?' she said out loud, although she knew her husband was sleeping. 'I have never seen anywhere so full of life.'

'Anybody here ever changed a baby's nappy before? Mummies? Daddies? Come on, don't be shy.'

Cat looked at Rory.

'Go on,' she hissed. 'You told me you changed Jake all the time.'

'But that was years ago.'

'You told me your ex-wife was a lazy bitch who wouldn't get up at night.'

'Leave me alone.'

'Put your hand up!'

'No!'

The teacher of their antenatal class smiled at her students. They stared back at her, or at the pink doll flat on its back on the mat between them. The doll was wearing a sodden nappy. It was one of those dolls that sold itself on the fact that it could cry and pee its pants. Just like the real thing. Just add water.

The teacher was one of those earth mother types that always made Rory feel uncomfortable. A big body in a floaty dress. Long, flowing hair that was probably meant to signify her belief in personal freedom, but just looked unkempt and dirty. Ethnic earrings and a beatific smile, as if she knew the secrets of the universe.

'Changing baby's nappy when she has done a wee or a poo is one of our most fundamental parenting skills.'

'I watched me sister change her baby,' said one of the expectant mothers. She was typical of the class. Hardly out of her teens, bedecked with tattoos and pieces of metal that suddenly peeked out at you from ankle, breast and buttock. She was accompanied by a surly-looking young man with bad skin.

Babies making babies, thought Rory, thinking of an ancient Sly and the Family Stone song that must be – my God! Almost forty years old! Your granny might know it, he thought. These kids. They don't know what they're letting themselves in for.

'Anyone?'

Cat elbowed him in the ribs.

'Ah!' he said.

The teacher turned her smile on him. The expectant mothers and their blank-faced men all noticed him for the first time.

'Ah, ah, ah did it once, years back. My son.'

'Real hands-on experience,' the teacher said, all mock-impressed. 'Let's see what you remember.'

Rory joined the teacher on the mat. Smiling still, she gave him a new nappy, a box of baby wipes and a jar of cream.

'Most newborn babies have erythema toxicum,' she said.

Rory must have looked alarmed.

'Nappy rash. Crucial to keep baby clean.' She nodded briskly. 'Off you go.'

Rory thought back. It wasn't so difficult. It was true he had been the one to get up in the middle of the night while Ali slept off a few glasses, or perhaps a bottle, of something white and fruity. Feeling a surge of confidence, he tried to straighten the pretend baby, ready for changing.

Suddenly the doll's head came off in his hands.

'Bugger.'

The class roared with laughter.

'Never lift baby by her head,' the teacher said sternly, her smile finally vanished.

'I was just straightening it,' Rory said, desperately trying to put the head back on. 'Obviously in real life I wouldn't –'

He had managed to get the head back on but as he fumbled with the wet nappy he realised it was the wrong way round. The class laughed again. The teacher looked disappointed.

'Stone me,' said one cockney wag. 'It's *The Exorcist*. That head will start going round and round in a minute. *Your mother sucks cocks in hell! Your mother sucks cocks in hell!*'

Oh, that's lovely talk in a parenting class, Rory thought.

He angrily pulled off the head and jammed it on the right way. He placed the doll on the mat and tore off the soiled nappy. Its pink plastic private parts were flooded. Rory delicately swabbed them with a baby wipe, controlling his breathing so that he calmed down a little, then quickly applied a layer of cream and began fumbling with the new nappy. He bent over the pretend baby, smiling proudly, the nappy ready to go. Then the doll squirted a jet of water in his face.

The class applauded and cheered.

'Incidentally,' the teacher said, smiling calmly through the laughter, 'fresh urine is sterile and not at all harmful.'

Oh yes, I remember it now, thought Rory, it's coming back to me.

It's all a nightmare.

* * *

The class ended with the teacher telling them that next week they would be dealing with the colour of stools – vivid yellow to pale green, apparently – and, as a special treat, they would be meeting a baby, the six-month-old offspring of a graduate of the class.

On the way back to the car, Rory chose to make meeting a baby the focus of his discontent.

'How can you *meet* a baby? You don't *meet* babies. What's he going to do? Stand around with a cocktail in his hand, making small talk and chatting about the weather?'

'Maybe he'll give you a few pointers on changing nappies.'

'It's all rubbish.'

Cat stared at him. 'You really don't want to do it, do you?'

'Of course I do. It's just these stupid classes. All that talk about mummy and daddy and baby. That's not who we are.'

She shook her head, thinking it through. Really thinking it through for the first time.

'No, you really don't want to do it.' She stared at him, and it was if she had realised he was someone she didn't really know. 'It's not your fault. I should have seen it coming. I forced you to do it. And now it's all coming out.'

'Come on, Cat, let's go home. Your hormones are running wild.'

She smiled sadly.

'It's not my hormones that are the problem. It's you. All your doubts.'

He tried to take her hand. 'Come on. We're in this together.'

'I wonder. Because it feels like I'm in it alone.'

'Cat, stop it. You know I don't like these women with big earrings.'

'It feels like you're here because – I don't know. Because of your conscience, or because you would feel guilty about leaving, or because I trapped you. That's what it feels like. Do you know what I think?'

'Let's stop this. It can't be good.'

'I think you don't have the guts to go the distance.'

'That's not true.'

'I think you're not really here for this baby and me. If you were, some old hippy in an antenatal class wouldn't matter at all. I think your luggage is packed. I think – sooner or later – you're going to leave.'

'I want this baby as much as you do.'

She smiled sadly, shaking her head, and it broke his heart.

'I think you're just like my mother,' she said, and he knew it was the very worst thing she could ever say.

The traffic was insane.

Bicycles gliding like schools of fish through the teeming streets – she had been expecting that in mainland China, but not all the cars beyond number, none of them keeping to their lanes, all of them constantly sounding their horns, even when they were stuck in one of the apparently permanent gridlocks and going nowhere. What would happen when the bicycles were gone and they all got cars?

As the traffic ground to a halt again, a pick-up truck pulled alongside their taxi. The back was a high, wire mesh cage, the kind of thing that her gardeners used back home. But this cage was loaded with pigs.

Overloaded with pigs, grotesquely overloaded, because there were twice as many of the curiously small animals than could be comfortably contained by the truck's cage. They had been thrown on top of each other, as if they had no more rights or feelings than her gardeners' sacks of compost, and now they fought for space, stepping on each other, their eyes gleaming with wild panic as they desperately lifted their heads for air, and shrieked with a terror that turned Jessica's stomach.

She wanted to go home.

This wasn't what she was expecting at all, this wasn't like Hong Kong. China was dirty, and desperate and cruel. Beijing was a hard place, choked with dust from the ever-encroaching Gobi desert. If Hong Kong had seemed full of life, then here everyone seemed to be fighting for their life. Struggling for life, scrabbling for it, stepping on each other without thought or pity.

The old taxi driver was contemplating Jessica and Paulo in his rear-view mirror.

'Meiguo?'

The young translator in the passenger seat shook his head.

'Yingguo.' He turned to grin at them. 'They are English. Not American.'

He had attached himself to them in the vast concrete expanse of Tiananmen Square, as they stared across at the epic blankness of Mao Tse-tung's giant portrait, and for the last few hours he had acted as their guide, translator and chaperone as they wandered the Forbidden City, ancient *hutong* back alleys and tacky tourist shopping malls. He was a pleasant, good-looking young man, an architecture student who called himself Simon. When they asked for his Chinese name, he said it was too difficult for them to pronounce.

'What you do?' he asked Paulo. 'What you do in England for job?'

Paulo sighed, staring grimly out of the window. At first he had been happy to respond to Simon's constant questions. But it had been a long day. And the questions never stopped.

'He sells cars, Simon,' Jessica said. She shoved Paulo. 'There's no need to be rude.'

'Well. It's like the Spanish Inquisition with this guy.'

'How much money make?' Simon said, as innocently as if he was asking how they liked the weather.

'None of your bloody business,' Paulo said.

Simon turned to Jessica.

'You marry? Or boyfriend-girlfriend just partner?'

'We're an old married couple,' Jessica said.

She smiled and lifted her left hand, displaying her wedding ring.

'See?'

Simon took her hand and inspected the ring. 'Tiffany. Very good quality. Cartier better though. How long marry?'

'Five – no, six years.'

Simon nodded thoughtfully.

'Where the baby?' he said finally.

'Jesus Christ,' Paulo said. 'Not here too. We're on holiday, mate.'

'No babies,' Jessica said.

'Six year no baby?' Simon said.

'That's right,' Jessica said. 'What a pair of freaks, right?'

She took her husband's hand, and he squeezed it, still staring out of the window at China.

Simon turned in his seat and said something to the driver. The old man nodded.

The stalled traffic began to move.

When morning surgery was over, Megan called in her extra patient.

'There's a man in your reception area with a *dog*,' said Olivia Jewell, coming into her office, 'and they are *sharing* a packet of *potato crisps*.'

'Don't worry, Mother. I don't think he'll bite you.'

Olivia shot her a look that made Megan smile – the same startled double take that had tickled the watching millions thirty years ago.

'We *are* talking about the dog, aren't we, dear?' Olivia looked around Megan's tiny room. 'Is this where they make you work every day?'

'I know it's not quite what you're used to. So why didn't you go to see Dr Finn?'

Finn was the private doctor her mother had seen since they were children. Megan remembered the reception area of his practice on Harley Street. Deep-pile carpets, glossy magazines, comfy sofas and a chandelier that had impressed Megan deeply. It was more like a hotel lobby than an NHS waiting room. It was only years later that she realised the most luxurious thing of all was that Dr Finn could spend thirty minutes with every patient.

'Dr Finn retired last year. I don't like the one who replaced him. Keeps going on about my smoking. And besides. I wanted to see you.'

Megan rubbed her eyes. 'What's the problem?'

'God, you look awful.'

'Poppy was up for most of the night. She seems unsettled with Jessica away. Kirk's taking time off to look after her, but she misses Jessie.'

'They're just so much work, aren't they?'

'How would you know?'

'Charming bedside manner.'

'You should come and see her some time.'

'I keep meaning to. It's your flat. It depresses me, Megan.'

'Yes, it depresses me too. Look, can we get on with it? I have to go home and take over from Kirk. What's wrong?'

What was wrong was that the pins and needles in her mother's arms were getting worse. She had blurred vision in one eye. Sometimes she was so overcome with fatigue that she could hardly light a cigarette.

Megan's face was an unreadable mask, but she was shocked. She thought the old girl was lonely. It was worse than that.

'You need to see a specialist.' Megan started scribbling a name and address. 'A neurologist. Someone I use in Wimpole Street. Very close to where Dr Finn used to be, in fact.'

'What is it? What's wrong with me?'

'You need to see a specialist. You can talk to him about your symptoms. He will almost certainly ask you to have an MRI scan. You should also prepare yourself for a lumbar puncture.'

'What the fuck is a lumbar puncture?'

'Don't be alarmed. Please. A sample of fluid is drawn off from around the spine and given a series of tests.'

'Megan, what's wrong with me?'

'That's what they're going to find out.'

'But what *is* it?'

'It's not my place to make guesses.'

'You know what it is, Megan. You *know*.'

'No, I really don't.'

'I'm not going until you tell me.'

Megan took a deep breath. 'Okay. From what you're saying, it looks like the early stages of multiple sclerosis.'

Her mother reeled.

'Am I going to end up in a bloody wheelchair?'

'It's unlikely. Most people diagnosed with MS never need to use a wheelchair. But it's unpredictable. No two people with MS experience exactly the same symptoms. If MS is what it is – and we don't know yet.'

'Is it curable?'

'No.'

'It's incurable? They can't cure it? Oh, God, Megan!'

She took her mother's hand, feeling the bones and the tired skin.

'Incurable but not untreatable. There are some very effective beta interferon products. They're self-injected.'

'Stick a needle in my arm? Are you serious? I couldn't possibly –'

'And there's a school of thought that says what works best of all for controlling MS symptoms is cannabis. But you can't get that on the NHS. Or on Harley Street.'

Olivia hung her head.

'I could be wrong. Please. Please see this specialist.'

Her mother lifted her head.

'I'm so sorry, Mum.'

Her mother held out her arms, and Megan went to her, but just then there was the sound of screams and breaking glass and a barking dog. Megan ran outside.

Lawford was on the ground grappling with Warren Marley. He appeared to have recently thrown the surgery's ancient coffee table at the receptionists. There was broken glass and shards of cheap wood all over the carpet. When he saw Megan, Marley's face warped with fury.

'Because of *you!* My sister lost her girl! Daisy! In fucking care because of *you!'*

When Megan got home that night she talked to Kirk about his dream of getting out.

How would it work? Where would they go? All these little slices of paradise where he could teach diving, and she could do what she had been trained to do – could they really live somewhere like that? She pushed him, seeing if the dream could survive in the real world. What about visas? Work permits? Day care? She was ready to get out of London.

She was ready for another kind of life.

Because she saw now that Kirk was right.

When you had a child, it changed everything. You couldn't worry about the rest of the human race. You had to be selfish, you had to think about your baby, and find a place that was safe for your own flesh and blood.

As soon as you became a mother or father, then everything was about the next generation. The new family.

You couldn't even worry too much about your own parents.

* * *

No tears.

That was the first thing Jessica noticed.

Not exactly silence, for it was a long, poorly lit dormitory with cots pressed close together on both sides, every one of them occupied by a baby or a toddler, and the musty air was full of the singsong chatter of small children talking to themselves. But there were no tears.

'Why don't they cry?' she said.

'Maybe happy babies,' Simon said.

No, not that.

'What is this place?' Paulo said. 'This is some kind of home. This is an orphanage.'

She had been afraid to enter. She had been afraid of what she might find. Negligence and cruelty and filth. Like the pigs piled on top of each other in their wire-mesh cage, and nobody even looking at them. But it wasn't like that in here.

As they slowly walked through the dormitory, she saw that these children were clean and fed. They regarded Jessica and Paulo with baffled curiosity, but they were not frightened or cowed. They had been treated with affection and kindness.

But there were so many of them that they had realised there was no point in crying. Their tears were not like the tears of a baby outside, not like the tears of Chloe or Poppy. Their tears were not the end of the world for a mother and a father, and those tears would only be ignored.

Because they were so many.

'Four million baby girls,' Simon said. 'Four million baby girls like this in China.'

'They're all girls? All these children are girls?'

He nodded. 'Because of one child policy of government. People only have one son or daughter. Many prefer son. Especially in countryside. Low people. Uneducated.'

Four million baby girls in care because of the one child policy.

And yet everywhere from Tiananmen Square to Beijing McDonald's, they had seen the other side of that policy – a generation of overweight, overindulged children, the biggest spoilt brats in Asia, China's Little Emperors. And now Jessica thought of it, the Little Emperors had all seemed to be boys.

A nurse approached them from the other end of the corridor.

'You want baby?' she said.

'Oh, thank you, but we're just looking,' Paulo said. 'Jessica? We have to catch a plane.'

'Very difficult to have baby now,' the nurse said, ignoring him. 'Many Westerners come. Think easy. Oh – go China, get easy baby. But not so easy. Much paperwork. Need proper agency. Called international child programme.'

Simon cleared his throat.

'I have,' he said.

Jessica and Paulo stared at him.

'You run an adoption programme?' Jessica said.

'I know. Can introduce.'

'For a nice fee, I bet.'

Simon spread his hands. 'All have to eat.'

'Jessica, we're being scammed, can't you see that? I wouldn't mind if it was just a fake Ming vase and a jade dragon for the mantelpiece. But not a child, Jess. Not this.'

He gestured helplessly at the endless rows of cots. The cots were old-fashioned and heavy. Inside them the babies were wrapped up tight, swaddled like tiny Egyptian mummies, so their arms were bound to their sides, while the toddlers had a gap at the rear of their trousers where their bare little arses poked out, making it easy for them to go to the toilet. And Jessica couldn't help smiling, because they were beautiful. Serious, almond-eyed little angels, some of them with surprising shocks of hair, all these Elvis-like eruptions of jet-black plumage.

Paulo shook his head. You can't just bring home a baby from your holidays. You can't do it. This was madness.

'Don't forget, you dealing with the governments of two countries,' the nurse said.

'Now wait a minute,' Paulo said. 'Nobody said –'

'Your government and Chinese government. Need checks. Visas. Permission. Not so easy. Not so easy as Western people think.'

'Ah, but agency help,' Simon said to Jessica. He had given up on Paulo.

But Jessica wasn't listening to any of them.

She was walking to the end of the dormitory, where a small girl of about nine months was shakily standing in her cot, holding on to the bars for support.

Jessica watched her fall on her bum with a thump, then grimly drag herself up again. She fell again. She got up again.

Then they were standing by the baby's cot. Paulo thought she resembled one of those cartoons of what an alien is supposed to look like – huge, wide-set eyes, a tiny mouth and an even tinier nose that looked as though it had been stuck on as an afterthought. That tiny nose was streaming.

'This Little Wei,' said the nurse.

'What happened to Big Wei?' asked Paulo.

'Big Wei gone Shenyang.'

'Shenyang? Where's that?'

'City in north. Dongbei region. About ten million people.'

This country, thought Paulo. China. They have got cities of ten million people *that we have never even heard of.*

Jessica was staring at Little Wei. The child stared at her and then at Paulo. He looked away from those huge, wide-set eyes, and touched his wife's arm, as if he were trying to wake her. It was time to go.

'I know, Jess. I know how you feel. I really do. This child – it's tragic.'

'Is she any more tragic than I am? I wonder.'

'You want to help the starving millions? Make a donation. Write a cheque. I mean it. You know – sponsor her. These are poor people, Jess. They will be grateful for your help. Call Oxfam. Fill out a direct debit. Give a little something every month. It will be a good thing you're doing. But it's the most you can do.'

'You know why they don't cry, Paulo? Because they're not loved. There's no point in crying if you're not loved. Because nobody comes.'

Paulo watched his wife reach into the cot and pick up Little Wei.

Jessica gently touched the back of the child's head, clearly hoping that she would rest it against her chest, the way Poppy did when her aunt touched her in the same way. But Little Wei's head remained stubbornly upright as she considered the two big-nosed pinkies on either side of her.

'You were the one who talked about adopting,' Jessica said.

'And you were the one who said you would rather get a cat,' Paulo said.

'Look at her,' Jessica said. 'Just look at her, Paulo. This child needs someone to love her. And look at me. Just look at me. I want to be somebody's mother. It's as simple as that.'

Paulo shook his head, and stared at the pair of them. This was insane.

But he watched Little Wei as she placed a tiny hand on Jessica's chest, her fingers like matchsticks, and some chunk of ice buried deep inside him began to thaw.

Maybe she was right after all.

Maybe it was as simple as that.

part four:
born at the right time

twenty-three

When the baby was finally sleeping, Megan lay in bed imagining that she could hear the sound of the island's two oceans.

She knew that was impossible. Their apartment was in Bridgetown, on the west side of the island, where she tended to accident-prone tourists in the grand hotels of St James, next to the gently lapping waters of the Caribbean.

But Megan liked to believe that she could actually hear the other sea on the other side of the island, her favourite part, where there were no luxury hotels and only a few of the most intrepid tourists, and where the Atlantic whipped huge waves against the rocks of Bathsheba and the east coast of Barbados.

An island with two seas. She had never seen anything like it. And she wondered how many of the tourists who flocked to the west coast of Barbados were ever aware of the rough majesty of the east coast. Everything she had heard about Barbados was true – the postcard images of white sands, wild palms and endless sunshine. But there was another side to the place, untamed and unpredictable, and you would never find it in the glossy brochures. You saw it in the pages of *The Advocate* and *The Nation,* all the crimes featuring drugs and knives, sometimes guns, and you could hear it in the wind at night. The heart of the island was wild.

It was hard being so far from her sisters, and their absence left terrible gaps in her everyday life. She missed their phone calls, the ritual breakfasts in Smithfield, the knowledge that they were only a few tube stops away. She missed the selfless hours that Jessica devoted to Poppy, she missed the constantly reassuring presence of Cat.

For as long as she could remember, Megan had thought of herself as self-sufficient – the only one to come through her parents' divorce undamaged, the straight-A student, the med school princess, doctor baby sister, tough and smart. It was only when she moved abroad that she saw her self-image as the clever little sister had always been built on the unconditional support of her family. But Megan had come to this place to start a new family. She would have preferred someone to look after her daughter out of love. But if love was out of the question, then Bajan dollars would have to do. Poppy was already enrolled in the Plantation Club Nursery in Holetown, and Megan was interviewing prospective nannies. For the first time in her working life, she didn't have to worry about money.

There was work for her here. Lots of it. But it was a different kind of work from anything she had known in the past. Looking back, it felt like her patients in London had been the victims of poverty. In Barbados they were the victims of affluence.

Yesterday she had visited three different hotels in St James. She had tended a child who had been stung by a jellyfish, a woman who had broken her nose when her jet ski took off without her and a fifty-year-old man who had torn a cartilage in his knee while attempting to windsurf for the first time. The man's young wife – she had to be the second or third – stood by holding their brand-new baby boy while

Megan examined him and wrote a prescription for painkillers.

Typical, Megan thought. They sit in front of a computer screen all year and then imagine they are Action Man as soon as they reach the tropics. Oh yes, there would always be plenty of work for her here.

Megan was also called out to see the victims of sunburn, the ramblers who had blisters caused by touching the poisonous manchineel apple trees that grew all along the St James coastline, and of course the great raft of what back in Hackney they had called UBIs – unexplained beer injuries.

The suspected strokes, possible heart attacks and other emergencies were all shipped straight to the excellent Queen Elizabeth Hospital in Bridgetown. Disappointingly, there were no tropical diseases for her to cure – Barbados had wiped them out long ago. So the medicine that Megan practised in her new life felt curiously bland compared to what she had known in the past.

In Hackney she had looked after heroin addicts, stab victims, alcoholics, the chronically obese and all those residents of the Sunny View Estate who were smoking themselves to death. Here she was far more likely to administer to someone who had been brained by a falling coconut.

It was almost as though nobody could ever really get hurt here, and nobody ever had to die, and the holiday would never have to end.

She felt Kirk stir beside her and she lay dead still as he rolled over and moaned in the darkness, pretending to be sleeping, just in case he awoke and reached for her, just in case he might want sex and not give her a chance to prepare her excuse. They had never been able to get back to how it had been that first night.

But he didn't wake up, and he didn't reach for her, so Megan lay there in the Bajan night, listening to the winds whip and whistle around Bathsheba, on the other side of paradise.

Cat took the lift to her mother's flat.

Even a quarter of a century on, there was still a part of her that was for ever that bright, gawky eleven-year-old girl, all legs and arms and eyes, watching her mother apply her make-up, smiling at her in the mirror, her eleven-year-old world about to fall apart.

'Now you're my big girl, Cat. Yes, Jessie is big too but she's timid and Megan's still a baby. But you're my big, big girl, and I know you are going to be brave, aren't you?'

Cat had nodded uncertainly, and then the taxi was there with the man in the back seat, waiting to take her mother away for ever.

In the years to come, when Cat and her sisters suffered the thousand cuts of having an absent parent, she really tried – she tried so hard to be brave. And as the lift opened on her mother's floor, she was trying still.

But she was afraid that her mother would always have the power to hurt her, and that she would never be quite brave enough.

Cat rang the bell and Olivia's face appeared before her.

'Get it, did you?'

Cat nodded. 'I've got it.'

They went into the flat. It seemed far smaller than Cat remembered from that day long ago when she tried to move in with her sisters, but just as immaculate, just as untouched by any dirty childish paws. There were photographs of her mother, young and beautiful, in the smiling company of people more famous than herself. Once these photographs had seemed impossibly glamorous to Cat, and now they seemed rather pathetic, almost touching.

Those end-of-the-pier comedians, corny macho men from

the telly – so many of them, all those hard-bitten cops, wayward private dicks and sub-James Bond special agents – and fading starlets, most of them long forgotten now. Was that the best her mother could do? Was that why she had given up her children? For some little league hunk in the back of a cab, and a life of small-time glory? Yet even now Cat was stung to see there were no pictures displayed of Olivia's children. Cat was angry with herself and thought, why should I care?

In the next room there was the sound of some kind of domestic chore being performed. The dark face of a cleaner or housekeeper appeared in a doorway, and then was gone.

'You're having a baby,' her mother said, lighting up a cigarette.

'That's right,' Cat said. 'But please smoke anyway.'

'Do I know the father?'

'The father's out of the picture.'

'Oh dear. Chuck you, did he?'

I have been in the room for two minutes, Cat thought, and we are already at each other's throats. I must rise above this, she thought.

'I didn't let him stick around long enough to do that.' Her mother raised her eyebrows. Did that well-worn gesture actually mean anything? 'Do you remember what you once told me?' Cat said. '*Your parents fuck up the first half of your life, and your children fuck up the second half.*'

'Did I tell you that?' Olivia chuckled, clearly pleased with herself. 'It's true.'

'Well, what about your partners? It seems to me that they fuck it up more than anyone. But only if you let them. Only if you allow them to.'

Her mother laughed again.

'You're not one of those sperm bandits that I keep reading about, are you?'

'A sperm bandit?'

'One of those women who just wants a man for as long as it takes to get her up the duff.'

'Yes, that's me exactly. A sperm bandit. Here. This is what you need.'

Cat opened her bag, took out a cigarette pack and gave it to her mother. Olivia shut the door where the cleaner's face had been glimpsed and then she examined the contents of the pack – something wrapped in silver foil.

She glanced at the shut door, and then unwrapped the foil, revealing a sizeable chunk of hashish.

Olivia smiled grimly at Cat.

'It must have been difficult for you,' her mother said.

Cat shook her head. 'I've worked around kitchen staff for years. They can be a wild bunch, some of them. It wasn't so difficult.'

'I didn't mean buying me *drugs*, dear. I meant coming here.'

'No problem. There's also a telephone number. If it works. If ever you want some more.'

Cat gave her mother a Mamma-san matchbox with a mobile phone number scribbled on the inside flap.

'You call this number and ask for Dirty Dave,' Cat said.

Olivia shook her head.

'I ask for – *Dirty Dave*?'

'That's right. He's the one who takes care of my kitchen staff.'

'By "take care", you mean he sells them drugs?'

'No, I mean he comes in once a week and does their ironing.'

'Do you seriously expect me to call someone known as Dirty Dave and buy drugs from him?'

Cat sighed.

'I don't care what you do. This is for your benefit, not mine.'

'You're a hard-hearted cow, aren't you?' Olivia snarled, suddenly flaring up.

'Well, I had a good teacher,' Cat flashed back.

Then she bit her lip. She remembered that for the few years her mother had stuck around, she had never been a smacker, but when that temper boiled over, she was a big thrower of shoes. Cat didn't want her mother throwing shoes today. She was a sick woman, and Cat wanted to go home and lie down and feel her baby pushing against the limits of its little world.

'Do you know what to do with this stuff? You heat it up –'

Olivia raised her hand. 'I'm not your maiden aunt from Brighton, you know. My God. My generation invented your culture.'

'It's not my culture.'

Cat turned to go.

'I really do appreciate it,' Olivia said, her voice softening, her fingers fiddling nervously with the matchbox. 'You coming here. Doing this. I know it's been a long time. I see your sisters. But never you.'

Cat turned to face her.

'Well,' she said. 'I see that as your doing, not mine. And don't get too sentimental. I'm only doing this because Megan asked me to.'

'I thought you were beautiful, you know.'

'What?'

'The three of you. You and your sisters.'

Cat laughed.

'Megan's pretty. Jessie you could call beautiful. But not me.'

'Don't put yourself down, dear. You've got a great pair of pins. I have a friend – he's a shrink – and he thinks that was part of the problem. It's hard for a woman. Your daughters are turning into gorgeous women just as everything is starting to head south. Beautiful children who grew into beautiful women. My three girls.'

'Your three girls?'

Cat let her mother's claim hang in the air, and the silence said, *You don't have a right to call us that.*

Olivia squinted at Dirty Dave's phone number, her hands shaking. She's an old woman now, Cat thought. When did my mother become an old woman?

'It's difficult with them both away. Megan in Barbados. Jessica still in bloody China. How long is she going to be gone anyway?'

'I'm sure they'll both send you a postcard.'

'You know why I need this, don't you? You know why I'm turning into a drug user in my twilight years?'

'Megan told me.' A pause. 'I'm sorry.'

'Really?'

'Of course I am. I wouldn't wish that on anyone.'

'Don't turn your back on me, Cat. This specialist that Megan sent me to – it's not good. The pain is getting worse. And the tremors. And you know the funny bit? MS doesn't shorten your lifespan. Your muscles go, and you shake like a leaf, and you go blind as a bat. But it doesn't kill you. You have to live with it.'

It's a cruel world, Cat thought. Just ask the three children you walked out on. But it was hard hating her mother today. It was harder than it had ever been.

'I hope this stuff brings you some relief,' she said, indicating the cigarette packet. 'I really do.'

Suddenly Olivia took her by the arm. Cat could feel her mother's long, bony fingers digging into the flesh just below her elbow. It was the firm grip you would take on a recalcitrant child who was about to do something they would soon regret. The shock of unexpected physical contact with her mother made Cat catch a breath.

'I'm frightened, frightened about what's going to happen to me,' Olivia said, pleading now. 'I'm scared what I am going to become. The person I'm going to turn into. I need someone to take care of me. I need *you*, Cat. There's nobody else.'

Cat stared at her mother. Maybe if she had asked for her help twenty years ago – maybe then they would have had a chance. But you can leave it too late, Cat thought. You can run out of time.

As gently as she could, Cat tried to remove her mother's hand. But Olivia's grip tightened and Cat's heart fluttered with panic. It was like being held by the past, still feeling the sting from all those old wounds, and knowing you can never really be free of all those ruined years.

Their eyes met. Olivia's voice was soft, but her grip didn't weaken.

It wasn't the grasp of someone old, Cat thought. It was full of steely determination and physical strength. The clench of someone who was used to getting their own way, to bending the world to their will. Cat could feel her heart beating, could smell her mother's perfume, could see the old woman starting to fight for breath. Her mother's fingernails buried deep into her flesh, five points of pain that blurred into one, and her arm started to throb. Cat thought, *she is never going to let me go, is she?*

'Stay with me, Cat,' Olivia said. 'Do you want me to beg?'

But, more firmly now, Cat took her mother's wrist and pushed her hand away. The two women took a step away from each other, as if they had finally completed some ancient dance.

'That's not who I am,' Cat said.

When Paulo saw that the Baresi Brothers showroom was locked up and in darkness, he told the taxi driver to wait.

His head still fogged with jet lag from the flight, he rang the bell and pressed his face up against the plate glass. For a moment China felt like a dream. The stock in the window was exactly the same as when he had last seen it, over a month ago. Five weeks without a single sale? That wasn't right.

He had been gone too long, he saw that now. But it took a long time to become instant parents, and they were still not quite there.

Paulo went back to the taxi and gave the driver Michael's address. The cab crawled down the stalled Holloway Road, and Paulo felt a creeping sense of dread.

He had pushed London and work out of his head, and that had been wrong. But it was his only way of coping with the marathon that they had been asked to run before Little Wei could come home.

There had been countless interviews at the adoption agency, the orphanage and the British embassy. Their entire lives were under the microscope – their financial situation, their character references, their experience with children, their suitability for adoption. Everything had to be translated into English and Chinese, every evaluation, assessment and recommendation, and everything took far longer than expected.

The only thing that kept them sane were the moments of magic between all the bureaucracy and waiting, the days when they were allowed to take Little Wei for a walk in her new stroller around the Summer Palace and Beijing Zoo and Tiananmen Square, always back to Tiananmen, so big it felt that you were walking on the surface of the moon, pushing Little Wei until she slept, ignoring the gawping stares and smirks of locals and tourists alike. Spending time with their baby daughter, terrified at how much they loved her, no longer a family of two.

Now they were waiting for final approval from the Chinese authorities before they could apply for a temporary

British passport for Little Wei, and the thought that they could lose her now was too much to bear. There had simply been no room in Paulo's head for fretting about his brother and the business. But by the time the taxi pulled up in front of Michael's house, his heart was pounding and his head was making up for lost time.

Michael opened the door in his pants and a filthy T-shirt. He was unshaven and bleary-eyed. As the two brothers hugged each other, Paulo thought there was something metallic about his breath. He followed Michael into his home. The TV was blaring some daytime game show. The air was thick and stale.

'Want a grappa?' Michael said, reaching for the bottle on the coffee table.

'Isn't it a bit early?'

Michael shrugged, and poured one for himself. There is no word in Italian for alcoholic, their father had told them.

Paulo looked around the living room. Chloe's playpen was still there, containing a scattering of toys. But where there was once the odd Teletubby underfoot, there were now beer cans and unwashed clothes. Paulo picked up Chloe's penguin and pressed the button in its synthetic paw. But it no longer worked.

'Where's Naoko and the baby?'

Michael slumped on the sofa. 'Osaka,' he said, his eyes drifting to the television's canned laughter.

Paulo picked up the remote and turned it off.

'They went back to Japan?'

Michael looked at his brother, and nodded. Paulo sat down beside him, and took him in his arms, holding him very tight, rocking his brother as if they were still boys, and Michael had just lost his first fight.

'I told you, Michael,' Paulo said. 'I told you what would happen.'

'It's not as though I had lots of women,' Michael said,

his voice choking. 'I had one more than you're allowed. One extra. One more than normal.'

Suddenly disgusted, Paulo eased his brother away, catching a blast of grappa full in the face.

'Maybe she'll come back.'

Michael rummaged around on the coffee table, lifted a pair of discarded combat trousers and found the papers he was looking for. He handed them to Paulo. It was a letter from a solicitor. Cold and formal words swam before Paulo's eyes. *Unreasonable behaviour. Reasonable financial provision. Application for a divorce order. The family home.*

'I am so sorry, Michael.'

This will never happen to me, Paulo thought. This only happens to men like my brother.

'You never can tell,' Michael said, as if reading his mind. 'It's never going to work for us the way it did for Dad. Staying home every night. Happy with one woman. I know you think I'm bad.'

'I love you, you klutz.'

'But you think I'm a bad man. But I'm not, Paulo. This could happen to anyone. It could happen to you.'

'Michael – I'll be back soon. I appreciate what you've done for me while I've been away. If you could just hold the fort a little longer.'

'Thought I'd take the day off today.' He picked up the remote control and aimed it at the TV. It erupted into brassy music and wild laughter. 'Business is a bit on the slow side.'

'That's fine. Whatever you think best. Listen, Michael. My credit cards are all maxed out. We're staying in Beijing and it's no cheaper than London, no cheaper than Hong Kong. But another few weeks and I'll be back with Jessica and the baby. Are you sure you're all right until then?'

Michael refilled his glass.

'No problem,' he said. 'What else can happen?'

twenty-four

A cornflake hung from Little Wei's fringe.

Only Paulo was there to see it. Jessica was spending another day among the crowds queuing up at the British embassy in Jianguomenwai. Every day this week she had been down there, taking a ticket with her number on it, only to be told hours later that there was still no news. The passport application for Little Wei was not yet processed.

So in their modest room at the Beijing Sheraton, only Paulo saw the soggy scrap of cereal hanging from hair that had never been cut, and something about that cornflake hanging above the innocent perfection of that face tugged at his heart, and awoke feelings in him that he couldn't even name.

It was just a tiny moment in his daughter's life, a moment that would one day be lost for ever, but not until the day he died. He would always remember the cornflake in Little Wei's fringe.

And Paulo knew that he was becoming a different kind of man now that everything about his child – especially that scrap of cornflake in her wispy fringe – made him painfully aware of life in all its fleeting beauty. Paulo became a father and his heart was no longer his own.

She was their daughter now. They had the paperwork in two languages to prove it. What kept them hanging on in Beijing, what stopped them from returning to their lives, were the queues and the bureaucrats and the endless hours at the British embassy in Jianguomenwai. So the little family waited in limbo, tired of tramping Tiananmen Square, staying in their room, the air conditioning humming.

Little Wei began squirming in her high chair, suddenly roaring with protest. Murmuring reassurance, Paulo deftly wiped her face, removed her Hello Kitty bib and lifted her from the chair.

'Time for your nap, gorgeous.'

With the baby in one arm, he went across to the window – thirty storeys below, the clogged ring roads of Beijing beeped and tooted in the dusty light – and drew the curtains. Little Wei's huge brown eyes blinked at him in the darkness.

Paulo gently laid her on the changing mat and checked her nappy, sniffing the air and feeling for wetness with a tentative finger. When he was happy that she hadn't done anything, he placed her in the cot that stood by Jessica's side of the bed. Then he went over to the CD player that nestled under the giant flat-screen television and put on Little Wei's only record.

They had picked it up from a shopping mall on the Street of Eternal Peace. A collection of nursery rhymes that seemed unchanged from Paulo's own childhood. 'Bobby Shaftoe'. 'Incey Wincey Spider'. 'Bow Wow Says the Dog'. 'One, Two, Buckle My Shoe'. They seemed to come from some other century. Even to Paulo, their references to big fat hens and tending swine, masters and dames, misty moisty mornings and froggies a-courting seemed prehistoric. He couldn't imagine what Little Wei made of them. But as soon as she heard the opening chords of 'Bobby Shaftoe', she settled herself for rest.

* * *

Bobby Shaftoe's getting a bairn
For to dangle on his arm
'In his arms or on his knee
Bobby Shaftoe loves me.'

Paulo lay on the bed and closed his eyes. Where did these strange rhymes come from? Were they Victorian? When it was clear that Little Wei liked this CD very much, he had looked inside to find out who had written these songs, and who was singing them. But there was no information inside, and it was as if the nursery rhymes were just there, and would always be there, for generation after generation.

Paulo slipped into sleep, wondering if Little Wei's own children would listen to the same words and tunes that soothed her in the Beijing Sheraton's cot. Then the next thing he knew he was waking up because Jessica was bursting into the room, shouting and laughing, waving a red British passport, and inside the passport there was a mug shot of a child who looked like a rosy Buddha, chubby-cheeked and poker-faced, staring quite calmly at the world.

All the excitement woke the baby, and Jessica picked her up, smothering her with kisses, as Paulo rubbed the sleep from his eyes and tried to remember what he wanted to show his wife. Then it suddenly came back to him. But when he looked, he saw the cornflake in his daughter's hair was gone, vanished for ever, and next to the enormity of Jessica's news he felt silly trying to explain the feelings it had stirred in him.

So he just watched his wife holding his daughter and smiled, as Jessica laughed and showed the baby her passport, reading her name again and again. *Wei Jewell Baresi.* A lot of adoptive parents gave their Chinese babies Western names, but Jessica had always said that wasn't necessary. She had a beautiful name already.

All those nations and cultures and histories to make this

one little girl, Paulo thought, and he felt like exploding with pride.

My daughter, the future.

It was no place to be fat.

The magazine was staffed by fiercely trendy young people, or by older people who had been trendy for twenty years or more. The youngsters were uniformly pale, as though a thousand nightclubs had bleached their skin, while the older ones were strangely discoloured, almost orange in hue – their skin colour appearing to have been artificially darkened, while their hair colour appeared to have been cosmetically lightened.

But they all had that starved look of the terminally funky, and they stared at Cat curiously as she waddled among their desks, eight months pregnant, twenty kilos heavier than her normal weight and horribly self-conscious about her new walk – this strangely side-to-side rocking motion that made her feel like a giant bloated crab. She collapsed, gasping for breath, in the chair opposite the features editor.

All the bun-in-the-oven magazines and books made the pregnant woman's changing body sound like some empowering earth mother experience – in titles such as *You're Pregnant!* and *40 Amazing Weeks!* and *Congratulations! You're Up the Duff!* there were references beyond counting to 'your new sexy curves'. But Cat didn't feel gorgeous, or empowered, or deliciously curvy. For the first time in her life, she felt frumpy. Puffy, distended and uncomfortable. She felt as conspicuous as a whale at a Weightwatchers class.

At night her enlarged breasts made her feel like she was sharing her bed with two fat strangers who couldn't keep still. There was only one compensation for turning into the Elephant Woman, and that was the tiny enchanted kicks inside that seemed to come whenever she lay down to rest.

'Been looking at your clippings,' said the features editor. A mere slip of a lad in retro Adidas, far too cool to smile.

'I'm happy to do other stuff,' Cat said, touching her tummy with that instinctive triple stroke. 'It doesn't have to be restaurant reviews. I know you've already got a restaurant critic.'

'Travis, yeah? How do you like Travis?'

'Oh he's great, Travis. Oh, I love him. So . . . waspish. The way he manages to sound utterly disgusted with everything.'

'Yeah, he's good.' He scratched his goatee thoughtfully. 'I'd like to offer you something. But it's a bit awkward at the moment.'

'Why's that?'

A smile at last. Like an anorexic shark.

'How can I put it? Because I can't commission something from someone who is going to have a baby within the next half hour. Listen – I've got kids myself. Two boys – three and one.'

Cat thought, well, who would have believed it? Sometimes it seems like I'm the only person in the world who's having a baby.

'Soon you're going to be way too busy to knock out a thousand words on some clever little fusion joint. Don't you know that?'

'But I need a job. And I can't work in restaurants because it's all too late . . .'

She stopped herself. He was not a bad guy. She had warmed to him when she found he had children. But everything about his pained, embarrassed expression said one thing.

Not my problem, lady.

Cat felt as though the working world was suddenly passing her by. She also felt old, and although there were more ancient people than her in this office – all those forty-year-old groovers, Ibiza veterans and rave-hardened E-heads – they somehow seemed younger than Cat, with their bare midriffs and their unencumbered lives and artificially lightened hair.

Cat got up to go, touching her stomach again. Down, up, down. That almost imperceptible movement that said, *don't worry, don't worry, don't worry, baby.*

Poppy sat in her high chair, eating junior yoghurt with her fingers. A small plastic plate of grapes sat waiting for her on the table, just out of reach, the treat for finishing her breakfast, or at least successfully smearing it all over her face.

The nanny, a large Jamaican called Lovely, chuckled approvingly as Poppy pushed another tiny fistful of mush in the vague direction of her mouth.

At first Lovely had seemed to be everything Megan could have hoped for in a nanny. Looking after Poppy seemed like far more than just a job to her – she seemed genuinely mad about the child. Megan had been touched to see that Lovely even had a framed photograph of Poppy in the small guest room that she stayed in during the week, before returning on Friday night to her own enormous brood in the Scotland District. Lovely was perfect. There was only one tiny, tiny problem.

Megan just wished that Lovely could remember which one of them was Poppy's mother.

She watched Lovely popping a grape into Poppy's mouth.

'Lovely?'

'Yes, ma'am?'

'Do you remember what we agreed about grapes?'

Silence. Poppy contemplated her mother, her jaws chomping on the grape.

'We said – grapes must be peeled.'

'Lots of good things in the skin.'

'Yes, but she's too small.'

'One year old.'

'But she was *early*,' Megan said, starting to get rattled. 'We have been through this so many times, haven't we? With premature babies, you don't count from when they were *born*, you count from when they were *due*.'

Kirk came into the kitchen, shouldering a large kitbag full of diving equipment. He kissed his daughter on the head.

'We've got a night dive at the Sandy Crack,' he said. 'Don't wait up. Bye, Lovely.'

'Bye, Mr Kirk.'

Megan strode over to the table and snatched up a carton of fruit juice.

'And what's this?'

'Apple juice,' Lovely said, sulky and resentful. She tenderly wiped Poppy's face clean, and gently lifted her from the high chair.

'Lovely,' Megan said, 'this juice has got *sugar* in it. *Sugar*. Poppy has the *sugar-free* apple juice. I thought we agreed . . .'

They were watching her. Her daughter and her nanny. Holding on to each other, and staring at Megan with exactly the same look in their eyes.

Their look said, yes, that's all very well, complaining about sugar-free juice and peeled grapes and all the rest of it. But you're not here all day.

Are you, Mummy?

'Lower your pants,' Megan said, pulling on a pair of plastic gloves.

The woman gingerly lowered the bottom half of her bikini.

One buttock resembled an albino porcupine – pink, round and covered with countless black spikes.

'It looks like you sat on a sea urchin,' Megan said. 'You can pull up your pants. I'll write you a prescription for the pain.'

Megan began gathering up her things, glancing out of the window at the bright sails of the windsurfers. A dive boat was heading towards the hotel, its red flag with the white diagonal stripe fluttering in the breeze. She wondered if Kirk was on board.

'That's it?' the woman said.

She was in her mid-thirties, tanned and toned, expensive highlights in her hair, no doubt some kind of mover and shaker back in London. Accustomed to getting what she wanted. Megan saw a lot of her kind in Barbados.

'Painkillers are the best thing for you,' Megan said. 'With these sea urchin spikes, it's much better if you just let them dissolve. Trying to pull them out will do you more harm than good.'

The woman straightened herself up. No doubt she was quite formidable in an important conference. She didn't look quite as impressive with a bunch of sea urchin spikes in her bum.

'Please don't be offended, but are you a proper doctor?' she asked. 'Or are you just some kind of – I don't know – hotel nurse?'

Megan smiled. 'I'm a proper doctor. But if you're unhappy with my diagnosis, by all means get a cab to take you to the A & E at the Queen Elizabeth Hospital, in Bridgetown.'

The woman looked appalled. 'A local hospital?'

'They're very good at the Queen Elizabeth. Get them to take a look at you. Get your bottom a second opinion.'

Out of the window she could see that the dive boat had stopped near the shore. Figures in wet suits climbed or jumped into the shallow water. Kirk was among them. Good. They could have lunch together. Megan smiled pleasantly at the woman. 'Enjoy the rest of your holiday. I hope you feel better soon.'

The dive centre was on the far side of the hotel's beach. Megan walked through the palatial lobby, returning the greetings of the hotel staff, and down to the sand. She felt the sea winds on her face, and took a deep breath. This was a better life.

But when she approached the dive centre she saw that Kirk was sitting on the sand with a girl in a wet suit.

She looked like one of those Swedish girls that came to the island – sporty, independent, and younger than Megan could ever remember being. Kirk reached out and pushed a tangled strand of wet blonde hair from the girl's face, and it made Megan catch her breath. Before they could see her, Megan turned on her heels and walked back up the beach.

Then she drove clear across the island to the east coast, parked her little Vitara on a hill above Bathsheba and spent the next few hours watching the Atlantic smashing itself against the rock formations.

She couldn't go home just yet.

It wasn't time to take over from the nanny.

The flight from Beijing to London takes ten hours.

The British Airways girl at the check-in desk must have taken a shine to Little Wei, who was effortlessly making the transformation from cute baby to radiant toddler, because the three of them found they had been upgraded to the business-class cabin.

Jessica had visions of cuddling the child and sipping champagne all the way home. But it was like travelling with a wild monkey.

Little Wei screamed when she was strapped to Jessica's

lap for take-off. She howled with outrage when she was prevented from staggering into the cockpit. Three months on from that first meeting, her walking was becoming proficient, and she liked to try it out at every opportunity.

And although Paulo rocked her and held her and told her that everything was going to be all right, she sobbed her heart out during those endless hours above the black mountains of Mongolia where time ran backwards and the day seemed to go on for ever.

'Jesus Christ,' muttered a fat businessman who had had one glass of complimentary claret too many.

Paulo, still holding Little Wei, turned on him, his face white with fury.

'Babies are allowed to cry, you know. Babies are allowed to cry. I'm sorry if she's disturbing you, I really am, but *babies are allowed to cry*. And if you have got anything to say about *my daughter* – then you say it to me. You don't talk about her under your breath. You say it to my face or you don't say it at all. Understand?'

The frightened executive retreated behind his John Grisham. Paulo turned away, shaking with emotion as he rocked Little Wei.

Jessica had never seen him so angry. Her husband was a gentle, quiet man – that was one of the reasons she had fallen in love with him.

But when the fat executive in business class complained about Little Wei's crying, Paulo had found a ferocity inside him that she had never seen before.

And the funny thing, Jessica thought, is that it seemed like the most natural thing in the world.

twenty-five

It was hurricane country.

They were born somewhere to the east of Barbados, and though they could come at any time from June to November, they usually passed by far to the north of the island. But not always.

Megan parked her Vitara on a hill above Holetown. She had just picked up Poppy from the Plantation Club Nursery, and the child was now happily playing in her car seat with a purple dinosaur called Barney. Megan looked from her daughter to the skies out to sea, and watched them turning black.

The clouds rolled and churned towards land, and already the rain lashed against her window, and the winds whipped and howled through the bending palms.

'I don't know what to do, Poppy,' she said under her breath. 'I don't know if we should try to get home.'

The streets were already emptying. The Bajans were gathering their children, putting up their storm windows and taking cover. An old woman with a small child under one arm and a baby goat under the other tapped on Megan's window.

'You want to stay with us, miss? You and the little girl? Until it passes? This one looks like it's coming our way.'

'Thanks, but I think I'm going to try to get home.'

The woman nodded and turned away.

Megan stuck the car in drive, and slowly made her way down to St James, afraid she would skid on the torn palm leaves and sugar cane scattered across the road. The wind in the trees took on a shrieking pitch, and for the first time she was frightened, realising there wasn't much time to make it back to Bridgetown.

She glanced in her rear-view mirror and saw Poppy chatting to her dinosaur. Maybe if she was alone she would have pushed for home, but not with the baby in the back. Megan decided they would take refuge in one of the hotels until the hurricane either hit, or missed them and headed on to Martinique and Dominica.

She was nearly at the hotel when she saw the dive boat. It had been caught unawares by the storm, or perhaps had been at one of the further dive sites, and now bobbed uncertainly towards the shore, its red and white flag madly flapping.

Was it his boat? Megan felt her heart shiver.

She parked her car and quickly unstrapped Poppy from her seat. The hotel lobby was almost deserted but there was a young woman Megan knew on the reception desk.

'Take her for five minutes, will you?'

Megan placed Poppy in her arms, and the child started to complain, but began smiling when the woman began extravagantly admiring the purple dinosaur.

Megan ran and slid over the wet stone floor of the lobby towards the beach. The wooden shutters were already up on the tiny poolside bar. A blue beach umbrella tumbled past her and suddenly took flight. She looked out to sea, filled with panic when she saw that the dive boat had gone.

Moving slowly now, Megan trudged away from the hotel, towards the dive centre, the wind bringing tears to her eyes and the sand stinging her bare legs.

The dive centre looked abandoned. The jet skis and sea kayaks and the bright sails of the windsurfers had all been pulled up the shore, away from the storm. But it wasn't locked, and there was some kind of movement inside, and that's where she found him with the Swedish tourist, the same girl she had seen before, in the unlit back of the dive centre among the clutter of empty tanks and wet suits and the tangled rubber tubes of the regulators.

They were finished by then, and back in their T-shirts and shorts, and not even holding each other. But Megan couldn't kid herself. She knew what this meant. It meant that she was all alone again, all alone with her daughter.

And, Megan thought, there's nobody more alone than someone who is alone with a baby.

In the showroom window of Baresi Brothers, in full view of the busy north London street, two youths in hooded tops were working on the door of an Alfa Romeo.

Paulo stood on the pavement, dumbfounded, waiting for his brother to appear with a baseball bat in his hands, or at least a mobile phone, and a call to 999. But there was no sign of Michael, and the two hooded youths went about their business uninterrupted.

Paulo hammered on the plate glass. But by now they had the door open, and the sound of the alarm drowned out his protests. By the time he entered the showroom, they were in the car, and the one in the driver's seat was trying a selection of keys in the ignition.

'Hey! I've called the law, you little bastards!'

They peered at him from under their hoods, malignant creatures from Mordor, and suddenly bailed out of the car.

Paulo had been cautiously edging towards them and now he lurched backwards as they charged at him, the one with the jemmy taking a wild, warning swing at his head. Then they fled, and he let them go, happy to see the back of them, and he was all alone in the plundered showroom.

There were only two cars left. The vandalised Alfa Romeo, and an old Maserati. Two Ferraris and a Lamborghini Gallardo were gone. Half their stock was missing. The good, extremely expensive half. It had either been sold or stolen. They were either rich or ruined.

He found his brother in the office. Flat on his back, an empty bottle of grappa still in his hands.

Paulo got down on his knees and shook him.

'Where's the stock, Michael?'

'What? Eh? Paulo?'

'Tell me you sold it. You sold it, right? Everything we have worked for was in that stock.'

Michael sat up, groaning. 'We had a bit of a break-in.'

Paulo picked up the bottle and dashed it against the wall.

'You stupid, stupid bastard, Michael.'

'Relax. We're insured, aren't we?'

'You think they'll pay for this? You pissed out of your head, and half of the wide boys in Holloway in our shop window? The insurance boys will think we're in on it. We'll be lucky to stay out of prison.'

'Well,' Michael said.

'Well – what?'

'Three months you've been gone. Three months in China. Three months on my own, with one fleeting visit, and that was just to make yourself feel better about being away.'

'You *told* me you could handle it. You *told* me you could look after the business while I was gone.' He stood up and paced the room, tearing at his hair. 'Jesus, Michael, what's going to happen to us? I've got a family to support.'

Michael's eyes were mean, jealous slits.

'Lucky you.'

They had nothing when they started this business. A black cab driver and a minicab herbert, trying their luck with a loan from the bank. And now they had nothing again. He had wanted the best for his daughter. That was the plan. A lifetime of the very best. And he had let her down before they had fully unpacked their suitcases.

There was a sound in the showroom and Paulo stepped outside the office. A heavy-set man with close-cropped hair and a thick pink neck was looking at the damaged door on the Alfa Romeo.

'We're closed,' Paulo said, raising his voice above the alarm.

'Michael Baresi?'

Paulo suddenly knew the man was Ginger's husband. He thought of his brother drunk and broken on the floor, and his family scattered and gone, and he couldn't find it in himself to let one more bad thing happen to Michael.

So Paulo took a breath, and then released it with a sigh.

'Yeah, that's me,' he said. 'I'm Mike Baresi.'

Paulo watched the fist coming and would really have liked to get out of the way, but didn't seem to have the time, and felt it hammer full flush on his mouth, something hard and metallic – a wedding ring? that would be funny, wouldn't it? – splitting open his bottom lip. The blow spun Paulo around and almost knocked him off his feet. When he turned back to Ginger's husband, the man was waiting to say something. It was almost a speech.

'She's back with me and the kids now. I don't know what you did to turn her head. But that's not her. This – all this – is over.'

When the man had gone, Paulo locked the showroom and managed to disconnect the alarm on the Alfa Romeo. He went back into the office, and found Michael quietly crying. Paulo put his arms around his brother, and kissed him lightly on the head.

'I've lost her, Paulo. Lost the love of my life.'

At first Paulo thought his brother was talking about Naoko, the good wife who had left him, or perhaps even Ginger, the bored wife who had fucked his brains out, and was now going back to her husband.

But of course not. The love of his brother's life? Paulo had her pictures in a drawer somewhere.

It could only be Chloe.

Cat stopped at the window of a charity shop, her eyes drawn to an old-fashioned-looking pram.

It was the kind of thing you saw in black-and-white photographs of uniformed nannies pushing their charges in Berkeley Square between the wars.

Not a stroller or a pushchair, but a real perambulator. A retro product, of course – a modern version of the original, the way they made contemporary versions of the Beetle and the Mini. But Cat thought that was no bad thing.

She went inside and admired the pram. It was reassuringly solid and secure. It was all the things she wanted for her baby, all the things that she felt were missing from her life. But it was huge – it would be like pushing your baby around in a panzer tank. Cat could envisage struggling with the pram firmly wedged in the doorway of Starbucks, the baby howling, everyone staring.

'Cat?'

Then Rory was by her side, a shy, surprised smile on his face, and at first she thought he must have been following her. But then she saw the two bags he was carrying, stuffed full of frayed white pyjamas. Karate kit.

'Just dropping these off. Stuff my students have grown

out of. Sometimes kids are put off starting a martial art because of the uniform they need. You think of getting this pram?'

'Just looking.'

She could feel her cheeks burning. Shopping for her unborn child in a charity shop. What had happened to her? She felt like she had been pushed to the side of her own life.

'Stuff like this – I'm really happy to help. Whatever's happened between us. Whatever you think of me. I want to help. All you have to do is ask.' Rory stared dubiously at the giant perambulator. 'Maybe we could get something new . . .'

'I don't see second-hand stuff as a sign of failure,' she snapped. 'I've got two younger sisters. They grew up in my old clothes. Didn't do them any harm.'

'Of course not,' he said mildly. 'So – is everything fine?'

She touched her stomach, and it seemed like the strangest thing in the world, and yet also the most natural. This new life, joined to her, growing from her. Part of her that would live on long after she had gone.

'The baby's doing well.'

She saw the relief on his face. Someone who has been a parent, she thought. Someone who has some understanding of the thousand things that can go wrong.

'The scans have all been fine.'

'Don't shut me out of this, Cat.'

He was a good man. She could see that. It was why she had loved him. But it wasn't enough. Wanting to do the right thing just wasn't enough. Because what would happen when he left them? Her heart would turn bitter, and there would be one more fucked-up kid in the world whose parents hated each other.

'And I told you,' she said. 'I don't want someone who can't go the distance. They talk about women being too old to have babies, but I think there comes a point when a man is too old. Maybe not biologically. But emotionally. Psychologically. They don't have the puff. Know what I mean?'

She saw the exasperation and resentment flare up in him – *it's my child too,* written all over his face – but then it was gone, replaced by something that he was not prepared to give up on.

'I admit I had some doubts, Cat. I can't help that. But I don't think that's such a bad thing. I don't think anyone should have a child lightly. You want a lifetime guarantee. But nobody can give you that.'

'Go on, tell me to buy a toaster if I want guarantees.'

'You know what I realised? Families are messy. Even when they're good – they're messy. *Even when they're good.* Do you need money?'

'Can I help anyone?'

It was the old charity shop lady, peering at them through bifocals.

'I brought in these,' Rory said.

The old lady peered into the bags. 'Ooh, they look very *with it,'* she said, trying the expression on for size. 'Very *bling-bling.'*

'Actually they're clothes for karate,' Rory explained. 'I've had them dry-cleaned, but some of them are a bit worn out, I'm afraid.'

'Oh, kids are happy with anything,' chuckled the charity shop lady. 'That's the thing about kids – they'll take anything you give them.'

Cat thought the old woman's smile was sweet as a child's face on Christmas Day.

'What happened to your mouth?' Jessica said, tucking Little Wei under one arm so that she could touch his split lip.

Paulo flinched under her fingers. 'A jealous husband punched me in the face because his wife has been playing away.'

Jessica stared at him for a moment, and then she laughed. 'You're funny. He's a funny daddy, isn't he?'

Little Wei gurgled at him. She was carrying her usual three dummies – one in her rosebud mouth, and one each in her tiny fists. They were all luminous yellow, and when she was sleeping in her cot, which was pushed up tight against Jessica's side of their bed, the dummies would sparkle and gleam in the dark like golden fireflies.

She was a calm, happy child, and her addiction to dummies was the only sign of some nameless insecurity buried deep inside. It would go in time, Jessica believed. They would chase out the fear.

'I was about to put her to bed.'

'I can see that. All dressed up, the pair of you. Little Wei in her pyjamas. And you looking like Suzie Wong.'

Jessica was wearing a black Chinese cheongsam with red trim embossed around the high neck and across one shoulder. It was as tight as a surgical glove, with a slit up one side that reached all the way to her hip. She had taken to wearing the dress when putting Little Wei down for the night.

'Do you think it's silly?'

He smiled. 'You look terrific. To be honest, I think maybe she's a little young to appreciate it. You know. This nod towards her culture.'

It wasn't just the dress. In the hall there was a scroll of Chinese calligraphy where there had once been a framed poster of Gustav Klimt's *The Kiss*. Masks from the Beijing opera adorned the kitchen. And on either end of the shelf in Little Wei's nursery, sandwiching the talking frogs and dancing dinosaurs and effigies of Winnie the Pooh, there were two red Chinese lions, watching over this child who had somehow found herself in a leafy London suburb. And Paulo's heart ached because he knew it would all have to come down when they moved, all those lovingly placed things would have to be put into cardboard boxes when they moved to some other place because he had failed them.

'Is it mad?' Jessica said, touching the high neck of the cheongsam. 'Maybe it is. But we don't know anything about her. We don't know who her mother was. We don't know when she was born. Today might be her first birthday. Or maybe it was last month.' Little Wei looked at Jessica, as if she was following the conversation. Jessica absent-mindedly stroked her daughter's face. 'We don't know, Paulo. And the thing is – we are never going to know. Neither is she. But one thing she will always be certain of – she's not really our child. She's Chinese. And I want her to be proud of that.'

Little Wei stared up at them with her wide-set brown eyes, and Paulo wondered, how the hell could anyone give her away? How could anyone give any child away? And how could I let her down so badly?

'You love her as much as any real mother could,' he said. 'More than her real mother. That's what counts.'

'I just want her to be proud of who she is, proud of her heritage, proud of where she came from. I don't want her to feel like it's second best. Because, you see, I know what it's like to feel second best.'

Paulo touched his wife's side, and felt her skin beneath the silk of the dress, and he knew that he would never stop wanting her.

'You've never been second best. Not in my eyes. No one else comes even close.'

'And after that, after we teach her to be proud of where she comes from, all we have to do is love her. Then it should work.'

'It will work.'

And he believed it now. They had travelled across the world to find each other. He couldn't believe that it was just a coincidence. It was meant to be. *Born wrong stomach – find right door.* If only he could have kept his side of the bargain. If only he could have done his job. Then everything would have been perfect.

The three of them climbed the stairs. The house finally felt like a home. It had taken so long, but at last they had found their place. And now it will all have to go, thought Paulo bitterly, feeling like a failure for the first time in his life. He remembered when he was a child, and had just lost his first fight in the school playground, and that crushing sense of shame that comes when you have been on the wrong end of a beating. Michael had attempted to restore some of his brother's pride by ambushing Paulo's tormentor at the bus stop. But now they were grown-ups and there was no one to heal his battered pride. Now he was on his own.

Little Wei began whimpering when they were in the darkness of the bedroom. Jessica made soothing noises as she rubbed gel on the baby's gums where the new teeth were pushing through, and Paulo quietly left the room because he knew that his wife would stay with their daughter until she was sleeping.

When Jessica finally came back to the living room, he was waiting for her. He wanted to get it over with. The terrible news that he had let their little family down.

'Jess, we may have to tighten our belts.'

She nodded. 'Okay.'

'The business is not good. Michael – well, it's all gone wrong while I've been away. It looks like the business is over.'

'What about the house?' A moment of fear in her eyes. 'Can we keep the house?'

With the baby, the large house and its huge garden had just started to make sense. But with the business gone, the mortgage payments suddenly seemed astronomical, a mountain to climb every month.

Paulo hung his head. 'The house is going to have to go, Jess.'

Jessica nodded, letting it sink in. But she didn't look afraid any more. Paulo was the one who was scared.

'The mortgage – I just don't think we can do it every month. Not on what I'm going to be earning.'

'I understand. What are you going to do?'

He shrugged, the sour taste of humiliation in his mouth, as if he were undecided. But he knew what he would have to do. He would have to go all the way back to the start.

'All I know is cars. If I can't sell them, then I'll drive one.'

She reached out and touched him.

'It's okay. Really. You mean a black cab?'

'Yes. A black cab again.'

'What's wrong with that? London black cabs are the best taxis in the world. You told me that the day I met you. Remember that? You were driving one.'

Paulo smiled.

'I remember everything.'

'Don't worry,' she said, her voice full of feeling. For so long he had been the strong one – encouraging her, urging her never to give up, to keep fighting. And now it was Jessica's turn. 'We'll get a smaller place. Move back to the city. Be closer to our families.'

'But the baby would love the garden.'

His voice was calm, yet there was dread in his eyes, real despair in his words. The fear of being poor again, of doing a job he hated, and coming home from work so tired that he fell asleep in front of the television set. Then getting up the next day and doing it all over again. The fear of turning into his father.

'She can play in the park,' Jessica said.

'But Jessie – you love the house.'

'And I'll love the new one too.'

He looked at his wife and felt like he might come apart tonight. He heard his father's voice from long ago – *you boys will never get rich working for someone else*. The thing he wanted most in this world was to be a good provider for his family. He had been proud of making so much money in recent years. He had thought that's what made him a man. And now it was all over. Now he was going to have to find other ways to be a man.

'I've let you down, Jessie. You and the baby. What kind of man am I? You deserve better than me.'

She smiled. 'You could never let us down,' she said, taking his face in her hands, and he saw the thread of steel in her.

From the moment he first saw her, he had wanted to protect her, to take care of her. But perhaps all along she had been taking care of him.

'You think I love you because you're a good earner? Because we had a big house? I love you because you're kind, and you've stuck by me, and because you're not bad-looking, in a certain light. You've always been there, Paulo. All those years wanting a baby. All the tests and the disappointments. You never gave up on me, did you?'

He turned his face away from her, ashamed of the tears in his eyes. He had so much to be ashamed of tonight. But she held his face, and she wouldn't let him go.

'Why would I do a thing like that?' he said, his voice choking.

She came into his arms and he again felt the curve of her body beneath the silk of the cheongsam.

'You could maybe keep the dress on for a while,' he said, all the hurt and humiliation of the night giving way to something stronger. They looked at each other. 'If you're not too tired.'

'I'm not tired at all,' she said, getting that sly, sleepy look in her eyes.

It was good to make love again just as they had all those years ago, with their blood up and the lights on and their clothes all over the place, relaxed and excited all at once, and not worrying a damn about the future of the human race.

twenty-six

Kirk paced the floor of their bedroom, watching Megan pack her bags.

'Don't go,' he said. 'Don't leave me. Please don't take my daughter away from me.'

Now she had seen the ending, Megan felt strangely calm. She looked at Poppy's collection of swimsuits. She wouldn't need all those in London. One would do. She threw a frilly pink number in the case, and left the rest.

'You knew what I was like,' he said, his mood suddenly turning. 'Look how we met. Hardly a long courtship, was it? What do you expect from a guy you fuck on the first date?'

And then there were all her clothes. Her wardrobe had taken a decidedly tropical turn over the last few months. She wouldn't need all these T-shirts and shorts. Not in London.

'You can't support yourself and our baby,' he said. 'On the peanuts the NHS pays you? Even the poor cows drawing benefits on the Sunny View Estate will look down on you.'

We'll survive, she thought. I'm qualified and I've got my

family and we will survive. Although I'm not quite sure how. It was all going to be different, living on her own.

But she didn't feel the need to explain any of this to Kirk. There was an aching sadness in leaving, but this was a good thing. She didn't feel the need to explain anything any more.

'You would give up this life for that clapped-out city you come from?' he said, shouting now. 'You would give up the sunshine and beaches for those miserable streets and the rain and the bloody tube trains?'

There was so much that she could leave behind. Once she had accepted that she no longer had to carry all this surplus luggage, the sensation was actually quite liberating. All these summer clothes. All these swimsuits. And this man.

'We haven't had sex for months,' he said, pleading again. 'You and me, Megan – a couple whose entire relationship was built on what we did in the sack. And I'm sorry, I'm so sorry – but I missed that human contact. You can understand that, can't you? Some people can live without it. And some people can't. She was Swedish, in her twenties, and wagging her little tail at me. What was I meant to do?'

Megan closed her suitcase. She didn't need all this stuff. They could travel light. It was the best way. She turned to face him, trying to explain it.

'I just think we should have loved each other,' she said. 'You're basically a good guy, and you've been a good friend – despite your Swede. But that was what was wrong, and it was wrong all along. If two people are going to have a child together, then they should love each other.'

Then Megan went downstairs and took her daughter from the nanny.

'Everything all right?' said Jack Jewell.

What could Cat tell her dad? Could she reveal that the only knickers she could now squeeze into resembled a circus tent? Or that she was so constipated she felt that she had a plug up her bottom? Or that she had a few concerns about vaginal tears? You can't tell your father all that stuff.

'Everything's fine,' she said.

'Really? You look tired.'

'The baby takes a salsa class every time I nod off.' She smiled. 'But I'm fine. The baby's fine. So everything's great.'

Jack staggered into the flat, loaded down with bags containing new baby clothes. They opened them up on the coffee table, laughing at all these strangely mature numbers like a little denim jacket embossed with hippy flowers, and tiny white Nike trainers, and doll-size camouflage combat trousers, and Cat felt her heart fill up because the moment seemed as though it needed more people. Cat and her father didn't feel like enough people to enjoy the baby clothes.

'Are you okay, darling?' Jack said, his handsome old face creased with anxiety.

She nodded, accepting his handkerchief. Was her father the last man in the world to carry a handkerchief? Look at him, she thought, smiling at his blazer and tie, loving him for the formality of the clothes he put on for a casual visit to her flat.

'You look very smart, Dad. As always.'

He ran the tips of his fingers down a few inches of silk tie.

'Hannah's been trying to get me to loosen up a little. Dress more – well, like this.' He indicated the funky baby clothes before them. 'Maybe the baby can give me a few style tips.'

'I like the way you look,' Cat said. 'The only Englishman who would never own a baseball cap.'

Jack winced theatrically. 'Can't stand the bloody things. Make me look like Eminem's grandfather.'

Cat laughed. It had always amused his daughters that Jack

Jewell dressed like Edward VIII, and yet could always come up with the appropriate cultural reference.

'How is Hannah? Still seeing her, are you?'

He seemed embarrassed. 'Oh, yes. Still seeing her.'

'I like Hannah.' Cat kept her tone neutral. 'She's nice.'

'Yes – well. I like her myself. Like her quite a lot. She's a very special girl. Woman, I mean.'

Cat watched her father carefully, as the penny slowly dropped.

'Well, that's great, Dad.'

He nodded. It was almost as if he was working up the nerve to ask Cat for her consent. Would he do the same with Megan and Jessica? Or was it only her?

'I wonder how you would feel if we, you know, got hitched?'

Cat didn't know what to say. Ever since the break-up of his marriage, there had always been women in her father's life. Lots of them. She knew that. But over the last twenty-five years she had grown used to the idea that he would never marry again.

'If you think it will make you happy, Dad,' she said, choosing her words carefully. 'You didn't land us with a step-mother when we were growing up, and we were always grateful for that. But we're off your hands now. You deserve to be happy.'

'Hannah makes me happy.'

'But – no, it's none of my business.'

'What is it?'

She leaned towards him, and she felt the baby stir inside.

'Aren't you afraid that it could end again? Doesn't that frighten you? Your first wife left you, didn't she? What if the new one does the same?'

He shrugged. 'That's the chance you have to take, isn't it? That's the chance you take every time. If we were always afraid of being hurt and humiliated, we would never love anyone.'

Cat smiled, folding up the clothes her baby would wear. He will look like a little man, she thought. Like a little man before he can even walk.

'You're braver than me,' she told her father.

Jack Jewell looked shocked.

'Nobody's braver than you, Cat.'

She laughed, shaking her head.

'It's true,' he insisted. 'I remember coming back from a shoot when you were about twelve. A year or so after your mother left. Jessica and Megan were in the street. Some boys had been bullying them. Making fun of Jessie.'

'I remember that,' Cat said. 'Jessica was wearing a tutu. Wearing all her ballerina clothes, and crying. She thought the other kids would be impressed by her tutu.'

'You came storming out of the house in an apron and yellow gloves, and you chased those lads from one end of the street to the other. I thought you were the bravest person I'd ever seen. And not just because of that. Every day when the three of you were growing up.'

'That's not bravery, that's just getting on with it. And I liked taking care of my sisters.' How honest could she be with him? 'It made me feel stronger.'

He watched her folding the baby clothes he had bought for her unborn child.

'I'm sorry it wasn't easier. I wish it had been more settled. I wish I'd chosen someone who would have stayed.'

She laughed, trying to raise his spirits. She didn't want him to keep living with all that old sadness.

'But if you had married someone else, then I wouldn't exist, would I? Neither would Megan or Jessica.'

'No, you wouldn't exist if I'd married someone else.' He smiled, getting up to go. 'And that would be terrible.'

When they opened the front door they saw the brand-new pram parked in the hall.

It was a 3-series Mamas and Papas stroller, a metallic-blue three-wheeler. Cat thought it looked like something that Paulo might sell. Sleek and low slung, with the promise of speed. Cat pretended that she had been expecting the delivery.

Then she kissed her father goodbye and wheeled the pushchair into the flat, parking it at the end of her bed where she could watch it gleaming in the darkness as she lay awake all night stroking her stomach, and waiting for her baby.

Paulo had forgotten what it was like to live in a flat.

The bass of someone else's music. The smell of somebody else's meals. Footsteps on the ceiling. Laughter from under your feet. All these other lives seeping through the wall. The neighbours above liked Coldplay and lamb curry. Paulo had come to loathe Coldplay and lamb curry.

Jessica was bathing Little Wei, her sleeves rolled up to her elbows, building a mountain of bubbles for the child to play in. Little Wei waddled from one end of the bath to the other, her toddler's potbelly sticking out before her, carefully arranging her collection of plastic ducks and frogs and Teletubbies on the edge of the bath.

Paulo smiled for the pair of them, although he wasn't smiling inside, and kissed them goodbye. Night was coming and it was time for him to go to work.

The door of their home felt like cardboard. Such a flimsy protection against all the rubbish in the world outside. He double locked it behind him and came down the staircase hearing the sounds and smells of all those other lives that seemed to overlap with the life of his family. At the foot of the stairs was a discarded gas oven sprouting some kind of green fungus and a mountain of mail addressed to the tenants of long ago.

We have to get out of here, he told himself as he unlocked his black cab. *I have to get us out.*

Not because I am a big-shot businessman who should be working for himself. Not because I am too good for this place and these people with their Coldplay and their lamb curry.

But because I am a father, Paulo thought. Because I've got a family.

He liked working at night. He liked it that there was less traffic on the roads, and you could drive, and keep going, and not be stuck in the fumes and the clogged city.

Paulo started the evening down in the City, cruising Cheapside and Moorgate for fares, picking up all the financial types heading for the stations or the suburbs, then he moved across to the West End, which kept going until the middle of the night, when there would be a dead period of a couple of hours before dawn when the first overnight flights started landing at Heathrow from Hong Kong and Barbados.

In that time when the night had stopped but the new day had yet to begin, Paulo would head for the cab drivers' refuge that was hidden under the Westway, a place as exclusive in its own way as any gentlemen's club in St James's. There was a car wash, a garage and a 24-hour canteen that wouldn't let you through the door without a black cab driver's badge.

Under the Westway, Paulo would clean out the back of his cab. Vomit. Beer cans. The odd high-heeled shoe. Condoms, both used and unwrapped. Brown scraps of kebab and pearly puddles of semen. Mobile phones, umbrellas and – once – a Mr Love Muscle vibrator. He never talked to Jessica about what was left in the back of his cab.

When the taxi was clean, Paulo would have a bacon sandwich and a cup of tea with the other drivers, smiling when they called him 'butter boy' – meaning a new cabbie who was taking the bread and butter from more experienced drivers – and he would listen to their banter.

'So I picks this working tart up on Park Lane and when I gets to her place she's sitting there with her legs open and she says to me, *Can you take it out of that?* And I says, *Haven't you got anything smaller?*'

There were times when Paulo thought it was a great life, and that it would always be enough for him. When his stomach was full of steaming sweet tea and bacon sandwiches smeared with HP sauce, and his cab was newly cleaned and the laughter of the other drivers was ringing in his ears, Paulo would get in his taxi and feel like the city belonged to him.

London was beautiful. He saw that now.

To see the moon on the great parks, or the sun rising over the docks, or the early-morning mist on the river, and to witness all these things when there was no one else around to see them, to have it all spread out before you while you were driving alone through the empty city, was to feel completely alive.

That's when he was happy to be driving again, happy to be constantly moving, happy to be living a life that was free of VAT men and tax inspectors and all the soul-numbing bureaucracy of the small businessman. Paulo worked all night, and there were moments when he forgot everything and he felt completely free.

It lasted until he made his way to the airport for his final fare. The tourists and businessmen would stagger from their planes, grey-faced and hungover from the free booze, their minds still in some other place, emptied out from being spirited halfway round the world, and Paulo would deposit one of their number at hotel or home.

Then, with his yellow *For hire* sign finally extinguished, he would travel back to their little flat where Coldplay and lamb curry crept through the wafer-thin walls, and for a long time he would watch his wife and daughter sleeping, their faces his two favourite things in the world, wishing he never had to be away from them, his eyes spilling over, and feeling almost drunk with exhaustion and love.

twenty-seven

Megan went to see Dr Lawford, and it was as if years had gone by, not months. What was he? In his fifties? He looked like an old man, as though the sickness in this neighbourhood had started to seep into his bones.

'Go private,' he told her, sitting on his desk during a break between patients. 'Go away and don't come back.'

At first she thought he was joking. And then she saw that he wasn't joking at all.

He still smelled the same – that cigarette smell mixed with cheese and sweet pickle. Once that smell had repulsed her, and now she realised she had missed it. And missed him, and the generosity and wisdom he concealed under his cheap suits and fog of fag smoke.

'Go private?' she said, dumbstruck. 'Why would I do that?'

'Because nothing's changed around here.' He took a sip of something brown from a polystyrene cup. 'Too many patients. Not enough doctors. Not enough time. The reasons you ran away are the reasons you should go private.'

Megan felt her cheeks burning. 'Is that what I did? Ran away?'

'It's not a criticism,' Lawford said. 'I don't blame you. That pumpkin would have killed you.' Pumpkin – doctor talk for, *the lights are on but nobody's home.* 'You had your child to think of. But the reasons you went away are the reasons you should stay away.'

It had never occurred to Megan that Lawford would tell her to work in the private sector. *Going private* was one of the great dreams of the patients they saw at this surgery. It was like winning the lottery – something they would do one day, to escape the queues and frustrations of the overwhelmed NHS. If the doctors dreamed of going private, they had never mentioned it to Megan. It would have been a kind of blasphemy.

'You'll still be helping people,' Lawford said. 'Who knows? Maybe you'll actually help more people. How much good do we really do around here? Dishing out the antibiotics like sweeties. You were never very good at the assembly line medicine, were you? Wheeling them in and wheeling them out.' He smiled at the memory of the keen young GP registrar she had been. 'You always insisted on treating them like human beings.'

Lawford was scribbling something down on a prescription pad, as though the name and telephone number were just what Megan needed for what ailed her.

'I suggest you try your luck as a maternity locum. Stand in for all those clever lady doctors on Wimpole Street and Harley Street who take three months off to have their babies.'

Megan took the piece of paper.

'You don't want me to work here,' she said, trying and failing to keep the hurt out of her voice.

'I want you to have a happy life,' he said, making his voice hard to cover the softness and feeling in the words, and she thought, *he likes me.* Then he looked at his watch, and downed the cup of brown stuff. 'But now it's time to crack on.'

Megan briskly shook his hand. Any other form of physical contact – a hug, a kiss – was unthinkable. Then he was expertly ushering her out of his surgery and calling the name of his next patient. She wanted to thank him, to tell him that she could not have qualified without him, that she owed him everything. But Lawford had already turned his back, and was following a shuffling old man into his room.

The surgery was full and among the throng of faces someone was smiling at Megan. A woman with a young child trying to break free from her handcuff grip stood up to greet her.

'Hello, doctor!'

'Mrs Summer.'

The woman proudly stuck out her stomach. She must have been six months pregnant.

'Heard you were away,' she said. 'Glad to see you again.' Rubbing her stomach now. 'You can help me with this one.'

'That would be wonderful,' Megan said, before explaining that she was moving on, and this was just a quick visit. Mrs Summer looked crestfallen, but she smiled bravely and wished Megan all the best for the future, and Megan had to turn away.

There was decency and goodness here, she thought. Mrs Summer. Daisy. The boxer. And Dr Lawford. She wished that she could abandon the Sunny View Estate with a clear conscience, but ghosts tugged at her sleeve, and told her she was running away from everything she had once believed in.

I can't save these people, Megan thought. Just look at me. I have enough trouble looking after my little girl.

And as she left, she saw another face that she recognised, a man coming up the steps of the surgery as she was going down. Warren Marley caught her gaze, and she saw the hate and violence in his eyes.

Megan hurried out into the traffic, horns blaring all around her, to where Jessica was parked on the other side of the street in a battered old Punto. She quickly got inside, glancing at the back seat where Poppy and Little Wei were dozing in their baby seats. As the car pulled away, she saw Warren Marley standing on the steps of the surgery, the traffic between them like a river he couldn't cross.

Megan pushed herself deep into the passenger seat, feeling the prescription paper in her hand, and she didn't look back.

Her sisters were bickering.

Cat could hear them in the living room, their voices rising and falling, talking across each other as she leaned across her bed and zipped Poppy into her Grobag.

Little Wei was next to Poppy, already zipped up and on the threshold of sleep, and her three luminous yellow dummies – one in her mouth, one in each of her fists – glowed in the darkness.

Something inside Cat felt warm and shining as she watched her two nieces sleeping in her bedroom. It made her feel as though their little family, so long broken and different from everybody else's family, was finally renewing itself.

After returning to London, Megan and Poppy had moved into Cat's flat. It was unspoken but clear to both of the sisters. Cat had not given them a place to stay. She had given them a home.

Now Cat placed pillows on either side of the bed, a goose-down safety barrier to prevent anyone rolling onto the floor, even though Megan and Jessica had both told her it wasn't necessary, the babies were not going anywhere in those Grobags.

Cat murmured soothingly as she stacked the pillows,

telling them it was all right, and it was lovely to be in bed, and it was time for a nice nap, trying to distract the girls from the fractious voices of their mothers coming through the half-opened door.

'But you *said* you would look after her for me,' Megan was saying, and Cat thought she sounded every inch the much loved youngest sister, outraged at the unfairness of the world. 'You *said* you would.'

'But our boiler's gone again,' Jessica was saying, and her voice seemed to sigh with irritation that yet again she needed to explain the patently obvious. 'Nothing works in that flat. We've got no hot water, no heating, and tomorrow I have to wait in for the plumber, whenever he decides to show up.'

Nothing changes, Cat thought wearily. How many times had she heard those two squabbling when they were growing up? How many times had she played the mediator, the peacekeeper, the big sister? Except that once Megan and Jessica argued about who had pulled off Barbie's leg or Ken's head, and now they had other things to fight about.

Because everything changes, Cat thought, as she retrieved a dropped dummy from Little Wei's right fist, and gently placed it back in her hand, knowing she would go crazy if she woke up and found one of her dummies missing. Everything changes. Look at these two.

They were sleeping now. Poppy was still a bit underweight for her age, but with a long body, much more like Cat's gawky frame, all legs and arms, than Megan's cuddly roundness, her baby sister's body of circles. Like Cat, Poppy seemed to have a tiny head which made many children her own age look like the Incredible Hulk when they were next to her.

But after the scare of her early birth and the weeks in the Intensive Care Unit, they were not worried about Poppy now. So what if she was always on the light side? The entire

Western world wanted to lose weight, didn't they? Cat could already tell that Poppy was going to be tall and slim and gorgeous. Like a pretty version of me, she thought.

And Little Wei had settled into her new life better than any of them could ever have hoped. There were still signs of the insecurities of the past, like those three dummies during the night, and the way she organised her stuffed monkeys and talking frogs and Leapfrog musical toys with an obsessive love of order that seemed out of place in a child so young.

But Little Wei was bright and smart and happy, spending ages poring over her Maisy the Mouse books and contemplating her Baby Einstein DVDs, starting to show some affection – although her kisses were strictly reserved for Jessica – and she had learned to cry. Jessica and Paulo had done a great job with her, Cat thought. They had taught Little Wei that she was home.

'What's more important to you?' Megan was demanding, starting to play dirty, the last refuge of the youngest child. 'A plumber or your niece?'

'That's *really* unfair,' Jessica said, sounding on the edge of tears. 'After the days I spent sitting with her when she was in the incubator while you were moping in your room. After all the times I looked after her when you were working.'

The two babies were so different, Cat thought. Little Wei had dark eyes that looked like melting chocolate, and Poppy's eyes were icy blue, like the eyes of her father. Poppy's skin was so fair it looked as though it had never seen the sunshine, while Little Wei was the colour of honey. Even sleeping they were different – Little Wei throwing her arms above her head, her face in profile, a baby weightlifter ready to claim her place in the world, while Poppy curled up like a pale-faced comma inside her Grobag, sucking busily on her thumb, as if still missing her mother's body. So different in every way, Cat thought, and yet she had no trouble in believing that the two girls were part of the same family.

'You can't start crying just because you lose an argument,' Megan was saying, a note of mocking triumph in her voice.

'Only thinking of yourself,' Jessica said, her voice shaking with emotion. 'Bloody typical.'

Cat felt a double blow from inside, a baby-sized combination of foot or fist that said, *don't forget about me*. Stroking her stomach, Cat left the sleeping children and joined her sisters.

I could never forget you.

Megan and Jessica fell silent when they saw Cat.

'What's the problem?' she said, not knowing whether to be annoyed or amused. When I am seventy-five, she thought, I will be separating these two while they bitch about who stole the other one's walking stick, or whose turn it is to use the zimmer frame.

Jessica and Megan avoided her eyes.

'Come on, let's have it.'

'It's nothing,' Megan said, all haughty and authoritarian. *I'm not baby Megan any more.*

Jessica turned wet eyes towards her big sister.

'Megan's got these job interviews tomorrow,' she said. 'On Harley Street.'

'Wimpole Street,' Megan said, her eyes flashing angrily at Jessica, who could never be trusted to keep her cake hole shut. 'Maternity locum posts.'

'More interviews?' Cat said. She knew her sister must have had a dozen already. They had all told her that she was up against doctors who were older and more experienced.

'Once I get my foot through the door, they'll all see,'

Megan said bitterly. 'But Jessie's plumber is coming round. So she can't come and pick up Poppy.'

Cat could see the frustration burning in her youngest sister. All those years skating through exams, all those years being the star of every classroom she entered, and now the real world was unimpressed. Just when she needed it most.

And Jessie had problems of her own. Although she tried to keep it from Paulo, their new little flat was wearing her down. Just as she had to worry about money for the first time in her life, she was living in a place that seemed to hate her. She had rolled up her sleeves and dealt with the overflowing toilet, the leaking washing machine and the whims of the prehistoric cooker. But the lack of hot water and heating was too much.

'I'll take Poppy tomorrow,' Cat said, not even needing to think about it.

'But you've got to see the midwives tomorrow,' Jessica said.

'What's that?' Megan said. 'Fluid retention check?'

Cat nodded. 'I'll reschedule it. The day after. Whatever. It's okay, I don't mind staying home. I can hardly get my shoes on anyway. My feet act as if I've just got off a long-haul flight.'

'You should really keep these appointments,' Megan said.

'I'll keep them,' Cat said. 'When you've got your job back, and Jessie's got her boiler back.'

The telephone rang. Cat moved slowly across the room to pick it up, as if her legs could no longer carry the weight of both her and her baby. By the time she reached the phone, Rory's voice was speaking on the answer machine. Abashed, hesitant. No trace of the humour and warmth that used to be there, Cat thought. But then whose fault was that?

She made no attempt to pick up the receiver.

'I know you don't want me to keep calling you . . . but

I just wanted you to know that your father has kindly invited me to his wedding . . . and I'm going to go . . . unless you ask me not to . . . so, er, I guess that's it then . . . well . . . hope everything is okay.'

When his voice had clicked off, Cat looked up to find her sisters staring at her. Jessica's pretty face all pained, Megan shaking her head knowingly.

'What?' Cat said.

'He's such a lovely man,' Jessica said.

'Don't try to do it all alone,' Megan said.

Cat laughed. 'Look who's talking.'

'That's right,' Megan said defiantly. 'I know what I'm talking about. It's hard doing it by yourself.' She looked at Jessica, softening. 'I know I'm not alone. Not when you two are there. But still – there's no father around, is there? There's no partner.'

'What else could you do?' Cat said. 'You couldn't let him walk all over you. That's not who you are, Megan.'

'But it's not just me any more, is it? There's Poppy. And I tell myself, I need to be happy, so my child can be happy. And I keep telling myself that, but I don't know if it's true. Maybe I should have stuck it out, for at least a bit longer. For my daughter. For both of us. There's no back-up when you're on your own.'

'You did the right thing,' Cat said. 'Leaving him. Coming back.'

But Megan was no longer young enough to be so certain of everything.

'I don't know if I did the right thing, Cat. We expect these men to tick all our boxes. Romantic, sexual, emotional. Maybe we expect too much. Maybe we think about ourselves too much. Maybe we should think about our children.'

'You want Poppy to grow up with a father like that?' Cat

said angrily. *'Where's Daddy? Oh, Daddy's out banging a Swedish tourist.'*

'But Rory's a nice guy,' Jessica said.

'The world is full of nice guys,' Cat said.

'So why don't you get one?'

Cat shook her head with disbelief, collapsing on the sofa. 'You two giving me advice – I can hardly believe it.'

'I just think we should be kind to each other,' Jessica said. 'While there's still time.'

'When you go back to work, you can't leave a kid with your pride,' Megan said. 'You leave it with your family, or you leave it with strangers. I'm just saying – if you can avoid it, don't go it alone. Don't do it by yourself because you're afraid you'll get left again.'

Cat bridled at that. 'You mean – like I was left before?'

'No,' Megan said gently. 'Like *we* were left before. And why shouldn't I give you advice? We're not kids any more,' she said, and there was a kind of sweet sadness in her words. 'Look at us. We're all grown up.'

From the other room came the siren's wail of a baby screaming. Little Wei, caught in a nightmare or possibly dropping one of her dummies.

'I'll do it,' Cat said, struggling to get up. 'Then I'll knock us up something to eat. I think there's some pasta in the fridge.'

Megan and Jessica swapped a look. The look said, *look what she did for us*. Without talking about it, both of them remembered the sight of a tired twelve-year-old girl clearing up their mess, and a debt that they could never repay.

So Jessica went off to settle her daughter, and Megan made Cat lie down on the sofa, placing cushions under her head and her swollen feet.

'Keep your feet above your heart,' Megan told her. 'That will reduce the swelling.'

When Jessica came back, Megan took their orders for the local Thai takeaway, and it turned out to be like a meal from their childhood, consumed in front of the television, punctuated by their laughter, with no adults to tell them that they had to eat at the table.

Without saying the words, and for long after the children were sleeping, Megan and Jessica brought Cat tea and made her take it easy and in all these little ways tried to show her that, for now at least, their big sister didn't have to worry about being strong.

twenty-eight

His daughters were waiting for him, wreathed in smiles, wearing their special dresses, the confetti in their fists.

They pelted Jack Jewell when he emerged from the little Marylebone church with his gorgeous red-headed bride by his side, and Paulo noticed that the sisters all threw confetti in their own particular style.

Cat was methodical, taking careful aim, using her height and reach, and landing a fistful of confetti on their heads or chest almost every time.

Jessica had this cute underarm throw, giggling as she brought the confetti up under their guard, always getting in too close.

And Megan was just wild, pelting the bride and groom and anyone who was standing anywhere near them, then encouraging the children, Poppy and Little Wei, to pick up the fallen confetti and throw it again, until the confetti was getting mixed up with leaves and all sorts of stuff, and they had to stop.

When the laughter was subsiding and the car was waiting and the kisses had all been kissed, Jack Jewell's three daughters put their arms around their father, and prepared to let him go.

He looked at them with tears in his eyes and Cat waited for him to give them one final thought, say a few last words, a summing up of all they had gone through together and what it might have meant. She thought about what he said for a long time.

'You've all got families of your own now,' he told them.

And as they waved and watched the car's taillights fading, Cat knew that she had been wrong about what she wanted when she was that child in an apron and yellow gloves, clearing up after her two younger sisters.

Cat had always thought that she wanted her freedom, but she saw now that what she had really wanted was for them to be a real family.

And now, as she stood there with her sisters watching their father go off to his new life, she saw that they had been a real family all along. Maybe not a perfect family, with all members happy and present, or the kind of family you would put in commercials to sell breakfast cereal.

But a real family all the same, who loved and supported each other, who even liked each other, capable of helping each other through anything, even the changes that came with the passing of the years.

They were walking north towards Regent's Park when Megan took the call about their mother. The little wedding caravan ground to a halt while they watched Megan's face, knowing something bad had happened.

Jessica was carrying Little Wei, Cat was leading Poppy by the hand and Megan was holding her shoes, her feet sore from new, unaccustomed high heels. Paulo and Rory trailed behind them like two native bearers, lugging the pushchairs. The late afternoon sun glinted on their silver-wrapped slices of wedding cake.

'Mother's been busted,' Megan said, clicking off her mobile.

It seemed that while their father was marrying Hannah in that small church in Marylebone, their mother was being arrested a mile away in her St John's Wood flat, during her weekly visit from Dirty Dave.

'She's in a cell down in Bow Street Police Station,' Megan said. 'Somebody's going to have to go down there.'

Jessica turned on Cat. 'You *knew* this would happen. You *knew* this Dirty Dave would get her into trouble.'

Cat shrugged. Nothing could spoil her mood. At forty weeks, she felt the melancholic joy that you get at the end of a beautiful holiday.

She was looking forward to meeting her son, but she could not remember a time in her life when she had felt happier. She touched her belly – *one, two, three, don't worry, baby* – and reflected how much she loved having her child inside her. It was a shame the experience ever had to end.

'Apparently the police followed this Dirty Dave to Mum's place,' Megan said. 'She was helping him flush his stash down the toilet when they kicked down the door.'

'Is she going to *prison?*' Jessica said.

Cat felt her abdomen tighten. Yet another false alarm, or maybe it was more accurate to call it a dummy run. She had grown used to the Braxton-Hicks contractions over the last few weeks. Soon enough it would be time for the real thing. Next week she had an appointment at the hospital to have her cervix decorated with prostaglandin gel, the hormone produced naturally during childbirth, designed to send a clear message to her son, and her body – *we have lift-off*.

The midwife had cheerfully told her that semen was rich in prostaglandin, if she would like to think about the love-making option of encouraging labour. Cat had to tell the midwife that there wasn't a lot of semen coming her way these days.

'She says Dirty Dave has told her, if I go down, you go down,' Megan said.

Cat gasped as she felt another contraction, this one stronger, and longer.

'Are you all right?' Megan said.

'He's not cooked yet.' Cat smiled.

'I shouldn't be upsetting you,' Jessica said. 'But really. How can you turn your own mother over to someone called Dirty Dave?'

'It was surprisingly easy,' Cat said, as Poppy hugged her legs.

Megan smiled at the pair of them. They had become so close recently, with Cat looking after her niece while Megan had started working as a maternity locum in a beautiful office on Wimpole Street, standing in for a doctor in her early thirties who was having her third child. The money was terrific, but best of all was getting to spend thirty minutes with every patient. She felt as idealistic as ever, but the focus of her idealism had changed. She couldn't take care of the world, but she could take care of her family.

Cat was giving Megan and Poppy a home, Megan was making enough to support them all, and Cat looked after Poppy in a way that no stranger ever could.

Perhaps it would change one day, and it certainly made it easier that neither of them had a man in their life. But Megan knew they were lucky to have each other, and she wondered how she had ever casually wandered away from her family.

It was true they all had their own lives. Jessica's full-time care of Poppy had inevitably come to an end when she adopted Little Wei. No doubt Cat would be more occupied after she had given birth to her own child. Megan knew that it couldn't last exactly like this for ever. Other arrangements would have to be made. But she understood now that she would never be alone while her sisters were alive. And neither would her daughter.

'It's just – she's our mother,' Jessica said. 'Despite everything, Cat – she's still our mother.'

Cat said nothing. She didn't want to argue with Jessica. But in her heart, she thought, *it doesn't take forty weeks to make you a mother. It takes a lifetime.*

They walked up Portland Place until they reached Paulo's gleaming black London taxi, shining like the night. It was decided that Paulo would take Jessica and Little Wei to the police station in Bow Street. They watched them go, and Poppy waved until the cab was out of sight.

'Have a heart, Cat,' Megan said. 'Olivia's a sick woman.'

Cat realised she didn't want to be heartless. Because that would mean she was just like her. Exactly like their mother.

Stung, Cat picked up Poppy, kissed her cheek and looked at her sister.

'Have a heart? Listen, if there's anything wrong with my heart, then it's the fault of that old –'

Then Megan saw Warren Marley come round the corner, and she didn't understand how he had found her, but somehow it didn't surprise her, perhaps because she was so close to where she worked – how hard would it be to find her? – and then she didn't think about it any more because she saw the flash of some sort of blade in his hand, and she was suddenly aware how deserted were these wide, white streets, this neighbourhood of embassies and offices, all locked up and empty, everyone gone for the weekend.

They were quite alone.

Warren Marley came towards them, two women and a child and a man holding a pushchair. Marley's face was twisted with loathing, and he was saying something, mouthing his obscenities, then feeling braver, working himself into a fury, now shouting the same words in the empty city, the knife – it was a carpet cutter, Megan saw – in his fist.

He roughly pushed Cat and Poppy to one side and slashed at Megan's face. She backed off, her heart pounding, felt the pavement come to an end beneath her feet, and stumbled into the road, half falling, as he came at her again.

Then Rory was there, out of nowhere, the pushchair gone, launching a textbook roundhouse kick at Warren Marley's head.

The ball of Rory's shoe connected crisply with the side of the other man's head, and Marley went sprawling, but he didn't drop the blade.

Rory aimed another kick but staggered from the pavement into the road, and missed his target altogether, the momentum spinning him round, crouching him over. Marley, on his knees now, lashed out with the carpet cutter, a punch with a blade on the end of it, and Rory howled with agony as the blade buried itself in one of his buttocks.

Then Marley was on his feet again, turning away from Rory, coming towards Megan, more slowly now, dragging one leg, as Rory stayed down clutching his rear, the blood already seeping through his fingers and the seat of his trousers.

Cat threw herself on Marley's back but he leaned forward, throwing her over one shoulder, and as she fell he swatted her away with the back of his hand, sending her flying, and he kept coming at Megan, Rory down, Cat down, the blade of the carpet cutter held out before him.

Then Megan saw her daughter's terrified face as the child huddled by some railings, and she felt her blood begin to boil.

Marley slashed at her with a wild, windmilling blow. Megan saw it coming and brought her left arm up, blocking it hard on her forearm, and at the same time she drove the palm of her right hand up, as hard and fast as she could, into the fleshy tip of his nose.

It broke with a satisfying crunch.

That's a palm strike, Megan thought. Palm strikes are really good.

She watched him drop the carpet cutter and stagger backwards, his hands over his face, the blood already streaming, shrieking with pain and surprise. He collapsed against the railings where Poppy was standing, and the child rushed to her mother's arms as Marley buried his face in his hands, whimpering with pain and shame.

Megan picked up her daughter and stood above him.

'Now stay away from us,' she said. 'Stay away from us for good.'

She kicked the carpet cutter down a drain and carried Poppy over to where Cat was kneeling next to Rory, both of them in the prayer position, trying to stop the blood that was pouring from the wound in his behind.

'Please don't die,' Cat said.

That's when she felt it. The contraction that went on and on, like a really bad period pain, and then the surprisingly painless sensation of a small dam bursting inside her. Cat realised that she had probably been in labour since the afternoon's first hymn.

'Megan,' said Rory, wincing with agony, but grinning with pride. 'You finally remembered – *aw!* – a bit of your karate. Why was that, do you think?'

Cat stared at Megan in disbelief, clutching herself now, gasping for breath. And, holding her daughter in her arms, her sister stared back.

'Now it's my turn to take care of you,' Megan told Cat.

On the back seat of his father's car, Megan delivered an eight-pound baby boy.

* * *

Somehow the hospital bed seemed big enough for the three of them.

Cat with baby Otis in her arms, and Rory lying beside them, gently resting his son's head in the palm of his hand, the baby's hair as delicate as the feathers on a bird's wings.

It was a time of miracles. When Cat touched the skin on her baby's cheek, Otis turned his newly made face towards the sensation, seeking milk, and comfort, and life.

His blind eyes, gummy little mouth, miniature fingers and toes, blissful sleeps, rhythmic breathing – everything was a source of wonder to his besotted parents.

And for Cat the pride was bigger than the exhaustion, the joy was bigger than the pain, and the love, this incredible love that had somehow been released inside her, swamped all the fears and doubts that she had ever had about the future.

People came. Jack Jewell and Hannah, his new wife. Rory's son Jake. They brought flowers and muffins and clothes that seemed so big that surely Otis would never grow into them. And when Megan looked in on them, the two sisters held each other and laughed a lot, and cried a bit, and said, 'I love you,' to each other for the first time in their lives, and agreed that baby Otis would one day be the breaker of many hearts.

Then Jessica and Paulo and Little Wei came back from Bow Street Police Station, and Jessica held Otis in her arms and raved about his beauty and rocked him to sleep, as if she was some kind of expert now, which she was.

Jessica told them that the police had been very understanding, their mother had been released with a warning, and even Dirty Dave seemed likely to escape charges, under the circumstances, as the drugs were clearly being used for medicinal purposes.

Every now and then Cat stared at the door to her room

but there was one person who didn't come to see the new baby.

Their mother didn't come to the hospital to see her only grandson, and for a moment Cat felt as if her heart was still eleven years old and that it would never stop hurting. But it was only a moment. She would take the baby to her mother. She knew that now.

She would say, *look, your child has given birth to a child of her own,* and if her mother could not see the wonder and the joy in that, then Cat would not feel hatred for her any more, but only pity.

Cat looked from the baby in her arms, as scrunched up and perfect as a baby kitten, to the man by her side, this man desperately trying to avoid sitting on the rather ridiculous injury in his buttocks, this wound he had suffered trying to save them, and Cat understood why she was alive.

Paulo sat on the edge of the bed with Little Wei and Poppy and the two small girls solemnly contemplated this strange creature who was far smaller than them. Then he felt the gentle tap on his shoulder.

'Jessica's waiting for you,' Megan said, lifting up Poppy. 'In the corridor.'

Paulo stared at her for a moment and nodded. He took Little Wei by the hand and led her out of the room. Jessica was standing right outside.

'Guess what?' she said.

Paulo looked at his wife, still in her wedding clothes, confetti dusting her wide-brimmed hat, fresh from Bow Street Police Station, and he had no idea what she was talking about. And hadn't there been enough excitement for one day?

'Come here, stupid,' she said, and took his hand, placing it on her stomach. Then she looked at him with eyes that he knew better than his own.

He felt his jaw drop open. It could really happen. Your jaw could truly drop open.

'No?' he said.

'Oh, yes,' said Jessica. 'Oh, yes. Definitely yes. Megan will tell you. She will. My sister will tell you. There's one thing these doctors can never explain. And that's your luck.'

Paulo kept staring at his wife, her beautiful face suddenly blurring with his unexpected tears. He didn't know what to say. He couldn't express how he felt.

So he picked up their daughter, and with her brown eyes shining, the child turned her face towards the source of that feeling, that feeling as old as the world, that feeling of being held.

Inside:

Knocked Up With Julia Roberts:
Q & A with Tony Parsons

Exclusive extract from *My Favourite Wife*

Don't miss Tony's other books

Knocked Up With Julia Roberts: Q & A with Tony Parsons

The three protagonists in *The Family Way* are sisters – how much of a challenge was that?

TP: It was all a challenge. *The Family Way* is a book where the three main characters are women, and that was tough enough. But the subject was pregnancy – or rather maternity; the book is about getting pregnant and also not getting pregnant. It is about the creation of new life, or the longing to create new life, and the hard fact of being unable to do so. Every day I woke up thinking – I can't do this. It's just too hard. I knew what a Caesarean birth looked like. But I didn't know what it felt like, and I could never know what it felt like. And I felt that gap every time I sat down to write.

Why not write it from the male viewpoint? The sisters have a husband, a boyfriend and an on-off partner. Couldn't you have told the same story from the male point of view?

TP: I could have done, but that would have been cheating. And it wouldn't have been as good. If you decide you are going to write about pregnancy, infertility, birth, miscarriage, abortion and all the rest of it, you have to write it from a female perspective. You just have to. Take a Caesarean birth scene, for example. It would be completely different if it was just from the male viewpoint – this guy amazed at all the blood and gore, and desperately trying not to faint. That's okay, and worth touching on, but it is so much more interesting to write it from the perspective of the woman who is actually having a C-section.

So how do you approach a book where you can never experience what the characters experience?

TP: You talk to people. You talk to women who know. And women you don't know. And they are happy to talk. It's just that men don't usually ask. But when the tenth woman tells you, 'Having a Caesarean feels like someone is doing the washing up in your stomach,' then you have to believe them. And that's how I wrote *The Family Way*. Women talked and I listened. I listened to them talk about their experiences of becoming mothers and they were the most gripping stories you could ever hear. The wild extremes of joy and sadness. And the random nature of it all. Getting pregnant when you really don't want a baby. Failing to get pregnant when that's what you want most in the world. I remembered what women had said to me in the past. What they said about getting pregnant when they were teenagers. What they said about abortion. What they said about going through a miscarriage, and feeling like they had endured a bereavement that they would never be allowed to mourn. Conversations from five, ten, twenty years ago. Sometimes you are researching a book but you don't know it yet.

And I believe your wife was pregnant during the writing of the book? That must have helped.

TP: It certainly put me in the thick of things. Because we went through highs and lows of our own. It was all going pretty smoothly up until the end, and our daughter ended up being born six weeks prematurely. It was all fine, but she had to spend the first few weeks of her life in an incubator in an Intensive Care Unit – and that was an education in itself, seeing the babies and parents who pass through an ICU.

So you decided to write *The Family Way* when you learned that Yuriko was pregnant?

TP: No, it came later. Yuriko was pregnant, and we were both incredibly happy, but the idea for the book came a bit further down the line. We went for a Nuchal Scan after about twelve weeks; that's the one where they assess the chance of Down's syndrome. And Yuriko's obstetrician told us, you'll be fine, but prepare yourself. They can tell you anything in there. Some people go into a Nuchal Scan and leave learning they are not going to have a baby after all. And although everything was all right, thank God, and our baby was healthy and happy, there was a young woman and man standing outside the place where we went for the Nuchal scan, and they were holding each other and crying. I can see them as clearly now as if they were standing in front of me. They were young – only in their twenties. Both dressed for the office. And completely crushed by whatever they had just learned. I saw that couple and my heart went out to them, because it could have been us, it could have been anyone. I could not stop thinking about them, because seeing them proved to me that this was the great human drama. Longing for a baby, that thin line between incredible joy and the greatest sadness you will ever know, the randomness, the unfairness, that feeling of being held hostage by life – nothing comes close to this experience, the experience of wanting to create a new life, and nothing ever will. For me it is the ultimate subject. And when I saw that couple, I knew I was going to write about it.

When did you stop worrying that you might not pull it off?

TP: I am not sure that I ever did. If I was writing about something I had never experienced, I felt anxious until I had talked to someone who knew – like the women I knew who had been through a miscarriage, or IVF, or abortion – and then I felt anxious because I wanted to get it right, and to treat their memories with respect. But *The Family Way* taught me that it's not bad for a writer to feel like he has bitten off more than he can chew. I think it produces good work. I am proud of the book, but I couldn't have written it without help. A woman at a party came up to me and said, 'I hear you're writing a book about pregnancy' And when I nodded, she said, 'What you have to understand is that pregnancy is just like flying. The difficult bits are take-off and landing.' As soon as the words came out of her mouth, I knew it was true. I already knew that the beginning and the end of pregnancy were where things could go wrong, but she summed it up in a more beautiful and accurate way than I ever could. Because she had been there.

And what is the Julia Roberts connection to *The Family Way*?

TP: She read it when she was pregnant with her twins. Somehow my agent got a copy of the book into Julia's hands. And every few weeks the word would come from LA – oh, Julia Roberts is really enjoying your book. You try not to get too excited. You tell yourself – okay. Julia Roberts is enjoying my book. With that and two quid I can buy a cappuccino.

But she bought the film rights and asked you to write a screenplay?

TP: She did. It was my first experience of being in proximity to that kind of power. Complete and total power. No Hollywood executive was ever going to give me a job writing a movie. But because Julia Roberts wanted it, it happened. It was like being in the court of Queen Elizabeth I – give this man ten ships. A favoured courtier. And the first draft I did was self-consciously filmic – I was really aware that I was writing for a different medium, and tried to write accordingly. Until Julia Roberts said, 'Listen, just punch three holes in the book.' Meaning – just get the book and stick it in a screenplay cover. Which of course you can never really do, but I took her point, because it was a point well made and fantastic advice from a woman who had been making movies for half her life. And then she had her little boy and little girl and she eventually decided not to proceed with the project. Probably the experience of being pregnant was totally different from the experience of motherhood. Maybe she had so much baby stuff going on in her life that she didn't want to make a movie about it. But that's the way it goes in Hollywood. There's limitless disappointment. It's the only town where you can make a pile of money and still feel like a loser. But it was an adventure and I have nothing but good feelings towards her. I always say that I only have one true fan in America, but that fan is Julia Roberts.

Perhaps she will get pregnant again and take out another option on the book.

TP: The thought had crossed my mind.

Exclusive extract from *My Favourite Wife* – out now in paperback

Bill's father came through the arrivals gate at Pudong, his tough old face lighting up at the sight of his granddaughter.

'Granddad Will,' Holly said, squirming out of Bill's arms and running to him.

Picasso, Becca had said the first time she met the old man. That's exactly what Picasso looked like. Bald, broad-shouldered, eyes that stared straight at you and never looked away. Bill didn't know about Picasso. He thought his father looked like a bull. Old and strong. A tough old bull.

He had a suitcase in one hand – the only suitcase Bill had ever known him to own, the old man was very monogamous when it came to luggage – and tucked under his free arm was an inappropriately gigantic teddy bear.

'Dad,' Bill said, 'they have trolleys, you know,' and the old man said, 'Do I look like I need a trolley?' and so they nearly had a row before they had even said hello, which would have been some kind of record.

'Please be nice,' Becca murmured to Bill as Tiger led them to the car, and the old man listened patiently to one of Holly's meaningless monologues about a character she called her 'third-favourite princess'. Bill didn't remember that kind of patience when he had been growing up. Maybe everything was different with grandchildren.

Becca's father had been scheduled to be the first one to come out to visit, but a heart murmur and endless tests had kept him confined to London. It felt like more than ill health. For someone who had spent his life on the move with Reuters, Bill thought that Becca's father seemed very reluctant to stray far from home. But Bill's old man was hard as nails. He blinked back the effects of a ten-hour flight as if he had just woken from an afternoon nap.

'So what do you want to do?' Becca said as they drove to Gubei. The Bund was passing by the window. But the old man didn't take his eyes from his granddaughter. Bill felt he couldn't look at her without smiling.

'Well,' he said. 'I want to see the Great Wall, of course.'

Bill and Becca looked at each other.

'That's Beijing, Dad,' Bill said. 'The Great Wall is near Beijing.'

Becca was looking concerned. 'We could fly up there at the weekend,' she said to Bill. 'If you could get off work on Saturday...'

Bill shook his head impatiently. Silly old sod. He probably hadn't even looked at a guide book. 'What else, Dad?'

'How about the Forbidden City? That looks nice.'

'It's very nice,' Bill said. 'But the Forbidden City is right in the middle of Beijing.'

The old man looked at him. 'I don't want to be any trouble. If it's too difficult . . .'

'Oh, it's not too difficult at all,' Becca said happily.

'Granddad, Granddad,' Holly said, disappointed that his attention had been diverted. She kicked the back of the seat and Becca told her to please not do that.

'It's not too difficult, if that's what you want to see, Dad,' Bill said, with the exasperated impatience he knew so well. 'But it's like expecting the Tower of London when you're in

Paris.' He felt his wife's restraining hand resting lightly on his shoulder and said no more.

They were all up early the next morning. As Holly played with her grandfather, Becca took Bill to one side.

'Make the most of it,' she said, and Bill thought that she was thinking about her own father. 'He's not going to be around forever.'

'No,' Bill said, watching his father down on the carpet, doing one-arm push-ups with his granddaughter on his back. Holly squealed with pleasure. The old man's thick builder's hand pressed into the freshly cleaned carpet of the company flat. 'It just feels like forever.'

Holly lost her balance but righted herself by gripping what was left of her grandfather's hair. They both laughed. Holly held on tight and the old man changed hands and continued with his one-arm push-ups.

Bill made a move towards them but Becca stopped him. 'Leave them,' she said.

'But it's dangerous,' Bill said.

His wife shook her head, and he went to work before anything started.

Becca was making tea and toast when Bill's father came into the kitchen with Holly in his arms.

'His Lordship gone off to work?' he said, settling the child on the floor. She clambered up into her special chair.

Becca smiled and nodded. 'The pair of you were having such fun, he didn't want to disturb you.'

'Bill has an early start,' he noted, spooning three sugars into his tea.

'He has to work to get money,' Holly said, repeating the party line. She took a sip of her juice and half of it failed to go inside her mouth.

'Early starts and late nights,' Becca said, mopping the juice off the child's face with a piece of kitchen towel. Then she sat back in her chair and smiled at the unusual sight of three people sitting down for a meal. 'This is so nice,' she laughed.

'Long days,' the old man observed as Becca lavished butter on to a slice of toast, cut it into four triangles and placed them on a plate featuring the Little Mermaid.

'Well, he's either working late at the office or he's out with clients,' she said, placing the plate in front of Holly. 'So yes – they're very long days.'

The old man frowned with disapproval. 'He should slow down a bit. There's no end to that kind of life.'

Becca felt the need to gently defend her husband. 'He just wants a good life for us,' she said, buttering more toast for everyone. 'That's all. That's why we're here.' She picked up a tissue and wiped a greasy smear from her daughter's chin. 'That's what everyone wants, isn't it?'

The old man chewed his toast. 'Suppose so,' he conceded. 'I think Bill always thought I was a bit of a stick-in-the-mud.' He looked almost shy. 'That I shouldn't have been satisfied with our little house. My little job. My little life.'

Becca placed a hand on his arm. 'I'm sure he never thought that,' she said.

'Oh, he did,' insisted the old man, warming to his theme. 'And he still thinks it.' He looked defiant, a slice of toast poised halfway to his mouth. 'But that's the difference between me and His Lordship, Bec. He wants it all. And I only wanted enough.'

'But it was my idea,' she said. 'Coming out here. I pushed him. And he'll do anything I ask him to do. Because he loves me.' Now it was her turn to look embarrassed. She felt her face turning red. 'Because he loves us,' she amended. 'And he'll make it work,' she said, lightening the tone. 'He will. He's like you – a grafter.'

'Never got his hands dirty in his life,' the old man said, but with a rueful grin.

And Becca could see the pride that the father felt for the son, although she felt like she was the only person in the world who did.

Don't miss
Tony's other
books . . .

THE MILLION-C
BESTSELLER

Man and Boy

Harry Silver has it all: a beautiful wife, a wonderful son, a great job in the media – but in one night he throws it all away. Then Harry must start to learn what life and love are really all about.

'One of the finest books published this year... Hilarious and tear-jerking in turns' *Express*

'Parsons has written a sharp, witty and wise book straight from his heart. His characters are all nitty-gritty, bounce-off-the-page, real people; his dialogue is brilliant' *Daily Mail*

978-0-00-651213-4 • £6.99

'Packs an enormous emotional wallop'
Time Out

Save 10%
when you buy direct from HarperCollins

Call 08707 871724
Free postage and packing in the UK only

One For My Baby

Alfie Budd found the perfect woman with whom to spend the rest of his life – then lost her. He doesn't believe you get a second chance at love.

Returning to the England he left behind during his marriage, Alfie finds the rest of the world collapsing around him. He takes comfort in a string of pointless, transient affairs, and he tries to learn Tai Chi from an old Chinese man, George Chang.

Will Alfie ever find a family as strong as the Changs'?

And can he give up meaningless sex for a meaningful relationship?

978-0-00-651481-7 • £6.99

'Another brilliant novel that combines laughter and tears, love and sex – and real human emotions'
Evening Standard

Save 10%
when you buy direct from HarperCollins

Call 08707 871724
Free postage and packing in the UK only

Man and Wife

Harry Silver is learning to juggle his many commitments – to his wife and his ex-wife, to his son, his stepdaughter and his mother, to his own work and his wife's career.

And then someone walks into his life who is going to make it even more complicated...

A sequel to the international bestseller *Man and Boy*, *Man and Wife* also stands on its own as a brilliant novel about relationships in the new century – about why we fall in love and why we marry – about why we stay and why we go.

978-0-00-651482-4 • £6.99

'Funny, serious, tender and honest... Tony Parsons is writing about the genuine dilemmas of modern life'
Sunday Express

Save 10%
when you buy direct from HarperCollins

Call 08707 871724
Free postage and packing in the UK only

Stories We Could Tell

Sometimes you can grow up in just one night

On a hot summer night in 1977, London rages around three young men who are about to learn the true meaning of friendship.

Hip young gunslinger Terry is basking in his scoop on rock star Dag Wood. But Dag has set his sights on a photographer called Misty – Terry's girlfriend. Who gets the girl?

Ray is about to be sacked from his music paper from crimes against cool and the only thing that can save him is landing an exclusive interview with John Lennon. Can he find his hero in time?

And Leon seeks sanctuary in a disco called the Goldmine as he goes on the run from the meanest gang in town and meets the dancing queen of his dreams. But are her dreams the same?

978-0-00-715124-0 • £6.99

'The trio's rites of passage are handled beautifully and poignantly and Parsons brilliantly captures a bygone era'
Irish Independent